EROTIC CLASSICS FROM
CARROLL & GRAF

Nothing Sacred

Nothing Sacred

ANONYMOUS

Carroll & Graf Publishers, Inc.
New York

Copyright © 1993 by Carroll & Graf Publishers, Inc.

First Carroll & Graf edition 1993

Carroll & Graf Publishers, Inc.
260 Fifth Avenue
New York, NY 10001

ISBN 0-7867-0037-8

Manufactured in the United States of America

CONTENTS

Volume One   11

Volume Two   255

Nothing Sacred

Volume One

Part One

What a deep satisfaction it is to be free of the vain pleasures, frivolous amusements and dangerous passions that are so prevalent in the world today. Having regained my senses after so many perversions and aberrations and having won a tranquillity by abstaining from the former objects of my desires, I still shudder at the thought of the perils I escaped. On the other hand, their remembrance enhances my feeling of security.

Many, many times have I thanked the Almighty for His mercy in rescuing me from the abyss of libertinage into which I had plunged and giving me the determination to write down my transgressions for the edification of my fellow-man.

I am the fruit of the lasciviousness of the reverend fathers of the city of R.... I use the plural, because all boasted of having conceived me. Here I hesitate for fear of being censured for revealing the mysteries of the Church. But away with such scruples. A monk is still a man, and as such, he is able to propagate the species. And he acquits himself quite well in spite of the prohibitions.

I know, dear Reader, that you are impatiently waiting for a detailed account of my birth, but I am afraid that you will have to be indulgent and let me tell it in my own way and when I think is the right time.

To begin, I was living with a kindly peasant whom I considered my father for many years.

Ambroise, for that was his name, was a gardener of a villa that the priests owned. It was in a little village not far from the city. His wife, Toinette, gave still birth to a child on the very day I came into the world. The dead infant was secretly buried and I took its place. As is well known, money works miracles.

As I developed into a gawky youth, still believing myself to be the son of Ambroise and Toinette, I began to have vague doubts about myself. My inclinations were certainly not those of a peasant's son, but rather those of a monk.

Toinette was the proof. She was an attractive and lively woman. There was something very seductive about her Junoesque figure, sparkling black eyes, and retrousse nose. For a woman of her station, she dressed with an uncommon elegance. When I saw the coquette on Sundays in a robe that half exposed her two opulent breasts, I cheerfully would have forgotten that I was her son.

There is no doubt that I had the tastes of a monk. Prompted soley by instinct, there was not a pretty girl on the street that I did not try to kiss and caress. Although I did not know what the end of the matter would be, I sensed that there would be more if only the lasses had given me permission to experiment with them.

One afternoon while I was dozing in my bed – it was a hot August day – I was awakened by jolts coming from the next room. Not knowing what to make of the racket which doubled in intensity, I put my ear to the thin partition which separated my room and heard pants, grunts, and unintelligible sounds.

'Ah, not so fast, my dear Toinette. More slowly, please. Oh, you darling – you are killing me with bliss. Faster, now! That's it. My God! I must be dead.'

I was both disturbed and mystified by what I had heard. And, to tell the truth, I was slightly afraid. But my fear soon gave way to curiosity, and my ear was again pressed to the wall, through which I distinguished the same noises. Toinette and a man were repeating to each other the same expressions I had heard before. I was so determined to learn what it was all about that I would have gone into that room without knocking. It was not necessary, however.

Wondering about the best way to satisfy my aroused curiosity, I spotted a knot hole in the wall. Through it, I had a perfect view and what a sight met my eyes! There was Toinette without a stitch of clothing stretched out on her bed and Father Polycarpe, Procurator of the monastery, also naked as the day he was born, lying at her side. What were they doing? They were doing what our original parents did when God ordered them to people the earth, but only with a great deal more lubricity.

The spectacle caused in me strange feelings, a blend of misgivings and desires I had never experienced before. Whatever they were, I would have given anything to be in the monk's place. How I envied him! From the expression on his face, he was in a state of heavenly bliss. Now flames were coursing through my veins; my face was all red; my heart was pounding madly; and the pike of Venus that I was holding in my hand was so hard that it could have punched a hole in the partition. The monk seemed to have completed what he was doing, for he got up from Toinette, leaving her exposed to my feverish regards.

Her eyes were languid and her cheeks flushed. Seemingly exhausted, her arms were dangling lifelessly down the sides of the bed and her bosom was rising and falling. From time to time, she clutched her buttocks while emitting little animal snorts. Rapidly, my eyes took in every part of her delicious body, every one of which my imagination was covering with passionate kisses. I sucked the pink tips of her rounded, large breasts and licked her flat velvety stomach, but the spot that held my attention the longest – I could scarcely tear my eyes away from it – well, you know what it was. What a spell that charming sheath cast over me! What a fascinating flower! The bits of white foam that partially flecked it only enhanced the vivid colour as did the ring of black curly hair. I instinctively realised that that was the centre of lust. Never have I seen a woman in such a lewd position.

Apparently, the monk had regained his forces, for he began a new assault. But his ardour exceeded his abilities. When he withdrew the limp sword from the sheath, the frustrated Toinette grabbed it and began to shake it vigorously. She seemed to have been successful for the man of God was twitching as he had before.

I was bewildered as to what was causing the monk's convulsions. For some reason, my hand wandered to my prick and I was soon experiencing a completely new sensation that increased in intensity and ended with an explosion so powerful that I sank back on my bed with exhaustion. The white fluid I had seen on Toinette's fringed aperture was all over my trousers. Recovering from my ecstasy, I returned to the peephole, but I was too late. The last card had been played and the game was over. The two were now putting their clothes back on.

For days afterwards, I was in a sort of stupor, still amazed at what I had witnessed. It was a turning point in my life. For the first time, I recognised why the sight of a pretty woman aroused such sensations in me. Now the reason for the transition from rapture to tranquillity was no longer an enigma.

'Ah,' I cried to myself, 'how blissful they were. Joy transported them both. The delights they must have had! Yes, they were supremely happy.'

Thoughts of this kind absorbed me for some time.

'Well,' I continued to myself, 'aren't I big enough to do the same thing to a woman? I think I could give Toinette more delights than Father Polycarpe because I have so much more of that white stuff in me. But then again, I am so ignorant as to how to go about it. Maybe it goes automatically once you are on top of a woman.'

Suddenly, it occurred to me to tell my sister Suzon all about it. A few years older than I, she was a very pretty little blonde with indolent eyes. But they caused as much effect on men as a brunette's fiery, sparkling ones.

Strangely enough, I had never attempted to experiment with Suzon, because I lusted after every girl I saw. Maybe it was because I did not see her often. Her god-mother, one of the wealthiest women in the city, had sent her to a convent for her education for a year and she had just finished her schooling. Now that she was home, I was inflamed with the desire to indoctrinate Suzon and enjoy with her the same delights that Father Polycarpe had with Toinette.

Now Suzon appeared to me in a new light. She had charms that I had never noticed before. Her bosom, rounded and firm, was whiter than a lily. While I was mentally sucking the tiny strawberries at the tips, my mind was on that centre, that abyss of bliss.

Animated at such a dazzling prospect, I set out to find Suzon. The sun was setting and the fog was coming in. I flattered myself that when it was dark, all my desires would be fulfilled. In the distance, I saw her picking flowers in the field. When she spotted me, little did she realise that I was intending to pluck the most precious blossom of her bouquet. As I hurried to her, I was turning over in my mind how to let her know what I wanted from her. My indecision slowed my steps.

'What are you doing, Suzon?' I asked as I tried to kiss her.

'Can't you see that I'm picking flowers,' she replied with a laugh as she escaped my arms. 'It's God-mother's birthday tomorrow.'

Now I was not so sure of my conquest.

'Why don't you help me get up a bouquet,' she suggested.

As a reply, I threw some flowers at her face and she retaliated the same way.

'Suzon,' I sternly warned her, 'if you do that again, I'll ... you'll pay for it.'

To show that she did not give a fig for my threats, she hurled another handful at me. At that, I lost all my timidity. Also, I was not afraid of being seen for it was getting dark. I threw myself on her and she pushed me back; I kissed her and she slapped me on the cheek; I forced her to the ground and she writhed like a snake; I held her tightly in my arms, kissing her breasts through her bodice, and she struggled like a wild cat; I put my hand under her skirt and she screamed like a banshee. She defended herself so successfully that I had to abandon my efforts. I released her with a laugh to show that I bore her no ill will.

'Suzon,' I said meekly, 'I didn't want to hurt you. I just wanted to teach you something you would like.'

'I can imagine,' she replied in a shaking voice. 'Look, there's Mother coming, and I'm going to ...'

'My dear sister,' I quickly broke in. 'Please don't say anything. I'll do anything in the world for you if you keep quiet.'

Her little kiss on my cheek was her tacit assent. When Toinette came up, she did not say a word and the three of us returned home to supper.

When Father Polycarpe had been to call, he had given new evidence of the monastery's bounty for Ambroise's alleged son: I had just been given a complete new outfit of clothing. His conscience bothered him at times. Such prodigality towards me could have aroused suspicions about the legitimacy of my birth in certain circles. But the local peasants were simple souls, and they were not allowed to learn more than what was good for them. As for the others, who could suspect the ulterior motives of the benevolent monks? They were truly beloved in the village. They were helpful to all and consequently enjoyed respect and affection.

But now I should return to myself.

I had a roguish air, but it was not held against me. My eyes were mischievous and my long black hair falling down to my shoulders set off the clearness of my fair complexion. And now I was neatly dressed.

As I mentioned, Suzon had made a bouquet for Madame Dinville, her god-mother, who was the wife of a councillor in a neighbouring town. She was in the habit of coming to her chateau to drink the fresh milk and breathe the fresh air as a cure for the ailments caused by too much champagne and other excesses.

Suzon, dressed in her best which made her even more desirable in my eyes, asked if I would like to go with her to the chateau. I was more than happy to accept the invitation. When we got there, we found the lady of the house in the pavilion ejoying the cool of the evening. Picture to yourself a woman of medium height, brown haired, white skin, unattractive features, but alert and sparkling eyes that had that come-hither look, and a generous bust. It was the latter which first caught my attention, for I have always had a weakness for those celestial globes. One of the supreme delights in this vale of tears we call life is to have one in each hand. But enough of that.

When she saw us approach, she gave us a wave of her hand in welcome, but she did not change her position on the canape on which she was reclining, one leg on the couch and the other on the ground. Her skirt was so short that it was almost possible to see what every red-blooded man desires to regard. Also, she had on a flimsy, almost transparent bodice. With my memories of Toinette and Father Polycarpe fresh in mind, I regarded her avidly.

'Good evening, my dear child,' Madame Dinville

cheerfully greeted her god-child. 'So you have come to see me, and you were not forgetful of my birthday. Thank you ever so much for the flowers. Come over here and give me a kiss.'

Suzon did as she was bid and planted a kiss on each cheek.

'But,' she asked, looking at me, 'who is that nice looking lad with you. A young girl like you with a beau already. Shame on you.'

As I lowered my eyes, Suzon explained that I was her brother.

'Welcome, then,' she said. 'In that case, I'd like to get to know you better. Give me a kiss, too.'

When I was close to her, it was she who kissed me and full on the lips. Her tongue darted into my mouth, as her hand played with the locks of my hair. I had never kissed that way before, but it sent thrills running up and down my spine. Bashfully looking into her eyes, I saw sparks of passion, and I lowered my glance. I was reassured after a second kiss of the same nature. After all, it was nothing but a friendly greeting, but I was a little surprised at its vivacity.

She resumed her conversation with Suzon, which consisted mostly of admonitions to come and kiss her again.

Out of deference, I respectfully stood apart.

'Well,' Madame Dinville remarked not without sarcasm. 'So the boy is not going to kiss me again.'

I again advanced and put my lips to her cheeks, not daring to do what had so exhilarated me. But I was a little bolder than the first time. I could see that the lady was getting simultaneous enjoyment from my caresses and those of her protégée, but it soon became obvious

21

that she was getting more pleasure from me.

We were seated on the divan, chatting, and Madame Dinville loved to prattle. While Suzon was gazing out into the garden, the lady amused herself by curling my hair with her fingers, pinching cheeks, and giving me playful slaps. All that excited me and gave me the courage to touch her neck. She did not reproach me, and my hand descended down to her bosom, where it rested on a delightfully pneumatic breast. I was overjoyed. Finally, I was in possession of one of those glorious orbs I had always so desired. And I inwardly knew that I could do with it as I wished.

I was about to put my mouth on it, when misfortune occurred. A servant announced the visit of the village bailiff, an ugly, wizened monkey of a man.

Startled by the interruption, Madame Dinville pushed me away, saying: 'What do you think you are doing, you little scamp.'

Thinking all was lost, I turned a deep red. Noticing my embarrassment, she gave me a smile which seemed to say that she was not really angry and that the bailiff's unexpected appearance was as displeasing to her as it was to me.

The bore came up to us. After coughing, spitting, sneezing, and wiping his nose, he delivered a wearisome speech felicitating the lady on her anniversary. To top it all, he had invited all the tiresome dignitaries of the village to come and pay their respects. I was furious.

While Madame Dinville was responding to all sorts of stupid compliments, she turned to Suzon and me and said: 'My children, you'll have to come and dine with me when we can be alone.'

She looked me straight in the eyes when she said that.

I am sure I would have acquitted myself with her if it had not been for those damned callers. What I felt for her was not love, but the violent desire to do with a woman what I had seen Father Polycarpe do with Toinette. The date Madame Dinville suggested for our dinner – the following day – seemed an eternity away.

On our way back home, I tried to set Suzon straight about my intentions with her the day before.

'You got me wrong, Suzon,' I earnestly told her. 'I hope you don't think I wanted to harm you yesterday.'

'It certainly seemed like it. What did you want to do with me then, Saturnin?'

'I just wanted to give you pleasure,' I simply replied.

'What!' she exclaimed in surprise. 'You thought you would give me pleasure by putting your hand under my skirt?'

'Of course. And to prove it, let's go somewhere where we won't be seen.'

I looked at her closely to learn what reaction my proposal might have produced in her. Apparently, it had left her cold.

'Please give me a chance,' I pleaded. 'I assure you that you won't regret it.'

'What is this bliss that you seem to prize so highly?' she asked, seemingly still mystified.

'It is the union of a man and a woman. They hug each other tightly until they both swoon at the same time.'

This time, my words had some effect, for her bosom was heaving.

'But,' she protested, 'Father held me the way you

describe and I didn't have any of those sensations.'

Her comment was a good omen.

'That's because he didn't feel the same way about you that I do.'

'What do you want to do?' she asked in a trembling voice.

'I'm going to put something between your legs,' I boldly informed her.

She blushed and remained silent.

'You see, Suzon, you have a little hole there,' I continued, pointing to the spot.

'Who told you that?' she asked with lowered eyes.

'Who told me that . . . ?' I repeated, slightly embarrassed at the question. 'It's . . . well, all women have one.'

'How about men?' she demanded.

'Men,' I answered authoritatively, 'have a projection that fits in perfectly with the slit of the woman. Putting them together is what produces the raptures. I'll show you mine, but only on the condition you show me yours. We'll touch each other, and then you'll find out what fun it is.'

Suzon was now as red as a beet. I had impressed her, I knew, but she was still reluctant. I had failed this time, because we were now at home, but I was confident that the next time I would have better luck.

We were scarcely in the house when we saw Father Polycarpe arrive. I guessed that he had come to have lunch with us, for he knew that Ambroise was away. Not that Ambroise ever bothered him, but one feels more easy with the husband absent if he has intentions on the wife.

Confident that I was going to enjoy the same

spectacle this afternoon that I had the previous day, I decided to let Suzon share the pleasure with me. Only after lunch did I extend her the invitation. If anything could persuade her to accede to my wishes, this would be it.

The monk and Toinette, believing us too innocent, were not constrained by our presence. I saw the Father's hand slip down and then up Toinette's skirt, and it appeared that she was spreading her legs to provide him easier access. Then one of her hands disappeared and it was not difficult to imagine what she was doing to him. Now they were so excited that they could not hold themselves back, and they told Suzon and me to go and take a walk. I knew what that meant.

We immediately rose from the table, leaving them the freedom to do other things. I was envious of the fun they were going to have. Before offering her the tableau, I tried first to gain my ends with Suzon without having to resort to that ammunition. I tried to escort her to a grove whose thick foliage provided protection against prying eyes. She was still reluctant.

'Look, Saturnin,' she said ingenuously. 'Tell me more about what you were talking.'

'Do you like to hear such things?' I asked.

Her silence was assent.

Looking deeply into her eyes, I took her hand and pressed it to my breast.

'But, Saturnin,' she said worriedly, 'maybe it will hurt.'

'How can it hurt?' I replied scornfully, delighted at having one last feeble resistance to overcome. 'On the contrary. It is the most enjoyable thing imaginable.'

25

'Maybe you would make me a baby,' she murmured.

That observation jolted me somewhat. I did not think that Suzon knew so much, and I was unable to give her a satisfactory answer.

'Do you mean pregnant?' I asked. 'Is that how women get swollen bellies?'

She assured me that it was so.

'Where did you learn about that? I guess it's your turn now to tell me a few things.'

'I think I can trust you, Saturnin, but if you ever tell a soul what I am going to say, I'll hate you for the rest of my days.'

I swore to her that I would never breathe a word.

'Let's sit down here,' she said, refusing to go with me into the arbour. 'Now, I'll tell you what I know. You thought you were going to teach me something, but you are going to find out that I have more knowledge than you. But don't think I didn't like what you said to me. And a girl is always pleased to feel that a boy wants her.'

'I thought you were in a convent,' I cried. 'Is that what the nuns taught you?'

'I learned many things there,' she admitted.

'Well, hurry up,' I impatiently urged her.

'One night,' she continued, taking her time, 'I was awakened from a deep sleep by a naked body crawling into my bed. I started to scream, but a hand was clapped over my mouth, and a voice said: "Suzon, I mean you no harm, so keep quiet. It's your dear Sister Monique." This nun had just assumed the veil and she was my best friend. "Mother of Jesus," I whispered, "why are you here in the dead of night?" "Because I love you," she replied, amorously embracing me. "And why are you naked?" I inquired. "It's so hot that I couldn't stand any covers. Besides, there's a terrible storm. Don't you hear it? I get frightened stiff at the sound of thunder. Take me in your arms, my dearest, and let's put the sheet over our heads so that we won't see the lightning. That's fine. You have no idea of how terrified I am, Suzon."

'Since I am not afraid of thunder or lightning, I did my best to comfort Monique who, in the meantime had stuck her tongue in my mouth and was rubbing my thighs with hers. Also, she was gently slapping my derriere. After a time, I felt her twitch violently, and my legs were wet with a sticky liquid. She was sighing and groaning which I thought was due to her fear of the tempest. I caressed her more in order to calm her. When her spasms ceased, I told her I was tired and I was going back to sleep.

'"So you're going to let me die of fright!" she whispered in my ear. "You won't see me alive tomorrow if you leave me by myself. Give me your hand."

'I did as I was asked, and she guided it to the slit you were talking about. Then she requested me to tickle the little button near the entrance with my finger. Because of my affection for her, I did that, too. After a time, I expected her to tell me to stop, but she didn't say a word. All she did was spread her legs apart and pant. At times, she moaned and wiggled her backside. Thinking that it was hurting her, I stopped.

'"Ah, Suzon," she murmured in an anguished voice, 'finish it, finish it, I beg you.' Her voice was so urgent that I went back to my curious task. "Oh, oh!"

27

she sobbed, her entire body vibrating as she embraced me more tightly, "Hurry! Faster! Oh yes, that's it. I am dying!" Her body stiffened, and I felt again that fluid on my thighs. With a sigh, she relaxed and remained motionless.

'You have no idea, Saturnin, how puzzled I was at what she made me do.'

'Didn't you have any feelings yourself?' I asked Suzon.

'More than you know,' she replied. 'I realised that for some reason, I had caused her intense pleasure, and that if she did to me what I did to her, I would have the same raptures. But I didn't have the courage to suggest it to her, even though I was burning with desire. So I put my hand back on her hole, and that gave me much pleasure. Then I took hers and placed on several parts of my body, but not on the spot where I most wanted it to be. Monique well knew what I wanted, but she mischievously refused to do what I wanted.

'Finally, taking pity on me, she kissed me and said: "I can guess, darling." She lay herself on me and I eagerly pressed her body close to mine. After obeying her command to spread my legs, she inserted her finger into the aperture where I had given her such esctasy in hers. By degrees, I felt the bliss intensify with each jab of her finger. Then she ordered me to raise my buttocks in time with the insertions of her finger. I was in heaven, Saturnin, or at least, I was dead. When it was over, and we were lying without a sign of movement, she still on top of me, and I felt the same liquid dribbling out of me.

'I thought it was blood, but I was so exhilarated that I did not mind. In fact, I couldn't wait to start all over again. But Monique said she was exhausted. After a few moments, I lost patience and straddled her. Rubbing my button against hers, I soon had another spasm of rapture.

'"Well," Monique asked me, "are you sorry that I came into your bed? Are you angry that I woke you up?" I replied that I owed her so much for teaching me what pleasure really is. She answered that I was not in her debt, for I had paid her for what she had given me.

'"Tell me, dear Suzon, and don't hold anything back," she said, "but haven't you ever had any idea of what we have just done?" I told her no. "You never put your finger in your little cunt?" she wanted to know. I replied by saying that I did not know what the word "cunt" meant. "It's that little slit we titillated each other with," she informed me. "Didn't you know that? I see that I knew more than you when I was your age."

'"I never knew that such delights existed," I admitted. "You know Father Jerome, our confessor. It is he who always prevented me. I am always scared stiff when I go to confession with him. Without fail, he wants to know if I have done anything impure with my friends, and he expressly forbids me to do anything to myself. I was stupid enough, I know now, to believe him." Monique then wanted to know how he explained those lewd acts he prohibited. I told her he said I should not put my finger you know where and look at myself naked in a mirror. And lots of things like that. Monique said that he was nothing but an old lecher.

'"Well, I'll tell you more what goes on in the confessional," I said to Monique. "I always took his acts as marks of friendship, but after what you told me,

I know better." Monique was all ears. "He tells me to come closer to him so he can hear better, and then he kisses me on the mouth. After that, he looks down into my bodice, and as I am talking, he sticks his hand inside, all the way down to the nipple. Then he pulls out one of my breasts and starts rubbing it. That gets him so excited that I can't understand a word he is saying.

"'I remember one day, he covered my whole bosom with a hot, viscous liquid. I dried myself with a handkerchief which I had to throw away afterwards. Father Jerome said it was sweat from his fingers. What do you think, Monique?'

"'I had the same experience with him,' Monique replied. 'The old goat. That's the reason why I no longer go to him for confession. I'll tell you more about him, but you have to promise to keep your mouth shut. If you blab, I am ruined.'

'Saturnin, I know I am breaking my promise, but I'll tell you what Monique confided in me only if I have your solemn oath to keep it to yourself.'

Without hesitation, I crossed my heart, so eager was I to hear the rest of a story with such an enchanting beginning.

What follows is tale of Sister Monique as my sister Suzon rendered it to me.

The Story of Sister Monique
(as told by Suzon)

'We women,' Monique began by telling me, 'are not the mistresses of our hearts. Seduced from birth by pleasure, we cannot control ourselves. But I don't envy those who let themselves be swayed by wise counsel. They pay dearly for their austerity. The rewards for their virtue are imaginary. It is old women no longer able to satisfy a man who preach these false doctrines. But let them talk, Suzon. When a girl is young, she should obey no laws except those dictated by her heart. Follow its advice.

'You would think that a convent would be the ideal spot to stifle any nascent lasciviousness, but that is the very place where I discovered it.

'I was very young when my mother came to this convent after the death of her fourth husband. Although I did not say anything, I was dismayed at the thought of life in a nunnery. One could not even get a glimpse of a man. What a deprivation! Then I began to reflect on the difference between man and woman. What is there about a man, the sight of whom makes a girl's heart beat more quickly? Is he prettier than we women are? No, that cannot be it, for Father Jerome, ugly and disagreeable as he is, arouses certain sensations in me when I am with him. There is something about a man that produces this reaction,

31

and I did not know what it was. I made vain efforts to break the bonds with which my ignorance shackled me.

'Alone in my room with the door locked, my sole thoughts were concentrated on men. Taking off my clothes, I voluptuously examined my nudity. I cast inflamed looks on every part of my body in the mirror. To extinguish the blaze within me, I lay down on the bed and spread wide my legs, but that did not help. In my overheated imagination, there was a man whom I welcomed with outstretched arms because he would put out the fire in my cunt. Never did I dare put my finger on it, in spite of the unbearable itching, for fear of doing some damager to it.

'At times, I almost succumbed to temptation. I touched it with the top of my finger, but frightened at what might happen, I quickly withdrew it. Then I covered it with the palm of my hand. That was no good.

'Finally, I was no longer able to restrain myself. I determined to do it, no matter what might result. When I bravely stuck my finger in, the bliss was so great that I nearly died. When the first rapture was over, I did it again and again until my hand was so tired that I could barely move it.

'Overjoyed with my discovery, I felt that my eyes had been opened. If my finger could produce such ecstasy, the finger men have between their legs would give even greater satisfaction. I was now sure that this was the only true way to pleasure, and I was wracked with desire to view that masculine organ which promised so much.

'To attract a male, I became a true flirt, dressing

myself as seductively as I could, smiling enigmatically, casting inviting regards, and so on, but... alas!... there was no male on whom I could exert my charms.

'In the sitting-room, I waited with girls whose brothers would come to visit them. When they appeared, they were not oblivious to what I was inwardly offering them.

'One day, there was a handsome lad whose lively black eyes returned my regard. I felt a delicious sensation running through me. He tried to avert his glance, but it always returned to me. When his sister was not looking, he made certain signs to me. I had not the faintest idea of what they meant, but I pretended that I understood. When I smiled back, he became even bolder. With his hands stretched apart, he made it clear that he had an organ of such and such a length by pointing to the bottom of his stomach.

'Although modesty advised me to leave at such obscenity, I could not, for the gesture set me on fire. Besides, modesty is a weak opponent against desire.

'Verland, for that was his name, sensed what I was feeling. Then he joined his middle finger with his thumb and inserted the index finger of his other hand into the circle that was formed, and with inaudible sighs, he pushed it in and out. I understood.

'At that moment, his sister was called, and she left, saying she would be right back. Taking advantage of her temporary absence, he explained himself more clearly. Although the compliment he paid me was not very elegantly phrased, I shall always remember it with pleasure. Women are usually more flattered by a simple and straightforward declaration than by meaningless insipid gallantries.

'"We don't have much time," he exclaimed. "You are charming and I have a hard prick that is yearning to get into you. Tell me how I can sneak into this convent."

'Not only was I stunned by his words, but also his actions. He darted his hand through the bars of the grille and grabbed my breast which he feverishly fondled. I stood there as if petrified, absolutely unable to stop him. Just at that moment, his sister appeared and surprised us. She vilified us both, and I never saw Verland again.

'The whole convent soon knew about the escapade. Every time the girls saw me, they whispered, tittered, and looked at me knowingly. The pretty ones were kinder, for they realised that their homely fellow-students were simply jealous of me. No fellow would ever make an advance towards them.

'Naturally, the story reached the ears of the Mothers Superior who met to discuss what punishment should be meted out to a wanton who allowed her breasts to be touched. In the eyes of those withered mummies with tits so shrivelled that they could throw them over their shoulders, I had committed an unpardonable crime. It was a grave misdemeanour and I deserved expulsion. How I would have liked such a sentence!

'But my mother appealed to them, saying that if I were allowed to stay, she would force me to take the veil. As I had foreseen, the offer was accepted. I barricaded myself in my room, but the nuns forced open the door. I bit, scratched and kicked them and tore their wimples from their heads. I defended myself so effectively that the six sisters, including the Mother Superior, had to give up.

'Nevertheless, my rage was supplanted by fatigue. I was dispirited as I had been courageous, and I burst into tears. The thought of the jeers and mockery I would have to undergo plunged me into gloom. Then I determined to go to my mother for advice and help.

'As I opened the door and stepped out into the corridor, I tripped on an object on the floor.

'Fumbling in the dusk on the floor to learn what it could be, I found it. You can imagine my feelings when I saw an instrument which was a faithful reproduction of what so preoccupied me, namely, a prick.

'"What in heaven's name is that?" I asked the sister who was keeping guard on my room.

'"You'll soon find out," she calmly replied. "Because you are so attractive, many handsome young chevaliers will be more happy to instruct you in its usage. This is an artificial prick, my dear, and a prick is the name for the male organ. It is called the member *par excellence*, because of the pleasure it gives. If women would render it the adoration it deserves, the real thing, I mean, they would call it a god. Indeed, it is a deity worthy of worship, and the cunt is its domain. Pleasure is its element and it unerringly seeks it in the most hidden recesses. Penetrating and probing, it locates it and then dives into it, receiving and giving raptures. In the cunt it is born, lives, dies, and revives in order to continue its relentless task. But by itself it is nothing. Without the sight or thought of a cunt, the proud pike becomes flabby, cowardly, shrivelled, and ashamed to show itself. But when it meets its partner, it is arrogant, ardent and impetuous. It threatens, attacks and breaks down every barrier."

'"Just a moment," I interrupted the sister. "You

forget that you are talking to a beginner, and your eulogy of this merely confuses me. One of these days, I believe I shall worship this god, but I don't know much about it yet. Could you speak in simpler language so that I can understand?"

'"Gladly," the nun answered. "When inactive, the prick is soft, limp and short. But when men see a woman they want or get erotic fantasies, it is transformed. We can bring about this change by opening our bodices and letting the men see our breasts or revealing to their eager eyes a slender waist or a shapely leg. It's not necessary to have a pretty face. More often than not, it is a trifle that catches their attention, and then their imagination gets to work. It gives firmness to flabby breasts, flatness to swollen bellies, sleekness to wrinkled skins, and the flush of youth to withered cheeks. Then the prick swells, stretches out, and hardens, and the longer and harder it is, the more delight a woman receives from it, because it fills the hole more fully, penetrates more deeply, rubs more vigorously, and produces more divine raptures."

'I told her how deeply indebted I was to her for her information. And I said that I would display my legs and breasts on every possible occasion.

'"Be careful," she warned me. "That's not the way to arouse men. It's more of an art than you think. Men are funny. They don't like to feel they are indebted to us for the delights we give them. They think they are doing us a favour. And they always want something left to their imagination. And a woman loses nothing by indulging them. When a man wants a woman, she, to him, is the most desirable object in the world. There is nothing he wants more. As soon as Monsieur sees the Madame or Mademoiselle who strikes his fancy, he burns with a yen to insert his prick into her cunt. But he won't tell you that. He merely says that he is in love with you."

Delighted with what Sister Monique told me, I was more impatient than ever to hear the end of her story, and I urged her to continue. After catching her breath, she began to discuss the contrivance she had picked up.

'I had often heard of the dildo, and I knew it was the instrument with which the mothers superior consoled themselves for lack of men. It is an exact imitation of a prick and designed to perform its function. It is hollow and can be filled with warm milk to take the place of semen. After a bit of practice in using it, you can scarcely tell the difference from the real thing. The milk squirts when you squeeze it at the right moment and inundates you just like the man's juice.

'Apparently, in the ruckus with the nuns, the instrument had been jostled out of one of their pockets. I went back in my room and locked the door. As I held the article in my hand, all my grief and anxiety disappared. Although its size frightened me, it also fascinated me. I could not wait to try it out. A sweet warmth ran through my body in anticipation of the pleasure I was going to enjoy. Already I was shuddering and panting.

'Without taking my eyes off the dildo, I undressed with all the eagerness of a young bride about to enter the nuptial couch and then I got into bed with the instrument in my hand.

'But, my dear Suzon, you can imagine my despair

when I found that I could not get it in. In my desperate efforts, I thought that my poor little cunt was going to be ripped open. The pain was intolerable when I spread open the lips and tried to insert the contraption. But I did not give up. Then I was struck with the happy idea that some sort of grease would facilitate the entrance. I took some cream, which I rubbed both on the dildo and my cunt. That helped. I did not mind the indescribable hurt, so great was my pleasure. But it was so big that I could not get it all the way in. In desperation, I gave it one last mighty shove, but it bounced out, leaving me in frustrated agony.

'"Ah," I cried. "If only Verland were here. No matter how big his is, I would be able to take it. Yes, I would suffer anything, even help him torture me, and die happy as long as it was in me. The pains would be delights. I would hug him as hard as I could, and he would do the same to me. I would cover his lips and eyes with burning kisses. He would eagerly respond to my transports, and I would idolize him, adore him. Our souls would become one through the union of our bodies. Ah, Verland, why aren't you with me? You could do anything you want with me, anything. Why don't you come, you cruel monster. I'm all alone, alas, with nothing but a deceptive replica, a poor substitute, which serves merely to augment my despair and frustration.

'"Cursed instrument," I said, addressing the dildo and shaking it with a vengeance, "go and service some other poor creature, for you are of no use to me. My finger is a thousand times better than you."

'Immediately, I reverted to my finger and gave myself so much bliss that I forgot about the dildo.

Falling back with exhaustion, I fell asleep with my thoughts on Verland.

'The next morning, I got up, dressed, and to commence my emancipation, I ripped to shreds my veil which I regarded as a symbol of servitude. That done, my heart was lighter for I felt it was the first step to liberty. As I was pacing up and down my room, my eyes fell on that damned dildo. I picked it up and sat on my bed, where I began to investigate it closely. I could not help but admire its beauty. Caressing it, I was impressed by its length. It was so thick that I could barely wrap my fingers around it. What a shame it was so big that I could not make use of it.

'Although I realised I could not utilize it, I still lifted up my skirt and attempted to insert it. It caused the same burning pain as the night before. But it so excited me that I again had to resort to my finger. Never before had I masturbated so hard. My finger went in and out like a piston. When I had finished, I had an idea that I was very proud of. Since I had nothing to lose, I decided to depart from the convent in a burst of glory. I was going to take the device to the Mother Superior and enjoy her reaction.

'Going to the nun's suite, I relished in advance the consternation the sight of the dildo was going to cause her. Finding her alone, I saucily addressed her.

'"You realise that after what happened yesterday and the way you affronted me, I cannot honourably remain in the convent."

'She looked at me with surprise, and since she did not answer, I felt free to continue.

'"If I did something wrong, I would have deserved to be punished, but I did not. It was that vile Verland who wronged me, and I had no chance to defend myself. A simple reprimand would have been sufficient. You did not have to try and take me by force."

'"A reprimand?" she drily asked. "A simple reprimand for an action such as yours? You had to be made an example of, and if it were not for the consideration we have for your mother who is a saintly woman, you would have been expelled."

'"You don't punish all the wrongdoers," I accused her heatedly.

'"If you tell me who they are, I'll see that they will get what is coming to them," she answered.

'"You know I would not stoop that low," I retorted, "but among them are some of your nuns who so brutally tried to inflict indignities on me yesterday."

'"You're going too far," the Mother Superior cried. "Your heart and mind are depraved and corrupted. In addition to your base conduct, you are calumniating the chastest of women, models of virtue and piety."

'After permitting her to finish the eulogy of the sisters, I coolly took the dildo out of my pocket and presented it to her.

'"Here you are," I told her. "Here's evidence of the chastity and saintliness of at least one of your sisters."

'As she fingered it, I carefully examined her features. Returning my scrutiny, she blushed. From the look in her eyes, I had no doubt that the dildo belonged to her.

'"Oh, my dear child," she sighed, casting her eyes upwards, "how is it possible that there are women so abandoned by God in this house of the Lord to make use of such an infamous instrument. I can't get over it. But do not tell anyone about this matter. If you do, I'll have to take stern measures and make an investigation, but I would prefer to keep it under cover. But, my dear child, do you still want to leave us? Why don't you go back to your room, and I'll take care of everything. I'll say that it was all a mistake. You won't have to worry about the other girls. And I'll have a long talk with Mademoiselle Verland." Casting another look at the dildo, she muttered: "How cunning the devil is. What a diabolic, foul instrument. May God forgive her who made use of this."

'As she was finishing her speech, my mother entered the room.

'"What's this all about, Madame?" she asked, addressing the Mother Superior. "And you, Monique," she said, turning to me, "what are you doing here?"

'Not knowing what to say, I stuttered, turned red, and lowered my eyes. When my mother kept after me, the Mother Superior broke in and defended me with spirit. If she did not say that I was completely blameless, she made it clear that I had done nothing seriously wrong. My only error was my imprudence to let a young man slip his hand through the grille and grab my breast. And he would never again be permitted in the confines of the convent. She concluded by stating that it was Mademoiselle Verland who was in fault for having spread the story which should have been kept quiet, if not for the reputation of her brother, at least for mine. She would see to it there would be no disagreeable consequences for myself. I could not ask for anything more. I emerged from the escapade with my reputation unsullied. My mother was smiling with tenderness at me.

'Souls zealous for the glory of God are able to reap

advantage from everything. Although I was in the clear, my mother and the nun agreed that I would have to do the sacrament of penitence with Father Jerome.

'When I was locked up with the priest, I was reluctant to confess my sins and he had to force them out of me. Heaven knows what pleasure the old lecher had in hearing them. I did not tell him everything, for I did not think God considered it a sin if a poor girl tries to satisfy her desires by herself when they become too strong. Besides, whose fault is it that those erotic desires are planted in her? If she attempts to quench the flames that are consuming her, she uses the means nature has given her, and there is nothing wrong in that.

'In spite of the harmless secrets I revealed to Father Jerome, he refused to give me absolution, guessing correctly that I was holding out on him. When he permitted me to go, it was already night. I was so exhausted after the ordeal that I sat down on the *prie-dieu* near the altar and there fell asleep. During my slumber, I had the most charming dream. I was with Verland who was holding me in his arms. When he pressed me with his thighs, I spread open mine and lent myself to all his delightful movements. He was fondling my breasts in a delirium of joy, squeezing and kissing them.

'The bliss was so great that I woke up and, to my wonderment, I was really in the arms of a man. But it was not Verland. I could not see who it was for I was held tightly from behind. It did not matter, for I was ecstatic. Something hard and hot was penetrating me. Suddenly, I felt myself drenched with a hot fluid. Then I became aware that a similar liquid was gushing forth from my body in delicious jets and blending with what he was pouring out a second time. I fell forward senseless on the *prie-dieu*.

'This joy, if it lasted forever, would be a thousand times more delightful than the promised in heaven, but alas, it ended all too quickly.

'I was seized with terror at the thought that I was alone at night in the chapel with a man I did not know. Who could he be? But I was too frightened to make an attempt to learn his identity. In fact, I could not move. I closed my eyes and trembled like a leaf. My tremors became more violent when I felt my hand being pressed and kissed. Still, I could not move. But I was somewhat relieved when a deep voice whispered in my ear: "Don't be afraid. It's only I."

'The voice which I vaguely recalled having heard before restored my courage sufficiently so that I was able to ask who he was, but I still did not dare look at him. My assailant informed me that he was Martin, Father Jerome's valet. This discovery dispelled my fears, and I was now able to turn my eyes on him. Martin was a little blond fellow, quite good looking, and with flashing eyes. I could see that he was as nervous as I. He seemed unable to make up his mind whether to attack me again or take flight. He regarded me as if it were up to me to make the decision for him. I don't have to tell you that I certainly was not angry with him, and my eyes reflected the raptures I had just enjoyed. Perceiving that I bore him no rancor, he threw himself in my arms which warmly received him.

'We did not worry in the slightest about being surprised. Since love forgives anything, we felt no sense of impropriety when he stretched my body on the steps of the altar, lifted my skirt, and ran his hand over my legs and thighs. Just as stimulated as he, I extended my hand gropingly to his prick, and, oh wonder, for the first time in my life I had the ineffable pleasure of fondling that noble organ. How delicious my sentiments were. Slender but long, it was just the thing for me. Now I felt a voluptuous itch as I squeezed the beloved rod. I regarded it lovingly, fondled it some more, put it on my breast, brought it to my mouth, sucked, and tried to swallow it.

'During this time, Martin had his finger in my cunt in which he stirred as in a kettle of soup, then pushing it in and out, renewing and increasing my raptures at every motion. His kisses covered my stomach, my Venus mount, and my thighs. Abandoning them, he wetted my breasts with his tongue and gently nibbled the nipples. Of course, I made no attempt to resist these amorous attacks. Letting myself fall back, I dragged him down on me. Clutched firmly in my hand was the object of all my desires which I attempted to introduce into myself to obtain more solid pleasures. What we had been doing was merely the *hors d'oeuvres* of the main meal. Animated by the same urge, he pressed himself to me and began to shove.

'"Stop, dear Martin," I pleaded with him between my sighs. "Not so fast. Just a moment."

'Writhing under him, I spread my legs wide and wrapped them around his back. My thighs were next to his, my belly was glued to his, my bosom was squashed by his chest, our mouths were pressed together, our tongues were searching for one another, and our exhalations blended.

'"Oh, Monique," he panted. "What a wonderful

position! It is perfect for love-making."

'I was too engrossed in savouring to the full the thrill I was experiencing to answer him.

'Impatience prevented me from enjoying it at greater length. I had a sudden spasm at precisely the moment Martin did, and our bliss vanished. We were still locked together, but desire and pleasure refused our invitation to return.

'It is time, Suzon,' Monique continued, 'to tell you what that holy water was that Father Jerome sprinkled on you that time he was giving you absolution.

'My first reaction, when Martin slipped out of my arms, was to touch the spot which had received the most vigorous punishment. Inside and out, it was covered with the effusion that had caused my raptures. But now it had lost its warmth, and it was as cold as ice. It was fuck, as one calls the white matter that is discharged from the prick and the cunt. The emissions were the result of the reciprocal friction of our sexual parts. And a man or a woman can produce it by themselves with the hand. And fuck was what Father Jerome wetted you with.'

'What?' I asked Monique. 'Is that what you just spilled?'

'Of course,' she casually replied. 'And didn't you ever feel your cunt all moist? That dampness is fuck, my little one. The pleasure you experienced is much less than that enjoyed with a man for what he gives us, mingling with what we give him, penetrates us, inflames us, kills us, revives us, and sears us. Oh, what raptures, dear Suzon! But let me tell you the rest of my story.

'My clothing was all rumpled, as you can well

imagine after such strenuous activity. I straightened out my dress as best I could and asked Martin what time it was.

'"Oh, it's not late," he assured me.

'But I heard the bell ringing, announcing that it was time to go to bed.

'"I have to go, Martin, but before I do, tell me how you happened to be here and how you dared do what you did."

'"You know tomorrow is All Saints' Day and I had come here to put up some decorations. Then I noticed you and I said to myself that there is a pretty girl offering her prayers to God. But I wondered why you were here at such an hour, and when I came up to ask you, I saw that you were asleep. You were snoring, too. I stood there just looking at you for a long time and my heart went pit-a-pat.

'"I determined to take advantage of this unexpected opportunity. When I opened your bodice, I saw two petite hemispheres that were as white as snow. I couldn't help but kiss very gently their pink tips. Seeing that that did not awaken you, I felt the urge to do more. So I lifted your skirt and, damn it, I gave a shove, and well ... I fucked you, as you well know."

'Although a little shocked at his crude language, I was charmed by the ingenuous way he explained his actions.

'"Well, my friend," I asked him, "did you enjoy yourself?"

'"You have no idea," he answered, giving me a kiss. "So much so that I am ready to start all over again, that is, if you are willing."

'"No, not now." I told him. "I'll be missed at bed

46

count. And besides I am exhausted. But you have the key to the chapel. If you would like to come here tomorrow at midnight, leave the door unlocked and wait for me. All right?"

'"Oh, yes," he enthusiastically replied. "We'll have the place to ourselves at that hour. You can be sure I'll be here impatiently waiting for you."

'I gave him like assurance. Prudence won out over desire, and I turned a deaf ear to his plea for "one more little time". I consoled his grief by reminding him of the delights that he would have the next night. After exchanging kisses, I returned to the dormitory without being seen.

'You can imagine my impatience to examine my body and learn what condition it was in after the assaults it had undergone. I had such a burning sensation between my legs that I could hardly walk. Locking the door and drawing the curtains, I lit a candle and investigated myself with one leg on the bed and the other on the floor. I was surprised to find that the lips of my cunt which were so firm and chubby had become flaccid and shrivelled. The hair covering them smelt of his effusion and were now a mass of crinkly curls. The interior was an angry red and very tender. In spite of its sensitivity, it itched so much that I had to stick my finger in, but the sharp pain made me withdraw it immediately. I rubbed it against the bed post, covering it with the traces of Martin's virility. That so excited me that I forgot my suffering and tiredness. Gradually, my eyes became heavy, and I fell into a deep sleep broken only by the delicious dreams of what I had experienced.

'The next day, no mention was made of my absence

from classes and meals. When I went to Mass, I held my head high and regarded disdainfully the girls without paying any attention to the muffled whispering and looks cast in my direction. When I saw Martin enter the chapel, I forgot everything. More than one of my fellow students would have willingly exchanged the spiritual nourishment they were receiving for the raptures Martin could have bestowed on them.

'The regards I cast at my lover were more adoring than those I gave the altar. In the eyes of a woman of the world, Martin would be nothing but an impudent rascal, but with his youth and native charm, he was the epitome of love to me. I saw that he was running his eyes over all the girls, trying to pick me out. I did not want him to spot me, but I was pleased that he made the attempt. The sight of him made me all the more impatient for the rendezvous we had agreed on for that night.

'The hour that I so ardently yearned for finally came. The chimes sounded midnight. Trembling with anticipation, I tip-toed down the corridor. Although everybody was sound asleep, I felt as if the eyes of the world were on me. The only illumination to guide my steps was my love.

'As I quietly made my way down the hall, I was seized with a sudden fear that perhaps Martin might not keep his promise. If he did not show up, I thought that I would die of grief.

'But my dear Martin was there, waiting for me. He was as eager as I was punctual. I was very lightly dressed for it was warm, and also I had noticed the previous night that too much clothing was a nuisance.

'No sooner was I at the door than my heart began to

beat more rapidly. I was incapable of speech. All I could do was whisper "Martin" to announce my arrival to my lover. He swept me into his arms, and I returned caress for caress. We remained locked in each other's arms for interminable minutes. Recovering from these initial transports, we commenced to arouse one another to greater ones. I put my hand on the source of my desires while his hand groped to the spot where he knew I was eagerly awaiting him.

'We quickly stripped, making a bed of our discarded clothing, and lay down on it. Our ecstasies came in rapid succession for more than two hours. We gave ourselves up to each one as if we never would have another again. In the blaze of sensuousness, one abandons oneself completely. Excess is not enough. But Martin's forces were not the equal of mine, for finally he had to give up the battle.

'Our bliss lasted barely a month, but during that time, what rapturous nights we spent!

'Now hear me, Suzon,' Monique told me earnestly. 'Promise again that this is a secret between you and me. Nobody must ever know about it.

'I loved well but not wisely, but a girl loses her head with such an attractive boy as Martin was. The anxiety I suffered was a dear price to pay for the delicious pleasures I had tasted. How I repented those sweet hours! The consequences of my weakness seemed so horrible that I could do nothing but wail and sob the whole day long.'

'What was it?' I asked Monique.

'I noticed that I missed my period,' she replied. 'To my dismay, eight days passed without any sign of it. I heard that when it is that late, it is almost a sure sign of pregnancy. I was nearly out of my mind with worry, for I was positive that I was going to be big with child.

'Well, Martin had caused my condition and he would have to rescue me from my condition. My melancholy discovery did not prevent me from seeing him, however. Although I was anxiety-ridden and nervous, my love for him was still as powerful as ever. When he was in me, I momentarily forgot my woes. Besides, nothing worse could happen to me by going on with him as before. I had reached bottom which, in itself, was a sort of comfort.

'One night, after having received from Martin those tokens of affection that never abated in intensity, he heard my sad sighs and felt my hand, which was in his, shaking. He perceived that I was distressed. He worriedly asked what was wrong, and when he learned the cause of my melancholy, he tenderly commiserated with me.

'"Ah, Martin, you have ruined me. Don't say that my love for you has cooled, for I bear in my belly a proof which is driving me to despair. I am pregnant."

'His astonishment gave place to profound reverie, and I did not know what to make of it. Martin was my sole hope in the cruel circumstances. What was I to think of his hesitation? Was he considering ways to extricate himself from the situation? Perhaps he was thinking of flight, leaving me to face the consequences alone. Inwardly, I prayed that he would stay with me, for I would rather die loving him than hating him. At that thought, I started to shed warm tears. But he caused them to stop when he promised to do everything he could to help me. I felt as if I had been called back from the dead.

'Overjoyed at his reassurance, I was curious to learn how he was going to rid me of my burden. He told me that he was going to give me a potion he had found in his master's closet. Sister Angelica had used it successfully, he said.

'I was all ears at his casual remark. I was more than eager to learn about what had gone on between the monk and the sister. For the latter I nursed a mortal hatred because of her treatment of me the day of the incident with Verland. I had always thought her as pure as the driven snow, but it seemed that I was wrong. Apparently, she had been able to conceal her real propensities under a mask of unremitting devoutness. So she had been carrying on with Father Jerome.

'Martin told me all the details. While snooping among Father Jerome's effects, he came across a letter from Angelica in which she informed her lover that she was in the same embarrasing state I was. And Father Jerome had given her a phial of the liqueur he was going to purloin and give to me. Sister Angelica wrote him back, acknowledging the receipt of the potion and informing him that it had worked perfectly. The danger was gone and they could resume their relationship.

'"My dear friend," I urgently said to Martin. "Bring me that medicine tomorrow without fail. You will rid me of all my worries, and I'll be able to get my revenge on that hateful Angelica."

'Not realising what my imprudent request would cost, he brought me the next night the potion along with the damaging letters.

'I couldn't wait to read them, but I reflected that if I

lit a candle, I might be noticed, and so I restrained my impatience to read them until morning. When the sun cast its first rays into my room, I eagerly perused them. They were written in a passionate tone in which she described her erotic fury, using expressions and terms I never would have believed her capable of. She showed no restraint in revealing her feelings and ardour, for she counted on Father Jerome burning the missives, as she counselled him, but he was unwise enough not to have followed her advice. And I had some powerful ammunition in my hands.

'For some time, I pondered ways to make best use of this incriminating evidence in order to bring about the downfall of my foe. It was too risky for me to hand them over to the Mother Superior myself since I would have to explain how they came into my possession. And having someone else deliver them was also out of the question.

'I considered leaving them under her door, but I discarded that idea, too. Martin would come under suspicion, and he was too precious to lose. Finally, I decided to postpone my plans for revenge for the time being, that is to say, when I would be out of danger.

'I had asked Martin for an armistice of eight days, after which the elixir was to have had its effect. When the period was over, I could carry out my plans. And my success exceeded my fondest hopes. The Mother Superior found the letters slipped under her door. Summoning Sister Angelica to her apartment, she found her guilty on the spot. Perhaps she might have shown some mercy if it had not been for the rage that devoured the Mother Superior. She was envious of Sister Angelica. Although she did not lack, as I have mentioned, the means to blunt the points of the needles of the flesh, a dildo is a poor substitute for the real thing. And the Mother Superior could not forgive Angelica for having had the genuine article.

'Angelica was ordered to expiate in solitary confinement in a remote cell for an indefinite period and on a diet of bread and water.

'It was not long before I repented of what I had done. I had flattered myself that the storm would fall only on Sister Angelica, but it went farther than I had expected. Father Jerome, irritated at seeing his favourite mistress taken away, suspected that his servant, my lover, was the root of it all, and blamed him for the whole affair. He kicked Martin out of the convent and I never saw that delightful boy again.

'That's my story, Suzon,' she ended. 'Please keep it to yourself. Now you know the pleasures I enjoyed. If he were only here, I would suffocate him with my kisses.'

The memory of Martin excited her, and her recital produced the same effect on me. Unconsciously, we began games which compensated for her loss. They reminded her of the enjoyment that she had had with him. Momentarily deceived that I was only a young girl, she imagined that I was he. On me, she lavished the same compliments and endearments she had employed with her lover.

For myself, I could not imagine any greater pleasure than I was having with Monique. In her desire to recapture the past, she showed me the favourite position she and Martin had assumed. Our heads were at opposite ends. I learned later that the posture is commonly known as the sixty-nine. In that stance, we embraced each other until our fluids exuded. A momentary pause, and then we experienced new raptures. We were enchanted with one another, and it was only exhaustion that put an end to our games.

Both delighted, we separated with the mutual promise to repeat our revels the next day. Our games stopped only when I left to come here.

In Flagrante

Since Suzon had not been bashful about telling me her actions with Monique, my hopes for success rose immeasurably. But I determined not to rush matters so as not to ruin my chances. I tried to conceal my agitation, but it did not escape the eyes of Suzon.

I asked if Sister Monique was pretty.

'She is as beautiful as an angel,' Suzon declared. 'Her waist is slender, her skin white and satiny, her creamy complexion is set off by deep blue eyes and crimson lips, and she has the most adorable bosom in the world.'

'I feel sorry for her, now that she has lost you,' I remarked. 'I don't envy her, having to spend the rest of her life in a nunnery.'

'That's where you are wrong,' Suzon corrected me. 'She took the veil only a short time ago just to please her mother, but she has not yet made the final vows. Her fate depends on her brother who was seriously wounded in a brawl in a brothel. If he dies, which seems likely, Monique will be the only child, and her mother would not want to see the family come to an end.'

'A brothel!' I exclaimed. 'What is that?'

'I'll tell you what Monique told me,' Suzon answered. 'She seems to know everything about things like that. It's a place where girls and women of easy virtue gather. Their calling is to accept the attentions of lustful men and lend themselves to their caprices for a fee. That is how they earn their living.'

'Oh, I would give anything to live in a city with places like that!' I cried. 'Wouldn't you, too, Suzon?'

She did not answer, but I could see from her expression that she shared my desire.

'I bet that Sister Monique would like to work in such a place,' I added.

'I think so, too. She's mad about men,' Suzon concurred.

'How about you?' I asked suggestively.

'I can't deny that I have a yen for men,' she replied demurely. 'I adore them, but there are too many risks in having anything to do with them.'

'Oh, it's not as dangerous as all that!' I pooh-poohed.

'Come, come, Saturnin. If two women make love together, neither of them can get pregnant.'

'How about the lady next door?' I argued. 'She's been married a long time. She does it all the time with her husband, and she has never had a child.'

This example seemed to shake her convictions.

'Listen, dear Suzon,' I declared excitedly, for I had just been struck with a brilliant idea. 'Sister Monique told you that when Martin put his prick into her, she was flooded with his fluid, and I am sure it was that juice that made her pregnant.'

'Perhaps, but what is the point?' Suzon asked, averting her face to conceal the desire I felt was rising in her.

'What I am trying to say,' I went on, 'is that if this

ejaculation in the woman causes pregnancy, the man can prevent it by withdrawing his prick just before it comes out.'

'That's not possible,' Suzon demurred, although her eyes were sparkling with excitement. 'Didn't you ever set two dogs in action, one on top of the other? Even if you beat them with a club, they won't separate. They are joined so closely that it is impossible. Isn't that the same with a man and a woman?'

The objection took me aback for the example was apt. Suzon was looking at me as if asking me to give her a convincing rebuttal. She seemed to regret having pointed out a difficulty that I could not overcome. I wracked my brain.

Suddenly, I recalled that Father Polycarpe the preceding day had no trouble in getting off Toinette. I would have told Suzon about this, but I thought it preferable to let her see for herself.

'Come with me, Suzon,' I said confidently, 'I am going to show you how wrong you are.'

I got up, helping her do the same but first shoving my hand under her skirt. She pushed it away, but she was not angry.

'Where are you taking me?' she demanded as I led her down the path. The little wanton thought I wanted to bring her to some spot where we wouldn't be seen, and I think she would have liked nothing better. But to be sure, I wanted her to regard Toinette and the reverend father who must have been up to their tricks for he had not yet left. I answered that we were going to a spot where she would see something that would amuse her.

'And where is that?' she persisted.

'To my room,' I replied simply.

'To your room,' she repeated. 'Oh, I would never go there with you. You'll try to do something to me.'

She allowed herself to be persuaded when I swore that I would not do anything without her consent.

We reached my chamber without being seen. As we tip-toed down the hall, hand in hand. I could feel that Suzon was trembling. Putting my finger to my lips as a sign not to speak, I put my eye to the knot-hole in the partition, but they were not there yet.

'What are you going to show me?' she whispered, intrigued by my mysterious air.

'You'll see in good time,' I told her, and turned her on her back on the bed. I inserted my hand between her legs and was up to her garter, when she fiercely said that she would make a fuss if I did not leave her alone. She went so far as to pretend that she was going to go out, and I was simple enough to believe her. Dismayed, I began to plead with her, and in spite of my babbling incoherence, she consented to remain.

Then I heard the door of Ambroise's room open. I took heart and waited until Suzon's curiosity would do for me what I was not able to accomplish myself.

'There they are,' I jubilantly whispered to my companion, pulling her back to the bed near the peep-hole. Peering through it, I saw the good father beginning the game by fondling Toinette's magnificent breasts which had popped out of her bodice. Now they were motionless, locked in each other's arms. They were so totally absorbed in each other that it seemed that they were going to celebrate the great rite of contemplation.

I waited until they had made some progress before

nodding my head for Suzon to come and look. Bored with meditation, Toinette freed herself from the monk and let her chemise and dress drop to the floor in preparation for the ceremony. Oh, what a delicious sight it was! And because of Suzon's presence, it stimulated me all the more.

Burning with curiosity when she noticed my attentiveness at the aperture, she came up to me.

'Let me have a look,' she whispered, giving me a nudge.

I gladly relinquished my post, unable to wish for anything better. Remaining at her side, I watched carefully for the emotions that the spectacle was going to produce on her face. She blushed, but her eye remained glued to the hole.

While she was avidly regarding the scene in the adjoining room, my hand crept up her legs and met merely a token resistance. Now my hand was in the vice of her thighs, but as the amorous combat she was watching increased in intensity, she gradually relaxed them. I could have counted every stroke Toinette and Father Polycarpe exchanged by the twitches I felt on Suzon's satiny buttocks. Finally, I reached my goal. Now, without the slightest sign of objection, she spread her legs in complete surrender to allow my hand to do as it wished.

Taking advantage of the occasion, I put my finger on the sensitive spot, but it was so tight that it could barely go in. I felt her quiver as my finger worked its way in. She gave a start at each sign of progress.

'Now I have you, Suzon,' I thought triumphantly.

Immediately, I flipped up her skirt and what met my delighted eyes was the loveliest, the whitest, the most perfectly rounded, the firmest, the most delicious derriere it is possible to imagine. Never before or since had I paid my devotions to such an alluring altar. I paid those adorable hemispheres the worship due them with a thousand impassioned kisses. Never shall I forget that divine behind.

But Suzon possessed other charms which piqued my curiosity.

Getting back on my feet, I undid her bodice and released two little breasts, hard, firm, and seemingly fashioned by love itself. Rising and falling, they begged for a male hand to control their violent heavings. Mine came to their succour and tenderly squeezed each in turn and then both together.

Unable to tear her eyes away from the spectacle she was viewing, Suzon lent herself automatically to my manipulations. Her submissiveness charmed me at first, but her prolonged concentration on the performance taking place in the next room soon began to irritate me. I was burning with a fire that only she could extinguish, but she refused to leave her post.

I wanted to see Suzon completely nude in order to be able to take in all at once her exquisite body that I was kissing and fondling. To my experienced mind, that was all that was required to satisfy my desires.

Quickly, I summoned up enough courage to strip the unprotesting Suzon of every stitch of her clothing, and then I did the same to myself. Now that both of us were stark naked, I tried every which way to assuage my passions, but she remained unresponsive. Repeated kisses and tender but energetic caresses failed to stir her. Her thoughts were elsewhere.

Even though our position was uncomfortable, I

tried to take her from behind. Although she spread her legs and buttocks dutifully, my prick could not get in. I inserted my finger into her adorable little cunt, and when I withdrew it, it was dripping with the love liqueur. Again I tried to penetrate her with my prick, but my efforts were fruitless.

'Suzon,' I muttered, enraged at her preoccupation with our neighbours which prevented me from obtaining the satisfaction I was yearning for, 'enough is enough. Come now. We can have as much pleasure as those two.'

When she turned her eyes to me, they were glistening.

Taking her tenderly in my arms, I bore her to my bed and turned her on her back. Without my asking, she widened her thighs. My eyes were fixed on a tiny crimson button rise peeping out from a tuft of golden fleece which partially concealed a mound whose delicate tint the most skilful brush would have difficulty in reproducing.

Motionless but eager, Suzon awaited the marks of my passion which I was burning to bestow on her. But I was so incredibly clumsy, going either too high or too low, that my efforts proved in vain. Finally, her dainty little hand acted as a guide, and I felt that I was now on the right track. But I experienced an unexpected pain on the path that I believed was strewn with flowers.

A little squeak and start proved that Suzon was sharing my suffering. But neither of us was disheartened. Suzon seconded my exertions by trying to widen the road, and I shoved in all the harder. It seemed that I was half way there. Suzon, whose cheeks were flushed a bright pink, was panting heavily. The perspiration on our bodies mingled. From Suzon's sensuous expression, I could see that rapture was supplanting pain as it was with me. I was wallowing in the anticipation of approaching bliss.

Heavens! Why do such divine moments have to be ruined by the cruelest of misfortunes? We were both bucking in an erotic frenzy, when my bed, which I proudly thought was to be the site of my victory and delight, betrayed me. The slats under the mattress gave way under our vigorous bouncings, and we crashed to the floor with a frightfully loud thud.

The tumble could have helped me by forcing open the last barrier, but Suzon was terrified and made violent efforts to free herself from me. In a rage of desire and despair, I held her only more tightly, an action which was to cost us dear.

Toinette, alerted by the din, opened my door, entered and caught us *in flagrante*. What a sight for the eyes of a mother! She was petrified with astonishment and indignation. She was so dumbfounded that she could not budge. She regarded us with eyes inflamed not by anger but lust. Her mouth opened to speak, but no words came out.

Suzon was now in a dead faint. Wrathfully I glared at Toinette, and pityingly, looked at Suzon. Emboldened at my mother's immobility and silence, undoubtedly caused by amazement, I decided to salvage as much as I could from wreckage. I nudged Suzon who was showing some signs of returning life by heaving deep sighs, fluttering her eyelids, and wiggling her backside. Now she was at the peak of pleasure and flowing like a torrent. Her ecstasy soon aroused a similar sensation in me.

At the supreme moment, Toinette grasped me by the shoulders and I spurted on Suzon's stomach.

Father Polycarpe, also curious as to the cause of the ruckus, entered the room and was equally stupefied at what he saw: naked Suzon lying on her back with one arm over her eyes and the other over the seat of shame. It was an ineffective attempt to conceal her charms from the eyes of the lascivious man of God. It was such an enticing picture that I could not tear my glance from her. And my prick, regaining its pristine virility, stood up proudly.

In spite of fear, fury, and surprise, nothing had cooled my ardour. Looking down, I could see my prick, hard as iron, throbbing madly. There was longing in Toinette's eyes as she regarded it, and there was forgiveness in her expression as she looked at me. I was barely aware that she was ushering me out of the room. When I realised what she was doing, I felt some misgivings and uneasiness. Naked as I was, I followed her docilely. Not a word was exchanged between us.

When we were in her room, I noticed that she carefully locked the door. A sudden sense of fear snapped me out of my stupor, and I wanted to escape. Searching for some place of refuge and not finding any, I flung myself on the bed. Realising the cause of my terror, Toinette tried to reassure me.

'Don't worry, my dear boy,' she soothingly said. 'I don't mean you any harm.'

I did not believe her and kept my head buried under the pillow. She started tugging at me, and I could not resist, because do you know where she grabbed me? By the prick! There was no help for it; I had to emerge from my hiding-place.

When I came out into the open, my eyes popped open when I saw that Toinette was just as naked as I. She was as bare as a new-born infant.

She had my virility still in her hand, and she made it clear that she was not going to release it. Her expert fondling made it rise again. I don't think it ever was so hard. All thoughts of Suzon were gone, for all my desires were concentrated on the woman before me, particularly, on one special fringed spot.

Still clutching me, she lay on the bed, forcing me down on top of her.

'Come, my little Adonis,' she coaxed with a kiss on my cheek. 'Put it into me.' As I promptly obeyed, she sighed with deep satisfaction, 'That's perfect.'

Without any difficulty whatsoever, I was soon down to the very bottom of her. The flood I released in her was so copious that I nearly fainted as Suzon did. What a woman she was! A young man like me could not desire a better one for the first time. That I had cuckolded my father did not bother me in the slightest.

What food for thought this recital must give to those readers who had never experienced such erotic frenzies. But they can go their own moral way. As for myself, I like to fuck.

I was about to do a repeat performance, to which Toinette was more than agreeable, when we were disturbed by a loud screech coming from my room. Realising what was happening, she quickly got out of bed, dressed, and after telling me to hide under the bed, she ran out of the room, yelling at Father Polycarpe.

No sooner had she gone than my eye was on the peep-hole. Through it, I saw the monk apparently trying to ravish Suzon. Although she was now dressed, her petticoat and the priest's robe were both up to their waists. Apparently, the shrieks were caused by the amazing diameter of the monk's organ which was far too thick ever to effect passage into a dainty little cunt like Suzon's.

The skirmish ended with Toinette's appearance in the room. With a lunge, she was on the assailant and his victim, snatching the latter from the priest's arms and giving her several sound smacks on her bottom. Then she shoved Suzon out of the chamber.

One would have thought that she would be furious with Father Polycarpe, but she looked at him, panting heavily. One should keep in mind that a monk is always saucy and impudent. Nevertheless, Father Polycarpe felt a sense of humiliation at having been caught in the act with Suzon, and he inwardly quaked at the reproaches he was sure Toinette was going to rain on his head. He turned red and white and averted his eyes. Strangely enough, Toinette seemed similarly embarrassed.

From my observation post, I expected to witness some violent crisis, but nothing like that occurred. Although the monk was abashed, his prick did not go soft. But then, does the virility of an ecclesiastic ever go soft?

Although Toinette was beside herself with rage, she could not help stealing glances at the monstrous member. At the ravishing sight, her anger subsided to desire. His fears allayed, the monk approached her, and putting his pride in her hand, he whispered loud enough for me to hear: 'If I can't fuck the daughter, at least I'll have the mother again.'

Toinette, always ready to forgive an insult that was a

promise of pleasure, became again a willing victim of the divine's amorous attack. Tumbling on my messed-up bed, they sealed their reconciliation with mutually abundant discharges. At least they seemed copious from the way they were convulsing at the end.

The reader undoubtedly will ask himself what that imp Saturnin was doing while he was watching the events. Did he merely look without some fantasies being aroused?

I was still undressed and excited from the marks of affection Toinette had favoured me with, and the present spectacle stimulated me even more. What do you think I did? I masturbated, of course.

Enraged at not being able to participate in the game, I shook myself in a frenzy and discharged at the moment when the rise and fall of my mother's behind began to subside.

'Well,' commented the monk, 'how do I compare with Saturnin?'

'Did I do anything with Saturnin?' Toinette innocently asked. 'He's hiding under my bed. Just wait until Ambroise comes. He'll give him what he deserves.'

You can imagine with what little pleasure I heard that exchange of dialogue. I continued to listen, but more attentively.

'Now, don't get all worked up,' Father Polycarpe advised her. 'You know as well as I that he is not to stay here forever. He's old enough, don't you think? I'll take him with me when I leave here.'

'I hope he has not found out about us, for he is a real blabbermouth,' she answered. Suddenly, she let out a little squeal and pointed to the wall. 'My god! I never noticed that hole before. The rascal could have seen everything.'

Thinking that she would come to verify her suspicions, I hastily crawled back under the bed from where I was careful not to emerge a second time, despite my desire to hear the conversation which was getting more and more interesting. Impatiently, I bided my time to learn the outcome of their talk, and I had not long to wait.

Somebody entered my prison to release me. I shook with fear lest it be Ambroise, who really would have given me a walloping. But it was Toinette who brought me my clothes and ordered me to get dressed immediately. Although tempted to taunt her on her antics with Father Polycarpe, I held my tongue and quickly obeyed. When I was presentable again, she curtly commanded me to go with her. When I inquired as to where she was taking me, she simply replied that we were going to the parish priest.

I was not pleased with the prospect of seeing that old goat again. In fact, I was quaking in every limb. On more than one occasion, my bottom had received the honour of his attentions, a chore he did not dislike performing, and I was frightened lest he grant me the same favours. But I did not dare voice to Toinette my trepidations. But why she was taking me there, I did not know. Since I saw no alternative, I meekly followed her.

I entered the room and my fears were dispelled when Toinette, presenting me to the awesome character, asked if he would be good enough to keep me for a few days. The phrase 'a few days' reassured me.

'Good,' I thought. 'After a few days, Father

Polycarpe will take me away with him.'

At first, I was delighted at the prospect, but Suzon suddenly crossed my mind. She would be lost to me forever. The thought agonised me, and I was overcome with grief. The experiences and emotions I had just undergone had driven her out of my mind. But now my heart was rent at the idea of leaving her.

In my mind, I saw again all the beauties of her adorable body, her thighs, her rounded buttocks, her swan-like throat, and her firm little white breasts that I worshipped with my kisses. I recalled the delights I had enjoyed with her and compared them with those Toinette had given me. With the latter, I had fainted, but I knew I would have expired on Suzon if we had not been interrupted. What a happy death it would have been! What was going to happen to her, I wondered. How was Toinette going to get revenge on her? Was Suzon going to miss me? Perhaps she is weeping now. She is sobbing and cursing me, the cause of all her misery. I am sure that she hates me. Shall I be able to continue living with the knowledge that she detests me? I, who adore her, would cheerfully suffer the agonies of hell to spare her the slightest sorrow? Such were the gloomy thoughts that threw my soul into turmoil. My melancholy was dispelled at the sound of the dinner bell.

The Cure

Let us leave Suzon for a while. We shall meet up with her again, for she plays an important role in these memoirs. Let us go and have something to eat, and I'll acquaint you with some of the characters who are to figure in my life. We'll begin with the Cure.

The Cure was one of those figures whom it was impossible to regard without laughing. He was no more than four feet tall, with a moon-shaped face illuminated by deep red cheeks that did not come from drinking water, a squashed nose with a ruby tip, little brown darting eyes surmounted by bushy brows, a narrow forehead, and a frizzled beard. Add to all that a mocking air, and you have the Cure. In the village, he was noted for certain talents which are worth more than a handsome face.

Next comes the Cure's housekeeper, Madame Françoise. She was an old witch, as malicious as an old ape and more wicked than a senile demon. Her face showed her fifty years, but women being what they are, she admitted to only thirty-five. She used so much rouge she looked like a bedizened Jezebel, her nose dripped with tobacco snuff, her mouth was a slit from ear to ear, and the few teeth she had left in her gums were wobbly. In her earlier years, she had served the Cure in more ways than one, and in gratitude, he kept her on.

Being in complete charge of the menage, everything went through her hands, including the money, most of which remained stuck to her fingers. She never spoke of the Cure except in the collective pronoun. *We* shall do this and *we* need that.

Under the protection of this grotesque pair lived a girl, ostensibly the ecclesiastic's niece, but it was common knowledge that the relationship was much closer than that. She was a big girl with a beautiful pale complexion only slightly pocked, an admirable bosom, a prominent nose, and tiny but ardent eyes. She was not overly endowed with intelligence.

From time to time, a certain rogue of a theologian came to the presbytery to spend a week or so, less out of friendship for the Cure than his interest in the niece. Later, I'll tell you my role in that affair.

Mademoiselle Nicole, which was the name of the amiable lass, was adored by all the boys, but she gave her preference to the bigger and older ones. Unfortunately, my age and size were against me. It was not that I had not attempted on several occasions to launch a spearhead against this winsome creature, but I was always disdainfully rebuffed. The gift I offered was heartlessly refused. She would not let me prove that I was more of a man than I appeared. To add insult to injury, my amorous attempts were always reported to Madame Françoise who passed them on to the Cure, and the latter showed me no mercy with the rod. I raged at my size, which was the cause of all my woes.

I was getting discouraged at my lack of success with Nicole and with the thrashings I regularly received from the Cure. I did not think I could hold out. But every time I was near the girl, my desires were relit, and I knew that sooner or later something was bound to happen. It did, but before giving an account of it, I have to tell you about Madame Dinville.

I had not forgotten that this lady had asked me to dine with her the next day, and I decided to keep my promise because there was a chance I might find Suzon there. I reasoned that I had been turned over to the Cure because Father Polycarpe suspected that Toinette had given me something other than a beating for my escapade with Suzon and he did not want me to get too accustomed to such chastisements. Toinette had as much reason to remove Suzon from the monk as he had to get me away from Toinette.

As I walked to the chateau, I planned, if Suzon was there, to seduce her behind the bushes in the garden. I was already anticipating the bliss.

Finding the door open, I entered. A deathly silence prevailed. There was not a soul to be seen. Going down the deserted corridor, I opened each door in turn. Each time I went into a room, my heart beat faster in the hope of finding Suzon.

'She will be in this one,' I said to myself, 'and if not, in the next one.'

Sunk in these reflections, I finally came to a chamber that was locked but with the key in the door. I hesitated, but then I thought I had not come this far just to retreat. I boldly opened it. The first thing I saw was a large bed in which apparently someone was sleeping. As I was about to leave, I heard a woman's voice ask who was there. At the same time, the bed curtains were opened and Madame Dinville stuck out her head. I would have fled if the view of her breathtaking breasts had not deprived me of all powers of locomotion.

'If it isn't my little friend Saturnin,' she gaily greeted me. 'Come over here and give me a kiss.'

At this invitation, I became as audacious as I had been timid, and I ran into her outstretched arms.

'I like that,' she remarked in a tone of satisfaction after I had acquitted myself well of a duty which went beyond the bounds of courtesy. 'I like it when a young man is so prompt in obeying.'

Scarcely had she finished these words, when I saw come out of the dressing-room a little simpering figure. He was singing out of tune a popular air and marking the rhythm with little comical pirouettes that perfectly matched his ridiculous voice.

At the appearance of this harlequin whom Madame Dinville addressed as Abbot, I felt embarrassed at the thought that he might have witnessed my passionate kisses. But from his demeanour, he apparently had no suspicions. I now regarded him irritatedly as an intruder whose presence was going to postpone or prevent the raptures I was eager to enjoy.

Carefully examining him, I pondered his appellation of Abbot, for he was dressed like a Paris fop. But then the only ecclesiastics I knew were of the small-town class.

This diminutive Adonis, whose name was Abbot Fillot, was the son of the collector of a nearby town. He was very rich, but God only knows how he got his money. From the way he talked, it was obvious that he was filled with more fatuity than doctrine. He had accompanied Madame Dinville to this bucolic retreat to spend some time with her. To her, there was no difference between an abbot and a schoolboy.

Madame Dinville pulled the bell cord and, to my delight, Suzon appeared. My heart throbbed at the sight of her, and I was so grateful that my hopes had been realised. She did not see me at first, because I was partially hidden behind the curtains of the bed. It was a situation that the Abbot was beginning not to like, for he was smelling a rat.

When Suzon came forward, she immediately spotted me. The colour of her cheeks changed from a pale pink to a deep red. She turned her eyes to the floor, and she was so agitated that she could not speak. I, too, had lost the power of speech. Madame Dinville's charms, which she made no attempt to conceal, had inflamed my imagination, but they now paled in comparison with Suzon's.

If it came to a choice between Dinville and Suzon, how could anyone fail to pick the latter? But I was not given a choice. To have Suzon was only a faint hope, and the enjoyment of Madame Dinville was a sure thing. Her looks assured me so, and her words, although somewhat restrained by the presence of the Abbot, did not belie what her eyes were saying.

After dismissing Suzon to do some errands, Madame Dinville became bolder with me. When I felt her hands on me, I was both confused and disturbed. My desires were divided – one was for pure sensuous pleasure and the other for enjoyment which had something deeper to it. I was so upset that I did not notice the disappearance of the Abbot. Madame Dinville had seen him leave the room, but thinking that I had observed him, too, she did not think it necessary to mention it to me.

Reclining back on her pillow, the lady of the house gave me a languorous regard which told me clearly that she was mine if I wanted to take her. Tenderly, she took my hand and put it between her thighs which were lasciviously opening and closing. Her halfshut eyes were reproving me for my timidity. Under the impression that the Abbot was still in the chamber, I maintained an insane stubbornness that ended by irritating her.

'Are you asleep?' she asked sarcastically.

I told her that I was not asleep, an artless reply that delighted her. For her, I now had the charm of innocence, always appealing to lustful women. Ignorance and naivety gave pique to pleasure.

My continued indifference made Madame Dinville realise that her method of attack was ineffective and that some other stimulant was required to rouse me. Releasing my hand, she stretched her arms with a pretended yawn and exposed to me some of her charms. Her action dispelled the sluggishness I had felt since Suzon's departure. Returning to life, I sensed tingles running through my body. Suzon vanished from my thoughts. Now my regards and desires were concentrated on Madame Dinville. She immediately perceived the effect of her stratagem. To arouse me further and to encourage me, she said she wondered what had happened to the Abbot. I looked around, but I did not see him. That was the last thing that had been holding me back.

'He's gone,' she remarked and added, 'it's rather hot in here.'

With that, she threw off the covers, exposing a dazzling white thigh at the top of which was the edge of a chemise that seemed to have been placed there expressly to prevent my eyes from going any higher, or rather, to excite rather than to satisfy my curiosity. In spite of the covering, I did get a glimpse of a spot of vermilion which made me almost wild.

I shyly took her hand, and rapturously kissed it. There was fire in my eyes and sparkles in hers. One thing led to another without a hitch, but it was ordained that I was never to take full advantage of the opportunities offered me. That damned chambermaid Suzon had been asked to summon appeared just at the wrong moment. I promptly ceased what I was doing. The soubrette, standing at the door, was laughing her head off.

'What's so funny?' Madame Dinville asked, pulling the sheet back over her.

'Hee, hee,' giggled the maid. 'Monsieur the Abbot.'

'Well, what about him?'

So she was laughing at something that had happened to the Abbot, and not at us.

At that moment, the Abbot returned, concealing his face with a cambric handkerchief. The maid's titters increased when she saw him.

'What's wrong with you?' Madame Dinville demanded of him.

'See for yourself,' he answered, showing us a face that looked as if it had been worked over with a rake. 'That's the work of Mademoiselle Suzon.'

'Suzon!' Madame Dinville cried in surprise.

'That's what she did just because I tried to kiss her,' he replied coldly. 'Her kisses are expensive.'

I could not help but be amused at the free and easy manner with which the Abbot spoke of his misfortune, and he bore with indifference Madame Dinville's gibes.

As she dressed, the Abbot, in spite of the sad state of his face, flirted with her, made outrageous remarks, helped her arrange her hair, and told stories that made her laugh until tears came to her eyes. We then went down to dine.

We were four at the table, Madame Dinville, Suzon, the Abbot, and I. The one who cut the most miserable figure was I, seated opposite Suzon. The Abbot, next to her, maintained his composure in spite of Madame's continued banter. I could see that Suzon was confused, but from her furtive looks at me, I guessed that she would have preferred to be alone with me. Her wistful regard drove all thoughts of Madame Dinville from my head, and I impatiently awaited the end of the repast so that I could try to find some way to slip off with Suzon.

When we rose from the table after coffee, I made a little nod to her. She understood and was the first to leave the room. I was about to follow her, when Madame Dinville stopped me, saying she would like the Abbot and me to escort her on her promenade. A stroll at four o'clock on a hot summer afternoon! The Abbot found the proposal ridiculous, but it was not to win his approval that she made it. She knew what she was doing. Aware that he was too vain of his fair complexion to expose it to the rays of the sun, she foresaw correctly that he would decline, which he promptly did. I, too, would have liked to get out of it in order to be with Suzon, but I could not think of any plausible excuse. As a result, I made the sacrifice.

Slowly we walked, not in the tree-lined paths but

among the open garden beds where the rays of the sun were the hottest. The only protection Madame Dinville had was a little fan. I had nothing, but I suffered my tortures stoically. The Abbot was laughing at our foolishness, but he soon became discouraged after we went around several times. I still could not guess what Madame Dinville had in mind. Also, I could not understand how she was able to stand the burning heat which I was beginning to find unbearable. Little did I realise what rich reward I was to get for my faithful service.

Our stubbornness in continuing the walk soon bored the scoffing Abbot and he retired. When we were at the end of one of the paths, Madame Dinville led me into a pleasantly cool little arbour.

'Aren't we going to go on with our stroll?' I innocently asked.

'No, I think I've had enough sun,' she replied.

She regarded me searchingly to learn if I guessed the reason for the promenade, and she perceived that I had no idea of the blessing she was intending for me. She took my arms which she squeezed affectionately. Then, as if she were extremely tired, she rested her head on my shoulder and put her face so close to mine that I would have been a fool not to kiss. She made no objection.

'Oh, oh,' I thought to myself. 'So that's her game. Well, nobody will disturb us here.'

In truth, we were in a sort of labyrinth whose obscurity and turnings and windings would conceal us from the sharpest eyes.

Now she sat down under a bower on the grass. It was the ideal setting for the purpose I was sure she had in mind. Following her example, I seated myself at her side. She gave me a soulful look, squeezed my hand, and reclined on her back. Believing that the moment had come, I started to ready my weapon when all of a sudden she fell sound asleep. At first, I thought it was only drowsiness caused by the heat and that I could easily rouse her. But when she refused to wake up after repeated shakings, I was simple enough to believe in the genuineness of a slumber that I should have suspected because of its promptness and profundity.

'My usual luck,' I swore to myself. 'If she fell asleep after I had quenched my desires, I wouldn't mind, but to be so cruel at the moment when she had raised my hopes so high is unpardonable.'

I was inconsolable. There was sadness in my heart as I regarded her. She was dressed like the previous day, that is to say, with the diaphanous blouse which revealed her unbelievable breasts, that were so near and yet so far. As the strawberry-tipped orbs rose and fell, I longingly admired their whiteness and symmetry.

My desires were almost at the breaking point, and I felt the urge to wake her up, but I dismissed the desire for fear that she would get angry. She would have to awaken eventually, I reflected, but I could not resist the urge to put my hand on that seductive bosom.

'She is sleeping too soundly for her to awaken at my touch,' I said to myself, 'but if she does, the worst that she can do is scold me for my boldness.'

Extending a quivering hand to one of the inviting mounds, I kept an anxious eye on her face, ready to retreat at the first sign of life. But she slumbered peacefully on as I lifted her blouse up to her neck and let my fingers graze the satin-smooth contours. My hand was like a swallow skimming over the water, now and then dipping its wings in the waves.

Now I was emboldened to plant a tender kiss on one rose-bud. She still did not stir. Then the other was given the same treatment. Changing my position, I became even naughtier. I put my head under her skirt in order to penetrate into the obscure landscape of love, but I could not make out anything for her legs were crossed. If I could not see it, at least I was going to touch it. My hand slowly crept up the thigh until it reached the foot of the Venusberg. The tip of my finger was already at the entrance to the grotto. I had gone too far, I decided, but having reached this point, I was more miserable and frustrated than ever. I was so anxious to see what I was touching. Withdrawing the intruding hand, I sat up again and regarded the visage of my sleeping beauty. There was no change in her placid expression. It seemed that Morpheus had cast his most soporific poppies on her.

Did my eyes deceive me? Did one of her eyelids twitch? I felt a sense of near panic. I looked again, this time more closely. No, the eye I thought had momentarily opened was still tightly shut.

Reassured, I took new courage and began to gently lift up her skirt. She gave a slight start, and I was positive that I had awakened her. Quickly, I pulled the skirt back down. My heart was pounding as if I had narrowly escaped a disaster. I was terror-stricken as I sat again at her side and feasted my eyes on her admirable bosom. With relief, I saw that there was not a sign of returning life. She had just changed position, and what a delightful new position it was.

Her thighs were now uncrossed. When she raised

one knee, the skirt fell on her stomach, revealing her hirsute mound and cunt. The dazzling sight almost intoxicated me. Picture to yourself a rounded leg encased in a frivolous stocking held up by a dainty garter, a tiny foot in a saucy shoe, and thighs of alabaster. The carmine red cunt was surrounded by a ring of ebony black hair and it exuded a scent more heady than the rarest incense. Inserting my finger in the aperture, I tickled it a little. At this, she opened her legs still wider. Then I put my mouth to it, trying to sink my tongue to the very bottom. Words cannot describe the straining erection I had.

Nothing could stop me now. Fear, respect and caution were thrown to the winds. My passion was like a torrent, seeping away everything in its path. If she had been the Sultan's favourite, I would have fucked her in the presence of a hundred eunuchs armed with sharp scimitars. Stretching my body over her and supporting myself with my hands and knees so that my weight would not arouse her, my member gradually disappeared into the hole. The only part of me touching her was my prick which I gently pushed in and pulled out. The slow but regular cadence enhanced and prolonged my ineffable bliss.

Still carefully watching her face, I gently kissed her full lips from time to time.

But the raptures I was experiencing were so great that I forgot my caution and fell heavily on the lady, furiously hugging and embracing her.

The climax of my pleasure opened my eyes which had been shut since I had entered her, and I saw the transports of Madame Dinville, joys which I was no longer able to share. My somnolent friend had just clutched my buttocks with her hands, and raising hers which she convulsively wiggled, she dragged me down hard on her quivering body. I kissed her with the last of the passion I had left.

'My dear friend,' she moaned in a failing voice, 'push a little more. Don't leave me half way to my goal.'

I felt renewed vigour at her touching appeal and resumed my enjoyable task. After barely five or six strokes more, she really lost consciousness. For some unknown reason, that excited me and I quickened my tempo. In a matter of seconds, I reached the peak again and fell into a state like that of my partner. When we revived, we showed our appreciation of each other with warm kisses and tight embraces.

With the fading of passion, I felt I had to withdraw, but I was embarrassed for I was unwilling for her to see the sorry condition my prick was in. I tried to hide it, but her eyes were fixed on me. When it was out, she grabbed it, took it into her mouth, and began to suck it.

'What were you trying to do, you silly boy?' she murmured. 'Were you ashamed to show me an instrument you know how to use so well? Did I conceal anything from you? Look! Here are my breasts. Look at them and fondle them as much as you want. Take those rosy tips in your mouth and put your hand on my cunt. Oh, that's wonderful! You have no idea of the pleasure you're giving me, you little rascal.'

Animated by the vivacity of her caresses, I responded with equal ardour. She marvelled at the dexterity of my finger as she rolled her eyes and breathed her sighs into my mouth.

My prick, having regained its pristine rigidity from her lips on it, wanted her more than ever. Before putting it in her again, I spread open her thighs to feast my eyes on that seat of delight. Often these preliminaries to pleasure are more piquant than pleasure itself. Is there anything more exquisite than to have a woman willing to assume any position your lascivious imagination can conjure? I experienced an ecstatic vertigo as I put my nose to that adorable cunt. I wished that all of me were a prick so that I could be completely engulfed in it. Desire begat even more violent desires.

Reveal a portion of your bosom to your lover, and he insists on seeing it all. Show him a little firm white breast, and he clamours to touch it. He is a dipsomaniac whose thirst increases as he drinks. Let him touch, and he demands to kiss it. Permit him to wander farther down, he commands that you let him put his prick there. His ingenious mind comes up with the most capricious fantasies, and he is not satisfied until he can carry them out on you.

The reader can imagine how long I was content nuzzling that appetising aperture. It was a matter of seconds until I was again vigorously fucking her. She eagerly responded with upward thrusts to match my powerful lunges. In order to get farther in, I had my hands on the cheeks of her derriere while she had her legs wrapped around my back. Our mouths, glued to each other, were two cunts being mutually fucked by two tongues. Finally came the ecstasy that lifted us to the heights and then annihilated us.

It has been said that potency is a gift of the gods, and although they had been more than generous with me, I was squandering my divine patrimony, and I had need of every drop of the heavenly largesse to emerge from the present engagement with honour.

It seemed that her desires were increasing in proportion to the loss of my powers. Only with the most libertine caresses was she able to turn my imminent retreat into still another victory. This she accomplished by getting on top of me, letting her full breasts dangle above my face and rubbing my failing virility with her cunt which seemed possessed of a life of its own.

'Now, I'm fucking you!' she joyously cried as she bounced up and down on me. Motionless, I let her do what she wanted with me. It was a delightful sensation, the first one I had ever enjoyed in that way. Now and then, she paused in her exertions to rain kisses on my face. Those lovely orbs swayed rhythmically above me in time with her repeated impaling of herself. When they came close to my mouth, I eagerly kissed or sucked the rose nipple. A streak of voluptuousness shuddering through my body announced the imminence of the supreme moment. Joining my transports to hers, I gushed just at the moment she did, and our juices mingled with the perspiration on our bellies.

Exhausted and shattered by the assaults I had launched and withstood for more than two hours, I felt an overwhelming desire for sleep and I yielded to it. Madame Dinville herself rested my head on her abundant bosom, wanting also to enjoy some rest, but with me in her arms.

'Sleep, my love,' she murmured as she wiped the perspiration from my forehead. 'Have a good sleep, for I know how much you need it.'

I dozed off immediately, only to awaken when the sun was sinking on the horizon. The first thing I saw when I opened my eyes was Madame Dinville. She looked at me cheerfully, interrupting the knitting she had occupied herself with during my slumber to dart her tongue in my mouth.

She made no attempt to conceal her desire for a resumption of the sport, but I had little interest. My indifference irritated her. It was not that I was disinclined, but if it had been left up to me, I would have preferred repose to action. But Madame was not going to have it that way. Holding me in her arms, she overwhelmed me with proofs of her passion, but they did not arouse me, even though I tried my best to stoke the dead fires within me.

Disappointed at her lack of success, she employed another ruse to relight my extinguished flames. Lying on her back, she raised her skirt to her navel, revealing the object of the desires of most men. She well knew the effect such an exposure would produce. When she suggestively jiggled her buttocks, I felt something stirring in me and I placed my hand on the gift she was offering me. But it was only a token gesture of passion. As I was negligently titillating her clitoris, she was feverishly massaging my prick in a hysterical cadence dictated by her feverish eagerness. When my prick finally stood up, I saw her eyes sparkle in triumph at her success in reviving my ardour. Now aroused by her caresses, I promptly bestowed on her the tokens of my gratitude which she zealously accepted. Grasping me around the waist, she bumped up and down under me so violently that I ejaculated almost automatically, but with such raptures that I was angry with myself for having ended the joy so promptly.

Now it was time to leave the arbour which had been the scene of such transports. But before returning to the chateau, we took several turns in the labyrinth to allow the traces of our exertions to disappear. As we were strolling, we naturally chatted:

'How happy I am with you, dear Saturnin,' she remarked. 'Did I live up to your expectations?'

'I am still relishing the delights you were good enough to grant me,' I gallantly replied.

'Thank you,' she said. 'But it was not very wise of me to have surrendered to you the way I did. You will be discreet, won't you, Saturnin?'

I retorted that if she thought I was capable of betraying to others what joys we had, she must not have a very high opinion of me. She was so pleased with my astute response that she rewarded me with a long, lingering kiss. I am sure that I would have been rewarded much more richly had we not been in a spot where we could be seen. As an additional gratitude, she pressed my hand to her left breast with a meaningful expression.

Now we quickened our pace as the conversation languished. I noticed that Madame Dinville was anxiously looking from side to side and wondered why.

But who would have thought that after such an exhausting afternoon, she still wanted more? She wanted to crown the day with one last engagement, and she was on the lookout for some stray servant. The reader will probably think that she had the devil in the flesh, and he would not be far off the mark.

She tried to revive me with her tongue and mouth,

but the poor thing was lifeless. Sad but true. To attain her goal, what did she do? That is what we are going to find out.

As a youngster just getting to know the ways of the world, I flattered myself that I had made an auspicious debut and that I would be lacking in respect if I did not see her to her rooms. That done, I felt I could take my leave by giving her a final kiss for the day.

'What's that?' she demanded in a surprised tone. 'You're not leaving, are you? It's only eight o'clock. You stay here. I'll arrange things with your Cure.'

The thought of avoiding Mass appealed to me and I was agreeable to her interceding for me. Making me sit on the bed, she went to lock the door and returned to take her place at my side. She looked at me intently without uttering a word. Her silence disconcerted me.

'Don't you want to any more?' she finally said.

Because I knew I was finished, I was so embarrassed that I could not force out a word. To admit my impotence was unthinkable. I lowered my eyes to conceal my shame.

'We're all alone, dear Saturnin,' she said in a coaxing voice, bathing my face with hot kisses which just left me cold.

'Not a soul in the world can spy on us,' she continued. 'Let's take off our clothes and get into my bed. Come, my friend, down to the buff. I'll soon make the stubborn little prick stand up.'

Taking me in her arms, she actually carried me and deposited me on the couch where she disrobed me in a feverish impatience. She soon got me in the desired condition, that is to say, naked as the day I was born. More out of politeness than pleasure, I let her have her way with me.

Turning me on my back, she started sucking my poor prick. She had it in her mouth up to my testicles. I could see that she was in ecstasies as she covered the member with a saliva that resembled froth. She did restore some life to it, but so little that she could make no use of it. Recognising that that treatment was of no avail, she went to her dressing-table and got a little flask containing a whitish fluid. This she poured on her palm and vigorously rubbed it on my balls and prick.

'There,' she said with satisfaction when she finished. 'You aren't through yet by any means.'

Impatiently I waited for the fulfillment of her prediction. Little tingles in my testicles raised my hopes for success. While waiting for the treatment to take effect, she undressed in turn. By the time she was naked, I felt as if my blood was boiling. My penis shot up as if released by a powerful spring. Like a maniac, I grabbed her and forced her on the bed with me. I devoured her, scarcely permitting her to breathe. I was blind and deaf. Sounds like those of an enraged beast came out of my mouth. There was only one thought in my mind, and that was her cunt.

'Stop, my love!' she cried, tearing herself from me. 'Not in such a hurry. Let's prolong our pleasures and elaborate on them. Put your head at my feet, and I'll do the same. Now your tongue in my cunt. That's it. Oh, I'm in heaven.'

My body, stretched out on her, was swimming in a sea of delight. I darted my tongue as deep as I could into the moist grotto. If possible, I would have sunk my entire head into it. Furious sucking on her taut clitoris produced a flow of nectar a thousand times more delectable than that served by Hebe to the gods on Mount Olympus. Some readers may ask what the goddesses drank. They drank from Ganymede's prick, of course.

Madame Dinville was clutching my backside with both her arms while I squeezed her pneumatic buttocks. Her tongue and lips wandered feverishly over my prick while mine did the same to her nether parts. She announced to me the increasing intensity of the raptures I was causing her by convulsive spasms and erratically spreading and closing her thighs. Moderating and augmenting our efforts, we gradually progressed to the peak. We stiffened as if collecting all our faculties to savour the coming bliss to the full.

We discharged simultaneously. From her cunt gushed a torrent of hot delicious fluid which I greedily gulped down. Her mouth was so filled with mine that it took several swallows to get it all down, and she did not release my prick until she was sure that there was not a drop left. The ecstasy vanished, leaving me in despair at the thought it could not be recaptured. But such is carnal pleasure.

Back in the pitiable state from which Madame Dinville's potion had rescued me, I beseeched her to restore me again.

'No, my dear Saturnin,' she replied. 'I love you too much to want to kill you. Be content with the joy we just had.'

Not overly eager to meet my Maker at the expense of another round of pleasure, I followed her example and put on my clothes.

Feeling that Madame Dinville was not displeased with the way I had comported myself, I asked her if I would be permitted to play our games again with her.

'When do you want to come back?' she answered, kissing me on the cheek.

'As soon as I can and that won't be soon enough,' I declared spiritedly. 'How about tomorrow?'

'No,' she smilingly refused me. 'I have to let you get some rest. Come and see me in three days' time.' (She handed me some pastilles that she said would produce the same effect on me as the balm.) 'Be careful how you take them. Also, I don't have to tell you that you are not to say a word about what we did.'

I swore eternal secrecy, and we embraced one last time. So I departed, leaving her under the impression that I had presented her with my virginity.

As I made my way silently down the dimly lit corridor and passed through the antechamber, I was stopped by someone. It was Suzon. I was struck dumb with astonishment. It seemed that her presence was a reproach for my infidelity to her. In my feelings of guilt, I imagined that she had witnessed all that had occurred. Taking my hand in hers, she stood motionless without saying a word. My inner turmoil prevented me from looking at her. Uneasy at her silence, I raised my eyes and weakly asked the reason for her silence. When she refused to reply, I saw that she was shedding tears. The sight was like a stab in my heart. It also relit the flames that the caresses of Madame Dinville had just extinguished. Regarding Suzon with love in my breast, I wondered what I had seen in the older woman.

'Suzon,' I said with distress in my voice. 'Am I the cause of your tears?'

'Yes, it is you,' she sobbed. 'You heartless boy. You

have broken my heart and I am going to die of grief.'

'Me!' I protested. 'How can you reproach me this way? What have I done? You know that my love for you is as deep as the ocean.'

'So you love me, eh?' she replied bitterly. 'It would be better if you spoke the truth. I suppose you swore the same thing to Madame Dinville. If you love me, as you say, why were you with her? You didn't even try to find me when I left the dining-room. Is she more desirable than I? What have you been doing with her all this time? I bet you were not thinking of your Suzon who loves you more than life itself. Yes, Saturnin, I adore you. You have inspired in me a sentiment so profound that I would expire if you did not reciprocate it. But you don't say anything. I see it all now. Your conscience did not bother you when you dallied with my rival. I shall hate her until the end of time, for I know that she is in love with you and you have returned her affection. All you were thinking about was the pleasure she was holding out to you and forgetting the sorrow you would cause me. I can't get over it.'

I had to recognise the justice of her accusation, for indeed I had used the same terms of endearment with Madame Dinville as I had with Suzon.

'Suzon,' I said brokenly. 'Your harsh words are killing me. Please stop. Don't crush the one who worships you. And your tears plunge me into despair. Yu can't imagine how much I love you.'

'Ah,' she sighed. 'You have given life back to me. From now on, I forbid you to think of anyone but me. Since yesterday, you have been constantly in my thoughts. Your face has been following me everywhere

I go. Now listen, Saturnin. If I agree to forgive you for the wrong you did me, it will be on the condition that you promise never again to see Madame Dinville. Do you love me enough to make such a sacrifice?'

'Oh, yes!' I cried eagerly. 'I'll gladly give her up for your sake. All her charms put together are not the equal of one of your kisses.'

As I uttered those pacifying words, I gave her an impassioned kiss which she did not rebuff.

'Saturnin, now tell me something and be honest about it,' she softly said as she tenderly squeezed my hand. 'I am sure that my god-mother wants to see you again. When did she tell you to come back?'

'In three days,' I admitted.

'And you'll come, won't you?' she said sadly.

'Tell me what I should do,' I asked helplessly. 'If I come, she'll be annoyed at my indifference, and if I don't, I won't be able to see my beloved Suzon.'

'I want you to return,' she told me firmly, shaking her pretty little head in determination, 'but she mustn't see you. I'll pretend that I am sick and stay in bed. That way, we can spend the day together by ourselves. But you don't know where my bedroom is. Follow me. I'll show you.'

I let myself be led, but as I walked behind, I had the foreboding that something terrible was going to happen.

'Here is the apartment I have been given,' Suzon informed me. 'You won't be too unhappy with me here?'

'Ah, Suzon,' I sighed, 'what delights you are proferring me. We shall be together, just you and I, and we'll give ourselves up to all the raptures of our love. We shall have bliss such as you have never dreamed of.'

She did not reply, seemingly in a deep reverie. Wondering if I had said something wrong, I urged her to speak.

'I understand you perfectly,' she cried agitatedly. 'Yes, we'll abandon ourselves to our amorous caprices, but you can't look forward to them very much if you are able to wait three days.'

The reproach struck home.

The impossibility of proving her wrong dismayed me. My whole being was tortured. How stupid of me to have squandered all my resources on Madame Dinville! How I now regretted the pleasures I had showered her with. Desolate and crushed, I inwardly cursed her.

'Dear God!' I silently cried from the depths of my heart. 'Here I am with Suzon and I would give my life's blood to be able to make her happy. Here she is, just waiting for me, and I am helpless. I am drained dry. What can I do to take advantage of this unparalleled opportunity?'

Suddenly, I remembered the pastilles Madame Dinville had given me. Not doubting that they would have the same prompt effect as the lotion, I swallowed several of them. The anticipation of soon being able to satisfy Suzon's urges made me embrace her with an ardour that deceived us both. Suzon took it as a sign of my desire for her, and I believed it evidence of the revival of my virility.

In the expectation of imminent bliss, Suzon fell back on her bed. Inwardly praying that I would not disappoint her, I mounted her and placed my prick in her hand. Although it was still limp, I was confident that her dainty little hand would aid the action of the pills and the organ would soon be in the wished for state. She squeezed it, she massaged it, and she sucked it. Nothing happened. I exerted myself a hundred times more vigorously than I had with Madame Dinville, but it was to no avail. It was as dead as a door-knob.

'Here I have my dearest Suzon, the object of all my desires, in my arms, and I might as well be a corpse,' I reviled myself. 'I kiss her saucy breasts, those two adorable orbs, that I worshipped yesterday and that now leave me cold. Have they changed since then? No. They are as smooth, firm and full as they were. Her skin is still a delight to touch. Her open thighs should arouse me again to a fury. I have my finger in her delightful little cunt, but that's all I can put into it.'

As I heard Suzon sigh at my lethargy, I damned the gift that Madame Dinville had made me. I was sure that she foresaw something like this would happen when I left her and that she wanted to keep me in the same state of impotence until I saw her again.

I was on the verge of telling Suzon everything, when I was startled out of my wits. An invisible hand noiselessly opened the bed curtains and gave me a resounding smack on my behind. Gripped with terror, I abandoned Suzon to the specter, for I was convinced that it was a ghost, and fled for my life.

When I got back home, I was still shaking. Once in bed, I pulled the covers over my head.

Fright coupled with exhaustion soon brought me sleep. The next morning I awoke, but I was so fatigued that I could not get out of bed. Surprised by the lassitude that I could attribute only to the gymnastics of the previous day, I realised for the first time how necessary it is to ration one's self in amorous engagements and how dearly one pays for blindly heeding those lustful sirens who drain you dry and suck your marrow. How stupid to have such reflections only when it is too late, and remorse is no consolation.

But youth is resilient. I gradually regained my strength, gave up my lugubrious meditations, and turned my thoughts to the events of last night. I felt a sudden surge of anxiety as to the fate of Suzon with the phantom. With a sense of horror, I wondered what terrible things could have happened to her.

'She's probably dead,' I said to myself mournfully. 'She's so timid and shy that she surely died of fright. And I'll never see her again except in her coffin.'

Crushed by such thoughts, I burst into tears. At this moment, Toinette entered my room.

I shook when I saw her, for I believed she had come to confirm my worst fears. Her silence, however, gave me hope that my suspicions were unfounded. Perhaps Suzon had made good her escape as I had. The grief I had felt at Suzon's demise gave place to curiosity as to what had happened after my hasty departure. But Toinette had merely come to find out why I had not appeared for breakfast.

The two days of rest that Madame Dinville had prescribed for me were over and the third day had come. Although I felt my native vigour restored, I had little inclination for more gambols at the chateau. The recollection of what had happened there stifled my desires before they were born. Just so that I would not get any sexual urges, I gulped down the rest of the pastilles Madame Dinville gave me. They put me to sleep for several hours, and when I awoke I found myself with an erection, the like of which I never had in my life. My prick was throbbing and aching for satisfaction.

At the same time, I was exceedingly embarrassed. Yes, the reader can laugh. He can remind me that four fingers and one thumb were all that was necessary to assuage my pain. All right! Go ahead and say it: 'Dom Bougre, you have four fingers and a thumb, an infallible cure for the intemperance of the flesh. So why don't you use them? What do the priests do when there are no complaisant nuns or parishioners around? You do not always have a brothel or a devout at your disposal. So they masturbate until they are blue in the face. Simpletons assume that their pallor is the result of their austerity, but now you know what it comes from. So why not have recourse to the same remedy they employ?'

I was aware of all that. But I had been so crushed and impotent the past three days, that I was reluctant to relieve myself in such a solitary way. Nevertheless, I could not help myself. My fingers slowly embraced the quivering engine. Rubbing it up and down, I stopped just at the moment when all my pains would be dissolved. It became a game with me to see how long I could prolong the pleasurable agony. As I amused myself in this fashion, I pictured in my mind a shy young *grisette* who has not yet tasted the delicacies of love and who is unaware of your appetite for her. When I kissed her on the mouth, I saw her blush. She made no attempt at resistance when I unbuttoned her blouse and regarded her delightful breasts rising and falling. Then my hand descended to a hot little cunt that, in the beginning, fiercely defied my attacks.

Pleasure is sparkling, bubbling, and ephemeral. If it can be compared to anything, it would be those flames that suddenly jet out of the ground, dazzling in their brilliance, and disappear just at the instant you believe you have divined their cause. Such is pleasure. It shows itself momentarily and then vanishes.

The only way to capture it is to fool it, trap it, and force it to stay with you as you jest with it, then let it escape, summon it back, let it flee, call it back once more. That is the only method to enjoy it to the full.

I was so preoccupied with my diversion I did not notice night had fallen. I had ejaculated several times and was about ready to fall asleep when somebody in a nightshirt passed the foot of my bed.

At first, I thought it was the theologian I mentioned when I gave my description of Nicole.

'If that's who it is, he's probably on his way to fuck Nicole,' I said to myself. 'Well, I'm going to follow him.'

I sprang out of bed, dressed only in battle costume, that it is to say, a nightgown. Gropingly, I made my way in the dark to the corridor which I thought led to Nicole's room. I spotted the door slightly ajar and went in. With the utmost circumspection, I made my way to the bed where I expected the lovers to be engaged in amorous games.

I listened carefully, expecting to hear the usual erotic sighs, groans, and pantings. There was someone breathing heavily, but she appeared to be alone. Maybe the theologian had lost his way, I hopefully wondered.

I ran my hand over the body, and at the first touch, I discovered that it was feminine. I kissed her on the mouth.

'Ah,' she murmured in a voice that I could barely hear, 'I've been waiting for you so long that I fell asleep. But now that you are here, hurry up and get on top of me.'

Needing no further urging, I was soon atop my Venus. But there was a noticeable lack of enthusiasm on her part when she embraced me. Perhaps it was my tardiness that had incurred her displeasure, but I congratulated myself on the good luck that fortune had bestowed on me. Now I was going to get my revenge on that disdainful, haughty maiden who had so often rejected my advances. She thought I was somebody else, and that delighted me.

Kissing her full on the mouth and on her eyes, I gave myself up to raptures that had been denied me for what seemed an eternity. I gently massaged the resilient breasts, for Nicole possessed one of the most charming bosoms imaginable, delectable in their firmness and sauciness. Venus herself would have envied those hemispheres. I was in raptures. To reward her for the joys she was affording me, I spent in her a torrent the likes of which I wager she had never before felt. From her ohs and ahs, and from her spasms, I gathered that she had not expected such a royal munificence.

Scarcely had I crowned my labours with an initial transport than I felt myself incited to second effort, and I merited the praise she lavished on me. From her groans, I gathered she was in the mood for a third act to make this night stand out. Although I was still in good shape to give her the satisfaction she desired, the fear of being surprised by the theologian slightly dampened my enthusiasm. I was at my wits' end to give her an excuse for my procrastination. But as her desires became more urgent, I felt that the devil could take the hindmost and I proceeded again.

But two discharges slightly dispel the erotic fumes. Illusions vanish and the mind returns to normal. The shadows disappear and values resume their true value. It goes without saying that beautiful women win out over their less favoured sisters. For the latter, I have a bit of advice. If you give your all to a man, ration your favours. Don't splurge them. If you leave nothing more to be desired, interest is lost. Passion is extinguished by a too complete satisfaction. There should be always left something to be desired or wanted. But if you can hold out the prospect of something more, you can compete on equal terms.

It was indeed delectable to run my hand over the beauties of my elusive nymph. But I was astonished to find a difference from those I had manipulated with so much pleasure several moments before. Her thighs which I had found so firm and velvety were now wrinkled and flabby. The cunt that was so deliciously tight was now a yawning chasm and the delightful breasts, pointed and taut, were sagging and pendulous. The transformation flabbergasted me, but I thought it was just my imagination. In spite of the change, I was now ready for the third assault. Just as I was prepared to launch the attack, my partner and I were interrupted by a racket from the adjoining room which I assumed was that of the venerable Françoise.

'You wretch!' a voice cried.

At these words, my little sweetheart whose cunt I had already started to penetrate shoved me away.

'My God!' she exclaimed. 'What is happening to our daughter? Go and see what is the matter! It sounds as if she is being murdered.'

So Nicole had a daughter, I thought to myself. Strange.

I was so nonplussed that I could not move. As the hubbub grew louder, my bed partner, impatient at my refusal to budge, got out of the couch and lit a candle.

Now I saw who she was. It was not Nicole, but that hag, Françoise. Never shall I forget that horrible moment. I still become petrified at the recollection of the sight of that spook. Beside myself with rage, I now realised I had gone into the wrong room. And it was the Cure whom she had been expecting.

'God! What am I going to do?' I said to myself in a panic. 'How am I going to get out of this mess? If Françoise notices that it was with me she had her amusement, she certainly will tell the Cure, and what a whipping I shall get!'

Inwardly, I urged her to hasten and separate those dear enemies, but not to forget to leave the door open.

The bitch had locked it. I yanked at it with all my might, but it refused to open. Reduced to despair at my perilous condition, I tried to keep on my feet, but I sank to the floor. I was too young and inexperienced to realise that pleasure and misery are so closely interwined that in the depths of misery, one should not lose hope for a change in fortune. Often when you feel crushed by the cruel blows of fate, chance puts an end to them in the most unexpected manner.

At the moment when I was shivering with fear under

the bed where I had taken refuge, the wheel of fortune turned. The racket became noisier when the combatants saw Françoise, from whose hands fell the candlestick holder. The first thing she saw was the Curé who she thought was in her room. I could see the tableau in my mind.

There was the Curé wearing only his underpants and a nightcap on his head. His eyes were glittering and his mouth frothing as he viciously pummelled the squawling lovers, Nicole trying to protect herself by crawling under the covers. The theologian also under the blankets was not without courage for he occasionally stuck his head out and got in a punch on the face of the roaring Curé. And let us not forget the shrew in her nightgown, her eyes glazed with astonishment, slumped in a chair.

Judging from the sounds I heard, the theologian, for fear of being recognised, had bounded from under the covers and tried to escape in the darkness, for the candle had gone out when Françoise dropped it. The Curé was hot on his heels.

At that moment, I heard the door of my room quickly open and close and somebody throw himself on the bed. Trembling like a leaf, I thought it was Françoise and that the Curé would come to join her. But all was calm, except for the soft sighs of the one lying on the bed.

Now I was confused. What was I to make of those sobs? Why was Françoise weeping like that? Why did she come back? Would the Curé come or not, I wondered. Uncertainty is one of the cruelest of tortures. At times, I was tempted to try an escape, but the fear of discovery held me back. There was another

more compelling reason that kept me in the chamber: I
had another immense erection.

'So you're going back to your room with a stiff prick
like that,' the devil whispered in my ear. 'You're both
heartless and stupid. How can you abandon Françoise
to her sorrow, when you have the ability to console
her? It's the least you can do for her. Didn't she
overwhelm you with her caresses? And you are
unwilling to dry her tears? She's old and ugly, I agree
with you, but she still has a cunt, doesn't she?'

'By God!' I muttered. 'He's right. A cunt is a cunt,
no matter the age of its owner.'

Mephistopheles continued his exhortation: 'The
storm is over, and there is nothing more to fear. Get
into bed with her.'

Blindly I obeyed the injunction. Although I climbed
into the couch with all care, Françoise gave a little
squeal of fright. With my groping hands, I found her
cringing in the far corner of the bed. It was too late to
beat a retreat, and I put my hand between her thighs.

To my amazement, they had returned to their
former delectable condition. They had changed back
to a silken smoothness that was a delight to the touch.
Now I was at a peak of erotic excitement. My hands
wandered over her delightful resilient breasts, her belly
that was as flat and smooth as a young girl's, and down
to the cunt, and what a cunt! As I expected, there was
no protest at my exploratory fondling. Her charms
were so appetising that I had to put my mouth on all of
them.

My ardour aroused hers in turn, for her whimpering
gave place to sharp little cries of pleasure.

'How did you happen to find me here?' she

whispered, calling me by the theologian's name, as she opened her legs to make my entrance easier. So she was mistaken about the identity of her lover. But I was at such a pitch of excitement that I could not stop now. And from the way she responded to my jabs in her cunt, I knew that she was in ecstasies. Our mingled sobs and pants made a sweet harmony as we kept perfect time with our movements.

After the preliminary raptures had subsided, I recalled how she had addressed me. Was Françoise capable of sharing the theologian with Nicole? I ran my hand again over the body next to me, expected to find the same wrinkles and flaccidity, but no... the body was still as deliciously supple and firm as ever. 'What does this mean?' I asked myself in puzzlement. 'Is my partner Françoise or not?'

The moon briefly appeared at the window, and with its light, I saw who it was. Heavens! It was Nicole. She probably had also escaped from the other room and come here to hide, counting on Françoise's forgiveness. And she undoubtedly imagined that her lover had done the same. To my mind, that was the only logical explanation for her mistake.

With such thoughts in my mind, I felt rise within me all the passions I formerly had for her, but I regretted the resources I had wasted on Françoise.

'My dearest Nicole,' I whispered, attempting to imitate the theologian's voice, for I intended to continue with the deception, 'what good fortune that we should find ourselves together here. Let's forget that disagreeable incident by fucking.'

'What delights you give me,' she replied, quivering with pleasure at my caresses. 'Yes, let us calm ourselves in the only way possible. Let come what may, as long as I have that in my hand,' she continued, clutching my prick, 'I am not afraid of death itself. Besides, I locked the door and we won't be disturbed.'

Reassured by this precaution that love prompted, I began to fondle her beauties with renewed zest. My prick which she kept tightly in her hand was of a stiffness that overjoyed her.

I urged her to put it in her, but she was in no haste to comply. However, she did not release it.

'Wait a moment, my dear friend,' she said when I attempted to insert it myself. 'Wait until it gets even bigger and harder. I have never felt it in such a condition. Did it grow during the night?'

From this naive question, I gathered that the theologian was not as well endowed as I.

'I am sure that this is going to be the night of nights,' she gasped as she finally put the impatient member in her. 'Now push, push as hard as you can.'

It goes without saying that her injunction was unnecessary. I shoved in with all might and main. As I did so, I covered her sensuous lips and abundant breasts with hot kisses. For several moments, I was so blissful that I had to stop to savour the enjoyment.

'Go on,' she coaxed me, wiggling her buttocks so lasciviously that I was roused out of my ecstatic stupor.

I deepened my jabs so that she gave out little screams as she surged up to meet me. She panted that she thought it was going all the way to her heart. Her passionate responses plunged me into a torrent of rapturous fury. Flames seared every hidden recess of my body.

'Come, now is the time to gush out your elixir! You are a god from above, and I beseech you to let me remain in this state of bliss for an eternity. How is it that one does not die from such transports?'

I was as overjoyed with her as she was with me. What a difference between a hag and a girl! Youth makes love because of love, and age does it out of habit. You old people should leave fucking to the young. For you, it is a chore, and for us it is a delight.

Although there was not the slightest danger of my prick going soft, Nicole took every precaution to prevent such a sad occurrence. Her fiery efforts resulted in an unprecedented rigidity. She would not have surrendered me for a kingdom, and I would not have given her up for all the riches in the world.

Our simultaneous gushes were copious and relieving and the raptures ineffable. But it was not long before we hastened in pursuit of that which had just escaped us. Imprudence, though, is one of the characteristics of love. Intoxicated by ecstasy, you are unable to conceive that it can be lost. And we were betrayed by our blind desire for each other.

Our bed was right next to the wall separating our room from the one adjoining it, and we had not the slightest suspicion that Françoise was occupying it. Nor did we have any inkling that the sounds of our amorous gambols would penetrate through the partition and wake her up, enabling her to guess what was going on.

In a flash, she was at our door. When she found it locked, she called:

'Nicole!'

We were petrified by the terrifying voice. At our

silence, she began to screech, but after realising that that did not help, she remained silent. In spite of the knowledge that she was at the door, our desires outweighed our fears and we resumed our games. When she heard the bed creak, she began to shriek again.

'Nicole,' she screamed. 'You're nothing but a slut! Aren't you ever going to stop?'

Nicole seemed perturbed, but I comforted her by saying that since we were discovered, we might as well be hung for a sheep as a lamb. She tacitly agreed by joining her movements to mine. Slapping me on the backside and darting her tongue in my mouth, she got on top of me and began to fuck with all the valour of a brave soldier who is oblivious to the shells bursting around him. As we neared another climax, the hag's screams of frustration merely piqued our raptures. When it was over, we panted to each other that never before had we experienced such a thrill.

Five times in a very short period was not bad for a convalescent like myself. Although I felt that I was not yet completely *hors de combat*, I decided that wisdom was the better part of valour. The old bitch could get really angry and resort to severe measures such as ringing the tocsin on us. We would be in a pretty kettle of fish if she did that. We would have to come out of the room naked, hardly suitable for a youth and a maid.

The sagest course was to beat a retreat, which I did by going out through the window. But before regaining my bed, I thought I would be a fool to leave Nicole believing it was the theologian who was the hero of the exploits she had admired so much. I was vain, I admit, but if the reader puts himself in my place, I am sure he would do exactly as I did.

'My dearest Nicole,' I cooed in her ear. 'I hope you have not been dissatisfied with me.'

She assured me fervently that such indeed was not the case.

'I bet you never thought that that funny little fellow you always looked down on was capable of such feats,' I continued. 'How wrong you were about him, and he certainly did not deserve the treatment he got from you. Now you have learned that size is not everything. Good-bye for now, dearest Nicole. My name is Saturnin and I am at your service.'

With a final kiss, I left her with a baffled expression and a drooping jaw.

As I said, I think the reader, in my place, would do the same thing.

Still somewhat stunned by the bizarre adventures that had befallen me, I impatiently awaited the coming of morning to learn what the results, if any, might be. Because of my exhilaration at the theologian's humiliation, I did not sleep a wink.

With the exception of Nicole, on whose silence I could count, nobody could cast the slightest suspicion on me. I was chuckling in advance at the figure they would cut when I saw them. The Cure would look solemn and be in a vile mood, but I would not be among those who would feel the back of his hand.

Françoise would scrutinise carefully all the pupils, one by one, eyes scarlet with suppressed fury. Among the bigger fellows, she would spot a likely candidate for revenge, not for the joys she had but for those Nicole had received. Because of my size, I would be the last to be suspected. Nicole probably would not show her face, for if she did, she would be blushing, have a guilty look, and regard me with longing eyes.

I was so preoccupied with these happy reflections that I did not notice dawn spreading its rosy fingers in my room. Only then did Morpheus close my eyes and keep them shut until noon.

When I awoke, I was extremely surprised to find Toinette at my bedside. I turned pale and trembled with fear that my part in the night's escapade had been discovered.

'Don't you feel well, Saturnin?' she asked.

I did not answer.

'If you are sick, I suppose you can't go with Father Polycarpe, who is leaving today. He was planning to take you with him.'

The mention of departure dissipated all my trepidation.

'I never felt better in my life,' I shouted exultantly as I sprang out of bed and dressed before giving Toinette time to wonder at my sudden transition from depression to jubilance. When I had my clothes on, I followed her out of the room.

I left the Cure's house without the slightest regret. The thought that I would never see Suzon or Nicole again did not bother me in the slightest.

Father Polycarpe was delighted to see me, and Ambroise gave me an affectionate embrace. Seated behind the Reverend Father on his mount, I waved farewell to Ambroise and Toinette.

Part Two

Now I entered a new stage in my life. Destined from birth to augment the number of those holy swine whom the credulous stupidly nourish, I was perfectly suited by nature for this calling which experience perfected me in.

It is now my intention to recount some extraordinary events. If the reader argues that they are so improbable as to be untrue, allow me to assure him that they are veritable down to the last detail. All I am doing is describing what is done behind the seminary walls by mean, debauched, and corrupted monks who laugh at the gullibility of believers under their hood of religion. As hypocrites, they do in secret all that they condemn in public.

Since I became one of them, I have often reflected on the life they and I lead.

How is it that men of such varying characters and temperaments should come together in a monastery? There you find indolence, profligacy, mendacity, cowardliness, dishonour, and intoxication.

I pity those poor souls who believe that there is religion and piety behind those walls. If only they knew what goes on! The rampant iniquity would astound them, and they would despise those so-called holy men as they justly deserve. I am now going to lift the veil.

You have met Father Cherubim, that man of God whose vermilion bloated visage was the incarnation of lust. You knew him before he assumed the masquerade of the black serge cowl. What was his way of life?

He never went to bed before having downed nine or ten bottles of the best wines. It was not unusual to find him the next morning sprawled out under the dining-table he had been unable to leave. He abandoned the world, for God had showed him the way and he took it. I do not know if it was the Lord or one of His mundane deputies who effected this miracle, but I do know that Father Cherubim could more than hold his own with the most intrepid imbibers. That is how you knew him and he has not changed in the interim.

Perhaps you also glimpsed Father Modesto, puffed with his own self-importance. How has his character changed since he began wearing the triple cord around his pot-belly? You believe his words, but I know how he lies. Listen to him talk. In eloquence, Cicero is only an unconvincing babbler by comparison. He is more subtle than the most profound theologians. In his own eyes, he is another Saint Thomas, but in mine, he is nothing but a pompous ass. If you knew him as well as I do, you would agree with my opinion.

Now take Father Boniface, the crafty snoop who always walks with his head humbly bent down as if he were in silent communication with the Almighty. But watch out for him, for he is a snake in the grass. When he comes to call on you, keep an eye on your wife and daughters and send away your sons. If you are not present when he is there, your whole family will be fucked and buggered.

You have made the acquaintance of Father Hilary.

When you are with him, keep your hand on your purse, for he is the biggest swindler that ever lived. He will tell you of the urgent needs of the monastery in such a heart-rending fashion that tears will well in your eyes. The wretched friars are almost starving and the roof is about to collapse on their shaved pates. How could you allow such a piteous state of affairs to continue? Of course, you could not. In a burst of generosity, you open your purse until it is completely empty. Thus Father Hilary robs, pillages, and steals for the Church.

What a gang of rogues they are! You would think they would have changed for the better after they had taken the orders, but such is not the case. The drunk is still a drunk, the libertine still a libertine, and the thief still a thief. I'll go even further than that and aver that their vices are accentuated once they have donned the cowl, for they have unlimited opportunity to indulge in their caprices. How can they resist?

Although these monks hate and loathe each other, they are held together by common bonds. Even though rent by civil war, they present to the world a united front that is a model of discipline. And when it comes to stripping the gullible of their worldly goods, they have no peers. It is the same with the superstitions they invented and foisted on their flocks. In these efforts, they join forces with a common zeal.

After what I had seen of monkish frolics while living with Ambroise, I came to realise that the wearing of the cowl was the easiest way to gain admittance into the temple of pleasure. My mind reveled at the prospects such a calling would afford me.

With such thoughts, I eagerly donned the robe the

Father Prior gave me the day I arrived at the seminary.

I had learned enough Latin from the Cure to distinguish myself during my noviciate, but what good did it do me? I was made a porter.

As a writer who sticks to his facts, I should lead my reader, year by year, through my theologic career from novitiate to full priesthood. There would be many things to tell, but, alas, they would be of little interest. But I will mention a few amusing bagatelles.

After several years in the monastery, I was disabused of the high hopes I held when I entered it. If the monks had their fun, they certainly did not let a neophyte like me share it. Torn between repentance for having taken up a career which did not meet my expectations and eagerness for priesthood, I kept on the thorny path mostly because of the Prior who was the soul of kindness. More than once he told me that my abilities were unusual for the son of a gardener.

My first years in the seminary were not pleasant. There were the snubs I received from the other novices about my humble birth. There was no sex. Although Toinette came to see me, how could I enjoy her under the eyes of the ever present superiors? The loss of my beloved Suzon hurt even more. Although I knew that she was living with Madame Dinville, I had no news from her. I truly loved her, for there was an indefinable something about her. Every time I thought of our childish love-making, I was plunged into despair.

As I was attempting to console myself in my grief, there was one who was moved by my unhappy state.

'What are you doing, Saturnin?' he asked sympathetically.

As a matter of fact, I was masturbating. In those

unhappy days, my prick was the only thing that enabled me to forget my woes.

I thought I was alone while indulging in this voluptuous diversion. But a monk with an impish sense of humour was observing me. He was not a friend of mine. On the contrary, he never made any attempt to conceal his distaste for me. On this occasion, he came upon me so suddenly that I was frightened out of my wits. I thought I was lost for I was sure he would spread the story of what I was doing.

'Well, well, Brother Saturnin,' he remarked, rubbing his hands and raising his eyes heavenward, 'I never dreamed that you could stoop so low, you the learned theologian and the model of piety.'

'All right,' I brusquely interrupted him. 'That's enough of your sarcasm. So you caught me playing with myself, and I suppose you will see to it that everybody knows about it.' I took up where I had left off. 'Bring anyone you want here and laugh to your heart's content. I'll probably be on my tenth discharge by the time you are back.'

'Brother Saturnin,' he answered with the same sangfroid, 'I understand. There's nothing wrong. All the novices do it, and I did it when I was one.'

'If you don't get out of here, I'll...' I sputtered, clenching my fist.

My threat caused him to burst out into gales of laughter.

Extending his hand to me, he said in the most cordial tone imaginable: 'Take it, my friend. I never thought you had such spirit. Also, I feel genuinely sorry that you are so unhappy that you have to masturbate. You deserve better than such a feeble solace. I think I can find for you something more substantial and satisfying.'

His open and candid speech disarmed me, and I warmly shook his hand.

'I don't know what you have in mind,' I said, 'but I gratefully accept your offer.'

'All right,' he replied. 'Button up your trousers and don't expend your ammunition, for you'll have need of it later. At midnight, I'll be at your cell. For the moment, I won't say anything more. Don't follow me when I leave here, for nobody must see us together. It would cause talk. So, until later, then.'

I was slightly stupefied after Father André had left, so much so in fact, that I no longer had any interest in continuing with my game.

'What did he mean by "substantial"?' I wondered. 'If it's just some other novice, he can keep him for himself. That's not my cup of tea.'

My reasoning was that of an idiot, for I had never tried to get pleasure with a partner of my sex. Prejudice prevents us from so many delights. The thought of it disgusted me at first, but when I later tried it, I found it most appetising.

I happened to think of Giton. Is there anything more appealing than that pretty lad? His skin is like velvet and his rounded rump is as alluring as the most enticing little cunt. Yes, dear reader, you think I am breathing hot and cold by praising the cunt and then the male bottom. I suppose I am fickle.

Follow my advice, young fellow. Take your pleasure where you find it. My preference is to fuck a pretty, willing woman, but who in his right mind would reject a delicious pair of buttocks if they were offered him?

113

Take the famous philosophers of ancient Greece, for example, as well as some of the most distinguished men of our time – they will tell you the same thing.

As midnight sounded, there was a scrat̶c̶h̶ ̶a̶t̶ my cell door. It was Father André.

'I'm ready, Father,' I warmly greeted him. 'But where are we going?'

'To the chapel,' he curtly answered.

'Oh, no,' I balked. 'I'm not going there. Or are you making fun of me?'

He told me not to be a fool, and I meekly followed him.

Inside the chapel, we climbed up behind the organ, and, there, to my amazement, I found a table groaning under the weight of the finest food and wines.

The guests consisted of three monks, three novices, and a girl of about eighteen who seemed as lovely as an angel in my eager eyes. Father Casimir, who was the host of this cheerful gathering, gave me a cordial welcome.

'Greetings, Brother Saturnin,' he boomed as he wrapped in his arms. 'Father André has spoken very highly of you, and that is why you have been invited here. I don't think he mentioned our way of life here. Simply said, we eat, drink, laugh, and fuck. Are such diversions to your taste?'

'Good Lord, yes,' I instantly replied. 'You'll see that I won't be a wet blanket on your festivities and that I shall avail myself of the offered pleasures as eagerly as anyone.'

'Well, let's get the party going!' Father Casimir cried, and turning again to me, he said: 'I am going to seat you between me and this adorable little girl.'

Father Casimir, who was now uncorking a bottle, was of medium height, dark complexion, sharp features, and had the pot-belly from good eating that is common among prelates. Whenever he was near a good-looking boy, his eyes glistened with the lust of a bugger and he whinnied like a rutting stallion. And he had a clever and novel way of getting what he wanted without ever leaving his study. The novice who surrendered himself to him was rewarded with the favours of his niece, who willingly paid her uncle's obligations.

'We have chosen this spot for our orgies, because it would be the last place anyone would suspect,' he explained to me.

Father Casimir's niece was brunette, petite, and lively. Perhaps the first sight of her did not inspire immediate desire, but she knew how to guide a man's eyes down to an absolutely magnificent bust. She laughed easily, and she had something of the coquette that made her irresistible.

As soon as I was next to the charming maiden, I experienced the confused sensation I had when I happened on Father Polycarpe and Toinette. Also, my long period of continence had whetted my lubricity. For the first time in ages, I sensed life beginning to stir in me again, and I was confident that I was soon going to enjoy the pleasures of flesh. My confidence was confirmed by the merry, mischievous eyes of my partner.

I soon had my hand on her thigh which I pressed to mine. Then it went under her skirt. She took the intruder in her hand and guided it to the spot where I wanted it. The possession of a site that had been denied me for an eternity produced a shudder of pure joy in me. It was noticed by everybody.

'Get going, Brother Saturnin,' they encouraged me. 'You have it made.'

Perhaps I would have lost my self-assurance at their friendly jeers had not Marianne, for such was the name of the delightful creature, given me a warm kiss, unbuttoned my trousers, and squeezed my neck. In her other hand she now had my prick which was stiff as an iron rod.

'My reverend fathers,' she cried exultantly as she displayed my pulsating masculinity on the table, 'yours are nothing but little sausages compared to this prodigy. Have you ever seen its like?'

There was a muted murmur of undeniable admiration. All congratulated Marianne on the delights she was going to enjoy, and her eyes shone with enchantment at the prospect.

Now Father Casimir called for silence. After congratulating his niece on her acquisition, he addressed me:

'I don't have to vaunt the charms of my niece to you, Brother Saturnin, and she is all yours. I think you'll find the texture of her skin softer than velvet and her breasts inviting cushions. And, according to general opinion, there is no cunt in the world like hers. But to have her, there is one little condition which, I am sure, will give you great pleasure.'

My desires were stimulated to the breaking point and I cried: 'Anything, anything at all. Just tell me the stipulation. I'll give you my life's blood if you want it.'

'Don't you know what I want?' he exclaimed in unfeigned surprise. 'All I want is your adorable bottom.'

'Oh!' I cried. 'Whatever in the world do you want that for. Besides, I am bashful about even showing it to you.'

'What I'll do with it is my affair,' Father Casimir replied.

So eager was I to get on top of Marianne that I made no further objection and quickly dropped my trousers. I was in her in a flash and Father Casimir was in me. The pain I experienced in the rear was more than compensated by the bliss I enjoyed in the front. Also, I sensed that Marianne was suffering with as much pleasure from my organ as I was from her uncle's.

The three of us, with myself in the middle, were now bucking in perfect cadence. I felt like a conductor between uncle and niece. She was squeezing me, biting me, and scratching me as she felt the explosions I was causing in her. Her spasms astonished the company.

Father Casimir, who had long since abandoned the field, was also amazed at the ferocity of our combat. Everybody was ranged around us in a respectful silence. For myself, I was piqued that Marianne was standing up so doughtily against my repeated assaults, for I knew that I was at the peak of my powers after such a long abstinence.

As for her, she was annoyed at her inability to drain me.

Thus we continued the conflict, literally drenching ourselves with our emissions which were now starting to show flecks of blood.

After we had discharged simultaneously the seventh time, Marianne shut her eyes, let her arms droop, and remained still as she awaited the *coup de grâce* of my eighth ejaculation. After submissively receiving it and savouring it to the last drop, she sprang up and shook my hand to contgratulate me on my victory. In turn, I filled two bumpers with champagne, one of which I handed her, and we exchanged toasts in honour of the armistice.

After the finale, everyone returned to his place. I was again between Marianne, who had her hand on my prick, and her uncle, who had his on my rump.

Now the conversation turned from praises of our exploits to the subject of sodomy. Father Casimir vigorously defended it, eruditely citing its adherents who included Jesuits, philosophers, cardinals, and monarchs. Then he inveighed against those who frowned on pederasty, charging them with stupidity and blind prejudice.

His eloquent peroration was greeted with the praise it deserved. Then we made merry, drank and fucked, before the party broke up. We agreed to celebrate again in a similar fashion in a week's time. Such festivities were not possible every night for the monastery's revenues were not that great.

One day, after having held my first Mass, the Prior asked me to dine with him in his rooms. When I made my appearance there, I found him with some elders, all of whom greeted me with fulsome praise. The reason for the accolade was not clear to me.

We sat down to an excellent repast, and under the influence of the fine wines, the friars' tongues loosened, uttered words like 'cunt' and 'fuck' with a lack of restraint that astonished me. The Prior noticed my surprise.

'Father Saturnin,' he said to me, 'you are to feel as

free with us as we are with you. Now that you are a full-fledged priest, you are one of us. Now the time has come to reveal important secrets that have been withheld from you until now. You realise they could not have been imparted to young men who might leave us and have no scruples about baring mysteries that have to remain known only to the initiate. And it is to fill that obligation that I have asked you come here.'

This solemn exordium caused me to pay close attention to the words of the Prior.

'I don't think you are one of those prudes who are shocked by the thought of fucking, which, as you know, is as natural to a man as drinking or eating. We are priests, to be sure, but our penises and testicles were not amputated when we entered the monastery. But the imbecility of the founders of our order who laid down the rules of celibacy and the cruel insistence of our flocks that we follow those mandates have forbidden us the most natural of functions. If we were to conform to their tyranny, we would burn with flames that would be extinguished only with our deaths. But we don't accept that. We show an austere face to the outer world and indulge ourselves in the seclusion of the cloister.

'In a number of well regulated convents, there are some nuns who are willing to assuage the concupiscence we inherited from Adam, and in their arms we hurl ourselves to lessen the tortures of continence.

'Your words astound me,' I exclaimed.

The others burst out laughing.

'Why should we be such fools and give up the sweetest delight life has to offer?' the Prior continued. 'And we aren't about to. Here we have a refuge where we can escape the atrocities the outer world wants to inflict on us.'

'Have you no fear of being found out?' I inquired.

'None whatsoever,' he assured me. 'There is no chance of discovery. Who would ever think of snooping into a tranquil little corner such as ours? The eyes of the world pass us by. If you, who have been here nine years, had no idea of what was going on, how would an outsider have even an inkling?'

'When can I join you to console those lovely nuns you mentioned,' I eagerly asked.

'It won't be long before you give them the solace they are pining for. But these recreations are reserved only to full-fledged priests. We have to be sure of the discretion of those we accept into our inner circle. You are now one of us, and you join us whenever you wish.'

'Whenever you wish!' I cried. 'I'll take you at your word. Let's go right now.'

'Not so fast,' he said with a smile at my impatience. 'We have to wait until evening. That's when we go to assuage our desires in the piscina where the sisters have their retreat.'

'Now, Father Saturnin, I have another surprise for you. It is something you never even suspected. Ambroise is not your father.'

My jaw dropped at that revelation.

'Yes,' continued the Prior, amused at my dumbfoundedness. 'Ambroise and Toinette are not your parents. You are of much more distinguished lineage. You came into the world in our piscina from the womb of one of our sisters.'

Recovering from my surprise, I replied: 'Father, all along I had the feeling that I was not really a gardener's son. But I am slightly bitter that you withheld this truth from me so long. I would have been overjoyed with the knowledge, and you could have been sure that I would have kept the confidence. Is my mother still living?'

'We had our reasons for not telling you,' he said gently. 'Yes, your mother is alive and well, and in a few hours, you will be embracing her. It will not be a pleasure that you had lost, but one that you will find.'

'I can't wait until I have my arms around her,' I exclaimed.

'Just be patient,' he counselled me. 'It won't be long. The sun is already setting, and night will be here before you know it. We are going to dine in the piscina, and you are to join us.'

The desire to see my mother was not the only reason for my eagerness to penetrate the retreat. In reality, I was more eager to taste of the feminine charms of the beauties I pictured to myself enclosed there.

'So I have finally made it,' I congratulated myself. 'The moment to which I have looked forward so long has come. The long dreary days I spent are going to be more than made up for, if what the Prior says is true.'

When the bell tolled eight o'clock, I returned to the Prior's rooms where I found him with five or six monks, all sharing the same intent as I. Silently we left in single file and walked to those ancient chapels which serve as ramparts to the piscina. Without the benefit of a candle, we descended into a pitch black cellar. In this underground chamber, we made our way with the help of a rope fixed to the wall until we reached a staircase illuminated by a lantern.

Opening the door at the top of the stairs, the Prior

led us into a sumptuously furnished chamber in which were several couches specially designed for the combats of Venus. On the table, we noticed the preparations for a veritable feast.

The room was empty, but when the Prior rang a little bell, our nuns appeared, six in all. I found them delightful and charming. Each promptly threw herself in the arms of a monk, leaving me the sole witness of their transports. I was not a little hurt at their apparent indifference to a new monk, but it would not be long before I had my turn, as I was to find out.

The banquet was superb with the tastiest dishes and wines. Each guest had at his side one of the lovely nuns, and as they drank, ate, laughed, joked and kissed, they discussed fucking with the same casualness they would talk about the weather.

Feeling alone, I had little appetite. Although I naturally wanted to see my mother, I was more anxious for a skirmish with one of the sisters. I looked for the one who could have possibly brought me into the world, but they all seemed so youthful and fresh that it could not be any of those present. Although the six were most attentive to the reverend fathers, they began to cast coquettish glances at me from time to time which changed my original impressions of them. And my prick, now in a state of prime eagerness, yearned for all of them.

My discomfiture was a source of amusement for the whole party. After all had heartily filled their bellies, the Prior announced that it was time to think of fucking. At that, the eyes of the nuns began to glisten. Since I was the newcomer, I was given the honour of beginning the dance.

'Father Saturnin,' the Prior addressed me, 'we have to see what you are capable of with your neighbour, Sister Gabrielle.'

No sooner had he spoken than I started to make her acquaintanceship by exchanging passionate kisses. As we were thus engaged, her hand descended to the slit of my trousers. Although she was not the youngest of the six, she held enough allure for me to be more than contented with my lot. She was a big, voluptuous blonde, whose beauty was marred only by a little too much *embonpoint*. Her skin was a dazzling white and she had a ravishing face with big, blue eyes that were sparkling with delight. Add to all that a breathtaking bosom that was as proud and firm as a young girl's. I could not keep my eyes from those superb globes, and when I found the courage to take them and weigh them in my hands, I was in sheer bliss.

Gabrielle enthusiastically bent to her task of exciting me.

'King of my heart, come and present me with your virginity,' she ordered. 'Lose it in the very spot where you found life.'

Her words made me tremble. Without being a prude, I had acquired some prejudices that would not permit me to do with Gabrielle what I had done with Toinette and Madame Dinville. I was eager to fuck, but the scruple of incest stopped me at the edge of the precipice.

'Heavens!' exclaimed Gabrielle as she rose from her chair. 'Is it possible that this is my son? How could I have given birth to a coward like him? Is he actually afraid of fucking his own mother?'

'My dear Gabrielle,' I replied kissing her on the

cheek. 'Be satisfied with the filial love I have for you. I can imagine no greater delight than that of possessing you, but please respect a prejudice that I am just unable to overcome.'

The avowal of a virtue is respected and admired by the most corrupt and libertine hearts. My reluctance was approved by the monks who agreed that they were wrong in trying to spring such a surprise on me. Only one attempted to dissuade me from my decision.'

'You poor fool,' he told me. 'So you are frightened of doing such a simple thing. Let us talk sensibly. Tell me just what fucking is. You know that it is merely the union of a man and a woman. Is it or is it not permitted by nature? I don't have to wait for your answer, for you realise that the two sexes have an irresistible attraction for each other. It is nature's intention that this mutual urge be satisfied.

'Didn't the Lord command the mother and father of us all to increase and multiply? How did God intend that it should be done? Was Adam to do it all by himself? Adam made with Eve daughters whom he later fucked. Eve had sons with whom she did what her husband was doing with their sisters. Let's get to the Flood. The only family left on earth was Noah's. It goes without saying that the brothers had to copulate with their sisters, the sons with their mother, and the father with his daughters if they were to repopulate the world. And how about Lot and his daughters? In other words, indiscriminate fucking is a divine decree.

'Even Saint Paul counselled fucking, but he called it marriage. When you get down to it, what is the difference? Men and women wed for the sole purpose of fucking. I could go on indefinitely, but I suddenly feel a great need to follow the advice of Saint Paul.'

There was general laughter at the witticism of the monk who was now standing, and, with his prick in his hand, threatening all the slits in the room.

'Just a moment,' broke in one of the sisters whose name was Madelon. 'I just have had the most marvellous idea how we can punish Saturnin for his obstinacy.'

Everybody clamoured to know what it was.

'Well,' she demurely hesitated before continuing. 'He'll lie on one of the couches, Gabrielle will recline on his back, and in that position, our eloquent father will exploit Saturnin's mother.'

There was general hilarity at this whimsical proposal. Laughing myself, I said I would consent only if I could fuck the pleasing Madelon at the same time the father was having my mother on my back.

'Well, I'm agreeable,' Madelone said merrily. 'I have never enjoyed myself in such a position, and the idea intrigues me.'

And I was congratulated for my powers of erotic imagination.

Just picture to yourself the figure we cut. The monk did not give my mother a job without her returning it threefold, and her derriere, dropping on my buttocks, served to shove my prick deeper into Madelon's cunt. This copulative ricochet was immensely diverting for the spectators, but we performers were so busy at our task that we could not join in the merriment.

I could have obtained revenge on Madelon by letting the weight of three bodies fall on her, for she was at the bottom of our four-tiered group, but I liked her too well to play such a dirty trick on her. Besides, she was so conscientious at lending herself to my movements. I made the heaviness on her as light as possible, but when a moment of rapture seized me, I sank down on her with my load. Instead of causing her pain, the weight seemed to enhance her voluptuousness. When I sensed the pair on top of me reach their orgasm, I remained immobile from vicarious lust. At my rigidity, Madelon gave one last upward lunge which produced the same result for the two of us. It seemed that we four, our bodies now one, were swimming in the same lake of bliss.

The praises we made of the enjoyments to be had from making love in such a fashion made the watching sisters' and monks' mouths water, and soon the whole gathering was rapturously fucking in our position – one we dubbed the quatrain, to differentiate it from the *partie carée*, or four forming a square. The greatest discoveries are the result of chance.

Delighted at the improvisation I had come up with, Gabrielle confessed that she had almost as much pleasure as if she had done it directly with me. Then addressing the gathering, she said she was going to tell me before everybody something about herself and her son.

'My boy,' she commenced by addressing me, 'you cannot boast of a long line of illustrious ancestors. I am the daughter of a housekeeper who worked in this monastery and a monk whose identity I never discovered.

'When I was sixteen years old, I discovered love. One young monk gave me such sweet instruction that out of gratitude, I repaid his kindness the only way I knew how, and soon the other fathers were giving me the benefit of their lessons. It goes without saying that I paid them in the same manner. I was quits with all of them when the Prior suggested that I live in a place where I would have the freedom to return their favours as often as I liked. Up to then, I could do it only on the sly, such as behind the altar, in the organ loft, in the confessional, and, at times, in their cells. The thought of being able to indulge myself at will was indeed tempting, and I accepted their offer to come to the piscina.

'The very first day I came here, I was dressed like a young girl about to be confirmed. The thought of the happiness I was going to enjoy gave my face an expression that delighted the fathers. They all wanted to pay me their homage, and each vied with the others to be the first to have me. I was of the opinion that my multiple nuptials could end in a fiasco if I did not do something. Consequently, I suggested that their turn would be determined by lot.

'"My fathers," I addressed them, "your numbers do not frighten me, but my powers may not meet your expectations. Since you are twenty and I am one, the struggle will be unequal. To solve the predicament, I suggest that we all get down to the buff."

'I set the example by divesting myself of every stitch of my garments. It was a matter of seconds until the sisters and monks were in the same state as I. My eyes eagerly devoured the twenty upright pricks, erect, thick and hard as rods of steel. I wished that my cunt were big enough to accommodate them all at once. If only that were possible. I would have gladly accepted them all at the same time.

'"Well," I continued, "It's about time to start. I'll lie

down on this couch with my legs as wide as I can. Then each of you fathers will come in turn as determined by the lottery with your prick in your hand and fuck me in order, one after the other."

'I think it was you, Prior,' she said, addressing him, 'who made Saturnin, for of the twenty who had me, it was you who gave me the sharpest pleasure.' Turning to me, she remarked: 'You have this advantage over other men. They can tell you the date of their birth, but not that of their conception.'

Oh, the delights of the piscina! I savoured them to the full. I was the life of the parties we had there every night, and in no time at all I had fucked every one of the recluses except my mother.

At times, during the necessary pauses, I wondered aloud how such attractive women were willing to spend the rest of their lives in a retreat such as the piscina, which was a form of prison. They laughed at my puzzlement.

'You don't seem to understand our temperaments,' one of the prettiest of the nuns explained to me. 'Where else can we satisfy our fiery desires as well as here? There is the bordel, of course, but there, more often than not, you have to give yourself to the most awful men.' She wrinkled her little nose with disgust. 'You see, we have all the men we need here, and they are all gentlemen, courteous and kind. Five or six times is usual to exhaust a man, but women like us require double that many times. So when our first partner has to leave the field of battle vanquished, there is always another ready to take his place. Isn't that alone worth the price of loss of liberty? What woman with fire in her veins wouldn't envy us for the freedom we have to indulge our caprices? Women on the outside who give in to their desires always have to fear scandal and talk. Marriage, you say!' Here she gave a little snort. 'Just imagine the boredom of having the same man for all of your days. The piscina for us is a seraglio where we exchange partners to our hearts' content, and there are always newcomers, like you for instance. Could a womam wish for anything more? Ah, Father Saturnin, rid yourself of the notion that we are unhappy here in our voluntary bondage!'

I had never expected such sound reasoning from a girl whom I had considered merely a vessel of pleasure. And I had to admit to myself that she was completely right.

Man is not born for lasting pleasure. Having everything my heart could desire, I became nervous and irritable. In fucking, I was like Alexander in ambition. I wanted to fuck the whole world, and if I succeeded in that, I would have sought new worlds for new cunts to conquer.

For more than six months, I was the admitted champion in our amorous combats, but after that, I fucked with the same ennui that I used to masturbate. Soon, I was with the six sisters like a husband is with his wife. My mental lassitude now affected my potency and desire. It was soon noticed, and the sisters reproached me for lethargy, but I shrugged off their playful scoldings. My visits to the piscina became more and more seldom. The Prior urged the sisters to exert themselves to revive me, and they spared no efforts in the task.

Not only did they employ all their natural charms, but also all the refinements that the most lascivious imaginations could dream up. Gathered in a circle around me, they offered to my eyes the most lubricious sights. One would be negligently resting on the bed, half revealing an enticing bosom and letting me see alabaster thighs promising the most delightful cunt in the world. Another would assume an attitude of readiness for combat, letting me know by her sighs and convulsive motions how she was burning with desire. Others would assume different postures, some lifting their skirts and agitating their cunts, some spreading their slits wide open so I could see deep into their interiors, and one even went so far as to make me lie on the floor between two chairs on which she rested herself so that her cunt was directly over my face and then she worked on it with a dildo. Madelon, who had stripped herself completely bare, was vigorously fucking with an equally nude monk next to me so that I could follow every movement of their prick and cunt.

Sometimes they took off all my clothes and placed me on a bench. One sister then would get astride my chest so that my forehead was concealed in the hair of her cunt, a second would be on my stomach, and a third on my thighs trying to introduce my prick into her slit. Two others were at my sides so that I had a cunt in each hand. And then another, possessed of the loveliest bosom of all the sisters, pressed my face between her luscious breasts. All of them were stark naked and discharging so that my hands, stomach, legs, chest, prick, and face were inundated. I was literally drowning in fuck, but mine refused to mingle with theirs. The attempt was as vain as the others had been. From then on, I was considered a lost soul.

Such was my condition when, walking alone in the

garden with my gloomy reflections, I came across Father Simeon, a wise and scholarly priest, who had grown white-haired in the labours of Venus and the table. He came up to me and put his arms around me affectionately.

'My son,' he said, 'I can see that your grief is deep, but don't allow yourself to despair. In my long experience, I have found ways to revive the desire for pleasure, that voluptuous ardour characterising a good monk. You are in a bad way, that is obvious, and for severe ailments, desperate remedies are required.

'Cruel nature has granted us only limited powers, although it must be admitted that it treats us monks as favoured sons. But excessive dissipation, even in a monk, can produce the same result as in an ordinary man, and it is this dissipation which is the cause of your sickness and your disgust with sex. What you need to restore your jaded appetite is a succulent dish, and I know of nothing better than a devout woman.'

I could not conceal my surprise.

'I am quite serious,' he told me, 'and what I am telling you is not a paradox. You are still young, and you do not know devout women as I do. You have no idea, they have infallible resources to relight extinguished flames. They are able to arouse the ardour of the most jaded man. I know it from my own experience. I have fucked them, and more than one, I assure you.'

I looked at him unbelievingly, for he was considered a broken old man with ice water in his veins. He could barely walk, his testicles were empty, and his prick had disappeared. That was his reputation. And since his novitiate, he was renowned for his celibacy.

'Yes, my son,' he continued. 'You are still in that happy age when you can enjoy unlimited pleasures. Take advantage of it as I did. At my age, I have more important things to think about, namely, eternal life. Nevertheless, I do not refuse to give my advice to those who have need of it. I repeat that the only cure for your lethargy is a devout and the only way to get one is to obtain permission to hear confessions. I'll take care of that for you.'

Although I had my doubts, I thanked him for his advice and his offer to enable me to be a father confessor.

'That's not all,' he went on. 'Before you start your new calling, you'll need someone to guide your steps at first. I'll be happy to play that role, but before I continue, let's sit on this bench, where we'll be more comfortable.'

We sat down, and the good father, coughing to regain his voice, went on with his talk.

'You probably don't realise that this happy mania known as confession goes back to our ancestors, that is the first priests and monks at the beginning of Christianity. The practice is the most precious heritage they have left us. I have always entertained the greatest admiration for their genius. At first, priests did not know comfort and ease and monks depended on a few charitable crumbs to fill their empty bellies. With the advent of the confession, all that unhappy condition changed. Riches rained down on our heads, and we now lead happy, contented lives.

'You will soon learn the advantages of being a confessor. The people will bless you and the women will adore you. God, whose mercy they beg through your intercession, is less their deity than you are. One piece of advice I have to give you is to fleece those dowagers, those old bigots who come to confession not so much to make their peace with God as to see a handsome young priest.

'Be merciful with the young girls, for seldom are they able to make donations other than token ones. But they have something more precious to offer, and that is their maidenhead. Skill is required to steal this charming gem. Concentrate on these young devouts, for they are the only ones able to cure you. In spite of your understandable eagerness for recovery, watch your step. Don't openly express your desires. A woman can take a hint. Her heart more or less tells her your desires before you have uttered a word. But a young girl is different. Although her conquest is more difficult, the victory is sweeter.

'With all of them, you'll find a natural penchant for the joys of love. To handle this inclination is an art. The shy lass who appears before you with a demure dress, a humble attitude, and lowered eyes has coals smouldering within her that are ready to burst into flame at the first gust of love. If you are tender and adroit, your triumph is sure.

'With some, you have to paint the erotic delights in such vivid colours that they cannot resist.

'Perhaps you will object that it is difficult to succeed in such an art, but all that is needed is a little practise. Their inborn desires always win out over their modesty. And have no fear of their blabbing. As a man of God, they hold you in too great awe. The usual way is to casually put your hand on their breasts, regard them with longing eyes, and go up their skirt. If they have any scruples, dispel them by saying you know many ways to avoid the danger of pregnancy.'

Father Simeon's discourse so heated my imagination that I kept after him and the Prior until I obtained what I so ardently desired.

Now I was mediator between sinners and the Father of mercy. I pictured to myself the pleasure I was going to have hearing the confession of a timid young girl who would soon yield to her latent passions. I went to the confessional box to take up my post.

I had heard of a young priest, who, on finding his first penitent an ugly old woman, returned to his cell and stayed there the remainder of the day. I did not follow his example, fortunately, when a similar hag presented herself to me.

I suffered a torrent of twaddle and consoled her so successfully with hypocritical moral advice that she would have willingly granted me evidence of her gratitude. Fortunately, the grille was a barrier. I recalled Father Simeon's advice – fleece the old ones – and I obtained a generous contribution. She was a chatterbox and skilfully I led her to talk about her family. She cursed her husband and inveighed against her son, another ne'er-do-well, who was unfaithful to his wife as her spouse was to her. All her praise was reserved for her daughter, who was her only consolation. She was a model of devoutness, of angelic purity, who, in order to remain uncontaminated by the filth of the world, left her room only to come to church. Her sole pleasure consisted of prayer.

'Ah!' I exclaimed in a sanctimonious voice, 'how happy you must be to see yourself incarnated in such a daughter. But does this saintly creature come to our church? How happy I would be to meet such an example of virtue.'

'She's here every day,' the old woman informed me. 'You can't miss her, for she is a striking beauty. But I should not mention that because it cannot be of any interest to one like you who is of the saints.'

'We admire all the works of the Lord, including the beauty of women,' I assured her.

Encouraged by my curiosity, the old lady began to depict her virtuous daughter, whom I now recognised as the ravishing brunette who never missed Mass.

'Father Simeon,' I said to myself, 'that must be one of the devouts you were telling me about. I hope she comes to me so that I can learn if your prophecy is correct.'

I perhaps could have scared off the mother if in our initial talk I had tried to persuade her to have her child come to me for confession. I decided to postpone the suggestion until the next time, and to win her good graces, I gave her a general absolution, both for the past and for the present. I would have absolved her for future transgressions, if she had wanted. It would not have cost anything. As she left the box, I urged her to come often for the holy water.

It seems that I hear you crying: 'Go on, Dom Bougre, you are on the right track. You'll soon be cured.'

Yes, dear reader, the sanctity I had assumed was commencing to work. Praise the Lord for his beneficence. I was starting to have erections of sufficient vigour to lead me to hope that I would soon be my old self.

The next day, I did not fail to attend services, and

one can readily imagine why. There I saw my brunette praying to God with all her heart.

'There she is,' I thought with deep satisfaction. 'There is that paragon of virtue. Oh, what a delight it will be to munch on a morsel like that. What a rapture to give the first amorous lesson to someone like her. I am cured, for I have an erection like a Carmelite's.'

My devout was regarding me. Had her mother spoken about me to her? Quickly now. Let's put out the fires that her look lit in me.

I could not help myself. Her ecstatic gaze excited me almost to a fury, and my hand went to my prick which was as hard as rock. My pleasure when I discharged was almost as great as if I had been in her.

One day, I had been away from the monastery for some time, and when I returned, the porter, on opening the gate, informed me that a young lady had been waiting for me for several hours and insisted on speaking to me. I hurried to the reception room, where I found, to my utter amazement, the devout object of my adoration.

As soon as she espied me, she rushed to me and threw herself at my feet.

'Have pity on me, Father,' she pleaded as tears streamed down her cheeks. Her sobs prevented her from continuing.

'What is wrong, my child?' I asked as soothingly as I could as I helped her to her feet. 'You can confide in me. The Lord is merciful, and He sees your sorrow. Open your heart to me as His deputy.'

She tried to speak, but her sobs did not let her. Then she fell in a faint in my arms. What an idiot I would have been if I had followed my first impluse and gone to seek assistance! I had already taken a few steps with that in mind, but on second thought, I halted.

'Where are you going?' she unexpectedly asked. 'Are you waiting for a more favourable opportunity?'

Approaching my devout, I undid her bodice and regarded the most enticing bosom imaginable. The satiny globes with their pink tips were like the pillars to the gates of Paradise. In jubilation and ecstasy, I pressed my cheeks to their firm contours and eagerly took the points in my mouth. Our mouths met and our breaths blended.

Beside myself with desire, I retained my reason sufficiently to hasten to the street door which I opened and closed as if taking leave of someone, and then returned to my jewel. I clasped her in my arms with ecstatic tremors. Barely could I contain myself at the sight of her beauties.

'Dear God, second me in my efforts,' I cried as I reached my room with the beloved burden in my arms.

She was as light as a feather. Putting her on my bed, I locked the door, and lit a candle. In the dim illumination, I saw that she had swooned again. After completely removing her blouse to regard the enchanting hemispheres in their full beauty, I lifted her skirt and spread wide her legs. My mind was a combination of lust and delight. Holding myself back, I examined her charms and soulfully admired them. What a voluptuous spectacle! Love and grace were to be found on all parts of her body: whiteness, *embonpoint*, firmness, delicacy – all were there, and all were a delight to the eye. The snow of her skin strewn with little streaks of blue veins, the black fleece finer than velvet, and the vermilion which set off with exquisite nuances the enticing cunt, threw me into a veritable rapture. Picture to yourself all the beauties of the Greek goddesses, combine them, and they would not compare to what met my eyes.

But to admire them without enjoying them was unthinkable. I furiously put my mouth and hands on all that met my sight. As soon as I did so, my devout showed some signs of life by sighing and taking hold of my hand. When I kissed her again, she tried to free herself by shoving me away. Surprised and terrified at finding herself on my bed, she cast disturbed looks around the room and seemed to be trying to discover where she was. She attempted to say something, but it seemed that she had lost the power of speech. I was burning with such a passion that I could not release her. She made violent efforts to get out of my arms, but I held her more tightly and turned her on her back. Making a powerful effort to rise, she scratched and bit my face and pounded me with her little fists. By now, we were both perspiring copiously.

Nothing, however, could stop me. I pressed my chest against her bosom, my stomach against hers, and trying to keep her quiet under me with the weight of my body, I permitted her to do with her hands all that her fury and rage dictated. Oblivious to her blows, I slowly opened her stubborn clenched thighs. Momentarily despairing at reaching my goal, I redoubled my efforts, and I was successful. The thighs were spread wide and between them I inserted my prick which had popped out of my trousers as if released by a spring. With a mighty shove, it was in. At that sensation, all the anger of my devout vanished. She fervently put her arms around me, kissed me, closed her eyes, and fell back in a sort of faint. I no longer knew what I was doing, but nothing could stop me. I jabbed and shoved, and attaining my goal, I flooded the recesses of her cunt with a boiling torrent. She responded to my discharge with an equally copious inundation. Then we relaxed, savouring mutually what we had just enjoyed.

My companion was the first to return to her senses, and her first reaction was to resume the game. Her cunt was a fiery furnace in which my prick eagerly desired to become seared.

'I am dying,' she panted. 'I am suffocating.'

With that, she suddenly stiffened, wiggled her derriere to which I responded with two, and we again discharged.

We continued until nature made us stop. As is the case, our powers were not up to our desires. We had to pause. Taking advantage of the respite, I hastened to the kitchen to take the meal that was destined for a patient in the hospital, a repast that was to restore his vitality. I said I was the patient and took the food.

Returning to my room, I found my devout in regret and despair. Comforting her with renewed caresses, we shared the nourishing repast. Afterwards, I gave her the delights I was supposed to have only on the recluses of the piscina. In other words, I broke the rules of my order.

After the meal, we both thought we were too tired to continue. We returned to bed, still nude, but when I casually put my hand on her cunt, the source and tomb of the delights I had just enjoyed, all thought of sleep vanished. In turn, she touched my masculinity, admiring its size as well as the fullness of my testicles.

'You have reconciled me to a pleasure I had made up my mind to hate,' she told me.

Instead of answering, I made haste to give her new raptures before she could return to her former resolution. Eagerly she welcomed my advances with a vivacity that would have snatched me from the arms of death himself. Her backsides rose and fell like the ocean's waves in a tempest. Our bodies were like two iron bars just out of the fiery forge. So tightly did we hold each other that we could scarcely breathe. We felt that the slightest pause would annihilate our bliss. The bed was shaking and creaking ominously. A sweet intoxication soon crowned our exertions, and I fell asleep on top of her with my prick still in her cunt.

Dawn found us in the same position as when slumber had overtaken us. When we awoke, however, we found to our surprise that the sheets and even the mattress were drenched with fresh juices of love.

We could not wait to renew our sports. Sleep had restored my forces, so I was confident I could acquit myself like a true monk. I cannot tell you how many times I did it. I was so busy fucking that I lost count.

It is now time to tell how the devout had come into my arms.

After we were through, I saw that she had a worried, melancholy expression which touched me. Tenderly, I begged her to tell me what was wrong, and I promised her I would do anything to remove the cause of her sadness.

'Will I lose your heart, dear Saturnin,' she asked me slowly, 'if I tell you that you are not the first who has enabled me to taste the delights of love? Yes, it is that fear that is bothering me.'

'Of course not,' I replied in relief. 'Don't give it another thought. Even if you have fornicated with every man on earth, you would be the same adorable desirable creature. The pleasures you have granted others, did they diminish the delights you have just given me?'

'You have given me back life,' she said as she threw herself in my arms.

The Story of the Devout

'My misery has its source in my heart, in an insurmountable inclination nature has given me for pleasure. Love is my divinity, and it is the only thing I live for. My cruel mother got it in her head that the church should be my vocation. Too timid to expostulate with her words, I could only protest with a burst of tears. They had no effect on her cruel heart. I had to enter the nunnery, where I took the veil. The moment of my living death was approaching and I shuddered at the vow I was going to have to make. The horror of a prison-like convent and the despair of being eternally deprived of the greatest good in life caused an ailment that would have put an end to all my pains. At the last moment, my mother, reproaching herself for her severity, relented in her determination in her plans for me. She was living as a paying guest in the convent where she wanted me to take the nun's habit.

'Seeing my state, she left the retreat and took me with her. We returned to normal life and my mother was soon in search of a fifth husband.

'Knowing my mother as I did, I realised it would be dangerous for me to enter into competition with her. If any suitor appeared, I was positive that he would not hesitate to choose me over my mother, and that was what I was afraid of. Consequently, I decided to become a devout instead of a nun, for I knew I could have my pleasures under such a cover! I built a reputation of virtuousness for myself in order to indulge in my vices more easily. However, this reputation was sullied by an unfortunate happening with a young man at the grille.'

At this point of her story, I recalled what Suzon had told me about Sister Monique, her aversion to the convent, her passion for love, the scene she had with Verland, the stay of her mother at the convent, and I mentally compared Sister Monique with the pretty thing I had with me. Recalling that Monique, according to Suzon, had a rather long clitoris, I turned my devout on her back and carefully examined her cunt. I found what I was looking for – a vermilion clitoris slightly longer than average. No longer doubting that it was she, I embraced her with a new fervour.

'Dearest Monique,' I cried, 'is it you that good fortune has sent to me?'

Freeing herself from my arms and regarding me with a troubled look, she demanded how I knew the name she had assumed in the convent.

'A girl whose loss has caused me many tears,' I replied, 'and to whom you revealed all your secrets.'

'Suzon!' she exclaimed. 'The traitress.'

'Yes,' I agreed. 'That's she. But I'm the only one to whom she has told your story, and she only did so because I begged her so hard. I beseech you to forgive her.'

'So you're the brother of Suzon,' she said. 'Well, I can't complain because she told me everything that she did with you.'

Sighing at the pitiful lot of our poor Suzon, Monique picked up the thread of her discourse.

'Since Suzon left nothing out, including my skirmish with Verland, I may as well tell you the full story. Although he was banned from the retreat, he did not forget me. And when he saw me in church, all his desire for me was revived. On my part, I felt strange stirrings within me. I blushed when I discovered how handsome he had become, and I felt his eyes fixed on me. Quickly, he perceived my inner confusion. When I left the church, I took a little-frequented street down which he followed me as I expected he would.

'When he caught up with me, he said in a voice trembling with emotion: "Monique, can a man who did something wrong to you at our first meeting now pay his respects? I have repented of that ever since."

'I took pity on him and said that I considered it merely the act of an overly impetuous youth.

'"You do not know all of my faults," he went on. "Your kindness has just forgiven me for one crime. I now have need more than ever of your goodness since I am guilty of another offence."

'Falling silent after these words, he stood there with his head hanging down. I said that I did not have the faintest idea of what he was talking about.'

'"I have fallen madly in love with you," he declared, kissing my hand which I did not have the strength to snatch away.

'I let him know by my silence that I did not find this new crime unforgivable. Reluctant to show my feelings too openly at this first meeting, I left him, absolutely charmed and delighted by his avowal.

'I was sure that if Verland was sincere, he would

easily find ways to give me further assurances. He let me go, and as I went, I heard some sighs that I answered with those in my heart.

'We met again, at which time he asked me for permission to request my mother for my hand in marriage. I gladly consented, but she refused him, a decision that only enhanced my love for him. Verland, of course, was crushed. You have no idea of the reason for my mother's turning down my lover. She had become my rival for his affections. She betrayed herself by her continual praise of his charm and handsomeness. I was furious both with my mother and with myself. My love made me capable of doing anything. Although my mother suspected nothing, I saw Verland every day, for life without him was unthinkable. But would you believe that at that time, I had enough self-control not to yield to his insistences and to turn down his suggestion for the only method to bring my mother to her senses. Finally, touched by his tears, urged by my own love, and conquered by my own inclinations, I agreed to an elopement, and we discussed the day, the hour, and the means.

'The intensity of my love permitted me to picture only the pleasures that I would have with my lover. The gloomiest cave would have been a paradise if only I were with him. The momentous day arrived when we were to flee together. Suddenly, an invisible arm held me back. My passion had strewn with flowers the path to the precipice from which I was to make my leap. But when I was at the edge, and I saw how deep it was, I stepped back in horror. I did my best to overcome my lack of courage, and my tears were copious at my cowardice. The hour was approaching and I had to

145

make up my mind. What should I do? I was in such desperate straits that I could not think straight.

'Suddenly, a ray of light illuminated my brain; I saw the way to be with my lover and exact a sweet vengeance on my mother at the same time.

'I made the signal to Verland on which we had agreed in case I could not carry out my end. We met again the following day in the church where he approached me without saying a word, but the expression was eloquent. It frightened me.

'"Do you love me?" I asked him.

'"How can you even ask that?" he replied. His despair prevented him from saying more.

'"Verland," I continued. "I see the grief in your eyes. My heart is also torn. Find fault with me. Complain of my lack of courage. When I ask if you love me, it is not that I doubt your love, but I am afraid that you are unwilling to give me the sole evidence of it. Stop!" I commanded him when he tried to interrupt. "You want to reproach me, but if you do, you will be unjust towards me. I repeat that I have not the slightest doubt about your feelings for me, and please do not think that my love for you has altered. But what use is it to burn with a flame that a cruel mother refuses to let us extinguish? Ah, my Verland, doesn't the scarlet of my face tell you the means I wish to employ?"

'"Dear Monique," he replied, putting his hand tenderly to my mouth. "Does your love finally make you feel the necessity of a thing that I have asked you for so many times without success?"

'"Yes, yes. Your love will no longer have cause for complaint. No longer can I conceal from you the urge of my desires which are now at their peak. But before we enjoy our bliss, I expect only one word from your mouth."

'"Tell me what you want me to say," he cried impatiently. "What do you want me to do?"

'"Marry my mother," I told him simply.

'He looked as if he had been struck by a thunderbolt, so great was his amazement.

'"Marry your mother?" he repeated automatically, looking at me with bewildered eyes. "Monique, what are you saying?"

'"I'm just proposing that you do a simple thing that will overcome our difficulties," I replied, impatient at his incomprehension. "What I am proposing has cost me a torrent of tears, and you greet it with coldness and indifference. I now regret the profound love I had conceived for you. What am I to think of a man who is as cowardly as you?"

'"Monique," he said piteously. "How can you wish me to do such a despicable thing as that?"

'"You ungrateful idiot!" I retorted. "If I am able to overcome the horror of the thought of seeing you in the arms of my rival for the sole purpose of deceiving her, you can quiet her now and then. My proposal is made just so that we can enjoy each other, to have the pleasure of seeing you always, to have the bliss of always feeling your caresses. I am risking my reputation and I offer you for your happiness what I hold most dear. I don't give a damn about the tortures of jealousy, which I am stifling in my heart. But you are shaking like a leaf. Is it that I am stronger than you? Perhaps you don't have as much love for me as I have for you."

'"You're right," he replied with determination.

147

"I'm ashamed of my irresolution. Remorse is not for hearts as impassioned as ours."

'Delighted at his courage, I would have willingly granted him the marks of my affection if it had not been for the spot we were in, a place where we could have easily been surprised.

'The nuptials took place and the pleasure I showed caused my mother to overwhelm me with tender embraces and kisses. I returned them with ones less sincere. My soul was drunkenly anticipating both revenge and the pleasures of love.

'Verland appeared. He was utterly irresistible. Countless new charms animated all his movements. His slightest smile sent me into bliss and his most casual words made my heart pound madly. It was an agony to watch him and not take him in my arms. During the general hubbub, he was able to come close to me and whisper: "I have done everything for love. Will it do anything for me?" I answered him with a fiery glance that he immediately understood.

'We made our escape without being noticed. I entered my bedroom with him on my heels. After throwing himself on the bed, he pulled me down on him. I could not speak. Words fail me, and I am unable to describe to you the ineffable pleasures I had with Verland. Only, you, my dear Father, only you have been so far. "Oh, mother!" I cried during our transports, "how dearly your injustice to me is going to cost you!"

'My lover was a prodigy. For more than an hour we continued without a pause. Like Antheus who had only to touch the ground to regain his strength in his struggle with Hercules, my lover merely needed to touch my flesh to feel his forces returning.

'The others were looking for us for some time. There were even knocks at my door, at which we had to separate for fear of discovery. Verland slipped out into the garden where he pretended to be sleeping on the grass. The hilarity was general, because it was thought he was exhausted from the marital labours with my mother.

'Realising that I would be looked for, I took the key out of the door so the curious could peek in. They saw me on my knees fervently praying before a crucifix. Their respect for my piety increased. Recovering from the effects of my amorous exertions, I returned to the gathering without anyone suspecting what I had been up to.

'As soon as I conceived the project of marrying my mother to my lover, I made every effort to bring about ways that he and I could meet without being surprised. To effect this, I feigned an increase in my piety and insisted that I should never be disturbed during my devotions. Soon the entire household was accustomed to not knock at my door if they did not see the key on the outside. For his part, Verland got my mother to believe that he was not as arduous and vigorous as she had thought, and under the pretext of having to take care of some business affairs, he slipped off into my room.

'Our joys, children of constraint and secrecy, did not diminish after a year of mutually exchanged bliss. It was so ecstatic that I thought that all the men in the world together could not have added to my raptures. But, one time, I found out how wrong I was.

'One day, I met a young girl I had known before in

the town. We greeted each other and I asked what she was doing. She replied she was looking for a job, and I engaged her as a chamber-maid.

'Well, my dear Father, I won't conceal anything from you. I have to tell you that this so-called chamber-maid was none other than Martin, about whom your sister must have made mention while telling you my story.

'I had not seen him since our separation. He was still goodlooking. In the eyes of the world, he was merely a pretty girl but to me he was a male of inestimable worth.

'I did not hide from Martin my liaison with Verland. Only too delighted to enjoy me again, he was not averse at all to sharing my favours with another. For my part, I was pleased at his docility and enraptured with his virility. Playing no favourites, I divided my gifts: Verland was given the day and Martin the night. Thus the days began for me with a serene deliciousness and the nights were ended in pure voluptuousness. Never has a woman enjoyed such continued transports as I. But the characteristic of pleasure is that it is of short duration, and its loss is one of the prices that must be paid for its possession.

'As I told you, Martin was able to pass for an attractive lass with his girl's dress. But that faithless Verland, damn him! Well, I shouldn't say faithless for I was being guilty of the same sin. Verland found my chamber-maid more and more attractive, and soon my days were empty. Compensated by the nocturnal pleasures, I noticed the indifference Verland showed me during the daylight hours. My hands endlessly tried to arouse him to his former ardour, but my two young men met more and more. But Verland was sly and he made me believe the reason he gave for his indifference. When I attempted to scold him, a smile, a kiss, or caress was sufficient to dispel my nagging doubts. A day of repose, he assured me, was necessary to restore his vigour, and his absences made me believe that such was so. I agreed to them, and Martin satisfactorily took his place.

'Yesterday, oh miserable day which I shall always remember with loathing, was supposed to be Verland's day off. In my room with Cupid as our only witness, I was stretched out on my bed, my bosom bare and my legs wide open, waiting for Martin to regain his strength. In the nude, he was caressing my breasts and squeezing his thighs against mine. While his eyes and touches attempted to revive his desires, Verland unexpectedly entered the chamber and caught us in that position. Before we had time to disengage ourselves, he had closed the door behind him and come up to us.

'"Monique," he said to me, "I don't blame you for your pleasures, but you must share them with me. I'm in love with Javote (that was the name that Martin had taken), and I think I have enough forces to satisfy both of you."

'At that moment, he tried to kiss Martin. Dragging him from my arms, he put his hand ... and he didn't find what he expected. Without releasing Martin, he gave me an indignant look. He didn't dare to take out his anger on me, but his fury fell on the innocent cause. His love turned into rage, and he began to beat Martin mercilessly with his fists.

'Throwing myself between, I kissed Verland and

cried: "Stop! He is just a youth, and if you really love me, you will spare him. Have pity for his weakness and my tears."

'Verland ceased his pummelling, but Martin, who had now come to his senses, became furious in his turn. Grasping Verland's sword, he made a lunge at him. At the sight of that, I fled and came here.'

As she finished, she burst into a flood of tears.

'Alas, what is to become of me?' she sobbed.

'Stop your tears,' I comforted her. If it is the loss of your pleasures that is worrying you, more intense ones will more than make up for them.'

Realising that it was impossible to keep her much longer in my room for fear of discovery, I felt the wisest course was to take her to the piscina. Without going into details, I assured her that the pleasures reserved for her there would, in comparison, make her past ones pale. Such a retreat was ideal for a woman with a temperament like hers.

'Dear friend,' she said, embracing me, 'please do not abandon me. Tell me that I can stay with you. Your decision will determine my fate. If I lose you, I shall be miserable for the rest of my days.'

I assured her that we would never part, and, at her timid request, I said I would find out what had happened to her two lovers. I left, promising to return as quickly as I could.

Asking everyone who might have knowledge of the affair, I learned nothing. Apparently, the quarrel had ceased with Monique's flight and the two combatants considered it wise to hush up the matter. When I came back with the news for my devout, a servant ran up to me and gave me a letter and a little purse with some money in it.

I opened the letter and read the following:

'You have been found out. We suspected you and we opened the door to your room. There we discovered the treasure you were unwilling to share with you brother monks. We took her and put her in the piscina. Flee! You know the horrors our order is capable of. Flee for your life! Brother André.'

A clap of thunder over my head could not have stunned me more than the perusal of this missive. I felt that all was lost. Where could I take refuge? How could I save myself from their vengeance? Suddenly, in my consternation, the thought of Ambroise's house came to mind. It would be the safest asylum. I resolved to go there.

It was not without pangs of grief that I left the place that had been my repose, my happiness, and my pleasure. I bewailed the loss of Monique, but I consoled myself with the thought of the delights she was going to enjoy in the piscina.

When I arrived at Ambroise's, I only found Toinette to whom I told my woes. Touched by my account, she helped me the best she could. She gave me one of her husband's suits, and I decided to leave the next day for Paris, where I was confident I could find compensation for all that I had lost. For the sake of safety, I walked only at night, and after several days, I reached the capital of France.

Now I felt I could defy the vengeance of the monks. The money Father André and Toinette had given me would keep me for some time. My intention was to find a job as a teacher in a private home until fortune offered me something more suitable. Although I had some acquaintances in Paris who could have helped me, it was too risky to turn to them.

Even though I had decided to give up the pleasures of the flesh, a pretty little thing accosted me on the street one day and I immediately forgot my good intentions. She led me by the hand to a shabby building, in which we ascended a narrow winding staircase. The door was opened by an ancient witch who told me to wait for a moment in the room. In the meantime, my guide had disappeared. Although I had never been in one, I realised that I was in a brothel. A sudden anxiety and fear took possession of me when a coarse, plump woman approached me. Placing some money in her hand, I pushed her rudely away. She was indignant.

Then I heard a voice that was not unfamiliar to me. It penetrated to my heart. I began to tremble all over. I could not believe my ears. The door opened and there was... Suzon! Although the years had changed her features, I recognised her right away. Wordlessly, I fell into her arms and tears welled in my eyes.

'My dear sister,' I finally asked in an uncertain voice, 'don't you recognise your brother?'

After scanning my face, she fainted.

The hag tried to offer assistance, but I pushed her away. Pressing my lips on Suzon's mouth and wetting her face with my tears, I restored her to life.

'Leave me, Saturnin,' she cried. 'Leave a miserable wretch like myself.'

'My dear sister,' I exclaimed, 'does the sight of your Saturnin inspire you with such horror? Do you refuse his kisses and embraces?'

Touched by my reproaches, she showed her joy.

Happiness reappeared on her cheeks. She ordered the old woman to bring us something to eat and drink. I gave her some money. I would have given her all I had for was I not rich with the possession of Suzon?

While waiting for the repast, I kept holding Suzon in my arms. We did not yet have the strength to ask each other how it came about that we found ourselves so far away from home. Our eyes were the interpreters of our souls. Our hearts were so overflowing that our tongues were tied. We opened our mouths, but no words came out.

'Suzon,' I finally said, breaking the silence. 'How is it that you are in such a vile place as this?'

'You see before you one who has suffered all the vicissitudes of fortune,' she sadly answered. 'I see that you are impatient to hear about my miseries. Now that I am with you, I feel no embarrassment at telling you how I came to lead this life of shame. You are partially responsible, but I readily forgive you.

'I have always loved you. Do you remember that happy time when you told me so simply of your growing passion? How I adored you when I told you about Monique and all our secrets. My intention was to arouse you and instruct you, and I wanted to see what affect my discourse would have on you. I was a witness to your gambols with Madame Dinville, and the caresses you lavished on her were like stabs in my heart. When I took you into my room, I was consumed by a fire that you were no longer able to extinguish. It was then my misfortunes began.

'You don't know the reason for that horrible scene in my room. It was Abbot Fillot, that scoundrel of scoundrels. He had an urge for me that he intended to satisfy at any cost. During the night he had hidden himself in the space between the wall and my bed, and he took advantage of your flight to take your place. Since I had fainted from fright, he was able to do what he wanted with me. Revived by the pleasure I was experiencing, I was under the opinion that it was my dear Saturnin who was giving it to me. I overwhelmed with delight a monster whom I overwhelmed with curses when I recognised who it was. He tried to calm me with his caresses, but I shoved him away in horror. Then he threatened to tell Madame Dinville what I had done with him. Thus I had to give my all to a creature I detested, and fate snatched from my arms the one I adored.

'It was not long before I began to experience the bitter fruits of the incident. I concealed my shame as long as I could, but I would have betrayed myself by too obstinate a silence. After having repulsed his further advances, he consoled himself in the embraces of Madame Dinville. When concealment was no longer possible, I had to go to him and reveal my condition. Feigning sympathy, he offered to take me with him to Paris where he said he would do everything to help me. All I wanted was a place where I could rid myself of my burden, and I hoped that afterwards, he would assist me in getting a position with some lady. I allowed myself to be persuaded by his glowing promises and came with him here.

'But the shaking of the carriage had upset my calculations, and I brought into the world a league from Paris the hateful token of a villain's passion. Since I was disguised as a monk, everybody laughed at the miracle. My travelling companion immediately decamped, leaving me to my misery and woes. A compassionate woman took pity on me by taking me to the charity hospital in Paris. Although I had been saved from death, I was penniless. When I thought all was over with me, I met a girl who helped me by teaching me her trade, the one I am leading now. Although my life has been miserable, I have no complaints because I have found you. But how about you? Did you leave the monastery? And why are you in Paris?'

'A misfortune similar to yours is the reason for my being here,' I replied, 'a tragedy caused by your best friend.'

'My best friend?' she repeated with a puzzled look. 'Do I have any left? Oh, that must be Sister Monique.'

'You hit the nail on the head,' I said. 'But it will take some time to tell you the whole story, so let's eat first.'

The meal I shared with Suzon was the most delicious I had ever eaten in my life. But my desire to be alone with her and her eagerness to learn of my adventures prompted us to leave the table quickly. We retired to a room, where, on the bed with her body pressed to mine, I told her all that had happened since I left Ambroise's.

'Then I am not your sister,' she cried when I had finished.

'Don't have any regrets,' I consoled her. 'Even though you are not my sister, you are still my adored Suzon, the idol of my heart. Let's forget the unhappy past and consider the beginning of our life this day when we found each other again.'

At these words, I ardently kissed her breasts and my hand was between her thighs as I was about to turn her on her back.

'Stop!' she commanded, escaping from my embrace.

'Stop?' I cried, utterly amased. 'How can you possibly say that? How can you turn down the offers of my passion for you!'

'Stifle those desires,' she sadly said. 'And I'll set the example.'

'Suzon, you must no longer have any love for me if you say that. There is nothing to stop us from making each other happy.'

'Nothing, you say?' she sighed. 'How wrong you are.'

At that, tears streamed down her cheeks. I urged her to tell me the sorrow that caused them.

'Would you want to share with me the cruel price of my dissolute life? And even if you did, could I be so unfeeling as to let you?'

'Do you think I would let such a feeble argument influence me?' I exclaimed. 'I would gladly die together with my dear Suzon.'

Promptly I had her on her back and proved to her that I had no fears.

'Ah, Saturnin, you are a lost soul,' she wept.

'If I'm lost, let it be in your arms.'

Dear reader, I leave to your imagination the transports I enjoyed. I more than recaptured the lost delights.

Day appeared before we noticed that night had disappeared. Not once had I left Suzon's arms. I had forgotten all my griefs. In fact, I had forgotten the entire universe.

'We'll never leave each other, my dear brother,' she told me. 'Where will you find a more tender mistress, and I a more passionate lover?'

I swore to her that I would never leave her side, but we were going to be separated soon, never to see each other again. There was a storm hovering over our heads, but we were so dazzled with each other that we did not notice it.

'Save yourself, Suzon,' a panic-stricken girl panted as she rushed into our room. 'Hurry. Use the hidden staircase.'

Astonished, we got up, but it was too late. A burly soldier burst into the chamber. Suzon, with a screech of fright, threw herself in my arms. In spite of my efforts to hold her, he managed to drag her from me. God! The sight enraged me; fury lent me strength; and despair rendered me invincible. The andiron I instinctively grabbed became a lethal weapon in my hands. With a powerful blow, the would-be ravisher of Suzon lay at my feet. I was grabbed, and although I made valiant efforts to defend myself, I had to succumb. When they tied me up, they left me with hardly a stitch of clothing on.

'Good-bye Suzon!' I cried, trying to stretch my arms to her. 'Good-bye, my dear sister.'

I was shoved down the steps so harshly that the bumps on my head soon caused me to lose consciousness.

Should I finish here the account of my misfortunes? If there is any compassion in your soul, dear reader, you will consent to hear the end of my woes. Haven't I shed enough tears? I am safe in harbour, but still I regret the dangers of a shipwreck. Continue to read in order to learn the frightful results of libertinism. You will be lucky if you don't have to pay for them more

159

dearly than I did.

When I came to my senses, I found myself in a shabby bed in a hospital. When I asked where I was, I was told the hospital was the Bicetre. Heavens! Bicetre. I was petrified with terror and burning with fever. I had been cured only to find I had a much more virulent ailment than broken bones – syphilis. Without a murmur, I accepted this new chastisement from heaven.

'Suzon,' I said to myself, 'I would not complain of my lot, if you were not suffering from the same disaster.'

My ailment gradually became so serious that desperate remedies were required. In order to save me, I was told that I would have to undergo a slight operation. When informed of its nature, I fell into such a deep faint that it was feared my last moment had come. If only it had! When it was over, the operation, I put my hand where the pain had been.

'I'm no longer a man!' I screamed so loudly that it was heard in every extremity of the establishment.

Now my only wish was for death. I had lost the ability to enjoy life. I could only think with horror at what I had become. Father Saturnin, once the delight of women, was nothing. Fate, a cruel fate, had deprived him of his most precious possession. I was nothing but a eunuch.

Death did not heed my appeals. I gradually regained my health, and the head doctor said that I was now free to leave the hospital.

'Free?' I asked him in surprise. 'Free for what? But may I ask as to the fate of a young woman who must have been brought here the same day as I?'

'She was luckier than you,' he replied brusquely. 'She died during her treatment.'

'She is dead,' I muttered to myself in a daze, crushed by this last stroke. 'So Suzon is dead and I am still alive.'

I would have put an end to myself at that very moment if I had not been stopped. Then I was shown the door.

Shabbily dressed and with scarcely a sou in my pocket, I decided to abandon myself to fate. Let come what will. Taking the road leading out of Paris, I spotted the walls of a Carthusian monastery where a profound silence reigned.

'Lucky mortals,'' I cried to myself, 'who live in this retreat, protected from the storms of fortune, your pure and innocent hearts have no conception of the horrors that tear mine.'

The thought of their felicity inspired in me the yearning to become one of them.

Throwing myself at the feet of the Father Superior, I told him the story of my miseries.

'My son,' he said benevolently as he put his arms around me, 'this is the port for you after so many wreck. Live here with us and try to be happy.'

For some time I stayed there without being given anything to do, but soon I was being employed. Gradually, I rose to the position of porter by which title I am now known.

It is here that my heart has hardened in the hatred it has conceived for the world. Here I await death without either fearing or desiring it, and I hope that when I depart this vale of tears called life, there will be etched in letters of gold on my tomb the following:

Hic situs est DOM-BOUGRE,

fututus, futuit.

FINIS

II

A selection of extracts from anonymous
French erotic novels of the eighteenth
century, translated by Alan Shipway

The Memoirs of Suzon (1778)

SUZON, THE PRETTY YOUNG HEROINE OF THESE
MEMOIRS, HAS BEEN SEDUCED AND MADE PREG-
NANT BY AN UNSCRUPULOUS ABBÉ, HER GOD-
MOTHER'S SPIRITUAL ADVISER. HE IS BRINGING THE
YOUNG WOMAN TO PARIS IN ORDER TO AVOID A
SCANDAL.

The movement of the carriage had so much advanced
my pregnancy that I was obliged to stop at some
leagues from Paris because I had entered into labour.
Abbé Fillot chose this moment to acquaint me that it
was not so much consideration for my reputation as
fear of exciting Madame d'Inville's jealousy which had
prompted him to help me. For I had barely installed
myself in a nearby inn when that infamous scoundrel
took himself off and I have never set eyes on him since.

A lady who dwelt in the neighbourhood was moved
to compassion by my piteous state and she had me
conveyed to the Hôtel Dieu[1] at Paris. Hardly had I
recovered from the rigours of giving birth, than I was
ordered to depart, taking my few wretched belongings
with me. As my reader will no doubt realise, without

1. The oldest hospital in Paris, standing beside the church of
Notre-Dame.

165

money my state was truly wretched. Or, to express myself in another fashion, I did not know which way to turn.

Although my state of health was still much enfeebled, I passed the day wandering around almost all the quarters of Paris without any notion where I was going. At last, worn out with fatigue and hunger, I stopped in front of a wine-merchant's shop. Reflecting then upon my misfortunes, my tears flowed abundantly. The wine-merchant's young assistant, who at that moment was standing in the entrance, taking the air, approached me and with the greatest courtesy addressed me thus:

'Mademoiselle, may I, without being indiscreet, ask the cause of your tears?'

'Ah, Monsieur!' cried I, 'it seems to me that there is not a girl in the whole world to be pitied more than myself! I was brought here by a monster who has abandoned me! I have just been turned out of the Hôtel Dieu, I have not a penny to my name and, as a crowning misfortune, have not a single acquaintance in this town.'

My frank manner, my youth and whatever beauty I possessed engaged his interest in my favour. He invited me to enter the shop and immediately served me with a generous glass of his best wine. He fetched me a bowl of steaming soup from a nearby eating establishment and pressed me so earnestly to eat that at last I yielded. After I had taken some nourishment:

'I cannot lodge you here,' said he. 'This place is only what in Paris we call a town cellar, of which I have the charge. But I shall give you the name of an inn and pay whatever it may cost.'

When I had finished the soup and drunk a few glasses of wine, perceiving that I was fatigued, he acquainted me with the whereabouts of an inn and gave me a letter for mine host in which he said I was a relative. He spoke so warmly in my favour that the people at the inn treated me with every possible consideration.

Not a day went by without my visiting my benefactor. Every day he gave me some new mark of kindness. I found so much honesty in his behaviour, that I soon fell in love with him.

For several days he had been begging me to respond to his love, which he described in such sincere terms that I was only waiting for him to become a little more pressing in order to satisfy him. At last the happy moment arrived.

One evening, just as I was about to take my leave, he invited me to descend to the cellar with him. I suspected that his purpose in so doing was not simply to show me how tidy he kept it. As our hearts were in accord, I needed no pressing and went of my own free will, although there was no doubt in my mind as to his intentions. From the way he started to caress me as soon as we arrived there, it was easy to see what he wanted, but I pretended not to know. The place was not really suitable for what the young man had in mind, but necessity was the mother of invention.

He began by handling my bosom and devouring it with kisses. Another hand slipped under my skirt and began to explore other attractions, yet all that was but a sort of prelude to what he really wanted to do. I made some difficulty, just for the sake of appearances, for my desire was at least as keen as his. I complained about the liberties he was taking but all that I could do to defend myself served only to increase his ardour. Finally, noticing that we were near a barrel, he took me in his arms and placed me on top of it. Then, situating himself between my thighs, he pulled up my petticoats. Immediately the young man brought out of his breeches a prick fit to give pleasure to the least amorous of women and plunged it up to the hilt into my cunt. Although that part of my body was still sensible after my recent ordeal, it was not long before I began to feel the approach of pleasure. My dear Nicholas (that was the lad's name) was pushing so hard that had not my back been supported by the wall, I should have been quite unable to sustain his thrusts. He was holding my legs under his arms so that, pulling me to him at the same time he was thrusting forward with his bum, there was in truth not an inch of his prick which did not enter my cunt.

After three ample discharges without uncunting, and all the time in the same posture, we ceased our pretty game, well satisfied the one with the other, and promised each other that we should recommence our exertions the next day.

This agreeable mode of life might have continued much longer if the wine-merchant, who some ill-natured person had informed of our activities, had not threatened Nicholas with dismissal if he did not immediately put an end to our liaison. This honest lad, whose love for me was as great as mine for him, was quite unable to acquaint me with this devastating news without shedding many bitter tears. His chagrin was so great and appeared so sincere that, though I myself was inconsolable, I felt obliged to try to console him.

'What is to become of you,' said he, 'if we are forced to part?'

'I will return to my family,' said I, 'and let me assure you, my beloved, that the remembrance of your kindness shall ever be dear to me.'

Since my lover knew that this must be our last meeting, he had brought with him all the money which he possessed and, with the generosity which was so characteristic of him, offered it to me. I was unwilling to accept all of the sum and could be persuaded to take only four louis, which seemed a sufficient amount to see me on my way. That very day I reserved a place in the coach and set out upon my journey two days later.

The persons who were in the public conveyance were of very varied conditions. There were monks, abbés, officers and I was the only woman. During the journey, various subjects were discussed – very superficially, as is the way on such occasions. The officers spoke about their campaigns, the abbés about their good fortune in affairs of the heart. The monks, however, during this time, did not waste words and occupied themselves with paying court to me.

Among them there was a friar who was particularly pressing. During dinner, he made me a very advantageous proposition. He said that he would give me the money to rent a little house in a village close to the monastery where he would be living, that he would support me so well that I should be obliged in all fairness to praise his generosity, and that he could make my fortune. A perfectly natural desire to be my own mistress, and the fear of being discovered and sent back to my godmother's house after an absence which must have caused a great scandal, made this proposition seem extremely attractive to me.

Having concluded that he would give me an allowance of one hundred louis, not counting the little extra presents he had promised, we agreed that a preliminary payment should be made upon the occasion of our first lying together.

We had a care to choose two bedchambers which were contiguous in the hostelry where we were staying. It was nigh on one o'clock of the morning when I heard the friar give the signal which we had agreed upon. I opened the door with the least possible noise and he entered immediately. He had brought an excellent bottle of champagne with him, of which we soon disposed. Even as the lecherous monk was drinking, he was at the same time removing the fichu which covered my bosom and unlacing me. He went into ecstasies at the sight of my breasts, which in truth were very round, very firm and white as alabaster. Then, observing that I still seemed too much attired, he served me as my maid. Evidently, he was a true monk, and this was by no means the first time he had done such things. The libidinous man would not even let me retain my chemise, saying that it was his wish to see all my charms clearly.

As soon as I was completely naked, he made me lie down on the bed, on my back first, then face downwards. Then, holding a flickering candle in his hand, he examined all parts of my body, lingering over some of them in a manner which was very agreeable for him and applying passionate kisses everywhere.

At last, after having feasted his eyes and his hands, my lover and I sealed our bargain on the bed, several times, to our entire satisfaction.

As it was necessary for us to rise early the next morning, the monk withdrew to his own bedchamber. As for me, it was not long before slumber overtook me. The next day we left the coach after a distance of about two leagues, being obliged to quit the main road to reach the village where I should henceforth be dwelling. Our travelling companions, to whom I had acquainted our destination, were much surprised to see me descend with the monk. They appeared to be quite astonished at seeing me take the same road as him. An officer, being unable to contain his vexation, called out:

'You did not acquaint us that it was your intention to enrol the young lady in your order, father. If you were not a monk, I should demand satisfaction for the insult you have offered to myself and these other gentlemen.'

The monk showed more interest in putting distance between himself and the officer than in replying to the latter's gibes. The other monks said nothing but appeared furious to see the prey they had singled out for themselves filched from under their noses. As for me, I took my leave of the company by making them a deep curtsy.

As we made our way towards the village, my monk told me that he was conducting me to the house of one of his lady penitents, and that he would ask her to lodge me until such time as a suitable house could be found for my accommodation. He said that it would be prudent on my part to make a great display of virtue to that lady in order to hoodwink her.

When we arrived, the friar told her that he had frequently seen me at the house of some mutual friends in Paris, where he had learned that, since losing my husband, I desired to live in the country in order to improve my health. That he had advised me to choose the neighbourhood of his monastery for preference, as much for the excellence of the air as for the countryside, which was, it is true, charming, and that he had at last prevailed upon me to select that place. The lady received me with great courtesy, and I remained with her for eight days, which were employed in preparing the house which I was to occupy.

During that time, not a day passed without my friar coming to visit me. As his visits to that lady had been almost as frequent before my arrival, her suspicions were never aroused. And, besides, we both behaved with a great deal of prudence and caution.

As I was not deficient in at least some knowledge of religion, I always contrived to converse on that subject whenever I was with the good lady. Thus, without making a great display of piety, I soon led her to think of me as a very virtuous woman. What pleased her, she told the friar one day, was to see that my piety in no way diminished the gaiety of my disposition. So well did I play the part of Tartuffe, that my lover's penitent never spoke of me except to sing my praises.

As soon as all was ready in my little house, I went to take possession of it, accompanied by my new friend, who stayed to dine with me, as well as my monk. He never took a meal in my house but that Madame Marcelle (that was the lady's name) was also of the party. She herself expressed her admiration of the manner with which I managed to accord my pleasures with my reputation. The friar ceaselessly assured me of his amazement that one as young as I should be capable of so much prudence. Madame Marcelle was then the dupe of her Confessor's false piety and my hypocrisy. In a manner of speaking, she played the bawd for us, without the least realisation of what she was doing.

For six years I lived in that village esteemed by all the respectable people there. Never was a dinner given to which I was not invited; everyone vied with his neighbour to have the honour of my acquaintance. Husbands held me up to their wives as an example of virtue, and the mothers did the same with their daughters.

Undoubtedly, the reader is extremely curious to know how the friar and I managed to see each other in private without our liaison being discovered. He has no doubt that everything I was doing was only to give a varnish of decency to the most disorderly conduct. But did not gratitude also oblige me to safeguard my lover's reputation? Besides, should I have kept him long had I behaved differently?

In order to avoid boring those who may read these memoirs, I shall no longer postpone the satisfaction of their curiosity. This was the way of it.

Father Hercules (that was the friar's name) was the senior monk in the monastery. You may guess that, this being so, he enjoyed a much greater degree of freedom than the other monks. As he himself had chosen the house where I was living, he had given the preference to one which possessed a garden backing on to the open countryside. A gate at the end of the garden to which, naturally, he had a key, facilitated his nocturnal visits. When the monks had retired to their cells, Father Hercules left the monastery, entered by the garden gate and came to join me in my bed. Thus we spent every night together, if one overlooks a few which he judged necessary to the re-establishment of his vigour. The next morning, he would take his leave at a very early hour and return to the monastery without anyone having perceived his absence. How many delightful nights we passed together in this manner!

So much did I vary our pleasures, in so many ways did I provoke him to respond to my ardent desires, that at last I reduced the hapless monk to impotence. At length, exasperated at always finding between his legs a prick which was as slack and soft as a piece of wet rag, and disheartened by continually playing with it to no purpose, I resolved to give him an aide-de-camp. Thus I was myself the cause of all the misfortunes which have since befallen me and I have paid dearly for my ingratitude and the imprudence of my new lover.

It was not long before my choice was made. Whenever I attended mass in the monastery chapel, it had not escaped my notice that the organist always regarded me in a manner which plainly revealed the desire which he felt for me. He was a strapping fellow of a most healthy appearance who seemed eminently suitable to content a woman who had such a propensity for fucking as myself. The only problem was how to find a pretext for making him come to my house. But does an amorous woman ever lack stratagems for satisfying her passions? Dear reader, this is the one I employed. I shall leave it to your good self to decide whether it was adroit.

One day when Madame Marcelle and Father Hercules were dining with me, I steered the conversation towards the subject of the life one leads in the country. I said that it was necessary to have some manner of occupation in order to avoid boredom, especially in the winter when one was often confined to the house. That, for my part, I could not imagine how a woman could spend the whole year in such pursuits as embroidery, since that occupied only the fingers, leaving the mind in an unbearable state of inactivity.

'For myself,' I said, 'I should prefer to see a lady engaged either in drawing, or painting... or making music.'

'Do you like music then?' enquired Father Hercules.

'Yes, Father,' I replied. 'In fact, it is my passion. I have always desired to learn it but until now my affairs have always prevented me from doing so.'

Madame Marcel told me that she regarded the art of music as very innocent and that she should like to study it with me but now considered herself too old to learn. 'However,' said that good lady, 'you are still young and ought to succeed well in your studies.'

My lover, who was extremely pleased to have an opportunity of giving me pleasure, expressed his agreement with this opinion and said that he should send the monastery organist to me; he was a very good musician and a superior performer upon the pianoforte and had retired to the country with the express purpose of giving more time to his art.

You may easily imagine how agreeable this proposition was to me. What particularly pleased me was the fact that both of my guests had been so completely deceived, and that my lover was himself turnishing the means to render himself a cuckold, without even realising it.

The next day, Father Hercules sent the organist to see me. As you can guess he did not demand an unreasonable sum im payment for his lessons.

Our first eight encounters took place with such an air of cool reserve on my part that anyone other than a musician would have been most disconcerted. In fact my apparent indifference, far from discouraging him, served only to render him more enterprising. At last, he openly declared his passion to me, and intimated that he earnestly desired to give me another kind of lesson which had little to do with music.

When two persons both have the same desire, it is generally not long before they endeavour to satisfy it. We only deferred our satisfaction for the time it took to ensure the most complete secrecy, and then we agreed that the first meeting should take place in my bedroom on a certain night. I was quite sure that since I had not succeeded in giving Father Hercules a stiff prick the previous night, he would not yet be in a fit state to present himself for combat. Yet for fear of a surprise visit on his part, I took care to bolt the garden gate and having thus set my mind at rest was able to turn my whole attention to the joys of love. The long abstention which my monk had been constrained to impose on me filled me with longing for the moment when the organist should arrive.

How slowly time passes when one is waiting! Had I not been forever consulting my watch, I should have imagined that the hour of our tryst had long since passed and that my lover would not be coming. The period of waiting, however, had been as cruel for him as for myself. When at last he arrived, he said that those people who say that time flies can never have had an amorous rendezvous, or they would never say such a thing.

After the preliminary embraces which are usual on such occasions, having only a short time to do that which we wanted to do and not wanting to waste precious mometns, we went to bed ... What a splendid horseman my lover proved himself to be that night! He kept going for two or three hours and made eight prodigious gallops, the first four without quitting the saddle and the four others after very short rests! One may easily guess that in my whole life I have not often encountered such a vigorous athlete. I am even persuaded that had he not been obliged to take his leave of me at such an early hour, and had he been able to arrive sooner, he would easily have completed a dozen! My young organist seemed in no way fatigued by his amorous labours and even begged me to let him begin again. But realising that daybreak was approaching, and fearing besides to reduce him to Father Hercules' state if I were too immoderate in my demands, I refused to accede to his desires. In fact, I pressed him to depart, whereupon he dressed and left.

My new lover had not long taken his leave when I fell asleep, being greatly in need of repose. I must confess that having been accustomed for so long to a much less copious bill of fare, I was extremely fatigued after such a magnificent banquet of sensual delights. My slumber was deep and visited by the most delightful dreams imaginable. It seemed to me that I was still in the arms of my dear organist, that he was exploring my mouth with his tongue while, lower

177

down, his prick was doing its duty. My bottom was moving back and forth with an inconceivable rapidity. I was in fact near to discharging when Madame Marcelle entered my bedchamber somewhat noisily and woke me up.

One would have had to have been in such an agreeable state, experiencing such pleasure as I was feeling then to be able to form some idea of the vexation and ill-humour that this unexpected visit caused me. I controlled myself, however, and more or less managed to conceal my anger. Then the friar appeared, saying that he had called to pay his respects to Madame Marcelle and, finding she was not at home, presumed that she had come to see me. I requested them to pass into another room while I dressed myself.

Madame Marcelle stayed for no more than an hour and then departed, leaving me alone with the friar. As soon as she had gone, he told me that as his beloved prick had been showing some signs of life that morning when he awoke, he had made haste to acquaint me with the news, being persuaded of its giving me the greatest pleasure. He said that we must waste no time but make the most of this newfound vigour. Since I have never known how to resist such an appeal, I immediately consented to try our fortune.

After having felt my buttocks, my breasts and my cunt, the friar made incredible efforts to fulfil the fine promise he had made me, but all to no avail. It was in vain that I did my best to help him; everything we did fatigued us without raising even the ghost of pleasure. At last, seeing that his prick was losing even the slight firmness which at first it had possessed, I persuaded him not to attempt the impossible. In fact, I advised him to rest a week or two, in the hope that that period would suffice to restore his depleted forces.

Dear reader, could you bring yourself to believe that Suzon, who lives only to fuck, would have condemned herself to such a long abstinence had she not been sure to benefit by the monk's absence? Certainly not. I truly believe I should have preferred the risk of killing my faint-hearted fucker rather than consent to being constantly devoured by the ardent fires of unsatisfied passion. My advice, then, was far from being spontaneous. An opportunity to serve my own ends had presented itself and I was not going to let it pass by.

Safe in the knowledge that the friar would not visit me, that he was in no state to show himself to me without embarrassment on his part, I received the music-master every night. If that man did not have the Devil in him, he must have had a ton of spunk in order to support the life we were living. Every day he seemed to become more vigorous. Every day brought new delights: I have never known a man who displayed so much ingenuity in the ways of varying pleasures.

If it were my intention to recount all the different postures that we sampled, I should have enough material to compose a great volume of many pages. I will go further: even those of my readers who are familiar with the celebrated Postures of Aretino[1] have only a feeble idea of all that we did. However, it is not

---

1. This is a reference to sixteen drawings illustrating the various positions for making love, which inspired the famous Renaissance author, Pietro Aretino, to compose a series of short erotic poems.

my intention to leave this period of my life without describing one of them.

One particular day, after we had proceeded in many different ways, I was quite sure that all the resources of my lover's imagination were exhausted. So imagine my astonishment when I saw him attach the two ends of a piece of cord to the ceiling, thus making a kind of swing. He was careful to arrange the seat of this swing so that it should be at the height of his waist. Since I derived a lot of pleasure from these follies, I always lent myself to them with the utmost good-will. This one appeared to me to be so novel that I watched his preparations very attentively, but I must admit that their purpose escaped me.

When all was ready, he placed me upon the swing, urging me to raise my knees and spread my thighs as far apart as possible, and to make sure that my cunt was thrust well forward. As soon as I was sufficiently instructed in all that I must do, my lover set the swing in motion and stood at a little distance, his prick at the ready. He had prepared everything so well that as soon as the swing was in motion, he did not fail to hit the mark. Giving a thrust of his bum every time, when his prick touched my cunt-lips, he pushed it in as far as possible and caused the swing to move more and more rapidly as our pleasure grew in intensity.

When my lover felt himself to be on the point of discharging, in order not to lose that precious liquor, instead of pushing me away, as he had been doing, the lustful man took my legs under his arms and gripping me firmly by the bum, pulled my belly right up to his and inundated me with a positive deluge of spunk.

This manner of love-making has always greatly

pleased me and I have often repeated it in my life, not only with him but also with various other lovers...

The Letters of Eulalie (1785)

EULALIE IS A COURTESAN WHO HAS LEFT PARIS AND
GONE TO LIVE IN BORDEAUX. THE FOLLOWING
LETTERS WERE WRITTEN TO HER BY HER FRIENDS
AND COLLEAGUES WHO ARE STILL LIVING IN THE
CAPITAL.

Letter from Mademoiselle Julie.

Friday, 17th May, 1782.

My dear friend,

I have been to a pleasure party at the Duke of C's
country seat, at Monceau. There were eight of us in the
company gathered there, four men and four women.
After supper, we all went into a charming boudoir
surrounded by mirrors. Everyone was *in naturalibis* (it
is thus that these gentlemen express the idea of
removing all of one's clothes); then we each chose a
partner and taking up different postures, we all gave
each other the pleasure of watching charming
spectacles. After our amorous frolics, we danced and
did many foolish things until five o'clock in the
morning. Next Thursday we are going to repeat the
performance; how delighted I should be could you but
be there! How everyone would admire your beautiful
body!

Your former maid, who was in the service of that

Urbain woman, has just quit her. She came to see me this morning and told me that since little B . . . has been detained in his regiment by order of the King, there is often not a decent meal to be had in that insolent woman's house. I shall have to see whether I cannot find her a situation with one of my friends. She has charged me to assure you of her respect; she deeply regrets that she is no longer in your service. I must finish: my hairdresser has arrived and I cannot send him away. I am obliged to pay a visit to La Présidente[1] at four o'clock, you will most assuredly guess why. But more of this another time.

Your affectionate friend for life.

Letter from Mademoiselle Julie.

Monday, 20th May, 1782.

My dear friend,

What a strange desire men have! Yesterday, at La Présidente's establishment, I had to spend ages whipping an old government official whilst he, kneeling before me, gamahuched me. Barely had he departed than a young abbé arrived whose inclination was just as singular, although more pleasing. After we had both removed all of our clothes, I had to crawl around the floor on all fours while the abbé followed me in the same manner. When we had done several turns about the room in this fashion, this new Adonis became aroused and took me from the rear, whinnying like a stallion mounting his mare. I was on the point of

1. La Présidente was the nickname of one of the most successful procuresses in Paris in the 18th Century. Her real name was Brisseau.

bursting into laughter when his instrument, which was long and enormously thick, and which he was pushing back and forth with incredible force, deprived me of the power to do so. At that moment I experienced the most delicious sensations. Twice within a quarter of an hour I felt myself sprayed by the celestial liquor. How happy we should be, dear Eulalie, if all the men who have unusual tastes compensated us for our complaisances with such pleasure as that which my abbé gave me! Thus have I earnestly entreated the Brisseau woman to send for me when he shall come again. I sincerely hope that you may experience such pleasure at Bordeaux. Please write to me frequently.

Letter from Mademoiselle Julie.

Saturday, 25th May, 1782.

A most amusing thing happened at that Lebrun woman's establishment. An extremely elegant gentleman arrived in his coach and asked for a tall blonde woman. Immediately she sent for the Renesson girl. The latter made haste to appear, but imagine her surprise when she recognised her protector, with whom she had been living for a month! Mademoiselle Renesson did not lose countenance however and, immediately adopting a jealous tone of voice, began to heap reproaches upon her lover saying that, having for some time suspected him of infidelity, she had paid someone to follow him. And that, having been instructed of his whereabouts by her emissaries, she had come here to catch him red-handed. Having poured forth a long stream of words reproaching him for his unworthy behaviour and informing him of her bitter grief and disappointment, the hypocritical baggage swept out of the room, forbidding him ever to set foot in her house again. He replied that she need have no fear on that score.

The Lebrun woman was much grieved by this affair and in order to avoid such a thing happening again, is going to have a dormer-window made in such a manner that the young ladies may first see the persons intended for them without themselves being seen.

Always your friend.

Letter from Mademoiselle Julie.
                                        Wednesday, 29th May, 1782.
My dear friend,

What deceivers men are! You know that D ... has been my lover for two years and on his account I have refused several protectors, confining myself to brief encounters. Well, I was returning yesterday from my dressmaker and was about to enter my apartment when I heard a noise. Curious to know what it might be, I looked through the keyhole. Heavens! What a sight met my eyes! The infamous D ... was about to enjoy my maid who, her bosom uncovered and half lying on my sofa, was defending herself so inadequately that it was easy to see that it was solely to enhance the value of her capitulation. I made a noise at the door, causing them to cease their games and entered the room without saying a word of what I had just witnessed. In the afternoon my maid slipped out of the house without permission, thus giving me a pretext for dismissing her. As for D ..., I shall see about giving him his marching orders as soon as a suitable occasion presents itself ... if I have the strength to do so, for you know how much he means to me. Never become attached to anyone, my dear, if you wish to make your fortune, and do not follow the example of your unfortunate friend.

Letter from Mademoiselle Julie
                              Wednesday, 3rd July, 1782.
   Yesterday, I dined with Rosette at her invitation. As soon as I arrived, she asked me whether I should not like to earn five louis. I replied that such an offer could hardly be refused. 'Well,' said she, 'this is the way of it –
   'Some days ago, an ancient skeleton wearing an immense peruke accosted me at Nicolet's and addressed me thus: "My queen, you are very pretty and I should esteem myself happy to make your acquaintance." I did my best to discourage him but, persecuted by his insistence, I gave him my permission to call upon me. Addressing himself thereupon to my maid, into whose hand he slipped six francs, the ancient beau asked her for my address. Indeed, the very next day my admirer waited on me and showered me with a thousand compliments. Then he offered me ten louis, provided that I should indulge his penchant, which was, he told me, to see two naked women pleasuring each other, adding that I must surely know some young woman who would not refuse to second me. I expressed my willingness to fall in with his wishes and promised to give him satisfaction today at four o'clock. It occurred to me that you might be willing to lend yourself to this piece of foolery.'
   'Very gladly,' said I and, the soup being served, we sat down to dine.
   Our man arrived at four o'clock precisely. He

greeted us both in the most comical fashion, then wanting to play the gallant a little, he approached us and removed our fichus and handled our breasts. We thanked him for his courtesy and took off our remaining garments. When we were naked, Rosette and I pretended to amuse ourselves. Immediately, the old rake unfastened his breeches, revealing in the broad glare of common day a flaccid priapus which resembled crumpled parchment. Finally, after having rubbed it and shaken it for nigh on two hours, during which time he examined every part of our bodies, covering us with kisses, he managed to make a rather short libation. He praised the beauty and whiteness of our bodies with great enthusiasm and, thanking us for our complaisance, proposed that we should recommence our exertions in one week's time. We accepted, for lack of anything better. Adieu, I must finish for one of my regular visitors has been announced.

Letter from Mademoiselle Felmé.

15th August, 1782.

Last Monday, my sweet, La Présidente requested me to go to her establishment to dine and to spend the night there. Naturally, I complied. Imagine my surprise when I arrived and saw a man of some fifty or, perhaps, fifty-five years dressed like a child of three and who said to La Présidente, 'Mama, is that my new nurse?' 'Yes,' she replied and, turning towards me, she said, 'Here is my son, Mademoiselle, I am confiding him to your care, look after him well. He is a little rascal but all you need to do is to give him a good beating. Here is a cane and a strap, do not spare him. Go into that room with him.' So I went off with my big infant, who it was necessary for me to fustigate for two hours before he managed to make a tiny libation. Afterwards we dined. At one o'clock we went to bed and slept the whole night through. But in the morning we had to repeat the scene of the previous evening. You must agree, my beloved, that the tastes of some men are very *strange*, and impossible to comprehend. One could wish that the celebrated naturalist, Monsieur le Comte de Buffon, might be good enough to give us an explanation.

I am very cross with you because you have not written to me for a long time. Your man of law cannot occupy you to that extent. I imagine that you are not terribly faithful to him. One can easily catch that kind of protector: they are usually as well-regulated as a piece of clockwork. But be careful not to let yourself be caught, as you were with the Marquis de ... Or at least, if it does happen, be well-armed with a convincing story. Never have I known a woman who can put on such a bold face as you, a talent which is essential for women of our condition. Alas! I am unfortunate enough not to possess it: the merest trifle throws me into confusion. Please, my beloved, let me hear from you soon.

Letter from Mademoiselle Rosalie.

19th August, 1782.

This morning at about eleven o'clock, my maid informed me that a young man was asking to speak with me. I desired her to show him into the drawing-room where I joined him after assuring myself that I looked presentable. 'Excuse me for taking the liberty of calling on you without a preliminary introduction, but I have the greatest desire to possess those many charms with which you are endowed. May I dare to hope that you will not refuse me?' At the same time he placed a purse full of gold upon my mantelpiece and positively flew across the room to kiss me passionately and pull me down upon the sofa. Then he set himself to examine every part of my body and to cover me all over with burning kisses.

I was expecting him to take the supreme liberty at any moment and believed that these were only preliminaries, designed to heighten his desires. I tried to help him. But, merciful Heavens! What was my astonishment when I discovered that 'he' was a woman! I became angry, but she threw herself at my feet saying, 'Ah, I beg you, dear Rosalie, do not prevent me from becoming the happiest of mortals.' It was in vain that I endeavoured to resist; the sensations she had aroused in me were too sweet and I was curious to witness the dénouement of this scene. I weakened, she begged me to use my hands for her pleasure and, throwing herself upon me, she thrust her tongue into my love grotto! Ye Gods! With what dexterity did she penetrate every part! My pleasure was inexpressible and several times I filled her mouth with the bitter-sweet nectar of love. As for her, she inundated my hands.

After passing an hour in this pleasant exercise, we paused. We were extremely fatigued: she requested a dish of chocolate. As we sipped the steaming beverage, I expressed my surprise that such a pretty girl should have such an inclination. 'Ah!' returned she, 'if you only knew my history, your surprise would cease.' That piqued my curiosity and I invited her to tell me

189

her story. A little persuasion was necessary but at last she yielded to my insistences and recounted her adventures.

Afterwards she begged me to accord her my favours again. I made no difficulty about consenting. Ah! my dear friend, once more the young lady caused me to experience the most voluptuous pleasures. I must confess, however, that I should not like to indulge too often in such amusements for fear of becoming a tribade. After this second enjoyment, the good lady departed, leaving another five and twenty louis on my mantelpiece. As for me, I took a dish of beef-tea and retired to my bed from which, at seven o'clock in the evening, I have risen in order to recount these pleasant events to my dearest Eulalie.

Letter from Mademoiselle Rosimont.

Paris, 30th August, 1782.

My dear friend,

Last Thursday at Nicolet's I met a German baron who agreed to give me four louis to dine and sleep with him. We had reached the second course, when Victoire came to tell me that someone who was waiting in my antechamber desired to speak with me. It was D..., of the Royal Bodyguard, who had escaped from Versailles to come and spend the night in my arms. I tried to convince him that it was impossible but he would not listen. He announced that he was going to send the baron about his business. 'But,' I replied, 'you may well find that he will not give in without a fight.' I begged him to be reasonable, saying that he would involve me in a scandal; however, it proved impossible to talk any sense into him. I was truly at my wits' end when I hit upon an expedient to which, fortunately, the young man was willing to lend himself. Having first recommended that he should ply our Teuton plentifully with drink, I then presented him to the baron as a relative of mine who had brought me news from my family, and he dined with us. When the baron had become extremely tipsy. I helped him to get into my bed, and ordered that clean sheets should be put in my maid's bed, where I slept with D..., having arranged with her that she should lie with the baron. At six o'clock in the morning D... took his leave. Then my maid and I changed places. As soon as I had laid down beside the baron, I fell into a deep slumber, D... having greatly fatigued me. I did not wake up until eleven o'clock. You may imagine my surprise on finding that the baron was no longer there.

Ashamed of having made a spectacle of himself the previous night, he had risen quietly and quitted the house. Who would have imagined it? He is not like most of his fellow countrymen; that would be a mere trifle to them. I shall remember this episode for a long time. Farewell, my dear friend. You see, as I promised, I never write to you without recounting something worthy of your love of mischief.

P.S. I forgot to tell you about a man who I entertained at La Présidente's establishment who had a peculiar deformation: he had but one ball! Have you ever seen anyone like that? For me it was the first time. He informed me that *that had prevented him from becoming a priest*. Is it not extraordinary? As they are obliged to remain celibate it seems to me that their balls are an encumbrance. In my opinion, they all ought to be castrated. I'll wager that the number of them should then diminish with surprising speed.

Letter from Mademoiselle Felmé.

Paris, 27th September, 1782.

My beloved,

A few days ago something most diverting happened at the Lebrun woman's establishment. The Bishop of ..., dressed in secular garments had arrived there to indulge in a little dissipation. He had been but a few moments in a private room with a young woman, when a rather brutish man, wanting to have the same girl, and in spite of anything that could be said to dissuade him, went so far as to break down the door of the room where His Lordship had retired with his female companion. Hardly had the two men caught sight of each other they cried out, the one exclaiming, '*You*, abbé!' and the other, '*You*, Your Lordship!' The bishop, trying to assert his authority, said, 'I should never have expected to find *you* here.' But the abbé, visibly unimpressed, replied, 'No reproaches, please, Your Lordship; neither you nor I is in his rightful place. Let us come to an amicable agreement: keep your young lady, I will choose another and then we can all take our pleasure together.' The bishop agreed to the abbé's proposal and they had a merry time. It was in vain, however, that they requested the young ladies to keep the matter secret, for *they* had no greater desire than to render the affair public as soon as possible. Now it is the talk of the town. In fact, because of the scandal, the bishop has retired to his diocese. Farewell, dear heart.

Letter from Mademoiselle Julie.

Friday, 1st November, 1782.

One morning recently, my servant informed me that a woman describing herself as a dealer in second-hand ladies' garments desired to speak with me. I gave my permission for her to enter.

Approaching my bed, the woman expressed a wish to be alone with me. I asked Sophie to withdraw, and she began thus, 'Having seen you with my own eyes, Madame, I can easily understand why the person who has asked me to come and speak in his favour should be so passionately attracted to you. A Russian prince who has seen you several times at the theatre is positively dying to have you at his disposition for a few moments. He will be leaving soon to return to his country and says that, unless you render him happy he really will die. He has charged me to ask what price you put upon your favours and should you not wish to meet him here in your home, then I shall be only too happy to place my modest dwelling at your disposal. I live on a second floor, I sell dresses, so no suspicions will be aroused. The prince will come there and you can both use a room which is at the rear.'

I replied that it was not possible for me to accept this offer as my protector was a most honest man to whom it was my desire to remain faithful. 'Very well, Madame,' she returned, 'but you ought to seize such an excellent opportunity with both hands. They do not often occur. Youth and beauty soon pass and one ought to profit from them and put by sufficient to console oneself when autumn comes. Believe me, Madame, the prince is generous and a man of strong desires, he will give you whatever you want. Your infidelity will be a *sword-thrust in the water* which will leave not the slightest trace.'

At length, persuaded by her reasoning, I told her to inform the prince that if he would be kind enough to give me five hundred louis, I should lend myself to his desires. The woman returned three hours later to acquaint me that the prince had accepted my proposition and that he had even sent two hundred louis for me as an earnest of our agreement. I accepted the money and we settled that I should go to her apartment the next day at nine o'clock in the morning.

I was true to my word. The prince was already there and received me with all the caresses of a passionate lover. As he was anxious to proceed, we went into the aforementioned chamber which had been made ready for us and where, having made me sit down upon a sofa, the prince amused himself for a while by reviewing my charms. Then, suddenly uncovering himself, he displayed a virile member the size of which made me tremble. No, never in my life have I seen a man so strongly constituted! It seemed to me as if everything I had ever seen previously was but a pale shadow of what I was seeing now! My hand could not contain it, and I despaired of his ever being able to make use of such a formidable instrument with me but, laughing delightedly at my astonishment, the bearer of that mighty tool laid me down upon the sofa and set about putting it into the place designed by Mother Nature to receive it.

Only with the expenditure of a great deal of effort did he enter the grove of voluptuous pleasure. But after a few energetic thrusts on his part, my sufferings were speedily transformed into a torrent of delights. As for the prince, he had lost all self-possession, he seemed to exhale his entire soul with his sighs. Four times, without once quitting the place, had he inundated me when I requested that we might rest and compose ourselves. He complied and we partook of some refreshments, then a quarter of an hour after, we recommenced our exertions. I found the prince as animated and as vigorous as the first time. What a man! I have never seen his like, not even the abbé of whom I told you some time ago.[1]

Finally, after three assaults similar to the first, I was forced to beg the prince to cease his vigorous attacks, assuring him that I could do no more, that I was indeed vanquished. He thanked me in the most courteous manner, kissed me many times and gave me the three hundred louis we had agreed upon. Since then I have heard no more of him. Was I not fortunate, my dear friend? As you can see, Fortune and the Pleasures are uniting to render me the happiest of women. Farewell.

Letter from Mademoiselle Rosimont.

                                  Paris, 18th November, 1782.
My dear friend,

Two days ago Father Anselme, a Carmelite friar, came to visit me. Never have I been so *well-ridden*. I must admit that until then the idea of giving myself to a monk was repugnant to me, but his manner of approaching me proved to be irresistibly seductive: when he entered my room he placed five louis upon the

1. See the letter dated 20th May, 1782.

mantelpiece and, displaying a priapus of the greatest proportions to me, he said, 'For fucking with such an instrument one ought not to have to pay, *but the priest has to live off the altar.*' Whereupon he laid me upon my bed, without once detaching himself, he innundated me five times. And perhaps you think that was the end of it? Well, you are mistaken, he resumed his labours and did it three more times. My word, long live the Carmelites! If they are all as vigorous (and Father Anselme assures me that they are) their renown is well-merited. I was truly satisfied with him, as he was with me. He told me that he shall come and visit me again and has even promised to recommend me to one of his friends. Adieu, I hope that you too may find some Carmelites or, at least, men who resemble them.

Letter from Mademoiselle Julie.

Thursday, 2nd January, 1783.

Two days ago I made the acquaintance of a young officer in the Gardes Françaises who cannot be more than seventeen years of age. He has the most handsome features that I have ever seen. Yes, I admit that I am in love with him; I really should like to make him my own and spoil him with lots of presents. It seems obvious to me that he is a novice; how pleasant it would be to give him his first lesson in love! Yet how surprising at that age to be still a virgin; in Paris! I shall soon find out. He is coming to see me tomorrow and as I am positively dying to play my little games with him, I shall give him every encouragement to show me whether he knows very much. Moreover, if necessary, I shall make the first advances, whatever that might cost me.

Love listens to no remonstrances and ignores propriety. As you can see, my dear Eulalie, I am preparing to start the year in fine form. Certainly you may rest assured that I shall not let it pass without trying to obtain my share of happiness. I hope you are keeping well.

Letter from Mademoiselle Julie.

Saturday, 4th January, 1783.

Dear Friend,

Yesterday, my little officer arrived at ten o'clock in the morning, as I had requested him to do. I was still abed. Sophie brought the young man into my chamber and set a chair for him close to my bed. Straight away he seized one of my hands and, covering it with kisses, said that he loved me to the point of adoration, that since seeing me he had not slept a wink, that I was the sole object of his thoughts, a burning fire was consuming him and that should I not return his love, he was likely to die of chagrin.

Alas! his eyes spoke even more eloquently: they were animated by such emotion! His discourse, which he delivered with so much warmth and sincerity, together with the love with which the young man had already inspired in me, was arousing at least as much desire in me as in himself. I caressed the back of his neck, gave him a passionate kiss and told him that a young lady risked a great deal in putting too much confidence in the seductive words of a young man and that inconstancy and indiscretion were the least evils to fear in a tender commerce with men of his age and situation.

'Ah,' he replied, 'I do not know what others are like,

but for myself I swear to be discreet and to love you as long as I live!' Then he kissed me and straight away sank onto my bosom where he lay like one annihilated. He shortly recovered the use of his senses, however, and began to kiss me again, sighing tenderly. I realised then that he was a novice and sighing for something he dared neither take nor ask for.

I rang for Sophie and rose immediately, quite determined not to waste my morning, but to make my pretty boudoir the scene of our frolics. I put on a light quilted déshabillé, my corset was open and my hair hung down in a coquettish disorder. Thus arrayed, I passed into the boudoir with him and, having made him sit beside me on my sofa, I encouraged the young man to possess himself of my bosom and to kiss me as much as he would.

Perceiving that he was in fine mettle, I playfully undid the buttons of his breeches and there appeared before my eyes a wonder which caused me to shiver with both fear and pleasure. Whether by instinct or because my playful manner had rendered him more enterprising, he passed his hand under my skirts and explored there. His features suffused with a pleasing blush, the turbulent state of his spirits and his embarrassment were extreme when, drawing him suddenly on top of me and directing his amorous dart towards the centre of pleasure, I showed him what to do.

I believed then that he would tear me apart, so much did he make me suffer. Several times I begged him to cease, but in vain: like a bolting horse, nothing could stop him. But soon, exhausted by an ample effusion of amorous liquor with which I felt myself inundated, he remained motionless for a moment, as though intoxicated by pleasure. Then, recovering on a sudden from his lethargy, he began in earnest all over again. At last, after four sprinklings, he stopped. As for me, immersed in an ocean of delights, and no longer able to feel anything for having felt too much, I was in a kind of swoon.

My pupil occupied himself with considering my charms and the caresses and the kisses with which he was covering every part of my body restored me to my senses. Overwhelmed with fatigue, I went back to bed. My lover asked whether he could not join me there – a request which I granted, knowing that the Count was at Court, but upon the condition that he should allow me to sleep. He promised to leave me in peace, yet we had been in bed but one short hour when the rogue broke his promise. I would have scolded him if I had had the strength to do so, but that proved impossible. Finally, after another hour of savouring yet more pleasures, we rose and dined together. At four o'clock I sent him away and retired to bed, having great need to restore my depleted energies.

Farewell from your faithful friend.

Letter from Mademoiselle Julie.

Friday, 7th February, 1783.

My dear friend,

You must know that the Marquis de M ... had been living with the lovely Sainte-Marie for three months. Suspecting that she was unfaithful to him during the frequent trips which he was obliged to make to the Court, he paid someone to spy upon her. It was reported to him that the Bishop of ... often replaced

199

him in the lovely lady's bed. Piqued by this affront, he resolved to take an advantageous revenge. Consequently, he acquainted his mistress that he had to undertake a journey which would necessitate his absence for several days. The prelate, being informed of the absence of the Marquis went, as was his custom, to pay his respects to Mademoiselle Sainte-Marie.

The Marquis came in the middle of the night and, having a key of course, quietly let himself into the house. When he reached the bedside, he drew back the curtains and admirably counterfeited astonishment at finding His Lordship there. 'You are very welcome here,' said he, 'but in truth it is not just that I should pay for your pleasures. This three months past I have been living with Mademoiselle and she has cost me fifteen thousand francs. Now, you must return this sum to me or I shall send for the Watch to have you arrested and taken back to your palace.'

The Bishop tried to come to a compromise, but the Marquis was adamant. He parted with what money he had upon his person and wrote out a bill of exchange for the rest, payable the following day. The Marquis drew the curtains, wishing them a good night and informing His Lordship that he was ceding all his rights to the lovely lady to him. The bill of exchange being duly honoured the next day, the Marquis was in haste to publish his adventure, which is now the talk of the town. His Lordship is more mortified because of it than because of the money he has lost. It is generally believed that he will feel obliged to retire to his diocese for a while.

Letter from Mademoiselle Felmé.

Paris, 3rd June, 1783.

At last, dear heart, I have made up my mind. I shall
sell my diamonds and jewels; some of them shall serve
to provide me with a life annuity, and I will retire to the
provinces. I am tired of the life I have been leading. It is
my wish that I should be my own mistress and that if I
wish to give myself to someone, advantage should no
longer be my guide. Henceforth, love alone shall
perform that office. I shall never marry, for fear that
my husband might one day take it into his head to
reproach me for past misconduct. If some provincial
takes my fancy we could live together, but without the
sacrament. Those are the best kind of marriages, and
the ones which last longest. I know not yet where I
shall settle, but in a few days I shall set out for Roye,
which is my place of birth. My furniture has been
packed away in big boxes and is with a forwarding
agent who will send it to where I shall direct him.

My only regret is not being able to embrace you dear
Eulalie, before quitting the capital. It is my hope that if
you come back, you may be able to spend some time
with your friend. I shall write to you again, dear heart,
when I am settled.

Letter from Mademoiselle Felmé.

Roye, 20th July, 1783.

Dear heart,

I have settled in this town where I am leading a most
tranquil life. I am savouring the pleasure of bringing
happiness to my mother and father who, in their
declining years, had been reduced to poverty. It would
be impossible to describe their joy upon seeing me

again. They knew not what had become of me and believed me dead. My mother seemed like to die of pleasure in my arms. How moving were her caresses! I myself was quite overcome. Ah, dear friend, I have never before tasted such pleasures! In fact, I'd not change my lot with that of the great Guimar.[1] I have let it be known that my fortune was won on the lottery, with the result that I am now received in several respectable houses.

I am in disguise as it were and am constantly on my guard against using expressions which would be considered shocking here. It is something of a strain but it will undoubtedly become easier as time passes. If you return to Paris you really must come and see my contentment and the way one lives in the provinces. It is so different from the capital. I sometimes laugh to myself at the affected airs which the sociably inclined of both sexes give themselves.

I have caught the eye of a municipal councillor; it seems to me that he would like me to become Madame Councillor. I have never seen anything like his way of paying court to a lady: he is so measured in all his gestures and all that he says. One would think that he was always making a speech. As you may imagine, he is wasting his time with me.

You know my address now, dearest heart, so I am hoping to hear from you sometimes. As for me, I fear that my letters to you may prove to be rare since it is unlikely that there will be much of interest with which

1. A famous actress of the period who became wealthy and who was much sought after by the richest members of the aristocracy.

to acquaint you. But be assured that I am always your friend.

Letter from Mademoiselle Florival.

Paris, 31st October, 1783.

Dear Pussy,

Mademoiselle Victorine received me with the greatest marks of kindness. She presented me to La Présidente who, yesterday, arranged for me to sup with two Italians. Their passion, though it was quite extraordinary, had nothing unnatural about it however. What they liked was for one of them to get on all fours while I lay on his back so that the other one might fuck me. It was, in truth, a little fatiguing.

It seems to me that my affairs will prosper here. Believe me, my dear Pussy, I shall not forget the service you rendered me in furnishing me with those letters of recommendation. I should so much like to have the opportunity of demonstrating my gratitude to you. Please give my kindest regards to all our acquaintance.

Letter from Mademoiselle Florival.

Paris, 17th November, 1783.

Pussy,

You neglected to tell me that it was necessary for me to register with the Inspector of Police. He sent for me and started to reprimand me but my face pleased him and he took me into his private bureau. I had to give in to his desires in order to secure his protection. As he was passably handsome, it was not so terrible. The Superintendent of the quarter also sent for me but this time it was a much less pleasing experience: he was an ugly skeleton who pawed me for an hour and made me whip him until my arm ached and all that resulted was a discharge of a few miserable drops! Had I dared, I would have told him to go to the Devil. They are right who say that *every profession has its drawbacks.*

I am kept as busy as possible by La Présidente for the Gourdan woman's recent death has resulted in a lot of extra affairs for her. In her establishment I entertained a man who had the oddest desire: first of all I had to rub my derrière with gooseberry jelly, then he knelt between my legs and licked it all off while I was required to play with his chocolate-maker.

They are much less virile here than in Bordeaux. One has continually to apply the birch and the whip, even with young men. I pity the fuckstresses, they can find little to content them here.

Dearest Pussy, I hope to have the felicity of seeing you in six weeks at the latest and then I shall have the pleasure of assuring you of my everlasting attachment.

Letter from Mademoiselle Felmé.

Roye, 22nd November, 1783.

My dear heart,

One can be sure of nothing in this life, vanity has seduced me and tomorrow I shall become the Councillor's wife. In truth, what persuaded me is the fact that my future husband is a fool and I shall be able to twist him about my little finger. By this marriage I shall become related to some of the best families in the town. I will even have the honour of being a second cousin to Monsieur Le Lieutenant General. My wedding is to be a brilliant one: there will be a banquet in the town hall and a ball will be held in the evening.

My change of condition causes me a great deal of quiet laughter. I only wish that you might be among the guests tomorrow; you could not fail to be amused. As for me, I am preparing to be very bored. I shall be quite overwhelmed with civilities and must resign myself to being embraced from morning till evening.

But what vastly amuses me in advance is the thought of the foolishness which I shall be obliged to put on when my husband shall wish to try my supposed virginity. I have taken my precautions and made an ample use of astringent vinegar and chervil, which has been most successful. This morning, I was quite unable to introduce the tip of even my little finger into it. Thus all will appear to be as it ought to be, all the more so as I have remarked that my husband-to-be is well-endowed. But that is not because I have permitted him the least familiarity: I could judge of that by the state of his breeches when my presence inflamed his desires.

I must regretfully break off here, for my fiancé awaits me. Before long, you shall hear all about the wedding, and especially the wedding-night.

Letter from Mademoiselle Florival.

Paris, 7th December, 1783.

Dear Pussy,

Since last I wrote to you, a most unexpected piece of good luck has befallen me. An old man whom I encountered at La Présidente's has taken a particular fancy to me; he has provided me with a small furnished apartment for four months provided that during that period I shall be able to flagellate him whenever he wishes and satisfy his desires by hand. This is all he requires and apart from that I shall be free to employ my time however I will. We shall meet only about three times a week and then only for an hour or two at the most. I am so happy. My previous apartment was extremely expensive.

Please, Pussy, can I so far impose upon your good nature as to ask you to send on the things that I left in Bordeaux? For, you see, I have absolutely made up my mind to settle in Paris. It is quite clear to me that this is the only place where one can make one's fortune in a career of libertinage. Bordeaux is nothing in comparison, and one is so restricted there since the Duke de Richelieu is no longer in command. Yet people ought to realise that we are necessary, and that without us, honest women (if such there are) would no longer be in security. I hope to hear from you soon.

Letter from Mademoiselle Felmé.

Roye, 9th December, 1783.
My dearest heart,

It has been impossible for me to give you an account of the wedding before this since my time has been constantly occupied with parties and visits. All very boring! But I have done my duty now.

On the 23rd of last month, all my husband's relations and mine came to fetch me at ten o'clock in the morning. I was superbly attired for the occasion.

As for the bridegroom, he was wearing his black robe. Everyone was wearing his Sunday best, and there were clothes there which must surely have dated from the time of King Guillemaux and which had not seen the light of day for thirty years.

We entered the church at eleven o'clock. Upon our arrival, all the bells began to ring and the organist grievously maltreated a symphony. After the service, we repaired to the town-hall where we were greeted by a discharge of muskets. We entered a room next to the one where the banquet had been prepared, and I was obliged to abandon my face to everyone. Never have I been kissed so much in all my life! After these compliments, we went in to the wedding-breakfast. They started toasting me during the first course and that continued until we reached the dessert when songs were sung in my honour and once again everyone kissed me. At six o'clock the dancing started, which continued until ten o'clock then a light repast was served, after which I was conducted in triumph to my new home, amidst a thousand jokes about the coming night. As you may well imagine, I was exhausted after such a day and felicitated myself that the end was in sight.

My preparations for bed took an hour; I played the part of the bashful bride to perfection. I was hardly in bed when my new husband came to join me. I hid my head under the clothes and informed him I should not come out until he had extinguished the lights. He begged me most earnestly to keep them alight, but I did not relent until he had complied with my request. Then he began to caress me insistently. I resisted at first, as much as seemed proper, but then yielded and let him take possession of me.

Oh how I groaned then, how I shrieked, how I struggled! In short, I played my part so well that he was more than three hours putting it into me and had he not been exceptionally vigorous, there is little doubt he would not have attained his end that night. Because of my abstinence since leaving Paris, my pleasure was so intense that I was obliged to exercise the most severe control over myself lest I should abandon myself to my senses and run the risk of arousing his suspicions.

In the morning I was aware that my husband had woken up but pretended that I was still sleeping. He cautiously raised the sheets and began to examine my charms. Seeing that they were inundated with blood, he could not prevent himself from exclaiming, 'Ah, my wife was a maiden! How happy I am!' And immediately he began to cover me with kisses.

It was only with the greatest difficulty that I prevented myself from bursting into laughter. But I pretended that he had awakened me and gave a scream, as though shocked to see a man in bed with me. He threw his arms round my neck and overwhelmed me with tender caresses. Perhaps that might have led to other things had not someone entered our chamber just then.

You see, dearest, everything is for the best. My husband is all the time boasting of my virtue and publishing abroad my virginity. The next time you are in Paris, you really must come and see the Councillor's wife, who loves you quite as much as when she was just plain Felmé.

Memoirs of a Famous Courtesan (1784)

It is quite common for people to decry pleasures when they can no longer enjoy them. But why distress young people thus? Is it not their turn to frolic and feel the joys of love? Let us then anathematise these as they were in Ancient Greece only to multiply their charm and fecundity. Then the less unreasonable dotards, although prematurely aged, will be supportable and even amiable again. This philosophical idea must be sufficient to give my reader the key to those which I shall soon disclose to him. Thus, without any other preamble, I shall begin my story.

All thinking beings have a favourite penchant which drags them along willy nilly and seems to take precedence over all their other passions. I have mine, like other people: it is the love of pleasure, or to make myself clearer, the love of fucking. That is the cause of all my follies and disorders. These two words compel me to confess to the reader the nature of my profession.

I am a whore, I declare it without false shame. After all, is it such an evil thing? Let us examine the idea. What is whoredom? It is a way of life in which one follows nature without restrictions. After such a clear definition is a whore such a contemptible creature then? What am I saying? Does she not think better than other women? She has a deep understanding of nature and its various ways. Who could be more reasonable? I have said enough, I believe, to establish the excellence of my calling. For the rest, ask no more of me: it would be beyond my capacity to support my statements by grand words and solid logic. I have always detested long sentences. Provided that I can make myself understood, that shall suffice me. Thus I repeat then, I shall begin my story without any preamble.

There was nothing illustrious about my birth: this avowal is not however by any means habitual among women of my condition. I know many of my dear and venerable colleagues who have conferred a fine origin upon themselves, without being any the more noble for it. To hear them speak, it is impossible to wriggle one's bum effectively unless one is the daughter of a prelate, a councillor's niece, or cousin to a duke or peer. What folly such genealogies are! A true whore is interested in absolutely nothing but pleasure. She must despise both her birth and her parents and have no other ambition than that of assuaging her passion and making acquaintances which are both useful and agreeable. Let us come to the facts.

I was born in a village which is at a distance of two leagues from Havre-de-Grâce, where it is well known that there is a college. My father was a wheelwright. As far as education was concerned I was brought up as children always are in the country, that is to say very badly. I should have remained a simple country girl all my life had it not been for my natural talents. There was nothing extraordinary about my childhood, except that from my most tender years it was generally remarked that I had a vivacious manner which proclaimed a lively intelligence. So people in the village had a good opinion of me, and the master wheel-wright's daughter was considered to be a good girl. My worthy compatriots often referred to me in those terms.

In spite of that, I did not particularly distinguish myself from the other peasants until I reached the age of sixteen years. Until then, my most serious occupations had been learning to read and write. That was the extent of my knowledge, but I was reasonably good at it in that rustic community. Seeing how rapidly I was growing, my mother and father resolved to put me to work. They thought that I would be able to help them, but I was lazy by nature. It was from this natural inclination to sloth – which is innate in all my kind, let it be said in passing – that I derived so much love for my profession. Being good for nothing in my father's house, he resolved to give me some encourage-ment by sending me to the town. For a long time I had desired to go to market. It was only at the cost of much domestic upheaval and the shedding of many tears that I obtained this commission.

At last a day came when my father charged me with a basket of butter and eggs to sell at Le Havre. I went there with a lightness of heart which I soon lost when confronted with all those fine town gentlemen. How giddy I was at that time, and how different I am today!

Among the persons upon whom my father had instructed me to call was an old Admiralty official who liked our butter. When I arrived at the house, a young man, the old man's son, saw me and condescended to address himself to me. In fact, he flirted with me the whole time I was there. Of all the fine things he said I only fully understood one, which was a graceful compliment upon my beauty. A woman always has ears for that. Moreover, this young man was something less than handsome: sunken blue eyes, an extremely prominent forehead, a very short nose, a livid complexion and, above all, many of the scars left by smallpox. That is what the first man who uttered amorous words to me looked like. One can easily imagine how little I said in reply: I was far too shy as yet to say much. I had left my tongue at home in my village, which I was missing very much at that moment.

When I left that house, I sold what remained and returned peaceably to my village, without much reflection since I was so inexperienced that all the obliging things which had been said to me did not weigh much with me. When I arrived home, my mother enquired how I had found the town.

'Most displeasing,' I said.

'Why, pray?' asked that good woman.

'Ah,' I replied, 'Those gentlemen made me blush.' One may judge from this short dialogue how very naive I was. It ended with my saying that I should not go to the town again, but my father would not hear of that and obliged me to return there a few days later.

My task was the same and, as you can imagine, it was necessary for me to call upon the old naval official again. I was very much hoping that the son would not be there, but he was a cunning fellow: suspecting that I should be back the next market-day, he was watching for my appearance. My pretty face attracted him, and my maidenhead, for which he was making plans, attracted him even more. This time I was happier with him than on the previous occasion: he contented himself with staring at me, which made me lower my eyes, so naive was I then. However, I left his house feeling a little more bold and set off gaily for my village. You can picture my surprise when, having barely travelled half a league, I saw the young man coming towards me!

'Do you recognise me then?' said he, taking me in his arms and giving me a kiss.

My response was a most frightful shriek. I tried to disengage myself, but to no avail: he held me fast and said that he adored me, and that all he wanted was a little affection in return. All of his fine words were beyond me but I let him continue with his nonsense. Nevertheless, I derived a certain pleasure from what he was saying. I begged him to leave me however, but he said he would only do so on the condition that he might steal a kiss. It was impossible to deny him. Then he kissed me on the mouth with an inexplicable fire. He continued thus for some time, in spite of my struggles. At last, however, he let me go, leaving me with tears in my eyes.

During the rest of the journey, I reflected on what had just happened to me. The kisses which I had received deeply disturbed me. I knew not how or why but I experienced a secret joy deep within my heart. The very memory of those passionate kisses caused a glowing warmth to spread throughout my being which seemed to concentrate itself in *that noble part of my person* of which, at that time, I knew neither the usage, the charms nor any of the prerogatives, and upon which now and then, as if moved by an involuntary force, I placed my distracted and trembling hand. I pressed it through the veil which covered it in order to try to assuage the longing which was devouring me. I attributed these natural feelings to the young man's attentions and came to the conclusion that these town gentlemen were worth ten of my stupid village lads.

The more I visited the town, the more I was confirmed in this idea. My lover (for I think I can truly name him thus) then made me a thousand tempting offers. He desired to place me in the house of a lady who was a friend of his where, he said, it would be possible to see me very often and where he would give me material proofs of his tender feelings. Bit by bit, I absorbed the poison. Nevertheless, another three months went by before my final capitulation. I continually hesitated. But at last, obsessed by the young man's importunities, tired of living in my father's house, flattered by the hope of future happiness, I resolved to accede to all his desires the next time I should see him.

I did not have long to wait. The next market day, when I went to town, my lover redoubled his instances. My resistance was of short duration, then I gave in. He was overjoyed at the prospect of possessing an object as amiable as myself! His preparations had been made long since and he conducted me without delay to the house of the said friend, who was a dressmaker. It was in a distant quarter of the town and it was there that I abandoned forever my eggs, my butter and my poor basket.

Until now the reader has witnessed my simplicity, one might in truth even say my stupidity. From now on I shall be quite different, for Nature alone shall be my guide. What progress one makes when one follows maxims, precepts as indulgent as hers! The dressmaker's house was the first theatre where I shaped myself in the ways of pleasure: There I undertook my apprenticeship.

I must admit that the house impressed me when I first saw it. My eyes, it is true, were not accustomed to grand spectacles: a simple cottage, a hut with a few sticks of furniture had until then appeared to be beautiful. But when I made the comparison with the apartment my lover was offering me, I was very sensible of the contrast and a great happiness possessed me; the prospect of a brilliant future seduced me to the point where I believed myself to be blessed with eternal happiness.

My lover permitted me sufficient time to admire everything to my heart's content, then came the moment which was to be critical for my virginity. I knew perfectly well why he had brought me to that house, so I did not play the fool nor the prude. Besides, I was not experienced enough for that. Thus my lover placed his hand on my treasure, and fingered it as much as it pleased him to do, and he kissed me repeatedly without encountering any resistance on my part. I made no effort whatsoever to avoid his ardent caresses. But though he did not have to combat my will, yet he had other obstacles to vanquish. He was not of a size readily to ravish a maidenhead: his prick, which was bigger at the top than at the base, would have been excellent for a dowager. For some considerable time, he struggled to enter my plaything, without being able to force open the lips.

My lover had already made several libations, and

very copious ones, upon my thighs, which had not aroused the slightest emotion in me. At that time I did not know the preoccupation every girl and woman has in not losing a single drop of such a precious liquid. At last, after an hour of torment and combat, my champion entered the fort: he had conquered me, but at such an expense of suffering on my part that it seemed impossible to me that I should ever survive such a terrible assault. All the time I had been screaming, shrieking and begging him to desist.

'Is it in this fashion,' I sobbed, 'that you abuse my confidence? Will you not be content until I am dead?'

But no sooner had I uttered these words than a dramatic change occurred in my feelings: time seemed to stand still, my cheeks flushed, a warm glow suffused my body and a sweet intoxication took possession of all my senses. At last, I had been deflowered!

That was the most interesting period of my life. It was that happy time which witnessed the commencement of my pleasures, my chagrins, my joys, my misfortunes. But what am I saying? It was then that I started to live. After my first time everything appeared beautiful to me. Some of my readers may say that I did it too soon. But is it not at sixteen years that one should make one's debut in the world? Had I not done it then, would I at present have so much experience in that variety of pleasures which the public comes to savour in my different nooks and crannies? Undoubtedly no. Let people cease to denigrate what, in my humble opinion, ought to be and has in fact been my greatest happiness, that which has merited the approbation of the finest connoisseurs in these matters, which they have shown by giving me the glorious and flattering title of Nymph of the Day or, in other words: la Dumoncy, fuckstress par excellence.

My reader, seeing me thus separated from my parents, undoubtedly expects me to paint in the most vivid colours their sufferings at having lost me, and also the measures they took to bring me back. In fact, I feel at liberty to dispense with such tiresome details. Let me make myself clear: from the moment I entered the dressmaker's house, my parents no longer meant anything to me and I never heard any news of them. If they occasionally crossed my mind, it was solely pity for their fate that moved me and the hope of one day ameliorating it, thereby paying my tribute to filial piety and by the sentiments of my heart meriting on their part an indulgence for my escapade. But my condition then appeared to me to be much superior to theirs, for I was tranquil and lived without cares, without anxiety, indolent to the point of slothfulness, my sole occupation consisting, to speak plainly, of enjoying the sweet pleasures of amorous dalliance with my lover. Consequently, I did not often venture out into the great world, to avoid being noticed and perhaps obliged to return to my dreary village.

Thus six months passed during which time the only person with whom I had any close communication was my lover. I was most assuredly very virtuous, for a woman must be recognised as such when only one man renders homage to her charms. But that state of affairs did not last long; the moment was approaching when my lover would no longer suffice to satisfy all my desires. After having explored with him all the avenues of love, to the point of exhaustion, it was inevitable that I should have recourse to other men and, unfortunately for him, an excellent opportunity soon presented itself, and I did not fail to avail myself of it. This was the way of it.

A young cavalier, tall and well-built (he was, I believe, a captain of infantry), visited the dressmaker, my hostess, one day on the pretext of placing an order with her. I happened to be present and when he laid eyes on me, the officer addressed me in the most gallant terms, a stratagem for which military gentlemen have a particular talent. Neither did he confine himself to that, but stared at me so intently that I lowered my eyes, being quite unable to sustain such bold looks. That did not discourage him, however; on the contrary, it prompted him to request the dressmaker to go and buy some muslin for wristbands, adding that he had ordered some from a woman whom he named, saying that the dressmaker should bring as much as was necessary and that he would await her return to settle with her. My hostess, being always zealous in the prosecution of business, was only too eager to comply with the gentleman's wishes and she ran off to fetch the muslin, leaving me with the officer.

One may easily guess how embarrased I was! I stood up, went into my room, came back, sat down again and knew not how to keep myself in countenance. Observing my confusion, the officer undoubtedly came to the conclusion that my conquest should not prove to be difficult. He spoke to me in a tone of wheedling flattery for a few moments without being able to draw much response from me. Then, as though we were making a supreme effort to chase away my timidity, he said,

'Look at me, Mademoiselle; please, I beg you!'

I raised my eyes to look at him. But, merciful
Heavens! What did I see? Dare I tell? Yes, undoubtedly. For what use would it be for me to affect an
untimely bashfulness? After what I have said concerning my situation, it would hardly suit me. Very
well then, what I saw was a priapus of the most
majestic size. In brief, the biggest and most beautiful
prick in the world.

'Oh! Monsieur!' I cried. 'Pray, cover yourself.'

'Very well, O queen of my heart,' said he, 'your wish
is my command.'

Then he gave me a hard slap on my buttocks with his
left hand, and with his right hand obliged me to lie
down on the bed.

'Will you have done, Monsieur?' said I angrily.

'In a trice, my pretty one.'

Whereupon, he took possession of my treasure,
caressed it briefly then threaded me with his fine
upstanding needle, as though I had been some
voluptuous pearl. He moved back and forth furiously,
fucking me mercilessly and soon inundated me with a
torrent of amorous liquor which filled me with an
incomparable voluptuousness. Heavens! What an
indefatigable jouster! His priapus, still in form,
continued to work hard in order to deserve the homage
that my heart and my cunt could not fail to render it.
This man had had a great deal of experience with
women and knew that it is sometimes good to be a little
rough with them. I was happy beyond my wildest
dreams. How could it have been otherwise? The
spermatic liquor came out in great spurts from my
amiable fucker's hot balls and communicated an

unspeakable ardour and voluptuousness to every part of my body...! Ye Gods! So much pleasure at one time! Never shall I forget it. I shall remember that gallant officer for the rest of my life...

The Adventures of Laura (1790)

(MADAME DE MERVILLE, THE ABBESS OF A CORRUPT
NUNNERY, IS PLANNING TO INTRODUCE THE SIXTEEN
YEAR OLD LAURA TO THE DELIGHTS OF LESBIAN
LOVE.)

I visited Laura again, determined to risk more this time
than the first. My passion was increasing and so was
my desire! It was clear from what she said that the girl
was as innocent as she was lovely. Quite evidently she
did not understand my ambiguous remarks. A plan
was forming itself in my mind which should not prove
difficult to execute. I left her, and as soon as Brother
Bigprick arrived I acquainted him with my scheme. I
said that his assistance was essential to the success of
my enterprise. His deference to me, which was so often
rewarded, was boundless, and he made no difficulty
about falling in with my plan. I told him then that he
must seek to instruct Laura by questioning her, in the
confessional, upon the matter of impurity; that he
should subtly inculcate her with the desire to read
certain books, actually naming them while appearing
to proscribe them; and that I should be responsible for
the rest. We agreed that the confession would take
place the following day.

What a delightful night I spent in his arms! I

accorded him everything that his lewd passion inspired him to demand of me. Dawn arrived, and we went our separate ways. He promised me to spare no efforts to bring my affair to a successful conclusion and, hoping that I should procure Laura for him after her initiation into our mysteries, he departed feeling happy and satisfied.

I had to attend morning service. How long it seemed to last! 'But nothing that is worth having is ever gained without some difficulty,' I told myself, and bore my suffering patiently. In truth, my dear prior, the public who regard us as vestals are much mistaken. Can they really be so completely unaware that we are women, and that Nature speaks as loudly in our hearts as in those of people whose married state authorises the pleasures they wish to deprive us of? For myself, I do not know why this illusion should prove so enduring. But let us leave this trusting public in its state of naive credulity, for we profit by it. Let us come voluptuously in secrecy and silence, and by our pious mummery continue to hoodwink the people who are only too willing to be deceived.

Bigprick kept his word. After his young penitent had acquainted him that she'd three times lost her temper with the cat, stamped her foot, eaten a pear before going to mass and other childish things which proved the girl's innocence but which she took for great sins, the prior brought the conversation round to the desired subject. It was all Greek to our novice: she did not understand a word! As for me, while Laura was thus engaged, I profited by her absence and entered her cell: there I put that charming novel

Thérèse Philosophe[1] on her bookshelf. Some expressive plates illustrated this agreeable volume: thus did I hope to pique her curiosity and lead the unsuspecting girl to my ends. I watched for a favourable moment. As that cell adjoined mine, I had made a small opening in the wall. That aperture, of which Laura was of course totally unaware, would enable me to see everything she did when she was alone.

At length, the young lady returned and knelt for a few moments on her prayer-stool. Then up she rose and went across to her bookshelf. The new volume attracted the girl's attention by the freshness of its binding. She opened it and the illustrations immediately caught her attention.

Her cheeks flushed, which seemed to me to be a good sign. She did not know what to think of those diverse postures, then suddenly, realising that this must be one of those books which the confessor had warned her about, she threw it from her with an air of vexation, an action which pained me greatly. The girl remained motionless for a few moments, a prey to conflicting emotions, then the sentiment which I had so artfully inspired in her began to manifest itself.

Curiosity triumphed over piety: she ran across the room and picked up the book. The flush which graced her cheeks spoke eloquently of the state of her emotions. She was quite fascinated by the illustrations.

1. *Thérèse Philosophe* was one of the most well-known and widely-read erotic novels in eighteenth century France. There are good reasons for believing that the Marquis de Sade was influenced by it.

The desire to increase her knowledge swept aside Bigprick's hypocritical moralising. She placed a mirror on the floor and put the book on a table. My young pupil wished to verify that Mother Nature had in fact endowed her with the same attractions as those which the women in the plates were making use of.

With trembling hands she raised her skirts and looked into the mirror to see whether she too possessed that centre of pleasure. My dear prior, you may imagine the state in which I found myself at the sight of so many charms! I pressed my eye to the aperture and just a few feet away saw the prettiest mound, the most delightful cunt in the world! Its sealed lips, so rosy and so tender, confirmed its virgin state, a light covering of hair cast a shadow over that charming spot, and the whiteness of her thighs contrasted with the darkness of her pubic hair.

As she made this inspection, her naturally expressive eyes became animated by the fires of passion. If ever a woman has realised the charms with which the poets have endowed Venus, it cannot be doubted that Laura was that woman in those first innocent moments.

The love which was beginning to express itself in her heart, the modesty which seemed to reproach what she was doing established a conflict within her whose effects were extremely seductive. Finally, I could bear it no longer: I left my post for another which promised a thousand delights.

Naturally, I had keys to all of the cells, including Laura's. It was with the greatest stealth that I now opened her door in order to surprise her in the same posture. The application with which she was concentrating both on her own nature, and that represented in the illustrations served me well: I managed to open the door without disturbing the young lady. Then she discovered my presence. You may easily guess how embarrassed she was and visualise her confusion, which was filling me with delight. She lowered her eyes and sought to hide the book. I wished to amuse myself for a moment and expressed an anger I was far from feeling:

'Well now,' I said 'what are you doing, mademoiselle?'

She threw herself at my feet in tears. In truth, at that moment my resistance crumbled: I raised the girl gently to her feet, pulling her against me and placing my hand on a firm breast. I pressed my lips to those of my young charge.

After a brief silence, I said, 'Lovely Laura, the time for play-acting is over. You are of an age when your charms should inspire your happiness. It is my desire to make you aware of what treasures are in your possession, to intoxicate you with the sweetest of pleasures.'

I conducted her to the bed and pressed her down upon it. She was too astonished, too troubled to think of resisting. I covered the dear girl with kisses while my hands eagerly sought out her holy charms. When she felt me raising her skirt, she put up some slight resistance, whereupon I said, 'Divine Laura, until now you have been unaware of the transports which love inspires. It is my desire to introduce you to such delights: you are beholden to love for your beauty and cannot resist its delights. What I am saying surprises you, no doubt, but Mother Nature never loses her rights. We are women and subject to the most tumultuous passions. Give yourself over to those pleasures whose existence you have hitherto been aware of but from which you will derive the greatest happiness.'

Even while I was speaking, my fingers were busily engaged in exploring the most adorable little cunt. I tried to push one of them right in but Laura's protests and cries of pain reminded me that I must have a care since this was a virginal flower; therefore I contented myself with gently rubbing that plump little mound, which gave inexpressible pleasure to my young conquest.

She abandoned herself to me entirely. We gradually revealed our bodies to each other. I repeatedly kissed and caressed her perfectly formed breasts which were as white as alabaster. Her nipples seemed to my eyes to be as pink and delicate as rosebuds. Every part of her received my homage. Her snowy buttocks were firm to my touch. I placed her hand on my cunt, and an agile finger set my senses on fire. I said, 'You will observe dearest Laura, that you do not meet with the same obstacle in me as within yourself. That is an enigma which our prior will resolve for you.'

Oh, how ingenious is love! That gentle virgin masturbated me delightfully! Two hours did we spend, and more, in those delightful pastimes. We each succumbed in turn to the excess of pleasure. When we had recovered our lucidity, she asked me several questions and ran to fetch her volume of *Thérèse Philosophe*. We turned the pages together, pausing when we came to the illustrations. The virile member seemed particularly to draw her attention. I told the lovely girl that it was popularly known as a prick.

I pointed out the two little globes which hung down below the generative organ, telling her that they were enclosed in thick flesh, that these globes were called 'testicles' in surgical terms, and 'balls' in the vulgar tongue. I said that these balls were full of a seed which served for the propagation of the human species. I also told her that the sudden shuddering which overcame both of us when we were touching one another was also produced by the motion of that fluid, which took violent possession of all our faculties and whose emission plunged us into the state of voluptuous exhaustion that she had just experienced.

I spoke to her of the manner in which men and women complement each other, saying that Nature, desirous all the time to be uniting these two different creatures, had distributed her favours equally between them: the one possessing the miraculous tool of our existence, the other the pleasing cavern which so delightfully encloses the productive staff.

Laura asked me the following question: 'But how can that member enter such a tiny nook? It appears to be bigger than a finger and when you tried to put yours inside me it hurt me most dreadfully.'

'Ah, Laura!' I cried, 'how ignorant you are and how delighted I am to have such agreeable lessons to teach you! You must know then that the Creator has made these pleasures, of which I am the apostle, the most exquisite of all. I sing of their delights with both joy and gratitude. Your present state, my child, is one of innocence. You still possess what is known as your maidenhead. It is a precious favour which Nature reserves for a man and of the enjoyment of which you cannot deprive him. A certain amount of suffering is inevitable but will be succeeded by the keenest of pleasure. Those which we have just experienced are only a foretaste of those that you are destined to feel. You have seen that your finger entered without any difficulty into *my* nook. Well, that is the consequence of the sacrifice of which I have been speaking. I used to be as you are now, but an amiable man skilfully ravished my flower and rendered me capable of coupling with my fellow human beings.'

'What is this? A man has caressed you as I have done?'

'Most assuredly. Brother Bigprick does so every night. And I intend to recompense his tenderness for me by helping him to pluck the sweet flower of your virginity. As you will observe, jealousy is not one of my vices.'

'What! A man ... with me? I cannot even think of such a thing without blushing ...'

'What nonsense! In this world excessive modesty only serves to frustrate us of the sweetest advantages. We were born for pleasure. My dear young friend, pray let yourself be guided by me and one day you will realise how much I have done for you. In this cloister we may fearlessly give ourselves over to all the joys of love. For us, inquisitive busybodies do not hold the terror that they do for those who live in society. This evening I desire you to be present at one of our orgies which, as I shall inform our sisters, will start at eight o'clock. The chapter-house shall be prepared for that purpose, for I desire that your maidenhead should be sacrificed with pomp and ceremony ...'

Laura interrupted me, begging me most earnestly not to carry out my plan, saying that it would be impossible for her to appear thus before all her companions, that she would gladly do with me in private what we had already done, but that in public she should never have the courage. I reassured the poor girl by taking her into my arms again and overwhelming her with caresses to which she responded ardently.

I spoke no more to her about my project but instead concentrated upon putting it into execution. It was time for the evening service. We made our ablutions and adjusted our clothing then, carrying our prayer-books, our hands crossed upon our bosoms, eyes fixed humbly on the floor, we went to fulfil our duties.

A nasal and lugubrious chanting led the congregation to believe that we worshipped only one divintiy and that the very name of love was forever banished from that place.

I shall not conceal from you the fact that the celebration which I was preparing for the evening occupied my mind throughout the service. Frequent distractions acquainted the nuns with my state of preoccupation. When the service was at an end, I assembled them together and confided my project to them. Preparations speedily got under way.

I summoned Bigprick to my private quarters and addressed him thus, in a noble tone:

'Venerable fucker, your docile sweetheart wishes to prove how grateful she is to you. Come to our gathering tonight, come and savour the most splendid of triumphs. Come, I want to place Laura's arms around you. Her virginity is reserved for you; I desire to offer you an amorous combat worthy of such an athlete as yourself.'

At these words, his eyes sparkled, his cheeks flushed a deep red. He could only stammer, so great was his joy...

'What! Shall I hold such a ravishing creature in my arms? Shall *my* prick have the honour of such a maidenhead?... Can it be true? Or am I being deceived by some sweet dream?'

'No, my dear prior. No, you are not dreaming.' While affirming to him the reality of our conversation, my hand had disappeared under his robe and was seeking the sword of sacrifice... He understood at once what I required and threw me down upon my bed. You may imagine how well I did my duty and with what energy I moved my arse!

'I am satisfied,' I cried. 'You can see by the sacrifice I'm making that jealousy has no power over me. You know that I have always tried to be just in every way and have never wished to deprive my sisters of the joys which you have caused me to experience. This is the first time I have been able to procure a maidenhead for you and I have seized the opportunity with the greatest pleasure. Your triumph will please me prodigiously; we shall fan the flames of your ardour with fortifying drinks. But I cannot stay here with you any longer, for I must supervise the arrangements which will cul-minate in your victory.'

I did indeed go then and verify that all was being made ready. The most harmonious symmetry was what guided us, and we waited impatiently for the happy moment to arrive.

A repast arranged with taste and delicacy was to precede our delightful orgy. Excellent wines were on hand to increase our pleasure and I swear that not even the most aristocratic of libertines, not excepting d'Artois and d'Orléans[1], could have conceived of anything better. I left the good sisters to put the finishing touches to the preparations and went to fetch my amiable recluse.

I found her deep in reflection, *Thérèse Philosophe* lying open beside her. Laura's fascination with the novel seemed to me to bode well for our enterprise: the charming style of the lovable storyteller assured me in advance of the young lady's entire submissiveness to my desires. I did not mention my project. We chatted about *Thérèse*, and I made a few observations which further enlightened her. It seemed to me that her personality, which was predisposed towards the liveliest passions, would make little resistance to Bigprick's passionate advances and that afterwards our novice would become the most enthusiastic of hussies.

At last the longed-for moment arrived and I conducted Laura to the room where the banquet had been prepared. By now her fears were causing her some reluctance and so I told her Bigprick would be terribly disappointed if she refused to participate in the ceremony.

'Soon,' I said, 'you will fall under his spell. You are at an age when love speaks loudly in a girl's heart. However, if you wish to consider the matter a little longer, nobody will try to force you. But at least come and grace our gathering with your presence.'

---

1. The Count d'Artois and the Duke d'Orléans were both members of the French royal family.

At last I persuaded her. The company was already assembled.

Laura stopped short when she saw how elegantly the great hall had been decorated. A table, set with exquisite taste, cried out for the guests to be seated. The gentle light of the candles inspired our hearts with voluptuousness. Before us was the sofa which was to be the throne upon which Bigprick would soon triumph. When Laura arrived, she was surrounded by the sisters who all wanted to kiss her. Ah, my dear Hercules, how you would have enjoyed such a spectacle!... Your imagination must supply the deficiency of my description: see the lovely girl advancing with a timid and hesitant step, see the fires of love in her rosy lips, mingling with the blushes of innocence, see those great dark eyes modestly lowered beneath ebony eyebrows delicately arching on the ivory smoothness of a forehead, see round breasts, fashioned by the Graces, which are clearly discernible through the light wimple, straining against the cloth as though they wished to escape from their prison!

What mortal could remain insensible to the sight of so many charms? Bigprick was deeply impressed. I saw him make a gesture of surprise and, at the same time, his countenance lit up and he could not take his eyes off the young woman. None of us felt jealous, for we owed him too much to begrudge him this moment of enjoyment and, besides, we were certain that he would be grateful for our consideration and would reward us later on.

We all sat down. I had seen to it that Laura was seated between the prior and myself.

I addressed her thus, 'Dear child, you did not expect

to find such a sumptuously laden table in a convent. But you must know that we are extremely rich, that kings, queens and other imbeciles have made considerable donations to us. And we find ways to dissipate our revenue. Meals offer us endless resources and our dear prior is most accomplished in that sphere. He has already written two big treatises on the art of cooking: there is not a bishop who does not possess these nourishing works and who does not exhort his cook to consult them, to meditate upon these books which are more precious than a Holy Decree as far as they are concerned.'

The prior smiled at me and said, 'Dear lady, I shall become prodigiously vain if you continue to flatter me thus. But I know my true worth and I shall not let my head be turned by praise which I do not merit.'

Laura listened, ate, but said not a word. I had made sure that a drink which provokes amorous feelings was prepared and placed before her. Indeed, when she had drunk just a small glass of that philtre, her eyes began to sparkle, Nature repulsed shame, and we prepared ourselves to watch the most voluptuous spectacle.

The conversation became more animated, and words led to deeds. Sister Ursula, who was sitting next to me, kissed me passionately and our mouths remained positively glued to each other for some moments. Our tongues met and soon the whole company was similarly engaged. Bigprick audaciously placed his hand on one of Laura's breasts. The latter's first impulse was to push him away, but soon the example of her companions, and the philtre she had drunk, weakened her resistance to the vigorous prior's urgent caresses.

Sister Saint-Ange came to the aid of the prior and withdrew the pins which held the young lady's wimple in place. Then the most beautiful breasts were offered to our gaze: they were roses and lilies. Their precipitate movement clearly indicated the state in which our maiden found herself. Bigprick, who was impatient to come, had already exposed his long and vigorous member whose proud, rubicund head seemed to menace all the cunts assembled there.

Laura was led over to the sofa and placed upon it. We all surrounded her, covering her with kisses, and unfastened the young lady's clothing. Soon she was clad in nothing but her chemise. She did not utter a word, she blushed and her hands could not find the strength to repulse ours. We handed over the tender, almost naked victim to the great sacrificer.

Ah, my dear prior! What charms! What buttocks! What thighs! Bigprick hastily removed his garments and seized the trembling Laura in his arms. With one hand he pulled her chemise up to her waist, whilst with the other he presented his redoubtable cutlass to the entrance of her sanctuary. The poor girl screamed loudly. He stopped. I caressed Laura, persuading her that it was necessary to suffer a little, assuring her that it was an essential preliminary if ever she were to attain true bliss.

The prior tried thrice more, and thrice was he repelled. But he had managed to lodge the head of his prick ... he did not intend to lose that advantage: he gave such a vigorous thrust of the bum that he entered entirely. A piercing scream from the victim announced the triumph of the reverend brother. He held fast, however, and Laura became calmer. In fact, that young hussy was beginning to enjoy the proceedings and was in truth wriggling her bottom as I might have done. They both reached the supreme moment of delight together.

As for the rest of us, we could not be content to remain mere spectators any longer. Sister Ursula and I threw ourselves down on one of the mattresses which had been placed on the floor in accordance with my instructions. The others followed our example and soon one could see nothing but cunts, bums and breasts wherever one looked. After this pleasant exercise, we gave a dish of steaming broth to the happy couple, and a glass of excellent Cyprus wine.

I kissed Laura, who wanted to get dressed but I prevented her from so doing, telling her that Bigprick would never be content with just one bout. I made her change the chemise she was wearing as it was blood-stained. She wiped herself clean and remained in that agreeable disorder. I engaged the rest of the company to do the like and they applauded my suggestion. In less than no time all of our clothes were removed. Bigprick did the same and we seated ourselves at the table again.

It would be impossible for me to describe to you all the follies to which we abandoned ourselves. Laura was ravishing and was the prime mover of our passions. We all drank beyond the bounds of moderation. I intoned an ode to Priapus to which everyone contributed. At each strophe, every lady present kissed whoever was sitting next to her. Partly naked as we were, we rejoiced in the sight of our half-revealed charms, and to each of them paid a tribute of kisses and caresses.

By now we had moved the sofa nearer to the table. Bigprick and Laura were seated upon it with me by their side and Sister Ursula and Sister Saint-Ange were seated on either side of us. The prior pushed his young bride down on to her back, placed her legs on his shoulders, and endeavoured to bugger her.

'Ah, two maidenheads in one day is going too far!' I exclaimed.

He obeyed me, and directed his attentions to the young lady's cunt. Laura became violently agitated and seconded her fucker's efforts to the utmost limits of her ability.

As for the rest of us, we masturbated each other, since this was our only resource, but we went to it with such a will that we were like to swoon from joy. When this bout was over, we returned to our wine and our songs. Bigprick quoted almost all of Jean-Jacques Rousseau's epigrams to us. It was not long before the conversation, the liquor, and the naked women all conspired to renew his vigour, and he displayed a prick whose length and rigidity thrilled us all. Laura regarded it longingly but, addressing herself to the prior, said, 'It is not fair that I should be the only one to be so pleased today, and the Mother Superior deserves a reward for all her trouble.'

I did not wish to prove myself unequal to Laura in generosity, and told her that since this was her special day she should finish it. She raised more objections. Then I proposed another expedient: 'Very well,' said I, 'let us draw lots.'

Everyone agreed to this suggestion. I was the winner and hastened to lie down on the sofa. But I wanted Laura to participate in my pleasure: I took her in my arms.

I displayed a posterior to Bigprick which I well knew would tempt him. And I was right: he trussed up my chemise and buried his instrument in me. I masturbated Laura and Sister Ursula tickled the brother's testicles.

Never, no never, have I experienced so much enjoyment as fell to my lot that night: we passed it in voluptuous delights.

Daylight began to appear, it was now necessary to attend Matins. In truth, how well disposed we were to perform that office! So, after a brief hesitation, I took upon myself the responsibility of a general dispensation and we carried on with our orgy. Brother Bigprick rubbed all the sisters one after another, and still had enough strength left to shaft Sister Ursula and Sister Saint-Ange. He promised to make it up to the others later on, not wishing to excite their jealousy.

I said to him, 'You must be a very happy man after such a night, but do not count upon your new wife. Do as you will with the others, but I am taking charge of this young lady now. In a few days you may have her again, but before then you must fulfil your obligations and fuck the rest of us.'

As I finished speaking, I clasped Laura to me and could not resist caressing one of her firm breasts. I left off fondling her breast only to stroke her pretty mound. How well she responded to my caresses! And what pleasures her supple and ingenious finger induced in me!

For more than an hour we remained together on the sofa, locked in a tight embrace, gently rocking each other. Our tongues had no more strength. We were positively intoxicated with love. Our eyes closed and we remained in that state of utter prostration for so considerable a time that upon awakening, we found ourselves alone: the others had retired to their cells to seek some rest. We followed their example. I found Brother Bigprick sleeping soundly in Sister Ursula's arms. Their position convinced me that they had fallen asleep after intercourse had taken place.

'Come,' said I, 'we must not disturb them. Let us go to bed.'

I closed the door softly and we entered my quarters. We got into bed. I wished my young companion a good night and slept for about two hours. When I awoke, it was broad daylight. I made Laura get up. I went into all the cells and found everyone still sleeping. I told them that they must go to morning service, so they got dressed.

Bigprick and Sister Ursula were still in the same position and an idea came to me. I gently pulled back the bedclothes and revealed the naked lovers. Then I started to masturbate Bigprick. He did not awake but behaved exactly as men do when they are having voluptuous dreams. However, at the moment of ejaculation he stretched out his arms, I moved forward, he embraced me, and my touch awoke him. He opened his eyes. Imagine his surprise when he found me in his arms!

'Time to get up,' said I.

He obeyed at once and leaped out of bed. I desired to wake Sister Ursula in the same manner and succeeded marvellously. I gently introduced my finger into her cunt and titillated the clitoris. If only you could have seen how she flung herself about, how she moved her bum! She made the bed creak. Bigprick was laughing heartily. However, when she was satisfied, she opened her eyes and said, 'Where am I? What! In your arms!'

'Yes, yes,' said I. 'Come along, Madame libertine, get up; it is time for morning service.'

Bigprick said, 'Good. You go to the service but, as for me, it is impossible to leave at this hour. I shall return to the chapter-house: the remains of last night's feast shall provide me with a breakfast. After the service, you can come and join me there. Still, if you will take my advice, you will each have a little glass of something... to give you the strength to do all that praying and hymn-singing.'

We followed his advice. We went away and each took a glass of orange-water before going to perform our duties.

(Later that day Laura participates in another orgy and during the following week the young woman takes part in a great deal of such activities with the inevitable consequence that she becomes pregnant. Unbeknown to the Abbess, she also meets a young gentleman when he is visiting the convent, falls in love with him and agrees to run away with him.

One day, Madame de Merville finds that her charge has disappeared but soon after receives the following letter:)

'My dear abbess,
Your lessons, your example have awakened desires within me which it is not in my power to deny. Far from reproaching you, I must thank you for having

239

enlightened me, and if I have a regret it is that of not having become acquainted with you two years earlier, for then those years should not have been wasted in a culpable inactivity. Nature tells me at every moment that I was born for pleasure, and I should not wish to be deaf to a voice which is so much in accordance with my interests.

'Undoubtedly, you will think me guilty of the basest ingratitude for departing in this manner after all that you have done for me. I am aware that your reproaches are not without foundation, but you must believe that never shall I forget you. Here are the facts concerning my flight: Floridor came to the parlour with my parents, as you know; I saw him and was consumed with the ardent fires of love. Bigprick's caresses were only agreeable to me inasmuch as I imagined that they were Floridor's. It was not long before the latter, enamoured of my charms, expressed his passion for me. He bribed one of the sisters to deliver his letters to me. We agreed upon a day when I should flee with him and he brought his post-chaise to the new garden-door, I got into it and we sped away toward Paris. I bore in mind that I had a role to play and had a care not to let him see how much pleasure was mine at being in his arms.

'However, he caressed me a little in the chaise, and I pretended to resist. At last, after he had promised to marry me twenty times, I relented somewhat. We had just arrived at a delightful meadow. I perceived an arbour which decided me. We got out of the chaise. He led his horse close to the arbour, attached him to a tree, and we found ourselves under a sweet-smelling vault of leaves. This spot, which was shaded by hawthorn bushes and at a good distance from the road, facilitated our desires.

'He put his arms around me and drew me to his bosom. Again I played the coy maiden. One of his hands slipped under my skirts, I squeezed my thighs tightly together. At last, after a struggle of several minutes' duration, I contrived to fall. He profited from this circumstance and, pulling up my skirts, he proceeded to have intercourse with me. I struggled, I screamed; by my play-acting I made him believe that he had triumphed over my maidenhead. I appeared abashed, my eyes were lowered modestly, my bosom palpitated rapidly. In order to make my part seem more convincing, I even managed to shed a few tears. He hastened to dry them and, after many protestations of eternal love on his part, we got back into the chaise and continued our journey to Paris. It took us two days to complete the trip. When we reached the first town, I changed my clothes, for that was my first opportunity to do so, so precipitate had been our departure.

'When we arrived at Paris, we took rooms at the Hôtel de Tours in the Rue des Petits-Champs. A great deal more attentions and promises on his part were necessary before I would agree to share his bed, but at last I relented. We passed a delightful night together, and I abandoned myself to all the fire of my temperament. I have now spent two days in such delightful pastimes, but I have made time to write and acquaint you with what has happened so that you should not worry unduly. I can imagine your embarrassment with regard to my parents, but all will be well now, for I have written a letter to them;

however, since it would be foolish to let them know my real whereabouts, I have inscribed an address in Brussels on my letter in order to mislead them. I have charged someone who is instantly departing for that city to send it from that place.

'Adieu, my dear abbess. It is time for me to go to the Opera. I shall write to you frequently, please do the same for me. I kiss you all with the tenderness of both a friend and a lover.

Laura de Fondeville
Paris, 20th November, 1790.'

I summoned the whole community and acquainted them with this letter, at the same time revealing my fears to them ... fears which proved to be only too well-founded.

'This Floridor,' I said, 'appears to me to be a libertine, and I greatly fear that Laura has been duped by him. But one cannot avoid these first skirmishes in love. Had she consulted me, I should have advised the young lady to repress a passion which might prove to be dangerous. She lacked for nothing here, and this precipitate flight shows just how inconsiderate and thoughtless young people can be. She is only sixteen years of age. She might have savoured all the pleasures here for some years. During that time, her parents would have found a suitable match for her. She would have gone back to them with honour, and would have left the wimple for the bridal wreath: we have the means to repair broken maidenheads and the young lady's husband would have believed his new wife to be intact and pure. But what will become of her now? She is with child. As soon as Floridor becomes aware of that he will abandon her. Ah!' I continued, addressing myself to Sister Ursula, 'you conducted yourself far more prudently. You followed my advice and have profited by it. Your dear mother has arranged a most desirable marriage for you with a rich government official. You will pass from the embraces of Bigprick and myself to those of a husband who will believe that he is teaching you a game at which, in fact, you are already an expert.

'A few drops of our special medicine will soon make good all the ravages which the prior's weapon has made.'

Laura's disappearance affected me greatly, for I had become attached to her. However, I consoled myself to the best of my ability with Bigprick and my nuns: we continued our orgies. A month passed without any news from Laura. Her parents wrote to me saying how upset they were by their daughter's behaviour. I pitied them, and consoled them as well as I could.

Then, after an interval of about six weeks, a letter arrived from our fugitive. Here it is, faithfully transcribed for your benefit:

'Ah, my dear abbess, how foolishly I have behaved! I have been duped by my trust and my love! Floridor, who seemed to love me so much, is nothing but a monster. You know that a casket of jewels which were of great value was in my possession, well the scoundrel has made off with it leaving me with nothing but fifteen francs. You can picture my despair! Fortunately, I had already made the acquaintance of a distinguished gentleman, who is our neighbour. I did not hesitate to acquaint him with my misfortune and my lover's perfidious conduct. He sympathised with my situation and offered me pecuniary assistance.

"You shall be avenged," he assured me, "for the woman with whom he has departed has the most evil reputation and I wager he'll soon have good reason to repent his misdeed. But have a care lest he return and seduce you again, for then you would share his wretched fate. Let us leave this house."

'And indeed, that very same evening we removed to the Chausée d'Antin. I have nothing but praise for this gentleman's behaviour. Quite evidently, it is not his intention to deceive me.

'He said, "I can only remain in the capital for three more months, I cannot take you with me, but before my departure I want to reassure myself that you are provided for. You have a good voice and can read music. I know the director of the Opera and I shall use my influence to obtain an interview for you."

'Indeed, he spoke about me to his friend, who sent for me, listened to my singing and was satisfied with my voice. It was easy to see that I had made an impression upon him. He promised to give me some lessons and added, "I am sure that we can do something for you, mademoiselle. In less than two months you will be ready to join the chorus. Work hard and you will soon be earning money, you have a great deal of talent."

'He wanted me to visit him the next morning at ten o'clock. I promised him that I should keep our appointment punctually.

'I was true to my word. He had had a light meal prepared for us. He showed me into an elegant and ornate boudoir where we sat on a sofa. As you can guess, *Monsieur le directeur* wanted a reward for his protection. I made a show of resisting, as etiquette demands, but soon surrendered to his desires. The director, having no doubt of his triumph, had attired himself for combat: a voluminous dressing-robe enveloped him. But when he opened it, I perceived an extremely fine member thrusting against his shirt, which was all that covered it, for he was not wearing breeches. He grasped my hand and conducted it to that formidable engine. With his free hand he removed my *fichu*. He went into ecstasies at the sight of my breasts, which he found to be admirably white and firm. All the time my fingers were voluptuously squeezing his balls and he did not have time to throw me down upon the sofa, for he suddenly discharged.

'"Ah!" he exclaimed, "the next time we shall not waste time on preliminaries, but get straight to the point."

'He ordered his servant not to let any one enter, and the lesson he gave me had nothing whatsoever to do with sharps or flats, you may be sure. I removed my *fichu* completely and let him kiss and squeeze my breasts to his heart's content. We ate and drank, seated together on the sofa. I placed a little stool under my feet and trussed my skirts up to my knees. He admired my slender legs and his hand caressed my thighs, which he said were beautiful.

"My lover was determined to make love to me properly this time and he pressed me down upon the sofa, which was surrounded by mirrors. I regarded my reflected charms with pleasure and sought, by adopting a more lascivious posture, to render myself more desirable to my lover. At first the size of his prick caused me some discomfort, but that was soon transformed into a positive flood of joy in which we both drowned.

'After his ejaculation, the young man remained prostrate for a while and I endeavoured to restore his vigour. His prick was still lodged in my grotto and I could feel its power gradually returning. I invented a thousand little tricks to arouse him, nibbling, pinching and sucking his chest with my hot lips and my tongue seeking that of my lover. At last my efforts were rewarded and I felt my cunt filled once more with a powerful and vigorous prick. This time he put my legs on his shoulders and slapped and pinched my bottom with both of his hands. We came again and for two whole hours lay there annihilated.

'When I had recovered somewhat, I kissed him. I drank a glass of wine, then dressed myself, not without once more rousing my new lover. But this time I only wanted to kiss him.

'His prick was still bold and menacing and he said, "See the effect your charms have upon me, my pretty. Will you leave me thus without coming to my aid?"

'As he was speaking he guided my hand to his fearful tool. I am good-natured, I let myself be persuaded: I masturbated him delicately with one hand, while with the other I slapped his enormous buttocks. This time he was slow to discharge.

'When he had done so, I said, "You ought to be satisfied now; pray ask no more of me for I must take my leave."

'Then he showed me out by way of a little concealed stairway. I took a carriage and returned to my gentleman.

'The moment he set eyes upon me he began to laugh, staring at me all the while. I guessed the cause of his merriment, and blushed in spite of myself.

'He said, "You have been a very long time, Laura. The lesson would appear to have been an extremely strenuous one."

'"Yes," said I, "the piece was very pretty, and we played it several times."

'"Very good... Listen, Laura: I am not at all plagued by jealousy; you are at an age when the senses are violent. I know my friend: he is amorous and insistent. You were unable to resist him, admit it to me sincerely."

'"In faith, since you desire to know the truth, I shall not attempt to conceal it. I am naturally inclined to be frank and prefer not to dissimulate."

'And so I recounted to him the voluptuous scenes with which I have already acquainted you.

'"Very good, very good," said he, conducting my hand into his breeches. "Your naivety affords me the greatest pleasure and I would like us to repeat such a charming performance together."

'I could not refuse my favours to such an adorable man, especially as I was so indebted to him for his kindness to me. We went into his bedroom. He fetched a bottle of wine, drew the curtains to render the setting more mysterious and, after a small libation in honour of Bacchus, we turned our attention to love. I did exactly what I had done with the director: I removed my *fichu* and raised my skirts to my knees: In short, we followed the same path and experienced the self-same pleasures. However, when I endeavoured to reanimate his forces after the first act of intercourse, I did not find the same resources and we were obliged to let matters rest.

'"Lovely Laura," said he, "you are fertile in expedients, but you do not as yet possess sufficient power to combat exhausted Nature. I came well. I am no longer young and you cannot hope to experience the same pleasures with me as you have with my friend, who is less advanced in years than myself. Your age, your ardent temperament, demand vigorous attentions and, to be frank, with me you will only experience a pale shadow of the pleasures to which you are entitled. All I desire is that, although you may honour a more worthy object with your favours, you should continue to do the same for me. When it is necessary for me to leave Paris, I shall carry with me the memory of the sweet moments we have passed together."

'I could only respond by caresses to this speech which was at once frank and endearing.

'"The moment when we are forced to part will be a very painful one for me," I said. "I have the greatest affection for you. Your honesty has won my esteem."

'The next morning, he was quite insistent that I should keep my appointment with the director. The anticipation of pleasure lent me wings. This time, however, we went into his music-room where I had a proper lesson. When that was finished, we resumed our little games. I was quite enchanted by the new fashions of making love in which he instructed me.

'He showed me a new book of pictures dealing with the matter and said, "We must try all of them."

'Indeed not a day passed without him demonstrating how carefully he had studied the volume. We found some delightful ideas. It is my intention to send you this useful and important book. However I perceive that what started as a letter is turning into a positive treatise; nevertheless, encouraged by your last letter in which you requested me to conceal nothing from you, it is with the greatest pleasure that I am contributing to our correspondence. But if I am going to recount all my follies, you must tell me of yours with Bigprick, to whom by the way I send my affectionate greetings, as well as to your charming companions. Assure them that I shall always be, both for them and for you,

The tenderest of friends.

Laura de Fondeville.'

(Several weeks pass. Bigprick dies and is replaced by Father Ignatius. Laura appears at the Opera where she meets many admirers and becomes more and more promiscuous. At last, however, she realises that her aristocratic lovers are simply taking advantage of her. The unfortunate girl, now in a state of advanced pregnancy and almost penniless, agrees to the Abbess's suggestion that she should return to the convent. There Laura is delivered of her baby, her virginity is 'repaired' by the good sisters' skill in these matters, a reconciliation is effected with her parents and an advantageous marriage is arranged.)

Letter from Madame de Merville to the Reverend Father Ignatius.

'After two months of careful preparations, everything is at last ready for Laura's marriage: this Tuesday she will swear to her husband never to love anyone but him. Our remedy has done its work. In very truth, the most experienced libertine would take her for a maiden. Oh, how we shall laugh at the husband's expense! ... He has been here three times in order to pay his respects to the young lady and has been delighted with her. It is going to be a most advantageous union and I do not doubt that the affair will be concluded to the satisfaction of all concerned.

'The community is going to lose its most amiable hussies. Sister Ursula is also getting married, and we are going to administer the same remedy to her as we did to Laura: in other words, we are going to make a *new* woman of her. Thus you have only one more opportunity of enjoying the young lady. After that the box will be sealed and it shall only be opened to the desires of her legitimate husband.

'I have something to reproach you for: you took too little care, and I find myself in the same situation as Laura: in short, I am with child.

'Come to me in all haste and compensate me by redoubling your ardour. You have nothing to fear from me but my caresses.

'Farewell, until tonight.'

Letter from Laura to Madame de Merville.
'My dearest friend,
'The deed is done! I am now Monsieur de Blainville's wife. I played my rôle so well at the critical moment that he was completely hoodwinked and enchanted by his "triumph". I screamed so loudly that our neighbours must surely have heard me. He made three attempts and was positively bathed in his own sweat. Oh, what trouble I put him to! He would swear the most solemn oath that I am the most untried of

women. If only you could have seen my embarrassment, my blushes when he desired to put his tool in my
hand, how you would have laughed! One would have
sworn that never before in my life had I set eyes upon
such a thing. He admired my breasts, my thighs, my
buttocks. All received his homage, but in spite of all
my seductive charms, I was unable to obtain a second
audience. My word, if he thinks that a young person
with a temperament as ardent as mine is going to be
satisfied with just one enjoyment, he is greatly
mistaken, and I very much fear that my virtue will
succumb to the first agreeable man who tells me that
he loves me.

'And what a difference, dear abbess, between my
husband's prick and that of our dear lamented
Bigprick! *What* a difference!

'Imagine a poor little thing, all wrinkled, with an
insignificant head, dark, flaccid balls covered in sparse
grey hairs and you have a good likeness, although
perhaps still too flattering, of the present with which
my bridegroom honoured me. Am I, who have seen
such beautiful ones, likely to be content with that? As
yet I have not dared to reveal all the fire of my
temperament to him. I am waiting upon chance to
provide me with a favourable moment.

'During the wedding festivities, my husband's
nephew caught my eye: he seems as if he may be
eminently qualified for my purpose. But he is very
young and inexperienced and I fear that it is your
humble servant who shall be obliged to make the
advances.

'Yesterday, I was introduced into society by my
husband. The very first person I set eyes upon was the

gentleman with whom I lived in Paris, and who procured me for the director of the Opera. I blushed deeply. He noticed it, and drawing near to me, said softly in my ear, "Fear nothing, lovely Laura, I shall be the soul of discretion."

'How that reassured me! I learned that he had served in the army with my husband, and that his château was not far from ours.

'Whilst the other guests were gaming or conversing, we went into the garden. He enquired by what chance I found myself the wife of his friend. I told him everything binding him to secrecy by the most solemn promise. He laughed heartily and vowed that he would break off the marriage which he was about to enter into.

'"Oh," said he, "what a lesso   have learned today!"

'He entreated me with such good grace to accord him the same favours as before that, in very truth, I could not refuse him, and we made arrangements to meet again.

'It is my intention to try to ensnare the nephew as well: in fact, I want all the men in the district for my lovers.

'I shall come and pay my respects to you soon and tell you personally about all the exciting things which have happened to me and I hope to have the pleasure of taking part in one of your orgies again.

'Now there is no longer any reason for me to fear anything: my husband is no Argus, and a woman such as myself could outwit ten thousand of them.

'Adieu, my dear abbess, adieu, my tender friend, we shall see each other frequently and I shall kiss with delight your lovely breasts. The nuptial couch awaits me, but I am not counting on experiencing very lively pleasures there. You are more fortunate than me: Brother Hercules does not neglect you.

'I send you my love, and shall always be your friend.
Laura Blainville.'

Extract from a letter to Madame de Merville from Laura.

'A miracle has occurred, my dear abbess! A miracle! My elderly husband, like some new Tithonus has become young again in his Aurora's arms: last night was more abundant in pleasures than I had dared to hope it would be. Nature caused him to make an extra effort in my behalf, and he distinguished himself no less than three times. He was delighted with my little tricks and they were marvellously effective. My husband left me this morning to go to a place some ten leagues distant. He will stay there for three days to settle some family matters.

'I did not remain a widow long: my former lover, my gentleman from Paris, came to keep me company. I acquainted him with my good fortune, telling him that my lord and master had performed his conjugal duty with honour and during that time I had quite forgotten his sixty years. When this conversation took place, we were in my bedchamber, standing close to the bed.

'He looked at it and said, "This then is the throne of your pleasures? How I envy your husband!"

'"What are you complaining about?"' I said, "did you not, before him, taste those pleasures which you now seem to regret?"

'He said nothing but simply placed his hand upon

one of my breasts. Far from repulsing him, I pressed it closer to me. Emboldened by this gesture, he pushed me down upon the bed and pulled up my skirts; his burning lips kissed every part of my body.

'Once he had feasted his eyes upon my charms, he threw himself on me. I wound my legs tightly about him and wriggled my arse in perfect timing with his efforts. We both attained the moment of supreme enjoyment together. He wanted me to spend the night with him, but I would not agree to his request. It is my intention to be prudent in all my actions...'

Volume Two

CHAPTER I

WHAT THE NUNS NEEDED

CELIBACY, as it is enjoined in the Roman Church, is not only unwise as being opposed to nature, but it is provocative of the very evils that it is intended to banish and destroy.

Some individuals may have a spiritual gift in that way, but in the greater number of cases, young people, before they understand their nature or themselves, are induced, by reason of their emotional feelings being stirred up and directed by the Church, to take upon themselves vows which, when too late, they find it utterly impossible to carry out.

These emotional feelings are evanescent in their character, and are easily overpowered, either by the strong natural instinct of propagation, which becomes developed in most people as they grow to maturity, or when they are brought into contact with temptations of a lascivious tendency. And these very temptations, strange to say, they are sure to meet with sooner or later in the confessional.

There are abundant historical proofs of the truth of these statements in every country where that form of religion has prevailed; and nowhere more than in Italy, its great centre, and also among the ecclesiastics and religious bodies which there abound.

The following story, the facts of which are well authenticated, affords an interesting and amusing illustration.

There was, in the suburbs of a northern city, a handsome building, with well-kept gardens and grounds. This house was occupied by a sisterhood of nuns under the care of a Mother Abbess. She was a titled lady by birth, and in her younger days had been married to an old man. She was naturally of a voluptuous disposition, and not being satisfied by her husband, consoled herself in the arms of a young noble of their acquaintance. On one occasion they were surprised in the very act by her husband. The aged man made a furious onslaught on her gallant. In defending himself the younger man unfortunately ran him through with his rapier. The affair caused such scandal, and she, to make the best amend she could, took the veil, and retired into a convent. She had a brother, a Bishop; and by his influence and her own energy and talents, she was gradually promoted, until now, in her thirty-fifth year, she was made a Mother Abbess. She had under her charge twenty-four nuns, chiefly of her own selection. They were all good-looking young women, with the exception of four, who, being elderly, were chosen as examples of sanctity and strict adherence to convent rules and discipline.

The grounds and gardens were kept in order by an old man who slept outside the Convent bounds. He had managed to scrape together a little money, and at the time of our story felt that his years unfitted him for his work; and so he resolved to resign his post, and pass the remainder of his days in quiet and ease.

The position was a good and lucrative one, and was sought after by many. Among others was a nephew of the old gardener's named Tasso, who wished to obtain it. He possessed good qualifications for the post, as he had been trained on the property of a nobleman in the South, but he was a comparative stranger in the district in which the Convent was situated. He requested his uncle to recommend him, but the old man assured him that it would be of no use, for the objection would be that he was young, well-made, and altogether too good-looking; and he knew that the Mother Abbess, who prided herself on the reputation for sanctity which the Convent had acquired, would in all probability decline to engage anyone but a man, tolerably old, and not so prepossessing in appearance.

"And she is right," he added, "for among the holy Sisters are some young women that seem to me to be ready for almost any sort of mischief, – and from the way I have seen them sporting with one another, when they thought they were un-observed, I think that under their sober vestal garb they have as skittish natures as any girls I have ever seen."

This only made young Tasso all the more eager; for, like the war horse, he smelled the battle from afar, and his blood warmed for the fray.

"Well, uncle," he replied. "Don't oppose me. Give me your consent, and let me endeavour by my own wits to induce the Mother Abbess to give me at least a fair trial."

Now Tasso was not only a young man of enter-prise, but he was also singularly intelligent and wise in his generation. With great craft he determined to represent himself as being deaf and dumb, and to assume a heavy and stolid appearance. By what arts he persuaded his uncle to give him the desired recommendation, and by what means he obtained the old man's promise of secrecy, history does not tell us. We only know that when he went to the Mother Abbess with a note of introduction from his uncle, he had artfully disguised as much as possible his good looks and youthful appearance, and he communicated with her by means of a slate which he carried with him, and on which she wrote her questions to him and he replied in fairly legible writing.

She was pleased with the recommendations he had, and pitied his infirmities, but was rather repelled by his uncouth manner and unkempt hair; but on considering the matter she thought that after all, his not being very inviting in appearance, and especially his being deaf and dumb, might be of great advantage, as it would certainly render him less communicative either inside or outside the Convent.

So she finally engaged him on a month's trial.

Upon the following day Tasso entered on his duties. He knew his business well, and apparently thought of nothing else.

Now it was the custom of the Sisters to take exercise at certain hours in the Convent grounds. They looked at him in a friendly way, and some of them made bold to speak a few kind words. But to these advances he would always reply by a shake of his head, at the same time pointing to his ears and lips. Then he would hold out his slate, – which, when not in use, he carried in his pocket, – for them to write any commands they wished to give. But the Mother Abbess, ever on the watch, soon saw that he made no attempt to communicate with them of his own accord; and convinced that this was the right man for the place at last, and relying on his simplicity, she relaxed her vigilance, and gave her attention to more pressing duties.

After a while, the Sisters realized that he was deaf and dumb, and seemed to forget his presence, talking to one another just as if he was not there at all.

They thought him stupid as well as deaf, but all the while he kept his eyes open and his ears attentive, so that nothing passed unnoticed that came within their reach. Soon he had learned the names of all the Sisters, and could recognize them by their voices.

Two of the younger nuns, Lucia and Robina, seemed to have taken a fancy to him, for they often walked near where he was at work, and always gave him a smile as they passed.

There were many rustic seats scattered about, in shady spots, and these were much used by the nuns in their hours of recreation.

Whenever Tasso was occupied near any of these seats, the Sisters Lucia and Robina were sure to come and sit there and watch him, while they talked or worked at their embroidery.

Their usual conversation was of convent matters, such as their work or their teaching, – for nearly all the nuns took part in the instruction of the young ladies who attended the Convent School.

But on one occasion they commenced to talk of their Confessors. Lucia declared that she liked Father Joachim best, for he seemed to take more interest in the Convent.

"Only," she added, "He does ask such bothering questions."

"What kind of questions?" asked Robina, with a smile.

"Why, Sister! Don't you know we're not allowed to tell anything outside the confessional of what takes place within? However, you and I are such friends that we may disregard these hard rules when we are talking confidentially together, – may we not?"

"Yes, certainly. Go on."

Here Tasso, who appeared to be very busy,

moved a little nearer, and worked noiselessly.

"Well, the other night I had a queer dream. I had been looking, during the day, at a fine picture of St. Martin, painted by Titian; and when I was asleep, I thought that I saw him coming towards me with no clothing on at all, and Oh! he looked so very beautiful. As he advanced, I saw something between his legs, though I cannot tell you what it was like. But while I was looking at it, he came up and lay down over me. And I thought I felt his body pressing mine in a most delightful way, and I got a delicious feeling in the corresponding part of myself. Then I suddenly awoke, and – what do you think? I had one of my fingers pushed right up into myself, and I could not stop rubbing it in and out until I became all wet. Since then I have put my hand there several times, and it always gives me great pleasure. Now, of course, I know this is all very wrong, and I had to confess it to the priest."

"And what were his bothering questions?"

"Oh! He made me describe exactly where my finger was. I had to tell him, it was in my woman's slit, between the soft lips that we have there. Then he asked what was it I saw between St. Martin's legs, and if I knew what it was for? I felt annoyed at such a question, and said, 'How could I tell? I suppose it was what all men have there.'

"Then he asked, for these holy Fathers never seem to feel abashed, if I ever thought about a man's part, and whether I had any longing to see it, and know what it was like?

"I confessed that I had felt some curiosity about it, but that I always tried to banish such thoughts from my mind.

"He said that it was quite right, that such thoughts were natural to both men and women, and all that was required was not to allow them to dwell in the mind. Then he told me to come to him soon again, and tell him all my thoughts, and that he would hear my confession in the Mother Abbess' private room. Since then I have been thinking more than ever about these very things; and do you know, Robina, I have quite a longing to know what a man's thing is like? Haven't you?"

"Sometimes, dear. But it is very likely that Father Joachim may gratify your longing himself. I fancy he has some such intention in his mind, and that's why he said he would hear your confession in the Mother Abbess' private room. Meantime, let me tell you that these lusty priests use the confessional as a means of gratifying their own sensual desires. They know that we poor nuns are quite in their power, and they dearly love to make us tell them every secret thought which naturally comes

265

into our minds as women, with regard to the other sex. And more than that, they often suggest the thoughts themselves, and when we are at a loss, they supply the words too. It does seem strange to me, if these things are as wicked as they declare in their public teaching, why they encourage them so directly in their secret ministrations in the confessional. Now I'll tell you, Lucia, what I shall propose: Let us be true to one another; and consult together to get all the fun we can out of these holy Fathers, and at the same time enjoy any little pleasure that comes in our way, for indeed ours is a hard lot."

"I quite agree with you, dear Robina," said Lucia, "and gladly accept your proposal, for I too am heartily sick of the tiresome round of these vigils, fasts, prayers and penances, which instead of making us better, only drive us to something worse, as a mere matter of relief. We never see anything in the shape of a man, except these oily priests, with their sensual mouths and wicked-looking eyes. Somehow I don't trust them, and I can't abide them. Now there is some comfort in looking at this poor, honest, hard-working fellow, Tasso. And, Robina, have you noticed how well made he is? Look at his nicely-turned limbs!"

"You are right, Lucia," replied Robina.

"There is some satisfaction in looking at him. And indeed I was just thinking that, if we could see him as you saw St. Martin in your dream, we should behold a very satisfactory illustration of that special part which is most interesting to us as women. Is that what you were thinking of, you rogue?"

And looking at her with glittering eyes, she gave her a nudge with her elbow.

Lucia laughed merrily.

"Why not, my dear? Father Joachim says that such thoughts are only natural; and as we are forever shut off from the reality, it cannot be so very wrong for us to console ourselves with the thought."

"Quite so," replied Robina. "But let me tell you a notion which has come into my head, I don't know how. May we not try at least to turn our thought into reality? Could we not manage to induce Tasso in some way to gratify our curiosity? He is so simple that I am sure he would think nothing of showing all he has to us, if we could but make him feel that we would neither be frightened nor affronted, nor tell anyone. Now what do you think of that notion, Lucia?"

"Capital, dear! But how can it be brought about?"

"I'll tell you one way that we might obtain our

object even without his knowledge. I noticed yesterday when one of the Sisters brought him a glass of our light wine as a reward for moving her rose-trees so nicely, that after he drank it, he stole away among the laurels near our Little-house, (a name they had for a place of convenience in a corner of the grounds,) and I fancy he went there to make water. Now it occurs to me that if one of us got him some drink this hot day, and the other went to hide in the Little-house, she would have a chance of getting a view of that part of him which we would both like to see, and then she could tell the other all that occurred."

"You are very clever, Sister Robina," replied Lucia, "and you know many things of which I am ignorant. I cordially approve of your plan, and if you will place yourself in ambush in the Little-house, I will run for the drink. – But mind! You must describe to me afterwards everything you have seen, with the greatest precision."

"All right! Let us go away together, and I will steal round to the hiding-place without his seeing me."

Tasso fairly grinned with delight. His crafty device was already bearing fruit, and his manly organ bounded with exultation at the thought of anticipated triumph.

Lucia quickly reappeared with a cup brimming with love-inspiring drink. He took it from her hands with a grateful nod, and immediately drank it off. On receiving the cup again, she turned away to bring it back to the house. Tasso at once made off to the corner indicated, and having placed himself in full view before the door, which was pierced with holes for the purpose of ventilation, he took out his middle limb, and exhibited its full length and even the large appendages beneath. It was a splendid specimen of a flesh-coloured prick, large and strong, in the full flush of youthful power and beauty. Holding it in his hand, he made his water shoot out before him in a way that could not fail to be most interesting to a female observer. Then he drew down the soft white skin so as to uncover all the glowing head, now of a bright rosy tint. He shook it from side to side until the last amber drop had fallen, and then, as if yielding to some sudden impulse, he began to imitate the common fucking motion by vigorously working his posteriors and making his prick pass swiftly backwards and forwards through his hands.

The hidden watcher eyes it with the same regard a famished wolf has for a tempting morsel. Her bosoms heave and swell like the ocean billows scurrying before the storm. In vain she grasps them with her hands. In vain she tries to calm the rapid tumultuous beating of her heart. Her breath comes quickly. It is frequently interrupted by the soft sighs which escape her. Something within her seems to jump, and then a flame devours her. Instinctively one hand strays from throbbing bosom down to her robe. The black garb is quickly drawn up, and her hand touches the mossy charms beneath. Passion's hottest fires are already flaming furiously. Yonder, in the thicket, is the only solace that will afford her relief. Ah! If she only had it in her grasp! A rosy mist floats before her eyes. In its very midst, surrounded by a golden halo, she sees the gardener's own tool, – the glorious badge of manhood that Tasso alone possesses. Its ruby head turns toward her. Look! It quivers with passion. A few pearly drops ooze from it, glitter in the sunlight, and fall. Then the vision fades from her view.

For, with a faint sigh of satisfaction, Tasso has pushed it in under cover again, and has buttoned up his trousers. And the crunch of gravel under his feet a moment later informs the passionate girl that Tasso is returning to his work.

CHAPTER II
HOW THEY OBTAINED IT

TASSO'S great hope was that the two Sisters would return to their seat, and favour him a little more by their delightful conversation. Nor was he disappointed. The Sisters quickly reappeared, and bringing with them their embroidery, sat down in the seat they had occupied before.

Tasso was conscious that they now regarded him with peculiar interest, and that their eyes looked as if they were trying to penetrate that portion of his attire. He therefore pushed it out and made it prominent as much as he could.

Lucia was speaking.

"Well, Robina, you certainly had a grand success. How I envy you! It must have been delightful to watch him, when he thought he was all alone, first piddling and then actually playing

271

with his thing! But now, tell me, like a good dear, exactly what it was like: its size, its colour, and above, all, tell me its shape."

"You must try and see it yourself, my dear," replied Robina, "for it is not an easy thing to describe. It seemed about eight inches long, and nearly as thick as your wrist, but quite round. It is covered with a soft white skin which slips easily up and down. When he pulled this skin back, the top stood up like a large round head, shelving to a point, and of a purplish red colour. It was that which attracted me most, and, my dear, it had a most wonderful effect on myself. My hairy slit began to thrill and to throb in such a way that, for the life of me, I could not help pulling up my dress and rubbing it with my hand. And it grew hotter and hotter, until a warm flow came, and gave me relief."

"What a delightful time you must have had, Robina," commented Lucia. "Do you know your telling me all this has made mine frightfully hot, too?" And she twisted about, rubbing her bottom on the seat. "How I wish Tasso was not watching us. I would ask you to put your kind hand on my slit and afford me a little of the same pleasure."

Robina laughed.

"I fancy he's not thinking of us at all. He is too

272

dull to have any notions of that kind. Stand up, dear, as if you were pulling some buds from the branch overhanging us, and I will slip my hand up from behind, so that he can see nothing. Now, do you like that, dear?"

"Oh! Your fingers are giving me great pleasure!" replied the excited Lucia. "There! That's the place! – Push it up! – Oh! Wouldn't it be nice to have Tasso's delightful thing poking me there! – You said, Robina, that was Nature's intention, and that the mutual touch of our differently formed parts gives the greatest satisfaction. What fools we were to give it up!"

"What a child you are, Lucia! The holy Fathers will teach you that you may enjoy it now more than ever, and without doing anything wrong, either, only it must be done with them alone."

"Now! Oh! Now, Robina! – Push your finger up! As far as you can! How I long for Tasso's dear thing! – Oh! Oh! – That will do!"

And she sat down, and leaned her head against Robina for support.

It will be easily understood what an overpowering effect this scene had on poor Tasso. His sturdy prick, glowing with youthful vigour, seemed to be trying to break its covering and burst into open view.

The unsuspecting talk of the two Sisters almost maddened him. He felt that if he could only present his "dear thing," as they called it, openly before them, he might obtain from one or the other, or from perhaps both, the sweet favour he desired.

In this mood he gradually worked up close to them, and slyly unbuttoned his clothes down the front.

He restrained himself, however, for the present, that he might learn something more from the Sisters, who went on talking.

"But Robina, what shall we do about confessing this touching of ourselves and one another to the priests? If we conceal it, our confession is incomplete and sinful, as they tell us we ought to make a full avowal of all our faults and shortcomings. You know how they are always urging this upon us as a sacred duty. And if we give him the slightest hint, Father Joachim will be sure to worm out from us all about Tasso, and that might do him much harm, and cause him to be sent away, – and we too may be separated, and not allowed to walk with one another."

"Quite true, Lucia. We must do all we can to guard against these two evils. And there really is no way but to keep the whole matter a secret between ourselves. I, for my part, won't let that press upon my conscience, as I now know that there is so much humbug and deceit about the confessional that I have no faith in it as a religious duty at all."

"I am with you again, Robina," replied Lucia. "It would be an awful wrong to injure poor Tasso, who is quite innocent; and if you and I were separated, – why, I should die, and that would be the end of it."

Tasso was greatly pleased at hearing this, for his mind was now satisfied that so far as these two Sisters were concerned, he had no cause to dread exposure and its certain consequences.

"Well, Lucia, dear, we'll try to prevent that, at all events. We shall have to go to the priest, but we must carefully avoid all reference to anyone but ourselves. It will be great fun, I am sure, to confess our looking at and petting our own slits. We can tell him our dreams also. That will sufficiently please him, and perhaps draw him on to commit himself with us, and then he will have to keep quiet for his own sake."

And they both laughed at the thought.

Just then, a little accident happened to Tasso which gave a sudden turn to their conversation. As he was bending at his work, his foot slipped, and he rolled over on his back. This motion, in the most natural way, set his prick free, and it started out, looking very stiff and inflamed.

He quickly jumped up, and looking at his naked prick with stupid amazement, began to utter uncouth sounds, like an ordinary donkey: "Hoo! Awe!" And he made some ineffectual attempts to push it back into its place.

"There! Lucia," cried Robina. "Your wish is granted. This poor simple fellow has accidentally given you the view for which you were longing. Don't you admire it?"

"Yes! – But what should we do, Robina, if any of the Sisters were to come up now? What a hubbub there would be! – But see! – I declare, he can't get it back."

"Well, go and help him, Lucia. Make haste, and I will keep a lookout."

Lucia's eyes were intently fastened on the interesting object. Her face was flushed, and she looked altogether extremely excited. She had no time however, for reflection. So she jumped up, as her friend advised, went to Tasso, and tried to help to get his rebellious tool back into its hiding-place.

Taking advantage of his apparent simplicity, and wishing to expedite matters, she took hold of his prick with her hand.

But Oh! How the touch of that piece of animated flesh thrilled her! It felt so warm and soft, yet so firm and strong! She could neither bend it, nor push it back. And the more she made the effort, the more strongly did it resist and stand out.

"Oh! dear! Oh! dear! What shall I do, Robina? It won't go back for me!"

Robina laughed until the tears ran down her cheeks.

"Anyway, take him along," she replied. "Bring him into the summer-house."

This happened to be conveniently near, and was well screened by bushes. Lucia with a smile, pointed it out to Tasso, and still holding his prick, gently drew him on.

Tasso, putting on a most innocent look, went readily with her, and Robina followed in the rear.

As they entered the leafy shade, she said: "Now, Lucia, you have him all to yourself. If you don't succeed in getting him to do every thing you want, you are a less clever girl than I take you to be. If all else fails, just show him your mossy nest, and that will draw him as surely as a magnet attracts a piece of iron. Meantime I'll keep a sharp lookout here at the door."

But, in very truth, Tasso did not need much drawing. His prick was throbbing with desire. It was fairly burning to get into the folds of her soft recess. Yet he checked himself, in order to see what she would do.

She led him on until she backed against the inner seat. Then she sat down, and he remained standing before her. In this position his prick was now close to her face. She rubbed it softly between her hands, and then kissed its glowing head. She moved it over her nose and cheeks, sniffing up with delight the peculiar odour which exhaled from it.

Every time she brought it to her lips, Tasso pushed it gently against her mouth. Her lips gradually opened, and the prick seemed to pop in of its own accord. He felt her pliant tongue playing over its head, and twining round its indented neck. The sensation was so delicious that he could not help uttering a deep guttural "Ugh!" and pressing up against her.

She yielded to his pressure, and very soon he had her reclining on her back flat on the seat. Then bending over her he quickly drew up her nun's robes, and lifting her legs he pressed her thighs down on her body in such a way as to expose the whole of her beautiful bottom, and give him a full view of her delicious love chink, surrounded with luxuriant hair. Oh! How it seemed to pout out with a most unspeakable delight! He took his prick in his hand, and rubbed its glowing head between the soft moist lips.

This action proved just as pleasant to her as it

was delightful to him. She pushed upwards to meet him, and called too her friend:

"Look! Robina! There has been no failure, – he's just a-going to do it. Pity you could not come and watch it going in! Oh! It does feel nice! – Oh! So nice!"

"Ha! Ha! My dear," laughed Robina, "you will have to suffer a little before you know how really nice it is!"

Tasso now began to push in good earnest, and Lucia winced not a little as she felt the sharp pain, caused by the head of his huge prick forcing its way through the tight embrace of her vagina, for she was a true virgin, and her hymen had never been ruptured. However, she bore it bravely, especially as she knew her friend was watching.

"Robina," she called, to show her indifference to the pain, "I wish you would go behind and give him a shove, to make him push harder."

But just as she spoke, the obstructing hymen suddenly gave way, and his fine prick rushed up and filled all the inside of her cunt, and his hard balls flapped up against her bottom.

"Ah!" she cried, as she felt the inward rush of the vigorous tool. "Now it's all over! He's got it all in! – Well, it wasn't so bad after all. And now it feels delicious! – How nicely he makes it move in and out. – Can you see it, Robina?" she asked, as she noticed her friend stooping behind Tasso, and looking up between his legs.

"Yes, dear Lucia. I see your pretty slit sucking in his big tool, and I feel his two balls gathered up tightly in their bag. He certainly is no fool at this kind of work. I am sure he is just going to spurt his seed into you. – There! – Tell me, do you like it?"

"Oh! Yes! It feels grand! – He's shedding such a lot into me! And more is coming, too! It is the nicest thing I have ever felt!"

And throwing her arms about him she hugged him with all her might.

Presently he drew his prick out of her warm sheath. It was slightly tinged with blood, – the token of his victory and her pain. Robina carefully wiped it with her handkerchief, and coaxed him to sit down between them on the seat. Then they made signs to him to produce his slate.

Lucia wrote:

"Dear Tasso. I greatly enjoyed what you did to me. Have you any name for it, that I may know what to ask for when I want it again?"

He smiled when he read the question, and then wrote a reply.

"It is called fucking."

Then he handed her the slate.

"Doing this is called fucking," she said to Robina.

Then pointing to his prick, which was beginning to stand again, in all the pride of youthful vigour, she wrote:

"What is the name of this?"

"It is called a 'prick' and yours is a 'cunt'," he wrote, "and they are made for one another."

Lucia laughed when she read it.

"Why, Robina," she cried, "we are getting a grand lesson. His thing is a prick and our slits are cunts; but he need not have told us that they are made for one another, for all the world knows that. What a pity he can't talk! I would so much like to hear him speak of his prick and our cunts. But it is well that he can write about them."

Then she took the slate and wrote:

"Your prick is getting quite large and stiff again. Would you like to fuck Sister Robina?"

Tasso grinned.

"Do you know what I have just written?" said Lucia, turning to Robina. "I have asked him if he would like to fuck you?"

"Oh! You horrid girl!" retorted Robina. "Of course he will say he would. Men always love a change of cunts. I suppose we must use that word now when talking to each other."

Tasso's delight was almost insupportable. He longed to use his tongue, and give audible expression to his joy. But that would have spoiled everything. So he resolved to persevere with his role, and wrote:

"If Sister Robina will follow your kind example, and grant me the same favour, it will call forth the everlasting gratitude of poor dumb Tasso."

"Why, he has written quite a nice little speech, Robina," said Lucia, handing her the slate.

"He writes a fairly good hand, too," smilingly remarked Robina; and then handing back the slate, said, "Tell him to stand up, and let me kiss his prick as you did."

Lucia wrote accordingly:

"Stand up, Tasso, and let her kiss your prick first, and then you can fuck her cunt just as much as you like."

Tasso at once complied. He stood before Robina, and pushed between her knees so as to place his prick more conveniently for her eager inspection and caresses.

Taking it tenderly in her hands, she felt it all over, as if measuring its size and power to give pleasure. Then she turned her attention to the heavy bags which held his large stones, and pushed her fingers back even as far as the aperture behind.

Tasso repaid the caresses she gave him by bending to one side, and thrusting his hand up between her warm thighs. He grasped the fat lips of her cunt, and rubbed the hot clitoris which jutted out between them. Then, as they both became eager for the sweet consummation to which these thrilling touches led, he gently pushed her back. She yielded readily enough, for her cunt was already moist with the expectation of taking in the delicious morsel she held in her hands. She allowed him to uncover all her hidden charms, and spread her thighs to their utmost extent. But just as she felt him inserting his fiery tool, she called to Lucia, who, though standing at the door, was intently watching Tasso's interesting operation.

"Dear Lucia, keep a strict watch! It would be an awful thing if anyone caught us here!"

"Don't be afraid," replied Lucia. "I'll keep a good lookout. There's no one about now, and I only take a peep now and then to see how you and Tasso are enjoying yourselves. I love to watch you. I was just thinking, that next to being fucked one's self, there is nothing like watching another going through it. I never saw your cunt look so well as it did just now, when Tasso opened the lips, and rubbed the head of his prick inside the rosy folds.

And now he has got it all in. It is most delightful to watch it slipping in and out. But how is it that he does not seem to hurt you as he did me? For I notice that he got in quite easily, and you kept hugging him closely all the time! – Oh! How nice it must have felt!"

And Lucia pressed her hands between her own legs, and jerked her bottom backwards and forwards.

"My! How you talk, Lucia! But anyway, keep a good lookout, and you may watch me between times. I don't mind your seeing how much we are enjoying ourselves. Poor Tasso can't hear me, or I would tell him how well pleased I am. I am sure the squeezing of my cunt is making him feel that already."

She breathes heavily, and heaves her bottom up convulsively to meet his rapid thrusts.

"You might put your hand on us now, Lucia, if you like. – He's just finishing. – Oh! It's grand!"

And all her muscles relaxed as she reclined back, and Tasso lay panting on her belly.

Lucia sat down by them, and leaned over Tasso, squeezing her thighs together, for she felt her own fount of pleasure in the flow.

After a moment's rest, Tasso got up, shook himself, and having arranged his clothes, wrote on his slate:

"Dear kind ladies: You have made poor dumb Tasso very happy. Let me now thank you and return to my work, lest any harm should happen."

He then bowed himself out, and disappeared among the laurels.

285

CHAPTER III.

HOW ROBINA ENJOYED IT

ON THE following day, to Tasso's great delight, the two young nuns again sat near him, though in a different part of the grounds.

The sight of him naturally made them think of their late pleasures, and they began to talk of how and when they might safely meet him again in the summer-house.

Having been now fairly launched on the sea of pleasure, they felt irresistibly impelled to go on. They knew that they were running a tremendous risk, but the temptation was so great that they were ready to brave all the consequences.

So, watching their opportunity, they told Tasso on his slate that, if possible, they would come out that evening during the half hour allowed the nuns for private devotion before the usual service. It was his time for quitting work, putting away his tools, and retiring for the night, and the garden was then generally empty.

Lucia then reminded her friend that she had promised to tell her how it was that she felt no smart or pain when Tasso pushed his prick into her cunt.

"My dear Lucia," began Robina, "I think I may tell you, now that we understand one another, and have shaken off our terror of the confessional. Before I came here, I had for my Confessor a priest with a great appearance of sanctity; but, as I found to my cost, it was only a cloak to hide his real nature. He was of a strong lustful temperament. Why, dear, he actually forced me in the room of the Mother Superior, where he heard my confession. I often think he had me there with an evil design which the Superior not only had connived at, but helped to carry out. And strange to say, my confessions furnished him with the occasion he desired.

"I had to confess what arose out of a curious circumstance, – something like your dream. It happened thus:

"The evening before making my first confession after joining the Sisterhood of M——, I obtained permission to take a solitary walk of meditation in a field belonging to the Convent. Feeling tired, I sat down by the boundary hedge to rest. I had my Manual with me, and oddly enough was reading that part of the preparation for confession where the sins against chastity are referred to, and we are directed to examine our own conscience, and are asked if we have looked at indecent pictures, or touched either ourselves or others immodestly, etc., when I heard the voices of a man and a woman on the other side of the hedge.

"As they came up, the man said: 'See! What a fine sheltered spot! – Just what we were looking for!'

"Then they sat down and settled themselves on the grass. From their talk, they must have at once commenced playing with each other's private parts. They used such terms as 'prick,' and 'cunt,' and 'fucking,' which were then new to me. But I was at no loss to understand their meaning, from their talk, and the manner in which the words were applied.

"The man said: 'Pull up your petticoats as high as you can, and open your legs, so as to give me a full view of your pretty brown-haired cunt! – That's a dear! Oh! How luscious it looks! So hot and so moist! So velvety inside!'

"'I am glad you like it!' she replied. 'But don't keep it waiting too long! Put in your prick and fuck me!'

"I know it was a very wicked thing to do, to remain there, listening to all this, but my curiosity was so great that I could not tear myself away.

"I then heard sounds, as if they were struggling or working together, and then she spoke in a gasping voice.

"'Oh! I feel it up – ever so far!' she said. 'Push! My darling! – Push!'

"And then I heard their bellies smack together.

"'Oh! Oh!' she cried. 'Your dear prick is filling my cunt with the most unspeakable delight!'

"He panted loudly as she continued. 'Oh! My love! That is so nice!'

"I listened to this with breathless interest, and the effect upon myself was overpowering. Without thinking of what I was doing, I put my hand on my affair, and rubbed it until I obtained relief. And while I was so occupied, they departed.

"This touching and rubbing I later confessed to the priest, and then I had to tell him the occasion and the circumstances, and had to repeat every word which I heard used. But I objected to saying such names, on the score of decency. To this he replied that there was no such a thing as indecency in the confessional, for it was a holy place, and it imparted a holy character to everything that was said and done at that time. So he made me say 'prick,' over and over again, and then asked me what I supposed it was.

"I replied that it seemed to me to be the name for the private part of a man, and that the other word I had heard, 'cunt,' was the corresponding part of the woman, and that 'fucking' was the joining of them together, which Nature made us understand was a very pleasant thing.

"Then he made me describe the excitement I felt in my own cunt during the time I was engaged in listening to the man and woman who were fucking.

"And as if this were not enough, he told me he wanted to know exactly how I put my hand on my cunt, and to let him see me do it.

"This, however, I at first flatly refused to do. My obstinacy angered him; for his face, which had been very red before, now grew purple, and his eyes looked as if they were starting out of his head.

"He caught me roughly by the arm. – I was kneeling by his side, you know. – He shook me as he said:

"'Daughter, you have not yet learned the first of all virtues, – obedience. Stand up!'

"I did so.

" 'Now lift up your skirts and place your hand just as you have been describing it to me!'

"I jerked out the word 'Never!' through my compressed lips.

"He arose from the chair in which he had been sitting, and pushed me violently towards a sofa at the side of the room. He forced me down upon this, and then began pulling up my clothes.

" 'How dare you!' I said, in a very angry voice. 'If you were ten times a priest, I would not suffer you to take such liberties with me! Let me up, or I will cry out!'

"At this very moment, the Mother Superior walked in and came up, looking exceedingly vexed.

" 'Sister Robina! How can you behave in this unseemly manner? I am very sorry to find that I have such a refractory nun under my charge. Don't you know that you must obey this holy Father in all things?'

" 'But I won't obey him,' I retorted, 'when he wants me to do something that I believe to be wrong.'

" 'There you make a mistake,' was her reply. 'You may be sure that what a priest in the confessional requires you to do is always necessary and right. And even though the thought may be disagreeable to you, yet you are bound to submit.'

"'I won't!' I declared.

"'You shall!' she retorted, catching me by the shoulders, and pushing me over.

"I struggled with her, while the priest at the same time held my legs with one of his strong hands, and pulled up my clothes with the other.

"Between them both, I was powerless, and began to cry as I said:

"'You are making me break my vows!'

"'Not in the least, you silly girl. Don't you know he is under a vow as well as you are? And two vows, like two negatives, nullify one another. You are each only prevented from going with others, and your submission will be a praise-worthy act, for it will afford both him and yourself a necessary relief. Come, now! Show us that you understand the matter aright. Open your thighs, and let him see all that you have there. Nature meant that to be used, and in this manner; and with my sanction you can do so without blame. I heard what you just confessed, and approve of your using all those terms when engaged here with the holy Father.'

"But her fine sophistry did not quiet me. I still opposed them in every way I could.

"By this time the priest had forcibly drawn up

my skirts, and all my thighs, belly and bottom were exposed before him. He had even lifted my legs as well, and as I kicked them in the air in my struggles to get free, he pinched my naked bottom in the most savage manner, maddening me with pain, and making me jerk about in a manner that added greatly to his delight. I saw that his eyes were fixed upon my cunt, which I felt opening at every bound. He kept my legs wide apart, but I still struggled so hard that he was not able to place his hands upon my slit.

"Vexed at what she termed my silly obstinacy, the Mother Superior reprimanded me severely.

" 'You stupid thing!' she exclaimed. 'Keep quiet. Let him look at that saucy impudent cunt of yours. He shall do anything with it that he likes! – Now, Father Angelo, take your prick and thrust it well in! – It will be a good punishment, and only serve her right. – But show it to her first, that she may get the full benefit of the sight before she feels your hard firm thrusts.'

" 'He at once complied; and, taking out his prick, he stood up close to me. It was the first man's prick I had ever seen, and it terrified me by its extreme length, and its huge red head. All at once, he pushed it towards my face.

" 'Oh! Fie!' I cried. 'Take the monstrous thing away. – It is horrible!'

"And I shut my eyes.

"But the Mother Superior and the priest only laughed at me.

"'What a fool you are!' she exclaimed.

"And taking the prick in her hand, she rubbed it over my face, made it pass under my nose, and about my mouth. In vain I tried to turn from it. She always managed to keep the firm warm thing playing around my face, until it nearly set me wild. And yet not altogether with anger, for strange to say, though I certainly disliked the man, still the touch of his prick and its peculiar smell had an effect on me which I could not resist. I began to feel a kind of pleasure in having my cunt exposed to his view, and felt a thrill of delight run through my veins when he put his hand on my slit and caressed the lips and tickled the clitoris.

"Noticing this, the Mother Superior removed the charger, and addressing the priest, said:

"'Now, Father, you may try her. She seems tired out, or perhaps, – and I hope it is so, – she is coming to a better mind.'

"Then she put her hand softly under my chin, turned up my mouth and kissed me.

"'Come, Sister,' she said. 'Take my advice. Submit gracefully, and it will be all the better for you. Know then, that I am fully resolved that you

hall not leave this room until you have been well
ucked.'

"Father Angelo then drew me to the end of the
ofa, until my bottom rested on the very edge. He
hen fixed himself between my thighs, and spread-
ng open the lips of my cunt with his fingers, while
ie pressed the head of his big red tool firmly
igainst the entrance.

"Madame knelt on the floor beside us, and
ucking up my clothes as high as she could,
watched the operation.

"He pushed gently at first, then harder and
harder, and hurt me considerably. I moaned with
the pain, but I did not resist, for I now saw it was of
no use, and I began to be on fire, and wish his tool
was safely lodged inside.

"The Mother Superior now leaned over me and
opening my bodice, drew up my breasts, and
caressed the exposed bubbies with her hands.

"Then turning to him, she said, 'Can't you get
in? Is it too tight? – Just wet her cunt and your
prick, and you will find it easier.'

"He took away his prick, and in a moment I felt
his tongue moving around the inside of my cunt,
his lips sucking my clitoris.

"This had a strangely soothing and most
delightful effect, and I smiled with pleasure.

"'Ah! – You like that!' she said. 'You like t•
have your cunt licked and your clitoris sucked, d•
you? Well, you won't have the full pleasure until h•
gets his prick in, and drives it all the way up.'

"Meanwhile the priest was moistening his prick
with spittle, and again placed it between the lips o•
my anxious slit. This time I did not shrink from hi•
attack at all, but spread my thighs as widely apart a•
I could.

"'Now, Father, push,' she cried; and putting
her hand down, she grasped and squeezed my
clitoris.

"I could feel the great hard head forcing its way
in. You know now, Lucia, what a strange sensation
of mingled pain and pleasure a woman experiences
the first time a man's prick is driven into her cunt–"

"Shall I ever forget?" responded Lucia, with
animation. "But in my case, the pain was only for a
moment, for soon it was completely overbalanced
by the pleasure."

"Yes; so I was glad to see," responded Robina.
"But Tasso's prick is not by any means as thick as
that of Father Angelo."

Poor Tasso's jaw fell a little as he listened to this
confession.

"And somehow," she continued, "he uses his
in a more gentle and coaxing way."

"So he does!" assented Lucia. "And Oh! Robina! I am longing so for it now. – But go on. Tell me how they finished the job, and how you liked it."

"Well," resumed Robina, "the touch of Madame's fingers excited me greatly, and I met the next push he gave with an upward heave. I at once felt something give way inside, and the hot stiff prick glided up into my cunt and filled the whole cavity with such a sensation of voluptuous delight as I had never experienced before in my life. The Mother Superior kissed me again; and she squeezed the lips of my cunt around his prick as she asked me this question:

"'Now, Robina, how do you like that? – Could there be anything nicer than the feel of a man's prick stirring that way in your cunt? May he fuck you when he wishes hereafter?'

"'Oh! Oh! It's delicious! – Yes! He may fuck me as much as he likes,' I could not help adding, as I felt the great prick moving swiftly in and out. 'Oh! Oh! That is so – so – nice!'

"Madame seemed well pleased at her success. Nothing gave her so much pleasure, I afterwards learned, as seeing a woman fucked for the first time; and in the pursuit of this form of pleasure, she had had every one of her nuns fucked by one or another of the priests who acted as Confessors."

"I am sure," said Lucia, "that it is very pleasant to stand by and watch another woman being fucked. I know I liked to look at you while Tasso was fucking you. I dearly love to watch a prick working in and out between the hairy lips of your cunt. But go on, – tell me more."

"The Mother Superior asked me," Robina continued, "if I enjoyed the feel of her hand about my cunt while it was being fucked.

" 'It greatly increases the pleasure,' I replied.

" 'I expected it would,' she said. 'And now let me put your hands on mine, and perhaps that will not only add still more to your enjoyment, but also give me a little taste of the pleasure, as well.'

"Speaking thus, she drew up her clothes, and placed my hand between her thighs. I pushed it up until I met an immense pair of thick hairy lips, and, diving my fingers into the chink between I felt a cunt overflowing with moisture, and burning with heat.

"I rubbed my hand in and out of this crevice, – an operation which she informed me was called 'frigging,' – keeping time to the quick prods of Father Angelo's prick in my own cunt, while she kept pushing her bottom backwards and forwards.

"'That's a darling!' she said, with convulsive starts. 'Oh! Now it's coming! – Fuck! Father! Fuck! – Push your stones hard against her arse! – Drive your fingers into my cunt, Robina, – not one but two – three – four! – All you can! – Oh!!'

"And she squeezed the lips of my cunt so hard that I almost screamed out, while the Father actually bellowed with delight as he poured a flood of hot sperm into my throbbing recess.

"Madame finished up by leaning over me, rubbing her bare bubbies on mine, and darting her luscious tongue into my open mouth."

"Ah! Robina!" sighed Lucia. "That was a fuck! Your charming account of it has set me wild! My cunt is just burning!" – And pulling up her skirt in front, she continued, "Look at it, darling! – Tasso is watching, too, but I don't mind. – I would give all the world for a good fuck now! – Put your hand on it and frig me, darling, and let Tasso see you."

"Lucia! Are you mad?" chided Robina. "How

fortunate that the Sisters have gone in! – But we must not delay now. And see! Tasso is showing us his prick! Watch him, frigging it with his hands."

"Yes. Robina. Tasso is a dear fellow! How well he understands what to do! – Oh! How nice his prick looks! How stiffly it stands up! Wouldn't I like to have it in my cunt now? I love to watch it while you are rubbing me there! – Oh! How nice! Now faster! – Push your finges up! – Oh!! There!!! – Now let me rest, and I will go with you in a moment."

And with a sigh she leaned her head on Robina's shoulder.

Tasso was now in great need of relief himself. He felt his balls nearly bursting with their contained charge. Satisfying himself that there was no one in the garden but themselves, he stepped nimbly up to them, his fine prick standing out before him, and boldly pushed it up close to Robina's face. She put her hand upon it, and knowing well what he wanted, drew it to her mouth. Then she placed her other hand on his balls, which were also exposed. The soft touch of her fingers on those highly sensitive organs thrilled him with delight. He thrust forward his prick, and pressed its head against her lips. They opened, and in popped the prick, and she began to suck.

He gently worked his arse backwards and forwards, and thus fucked her mouth, as if it were a cunt. She held his balls firmly, and tightened her grasp around the roots of his prick. Her pliant tongue wound around its head, while she sucked with all her force.

Then came the gushing seed, which filled her mouth even to overflowing. She held all she could until he withdrew his prick, and then ejected the slimy sperm on the grass.

Tasso smiled his thanks, and at once turned away, but they detained him long enough to make an appointment with him for the evening. With a bow he left them, after which they also speedily retired.

CHAPTER IV.

OTHER NUNS DESIRE IT

THE two young nuns succeeded in having a pleasant meeting with Tasso not only on that evening, but on some days following. And by watching their opportunity, they several times enjoyed with him their favourite sport.

As they had done their utmost to avoid attracting observation, they thought that their friendly intercourse with Tasso had escaped the notice of everyone. But as is usually the case in such matters, they were very much mistaken.

The Sisters were not permitted to form special friendships; yet when they enjoyed any freedom together, they naturally fell into pairs or sets.

There were two other nuns, named Aminda and Pampinea, who had similar tastes and usually walked together.

They observed the intimacy which had sprung up between the Sisters Lucia and Robina, and the gardener; and feeling certain that there was something in the wind, they watched him closely.

So it was arranged that Pampinea was to hide among the thick bushes by the side of the summer-house one evening, to watch and report to her friend all that she could find out.

At their next meeting, Aminda at once asked:

"Well, Pampinea, dear, what news have you?"

"Most wonderful, – beyond our wildest imagination. Frightful in one sense, delightful in another. I must begin at the very beginning."

"Yes; do, dear."

"I found a capital hiding place, where I was quite concealed, and yet, by drawing aside a branch I could see right into the summer-house. Shortly afterwards, the two Sisters, looking as innocent as a pair of doves, came and sat down. And as soon as all the others had left the garden, Tasso marched in with a broad grin upon his face. They smiled on him, and let him place them as he liked. So without losing a moment, he had them both kneeling on the seat with their ends turned out. Then he whipped up their petticoats and uncovered to view their large white bottoms.

"Then, my dear, he took out his big red 'what-you-call-it.'

"I was horrified at first, and felt ready to sink into the ground with shame, but it is odd how soon one gets accustomed to these things!

"I could not keep my eyes off it. I wondered at its size, and its great red head. Well, my dear, he pushed it up against the bottom first of the one, and then of the other.

"They had no feeling of modesty, at all, for they poked themselves out, and spread their legs apart so as to let him see all they had, – their cute little bottom-holes, hairy slits, and everything.

"He smacked their bottoms with his tool, and then pushed it all into Lucia's slit. She seemed to like it well, for she laughed as she felt it going up. But she did not hold it long, for he quickly pulled it out and shoved it into Robina in the same way.

"Then when he had given her a similar prod, he went back to Lucia, and so on from one to the other.

"All the time they were thus engaged, they continued laughing and talking to one another; and, my dear, you would hardly credit the words they used. They said that Tasso had fucked them that way before, but they thought it very pleasant. They liked to feel his hairy belly rubbing against their bottoms and that his prick seemed to get even further into their cunts than ever before. – Tell me, did you ever hear such words?"

"I did. I remember hearing them when I was a girl at school. They are coarse words, and perhaps for that very reason all the more exciting. So go on, and use them as much as you please. Your description is very amusing, – and, do you know, it is causing me a peculiarly pleasant feeling in my cunt? You see I use them, too. – Would you mind putting your hand on it, dear, while you are describing what followed?"

"Not in the least. I shall quite enjoy it, and you can do the same for me, for my cunt too is burning with heat. And I have had to pet it. Twice I witnessed the wonderful enjoyment which both Lucia and Robina showed, when they had Tasso's prick poking their cunts."

Then the two nuns, in very un-nun like fashion, managed to get their hands on the other's cunt as Pampinea went on:

"After changing several times, I noticed that Tasso's prick looked larger and redder each time it came out. He plunged it with great force into Sister

Lucia; his belly smacked aginst her bottom. He remained as if glued to her behind, but Robina stood up, and pushing her hands between them, began 'fiddling with his stones and Lucia's arse,' as she called it.

"After a couple of minutes or so he drew out his prick, now all soft and hanging down, and some kind of white stuff dripping from it. Lucia then turned about and sat down, and made Tasso sit on the seat beside her, while Robina knelt on the ground before them, between Tasso's legs.

"Lucia put her hand on his balls and Robina took hold of his prick. And, my dear, she put it into her mouth, wet as it was.

"Lucia laughed: 'Ah! Robina, you are like me, – I love to taste the flavour of your cunt, and now I hope you won't find that the flavour of mine is disagreeable.'

"Robina lifted her head, and said: 'Not in the least. I like the salty taste, and the smell is delicious.'

"Then she recommenced her sucking, while Lucia's fingers played about the root of the prick, and occasionally touched the chin and sucking lips of her friend.

"Tasso's prick grew stronger, until its head seemed too large for Robina's mouth to take it all in.

Lucia remarked its size and said: 'I think, Robina, that you have sucked Tasso's prick into working order again. What would you think of getting him to lie down there on his back, and then for you to straddle over him, place his prick in your cunt with your own hand? – And I will help you if you like? Then go through the motions yourself and make him suck you at your leisure.'

" 'Capital notion! Let us at once put it into execution, for our time is nearly up.'

"They both stood up and soon had Tasso on his back on the ground. Then Robina, tucking up her skirts all around, straddled over him and made her cunt descend upon his standing prick.

"Lucia fixed it aright, and kept it steady as a candlestick with her hand, while Robina, with a downward push caused it to rush up into her to the very hilt.

"Lucia then laid herself down by Tasso's side and rested her cheek on his belly, so close to his prick that she was able to touch with her tongue at the same time both the little fleshy knot of Robina's cunt, and the prick as often as it was pressed down, while she allayed her own excitement by working a finger between the hairy lips of her own affair.

"Altogether it was a most voluptuous scene.

What, between their lustful motions, their wanton cries, and the sweet visible union of prick and cunt, nothing could be more exciting. I envied them with all my heart, and I am sure, Aminda, you would have done so too."

"I am quite certain I should, – and more. I know of no reason why we may not share in their sports – do you? But we must go, now. We will talk the matter over on the next opportunity."

CHAPTER V.

LUCIA GETS MORE OF IT

WE MUST now return to the two young nuns first mentioned in this narrative.

The day had come for Lucia to complete her confession to Father Joachim in the private room of the Mother Abbess. She and Robina had pledged one another, as you will doubtless remember, not to refer in any way during confession to their intercourse with Tasso, – but they agreed later that they might safely tell the priest how Lucia had seen his prick, and how they had talked together and petted each other's cunts.

Let us pass on then to the scene.

Lucia is kneeling beside the priest, who is seated on a comfortable arm-chair in Madame's private apartments. This little room is elegantly fitted up as a lady's boudoir. It had two doors, one opening into her reception room, – the other partially concealed, led by a secret passage to the Sacristy of the Convent Chapel. And by this way, the priests who officiated there could always visit the Mother Abbess without being noticed.

What a handsome man is Father Joachim! The bloom of youth is still upon his cheek. His white untarnished skin and full red lips had made many a voluptuously-inclined maid sigh with unrequited desire. Though somewhat of a tendency to embonpoint, yet his body might be termed a veritable cushion, in which a thousand dimples hid themselves until at the proper moment they were called into action. The fame of this handsome priest had travelled before him. For his celebrated amour with an angel was a stock story in monastries and convents. Robina and Lucia were not unacquainted with it, the Mother Abbess having retailed the gossip previous to Father Joachim's coming.

Lucia has just reached that part of her confession where she tells the priest how, having occasion to go to the Little-house, she saw through the perforated door, the gardener Tasso, coming up, unbuttoning his trousers, and taking out his tool and making water.

"Do you remember my daughter, the name

you mentioned in your last confession for a man's tool? I wish you to use it now."

"Well, Father, if you will have me use these naughty words, it was his prick that I saw."

The priest's eyes now began to glisten, and there was a slight tremor in his hand as he said:

"Yes; it makes your confession more real and exact. Now tell me precisely all he did."

Lucia could hardly repress a smile, for she felt that she now had the priest in leading strings, and she was determined to draw him on. So she spoke out more boldly as she continued:

"When he took out his prick, he held it in his hand and shot forth his water straight before him, and he looked down on his prick while he piddled. When he finished, he shook it two or three times. Then he drew the skin back from its red head, which made it grow larger and stick out more stiffly before him."

"Now tell me, my daughter, exactly and fully what effect the view of Tasso's prick had upon yourself, and use the terms you have already uttered in confession."

"Oh! Father! How can I tell you such things?" And she leaned her elbow on his knee.

"It is quite necessary, my child, and the more particular you are in every word and in every detail the better your confession will be."

"Well, Father, I suppose I must tell you every-thing. – As I kept looking at the prick, I felt a warm glow all between my legs, and my cunt began to itch so terribly that I pulled up my petticoats and squeezed it with my hand. Then I pushed my finger in and rubbed the inside as hard as I could."

"Were you standing up at the time?"

"I was, Father."

"Were your legs separated?"

"They were, Father."

"Now get up, separate your legs, and stand just as you did at the time."

Lucia stood up and straddled her legs.

"I am glad to find you so true a daughter of our Holy Mother Church, – for obedience to your spiritual guides is the very essence of her teaching.

"Now put your hand on your cunt just as you did when you were looking at the gardener's prick."

Lucia lifted her clothes at one side and put her hand on her cunt. The priest looked greatly excited, and said:

"But, my daughter, I want to see it."

"Well, Father you must raise my clothes yourself."

The priest's cheeks flamed with amorous desire; and the fire of lust flamed in his eyes as he lifted her petticoats in front, and stooping forward, he was enabled to gaze upon the revealed beauties of her charming cunt. Then with a quick motion of his other hand, he rapidly unbuttoned his breeches as he said:

"Now, my daughter, that the scene may be complete, I want you to look at my prick while you are rubbing your cunt. You know these things are no sin with a holy man like me. See! Here is my prick! Look at it!"

And placing his hand behind on her naked bottom, he drew her in towards him.

The priest's burly prick, still larger and stronger than Tasso's, stood up boldly before her.

"Does the sight of this prick excite you in the same way that the gardener's did?"

"Oh! It does, Father. But are you sure it is not wrong to look at it?"

"Quite sure, my daughter, and you may put your hand on it too, without fear of sin. My child, your confidence is most refreshing. Yes, I would like you to feel it all over, – and the balls too, if you will, while I explore your delicious cunt."

Then he pushed his finger up and began to rub it quickly in and out.

"Good! My child, now come over and rest upon this lounge."

With his arm round her, he drew her to the end

of the couch, laid her on her back, lifted her legs, and pushed her petticoats above her navel. He then stooped over her and with his hand directed his prick between the moist lips of her itching cunt.

As soon as she felt it in that sensitive recess, she panted out:

"Oh! Father! What do you want to do?"

"To push my prick into your cunt and fuck you. Isn't that the right word to use? May I fuck you?"

"Why, Father, you told me I must obey you in everything, and if you want to fuck me, of course I must let you."

The priest smiled approval, and gave a lunge with his prick.

"Oh! It's going in! – Oh! Father! – How strong your prick is! I feel it up to the very centre of my belly! – Oh! Do you like fucking me?"

"Yes, my daughter. Your cunt holds my prick deliciously. I have fucked many of the Sisters, but I like your cunt best of all. And especially because you talk so freely. – Now, heave your arse! – That's the way! – Now! – Oh! – It's just coming! – Put your arms around me! – Hug me! Tighter yet! Now tell me how you feel."

"Dear Father, your prick in my cunt feels lovely – I would like to keep it there forever! Fuck! Fuck! Fuck!"

314

The priest drove his prick up with his full force. His brawny loins smacked against the soft cheeks of her arse, and his hard balls pressed against the sensitive edges of her bottom-hole, while the flood of his fierce passion filled the recesses of her well satisfied and delighted cunt.

"Dear, dear Father!" she cries in her ecstasy. "Give me your lips to lick! – Oh! Blessed Virgin! I feel your lovely prick emptying itself inside of me! – Now I come! I come – There! There! – Oh! God! What pleasure!"

"Yes! Darling daughter! Suck my mouth!" shouts the delighted priest.

Then no sound is heard except the sucking of lips and the pleasing noise made by the priest's prick as it gurgles in and out of Lucia's cunt. His prick still remained stiff, though he had spent freely. This was too much for the partly distracted Lucia. She lost control of her senses, in fact, fairly swooned away.

CHAPTER VI.

THE MOTHER ABBESS DELIGHTS IN IT

WHEN she regained her senses, she looked about. The priest was gone. There was a feeling as if something were rubbing and titillating her grotto of love, and she opened her eyes wide. To her intense surprise she saw that the Mother Abbess was bending over her and she felt her fingers were playing with her dripping cunt.

"My daughter," she said, "you have behaved well. I am glad you showed such child-like obedience, and put your body to the holy service of giving relief to that worthy priest. It is no sin with him, you know, nor with me either. And I greatly commend your good sense in using all those terms which so increase and intensify these precious delights. And whenever you are with me, on similar occasions, I wish you always to use such words.

I saw you fucked, my child. I was close by, when Father Joachim's prick was prodding your cunt, and I heard everything you said. Now open your legs wide. I want to kiss your cunt while it is still wet with his holy seed."

Lucia lay as if thunderstruck. She did not know what to say in reply, but she willingly spread her legs as she felt the warm breath of the Mother Abbess blowing aside the hairs of her cunt. Then she felt her soft tongue licking all round the inside of the slit, and then the whole of the clitoris drawn into her mouth. This was very enjoyable, but when she felt her tongue actually penetrating the passage, she could not resist putting down her hand, and laying it gently on the head of the Mother Abbess as she said:

"Dear Mother, how good you are! You are making my cunt glow with as much pleasure as when the Holy Father was fucking me."

The only response of the Mother Abbess was to work her tongue more nimbly in and out, and to push a moistened finger into her bottom-hole.

This last act caused a new sensation to Lucia, and made her press up against the mouth of the Mother Abbess and cry:

"Oh! My! That's so nice! Dear Mother, I am just going to spend! – My cunt and bottom are all in a glow! – Oh! Oh! – There! It's coming!"

And the Mother Abbess skilfully frigged her arse, while she lapped up with her tongue every drop of the love juice which exuded from Lucia's hot little recess.

The Mother Abbess allowed her to rest for a while, then kissed her, and said:

"I am very glad you have had so much enjoyment. Will you not do the same for me?"

"That I will, dear Mother. I am indeed longing to see and pet your dear cunt, only I was afraid to ask you."

And Lucia stood up, as the Mother Abbess took her place.

"See then, here it is!"

And laying herself back the Mother Abbess drew up her petticoats and spread her legs wide apart.

Lucia had never before seen such a cunt as that which was now opened to her view. – So large, so hairy! Such immense lips! The thick fleshy clitoris stuck out like a boy's cock! And the red chink below it was deep and bathed in moisture.

She was of course familiar with her own little chink, which was young and fresh, and had a pert and innocent air about it. And she had often seen and closely examined Sister Robina's cunt, which was fuller and more open, and had a strong lust-provoking look about it, – but even Robina's was small and poor in comparison with the great shaggy affair of the Mother Abbess. From being long in the habit of affording relief to all these burly priests, its naturally thick lips had become enormously developed, and its capacity for taking in pricks of any dimensions was unlimited. Evidently nothing could startle this woman. In fact, she never saw a jackass with his tool extended, or viewed a stallion's telescopic tickler without wishing that she had it packed in her capacious hot-box.

Such was the cunt which Lucia now stooped over. She drew open the great fat lips, and as she looked into the deep rosy chink, she thought:

"Oh! That I had a man's prick, that I might plunge into these soft folds!"

But not having the prick, she could only do what little a woman could. So she placed her mouth in the open chink, sucked the clitoris with a will, and when she had forced an emission, she began to lick up the flowing juice.

She was however, suddenly interrupted. A man's hand pushed under her chin, and gently raised her head. Looking up with surprise, she saw another of the holy Fathers, named Ambrose, standing by her side, and his prick, still larger than Father Joachim's poking against her face.

In reply to her astonished look, he said:

"Let me, my child. This is what she wants. Pleasant as no doubt your mouth and tongue are, there is nothing like the real man's prick itself. Good Mother, may I take this sweet daughter's place? If you will permit, I am ready to serve you, and she can play with my prick and balls whilst I give full satisfaction to your heated and longing cunt."

"You are very welcome, Father Ambrose. I did not expect you for another full hour yet. Give me a satisfactory poke first, and by the time you are ready again, Sister Lucia will, I am sure, gladly avail herself of the services of your noble tool."

Without delay, Father Ambrose knelt close up to her great fat rump, now flattened out on the edge of the couch.

With one fierce, rapid thrust, he buried his enormous tool in her open cunt, while she, giving the fullest swing to her randy amorous inclinations, called out.

"Now Lucia, hold his prick by the roots. Keep a firm grip on his bollocks, – his balls, you know, –

and pinch his arse well. That's the way to make him fuck with life and spirit."

At each of these smutty words, the priest made a fresh plunge, and she as eagerly bounded to meet him.

Lucia gladly obeyed her Superior, and with a merry laugh pushed one hand between the Mother Abbess and the priest's hairy belly, and compressed her fingers as tightly as she could round the root of his prick. The other hand she put behind and took hold of the priest's cods, – first one and then the other, for they were too big for her hand to contain them both at once.

The holy Father now checked his speed, and, wishing to prolong the sweet joy, worked deliberately with a long steady stroke, pulling out the whole of his prick except the tip each time he drew back; while the Mother Abbess, more eager in her lust, crossed her feet over his back, and clung to him with arms and legs. But Lucia got so excited from watching his prick as it rushed in and out between the large clinging lips of Madame's voluptuous cunt, that she threw off all reserve, and pulled up her clothes and rubbed her naked cunt and belly against the firm cheeks of the priest's muscular backside. Then embracing him tightly round the loins with her arms, she joined in every push, tickling his arse most delightfully with the hair of her cunt.

This quickly brought on the climax, and the priest, with a loud exclamation of delight deluged the cunt of the Mother Abbess with his flowing sperm.

They rested a little, but with the secret parts of the bodies fully exposed, ready for either viewing or petting as might be desired.

Then the Mother Abbess produced some choice wine and spiced cakes. Each glass of wine which the good priest drank, he first seasoned by rubbing it on the cunt of one or the other, while they in like manner rubbed their glasses on his prick.

The Mother Abbess wanted them to hurry, and told Lucia to suck his prick to get him into fucking order.

Then the Father sat up, pointed to his prick and said:

"See how the fellow stands now!"

Then he cried:

"I want to fuck your cunt, Lucia! Let me see it! – It is just right! – Now kneel here on the edge of this lounge. Lift up your arse as high as you can. And will you, good Mother, put it in for me, and while I am fucking, play with us any way you like?"

The Mother Abbess knew what was implied in that permission, and at once began to finger both their bottoms.

The priest, however, did not get in as speedily as he expected. Lucia had not as yet taken in a prick of such abnormal proportions as that of Father Ambrose, and it stuck fast in the entrance of her cunt.

"Oh!" he cried. "This is grand! Her cunt is so tight that it won't let my prick in! But I like it all the more! – Does my prick hurt you, my daughter?"

"It does a little, Father. But I can bear it. – Ha! Oh! – Go softly! – Now push again! – I am trying to open my cunt for you. – There! It's getting in! Oh! Now I feel it going up! – up! – Oh! How immense it seems! I can feel it up to my very heart! My cunt is quite filled with it! Ah! Now it goes in easily enough! – Oh! Oh! That's delicious! Fuck me, Father! Fuck me! – More! More!"

She dwelt upon the word with such a libidinous accent as nearly set the priest wild, and caused him to drive his prick so forcibly in and out of her thrilling cunt as made the couch and everything movable near them vibrate with the violence of his powerful strokes.

In the meantime the Mother Abbess had worked

her passions up to an almost ungovernable pitch. She was visibly spending. In her frenzy of voluptuousness she almost tore their bottoms with her nails, as she urged on their mad ecstasy until Lucia's rolling eyes and heaving bottom told of the exquisite pleasure she was experiencing. Even the priest's eyes glittered and flashed, and his whole form quivered as he poured into Lucia's womb a flood of love's soothing-syrup.

"Ha! My pretty nun! What think you now?" shouts the Mother Abbess, apparently crazed with lust. "Do you know of another joy equal to this?"

With these words she secured possession of a rod and proceeded to lay it on the bounding arses of both priest and nun.

"Nice, plump arse!" she cries, lashing Lucia's posteriors severely. "Take that! And that! – So! – That makes you bounce, eh? – Now, Father, it is your turn."

So saying she cut the priest across the big fat cheeks of his arse so severely that he bounded like a rubber ball.

Lucia madly digs her fingers into its cheeks and holds the priest in such a firm grip that he cannot move. The Mother Abbess next gives Lucia a turn with the rod. Though the blows are quick and heavy, the girl is unmindful of them. She utters a loud shriek indicative of ecstatic pleasure. The priest expresses his blissful feelings in a pleased grunt. The Mother Abbess lays aside the rod, and then they all sank down, clutched in each other's arms.

CHAPTER VII.

IT IS THE CAUSE OF A MIRACLE

MEANWHILE, our friends Pampinea and Aminda held a consultation as to the best means of securing a share of Tasso's much prized services. Of course they neither felt nor acted as ordinary women. From the forced constraint under which they lived, their passions when aroused were almost uncontrollable; and the fact of Tasso's being unable, as they supposed, to either hear or speak, induced them to regard him as more of a machine than a man, and treat him so.

It was therefore agreed that Pampinea, the bolder of the two, was to write on his slate that she had seen all that he had done to the two Sisters in the Summer-house, and to invite him to go with them and do the same.

So waiting their opportunity, Pampinea went up and held out her hand for the slate. He gave it readily.

But what was she to write? After several abortive attempts she produced the following:

"I saw you in the Summer-house with the Sisters Lucia and Robina. I saw what you were doing. It seemed to please them so much that Sister Aminda and I would like you to teach us the same delightful game. – You may trust us, we will not tell any one, – no, not even confess it to the priest."

When he read it, he looked up with an amused but very pleased expression. Pampinea smiled in return, and pointed to the Summer-house. He nodded, and motioned to her to enter it.

The two Sisters looked carefully around; and, seeing no one about, sauntered up to the place, entered, and sat down.

Tasso quickly followed them. He assumed a half-witted expression as he stood before Pampinea, scratching his head, and at the same time making the huge bulkiness of his swelling prick as prominent as he could.

With an inquiring glance, she pointed to it as if asking what it was.

Oh! How his eyes did twinkle as he took her hand and rubbed it over his tool, letting her feel how it bounded and reared in its confinement. Her fingers began to fumble with the opening of his trousers. He undid the buttons, and with a dexterous movement brought the whole length of that stately machine into view.

The Sisters started! They had never seen a man's prick displayed openly before them in that fashion. It is true that Pampinea indeed, had seen it before, but then it was in the dusk of the evening, and was always popping out of one cunt and into the other, and she remembered that when he had finally drawn it out, it had an exhausted, shrunken and crest-fallen appearance. But now it stood erect, in all the power, and all the freshness, and all the beauty of its youthful vigour.

Their eyes devoured it. Their hungry little mouths of cunts began to water for it. They felt their quims throb with the first impulses of pleasure. They were quite ready even now, to fall on their backs, spread apart their legs, and allow him to fondle and view and pet their sweet treasures. They longed for that blissful moment when he should part their jutting lips, and then put in his dear prick and let it revel in the sweets within. Still, with womanly instinct they held back and let him make the first move, and select whichever of them he might choose to commence with.

He did not long leave them in doubt.

There was a bold dash about Pampinea which strongly attracted him. Men always admire courage in a woman, especially when it tends to confidence in themselves; and she had shown a freedom from fear, with respect to him, which was simply delightful.

Like an Eastern devotee he dropped on his knees before her, and with his hands reverently raised the coarse garment of the nun as if it were a costly veil which sheltered the object of his worship.

Having gone so far, Pampinea was not the woman to halt now. She therefore allowed him to proceed, and to act according to the instincts of his nature.

She suffered him to open her thighs, to draw her to the edge of the seat, and push her back. Then, when she felt his fingers amorously examining and probing her cunt, feeling its moist creases and soft folds, and was also conscious that his bold eyes were running over all the beauties of these secret parts, so blushed a rosy blush of pleasure from head to foot, and felt a thrill of delight pervade the regions of love, until the very lips of her cunt seemed to part in a gentle smile with the anticipation of the approaching joys.

Aminda looked on with great interest, trying to imagine how she would feel herself under similar circumstances, when she suddenly remembered that Tasso could neither speak nor hear, and so she said,

"Dear Sister, don't you feel terribly ashamed at his looking at you there?"

"Not at all, dear," replied Pampinea. "Strange to say, I don't mind it in the least. I really like it now, – it seems so natural."

"Well," said Aminda, "it may be quite natural; but at first – well, at all events – it does look very queer. Anyhow, I feel that I would love to watch what he is doing to you forever. You don't dislike it, Pampinea, do you, dear?"

"No. I like you to watch. – Oh! Now I feel him rubbing against me that part which Lucia called his prick, and I can't tell you, dear, how nice it feels! He's trying to get it in now! – Oh! It's hurting me a little. But the pleasure is just maddening. Oh! Aminda! He's just got it in! – Now the pain is over, and he has pushed it all up, it feels delightful! – I cannot tell you how delicious it is, now that he is moving it in and out! Can you see it, dear?"

"Oh! Yes! – I see it plainly enough! – How easily it slips in and out! – It must indeed feel very nice! My own cunt, – at least that's what Lucia and Robina called theirs–"

"Well! – What about your cunt, my dear?"

"Oh! My cunt is tingling all over at the sight! – I do hope Tasso will like mine as he likes yours. Oh! How delicious it must feel to be fucked! – Isn't that the word?"

"Yes! – Oh! I can't talk now. – Fucking is delightful. – No terms – can – express – how – delicious – it feels!"

These words were uttered in successive jerks as Tasso drove in and out his red and swollen tool, while the hungry lips of her quivering cunt sucked it in with all the eagerness of the highest and voluptuous enjoyment.

Aminda shared their transports, and putting her hand on her own itching slit, forced her finger for the first time up the thrilling passage of her cunt.

"Tell me now, Pampinea, how do you feel?" cried Aminda, vigorously working her excited cunt.

"I – I – Oh! You heavenly man! – I must move my backside, too! – Don't ask me, Aminda! It's just too sweet to talk about! – Oh! I am all wet inside of me! – But you won't take it out, will you?" she pleadingly asks of Tasso, forgetful of his being powerless to hear.

"His prick is covered with oil," remarked Aminda. "I guess he must be nearly done. – At least I hope so," she adds, in a slightly petulant tone.

Tasso was now fucking the long-deprived maid

with all his strength. His finely developed prick was as stiff as ever; and every time he thrust it in to the full, Pampinea uttered little shrieks of delight. At last he made a quick thrust, and buried his prick in the anxious and longing cunt to its fullest extent, and then ceased his motions.

"Oh! Aminda!" cried Pampinea. "He is squirting hot streams into me! – Oh! Oh! There he goes again! Oh! I can not tell you of the sweet, sweet feeling that is within me. I only wish he would not take it out! I want it right over again!"

"That is indeed unkind of you, Pampinea," said Aminda, poutingly. "You know I have been fingering my cunt until I am almost mad with desire. Come, now! Do let me have a taste of what you have just felt."

While she was speaking these words, Tasso withdrew himself from Pampinea's luscious cunt. The fact was, all this fucking was beginning to tell a littleupon the gardener's vitality. Yet such was the tempting nature of the feast which was being constantly spread before him that, to save his soul, he could not resist the offerings.

Pampinea was wildly excited by the workings of Tasso's prick. She still imagined that something was working within her, for after Tasso had taken his prick from her, she continued the motions just as though she were again being fucked.

The gardener now turned his attention to Aminda, who was eagerly awaiting her turn. She certainly was a very beautiful woman, and as fresh and sweet as a full blown rose. The red blood mantled her cheek; her lily white skin was without flaw. Her eyes were aflame with passion. Her position was such as to expose her most secret charms, the sight of which instantly made Tasso's prick arise once more.

"Do you like to look at my cunt?" inquired Aminda artlessly upon the slate.

Tasso nods his head vigorously.

"I love to look at your prick," she again writes.

This breathing spell gave Tasso a splendid opportunity to raise a stiff prick. He knew that he had spent heavily in Pampinea, and the result would be that his staff when it once hardened again, would remain stiff for quite a period. As he saw his prick become as hard as a stone, he could not contain himself any longer. The sight of Aminda's pouting little love-nest added to his joy.

Then he fell upon his knees between the plump white thighs, and exclaimed:

"Oh! Mother of God! What a glorious feast!"

As he spoke each word, he greedily kissed Aminda's quivering cunt.

"He speaks! He speaks!" cries Pampinea, awakened to herself at the sound of Tasso's voice.

But the gardener paid no attention to her. He saw only Aminda and her secret beauties. He opens the lips of her anxious cunt, and pushes his big stiff prick right into her without heeding either her cries or her protestations.

The girl's cries however, were not unheard by others. The Mother Abbess and Father Joachim, who were indulging in a little stroll through the grounds, were attracted to the Summer-house by such unseemly noises.

And what a sight it was that greeted their eyes!

There was Pampinea, lying upon the ground, with disordered attire, and vigorously rubbing the clitoris and stiffened inner lips of her still slippery cunnie, while not far from her, Tasso and Aminda were battling right royally in amorous warfare.

"By the Great God above!" shouts the intoxicated Tasso. "That was a fine return! – Ha! Ha! There is another for thee! Now, Now! My beautiful angel, give it back right quickly!"

"A miracle! A miracle!" shouts the Mother Abbess. "The dumb speak, and the deaf hear! Bear witness to this wondrous thing, Father Joachim!"

"Aye! Aye!" returns Father Joachim. "This must go upon the records. It will be recorded for all time in order to confound the erring ones and doubters. By Saint Anthony!" he shouts. "But that fellow fucks like a master of the art."

"'Tis a most entrancing sight!" observes the Mother Abbess, watching the two with amorous eyes. "How fortunate I am to witness it," she continues.

Pampinea in the meantime had arisen, and after arranging her attire, stood with downcast eyes and flushed cheeks awaiting her sentence. The Mother Abbess however did not pay any attention to her, and acted as though she was unaware of Pampinea's presence.

"Ha! That was an excellent shove!" she shouts. "Now, Aminda, return it with interest. Hold! I will stroke his arse, and fondle his balls. Now! Now! Gardener, show your mettle!"

Pampinea was overjoyed to witness the Mother Abbess' actions. She now felt more secure as she observed the conduct of her Superior.

With his arse being slapped, his balls fondled, and his prick tightly enfolded in an hitherto unfucked cunt, Tasso was in the seventh heaven of bliss. Nature could hold back no longer.

"Come! Come!" cried Father Joachim. "Spit

the contents of thy loins into the maid. This will but half satisfy her. By Saint Anthony! I will take a hand in the game myself."

The priest was right. When Tasso removed himself Aminda endeavoured to prevent it.

"What! Through already?" she cried, regardless of the company. "Bah! I am but half satisfied! – Oh! Holy Virgin! – Give me a prick! I am burning up with desire."

Aminda was in that state of feeling that few physicians seem acquainted with. The most modest and virtuous woman, left in an unsatisfied state, would without reluctance yield herself to the embrace of her most hated foe. 'Tis now that Father Joachim finds the best field for the display of his unrivalled talents.

"Fuck her, Father! Fuck her!" cried the amorous Mother Abbess. "Tasso is dry."

The gardener was highly indignant at the thrust.

"Madame," he retorts, "were you in my place, and beseeched constantly by a dozen prick-hunters such as your nuns here, upon my soul you would not have another drop within you."

"Ha! Ha! – Nice carryings on in my convent," remarks the Mother Abbess in a serio-tragic tone. "You are the deaf and dumb man, eh? – The modest one who dared not raise your eyes in passing us, eh? – By the Blessed Mother, I will have you to fuck me and no one else, – dost hear?"

"Alas! Madame," returns Tasso. "I pray you have mercy! You know the old saying, that 'one cock will do for ten hens, but one prick will not do for a dozen women,' for be it known to you that ten stiff pricks cannot satisfy one woman. Know you also that a disorder of long standing had deprived me of hearing as well as speech. The beautiful Aminda gave me such extreme pleasure that my senses were for a time dissipated. When they returned, I found myself a perfect man again."

"We will speak further of this in the future," said the Mother Abbess. "Just now we have no further time to waste on thee. – Ha! Observe Father Joachim! – See! He has already replaced thee. How well his handsome prick fits into Aminda's little cunt! – Watch them fuck! Oh! Is it not an entrancing sight? – Ho! Father! Work thy loins! – Ha! I know you are shooting into her. Halt her screams! Stifle them, or we may have unwelcome visitors!"

Father Joachim was enjoying himself to the fullest extent. Aminda's slit was eager for a prick, and when the Father placed his splendid tool into the hot and luscious cunt, it was indeed, the extreme of happiness for both. What a glorious sight it was! And how they all enjoyed it!

When Father Joachim had spent copiously into Aminda, he removed his fallen prick, and dropping on his knees between her thighs, pressed unnumbered kisses upon her still excited and palpitating cunt.

"The hour is late," spoke up the Mother Abbess. "Father, it is time to cry halt. You may enjoy this more in the future. – Tasso, away to your employment. – Pampinea and Aminda, go to your apartments."

"Were it not for an important engagement elsewhere," interrupted Father Joachim, "I would give you each such a rounding up as would make you utter shrieks of joy once more."

"Well," joined in the Mother Abbess. "In a few days we will hold high revelry, and participate in such a feast as you have never heretofore dreamed of."

A loud cry of approval greeted this bit of interesting information.

"I will inform you as to it at the proper time. – Oh! By the way, I might mention that letters have been sent from Madrid informing me that the famous Monk Pedro has been appointed one of our Confessors, and is now on the way here. I expect him the coming morrow. Rumour saith that he has been sent abroad as a punishment for engaging in an illicit amour with the King's daughter. – I am anxious to test his abilities. – Now, farewell."

Speaking thus the Mother Abbess and Father Joachim slowly wended their way conventward, while Tasso departed to resume his tasks.

Pampinea and Aminda walked towards their respective apartments slowly and with a somewhat halting gait, due no doubt to a little too-much of that pleasant prick-rubbing to which they had just been subjected.

CHAPTER VIII.

THEY ALL TAKE A HAND IN IT

CONVENT life in Italy at the period upon which our narrative touches, was anything but one made up of sacrifice, penance and devotion. The cloak of religion was but a thin disguise for the greatest immorality, and the greater the reputation for sanctity, the deeper would the inmates plunge into lecherous pleasures. The convent was the resort of the gay and dissolute youth of the sunny clime, who indulged in orgies and dissipation that would have done no discredit to their Roman ancestors, who had long been acknowledged by those competent to decide, to be veritable adepts in arts of fucking, sucking and buggering. The ancients practically made the science of fucking a fine art, and we who follow in their footsteps are naught but mere imitators. It therefore will not cause a shock to the intelligent reader to describe at length the riotous orgies which we are about to depict, for such sensual banquets were quite common in Italy, where the hot blood courses through the veins with lightning speed, and the passions at times become so uncontrollable as to rage with the fierceness of beasts or fabled centaurs.

The Convent in which the scenes of our story lay was an exception to the rule. It possessed an enviable reputation for sanctity and was frequently quoted as an example well worthy of imitation. The larger portion of its inmates confined themselves to sacred practices only, and the fall from grace of the Mother Abbess and the younger Sisters was totally unknown.

The Mother Abbess deferred to a week later the promised feast of love.

"It will give us time to recuperate," she said to Father Joachim, who impatiently awaited the evening of joy. "That fellow Tasso has been too devoted a follower of Venus," she added, with a suggestive smile.

"Hum! Lucky dog!" said the priest, a little enviously. "He is a fine gardener! – Ha! Ha!" he laughed. "What a nice crop of brats he will leave behind him! He has planted his seed to good advantage."

"I esteem it a misfortune that I was not acquainted with his talents before," observed the Mother Abbess. "But come! I must send you on a mission. Go and bid Robina, Lucia, Pampinea and Aminda to assemble here in this room tomorrow night. – Oh! By the way, forget not our Tasso. Ambrose is already informed, – and likewise the Spanish monk, Pedro."

"Why, he has but recently come from Madrid. What know you of him?"

"He is known as the Spanish Stallion, and I am informed that none can excel him in the gentle arts of love. By our Lady! I am anxious to test his virility. I already burn and itch with desire. Oh! I must play with your prick a moment, Father."

In compliance with this request, the priest undid his cassock; and showed to the amorous woman his ponderous engine.

She seizes it with greedily lustful hands, and works it fiercely, squeezing the heavy balls. At the same time Father Joachim buries his finger in her moist crevice, and they give each other exquisite pleasure for an extended period.

Finally the Mother Abbess recovers herself.

"We must not be backwards tonight," she says, giving his prick a last gallop.

Father Joachim then departed without any further delay.

Punctually at the appointed time they all assemble in the apartment selected for the meeting. The place chosen was a room in the most unfrequented portion of the Convent. Heavy curtains hid everything from prying eyes. A banquet table, spread with delicacies and luscious fruits first met the gaze of those who entered. The Mother Abbess was seated on a throne-like chair at the head of the table, and bade a most generous welcome to every guest.

"I introduce to you, ladies and gentlemen, (for that is what I will term you this festive night,) the Monk Pedro, also called the Spanish Stallion."

Shouts of laughter greet this sally.

"I will tell you my opinion when I taste his prick," observes the virtuous Robina.

'Yes! So will we all!" chime in the other pseudo-virgins.

Soon the wine was becoming effective, for all were presently partaking freely of the generous juice of the grape.

Modestly was quickly thrown aside with the vestments. The Mother Abbess was the first to set the example. A single motion, and she was entirely disrobed. One naked leg is placed upon the table. Then she falls back, sighing.

"Come, my Spanish Stallion! Fuck me before them all."

The handsome Pedro, a tall Hercules as it were, strips himself in a trice and displays a tool worthy of his title.

"Has he not a fine prick, Robina?" says Lucia, admiringly. "I would very much like to feel it inside me!"

"I am anxious to taste of it like yourself, Lucia," returns Robina, gazing with tender looks upon the Spaniard's prick.

Meanwhile the Mother Abbess was snatching frantically at the object before her. She would squeeze it gently, then draw her hand slowly backward in a most teasing manner.

The monk was pawing at her cunt in a most ferocious way. His whole hand grasped the fat lips, and pressed them tightly. Then he would insert two fingers, and titillate her clitoris until her arse jumped convulsively.

"They are getting in fine shape for a good fuck," says Father Ambrose, taking Lucia up on his lap and inserting his stiff prick between her naked thighs. Then with his other hand, he played with Robina's cunt.

Father Joachim had placed himself in front of Pampinea's lovely font, and rapturously kissed the ruby lips.

Tasso, whose stomach was filled with good wine,

seemed to be in fine fettle. His hand strayed to that delightful slit belonging to Aminda.

"That's right! Play with my cunt, dear Tasso, while I look at Father Pedro. See!" she cries. "He is about to fuck her now. Will it not be delightful for you to play with my cunt while they are fucking?"

The Mother Abbess now lost all sense of womanly modesty, for she caught hold of the Spanish Stallion's prick and pulled him by it to a couch conveniently placed, he playing with her cunt all the while. Look! She wrestles with him, twines her limbs about him like a vine, then she falls upon the couch and raises her limbs in the air. His mighty prick enters her veteran cunt without a halt. With a fierce wrench she throws him off, pounces upon his prick with her mouth, and mumbles her prayers over it as though Priapus were her God.

"Have at her, Monk!" gleefully shouts Father Ambrose.

"Hey! Stallion, your mighty prick will be conquered this time!" cries Father Joachim.

"Yea! Yea!" chimes in Tasso. "If she does not fuck you dry, she will suck you dry!"

Monk Pedro was oblivious to such jesting. He is wild with lust. He plays with his companion's splendid arse. He pushes up her ponderous titties, – squeezes, bites and sucks them.

The entranced Abbess is not a whit behind. Her tongue licks everything with which it comes into contact.

Again his prick enters her cunt. This time he will not be thrown off. He joins his stomach to hers. His big balls are close to her arse-hole. He keeps his prick in place, and moves his muscular arse from side to side.

The Mother Abbess gasps with pleasure. She cannot speak, but utters little shrieks expressive of the exquisite pleasure she is experiencing.

"See! See! He will not be halted," says Pampinea, whose arse is already quivering with delight from Father Joachim's ravishing fingering.

In vain the partly distracted Mother Abbess motions to her partner to move in and out.

"Beloved friend," observes Father Pedro, "I have her impaled, and as I am not yet ready to spend, I will stay as I am."

"By all the Saints!" shouts Ambrose. "If you will not oblige her, I will take a turn myself."

"An excellent suggestion," rejoins the Stallion.

Then he works his arse swiftly until his prick is streaming with the juices of his partner. He then withdraws his instrument, as stiff as ever.

Father Ambrose takes his place, and the Mother Abbess engulfs his prick at a single push. He rages like a bull; their bellies meet with a loud slap. Her tongue wags at him as an invitation to his own. Now they fuck with their mouths as well. His lunges are fiercely lustful, but he is not so well primed as Father Pedro. Off comes Father Ambrose with a mighty shout of unrestrained excessive bliss.

He withdraws his flabby prick and is pushed aside by the Spaniard, who again inserts his fine mettlesome steed into the willing cunt before him. He places a finger in her arse-hole and now works his backside with wonderful speed. Again she wags her tongue. He obeys the signal.

"His time is not far off!" cries Tasso.

"Nor is mine!" cries Aminda, whose clitoris is now in fine shape to be rubbed by a stiff prick.

Robina, Lucia and Pampinea are in like condition. They were all in such a state of sexual excitement that at the slightest motion, they all would have sucked their partners' pricks without a single note of protest.

"Fuck me harder!" shrieks the Mother Abbess. "Run your finger further up my arse, and work it up and down in time with your prick. Oh! Do you never mean to spend? – Hurry! I am dying to suck your cock! Now work your finger in my arse faster! That's it! That's something like it! – Ha! You spend at last! – Jesu! What a stream comes from you!"

"Ah! By Saint Iago!" shouts the now enraptured Monk. "I am spending! I will not lose a single drop to save your soul from perdition!"

Saying this he gave his body a violent wrench, followed by another and still more violent one.

"Once more!" he shouts, shooting his manly offerings into the innermost recesses of her palpitating womb.

Then he glued himself to his partner, and remained motionless for quite a period.

While the two were thus engaged, the others were by no means idle. Father Joachim had slipped his prick into Pampinea's tight little cunnie, and was pushing forward and backward in the pleasantest style imaginable.

"Your prick feels heavenly!" sighs his partner, embracing him in the most fervid manner.

"Yes, my daughter," he rejoins. "And your cunt is so tight and warm that I wish I could fuck it a whole day. Is it not delicious? – Now suck my lips and I will suck yours! – That is the way! – Now gurgle your tongue in my mouth! – I feel you spending, but that will only make you anxious to be fucked harder."

"Oh! Father! Just look at my cunt," says Pampinea. "See! Its lips are right against your hair. If your prick was larger I could take it all in with ease."

"Yes, my daughter. It is indeed a pretty sight. Now I will not move my prick, but just put my hands across your arse and press you tightly to me. Ah! God! – But this is heavenly! I will lay you down on the couch in a few moments, and fuck you hard, – very hard. I can now feel my prick moving gently away up!"

"Oh! Father! I want a good hard fucking! But before you commence, thrust your tongue way into my mouth. There! Yes! That is the way! – Yum! Yum! Yum! – Now fuck me as hard as you are able!"

Father Joachim at once obeyed the anxious girl's request. He laid her on the couch, and gave it to her in heroic style. His fine prick would come out only to be eagerly sucked back by Pampinea's greedy cunt.

While thus engaged, the Mother Abbess had placed Pedro's fallen prick in her lecherous mouth, and was sucking it with the appetite of a hungry beast.

"A prick! A prick!" she mumbles. "A prick to fuck me!"

Gentle remonstrances come from the rest of the fair ones. For as the reader knows, there were not quite enough pricks to go round, and each one was in great demand.

Father Ambrose appeared to have his nose in Robina's cunt, while his two hands were playing with Lucia's arse and crotch as well.

"I am suffering!" shrieks the Mother Abbess. "Hasten! Oh! Hasten! I am burning up!"

Father Ambrose could not resist the appeal. He now left Robina and Lucia, and placed himself between the thighs of the Mother Abbess. Her cunt was all wet with sexual dew, but this only excited the priest onward. A lecherous cry came from him. His large and thick tool was as stiff as a rod of ivory, and in fine shape to satisfy a wanton woman. With a vigorous shove, he placed his prick home and then started to fuck with all his power.

"Ah!" cries Aminda to Tasso. "The Mother Abbess is in heaven. Look at her eyes! She appears to be enjoying herself beyond expression. She has one prick in her mouth, and another in her cunt."

"Yes!" returns Tasso, who was fucking Aminda vigorously all the while. "She ought to have something in her arse-hole, too."

"Oh! Tasso!" cries Aminda. "Turn me on my side, and then I can see the Mother Abbess being fucked whilst you fuck me."

Tasso at once complied with the request. He proceeded to give her a good prick-drubbing as she watched the others. He gave it to her so finely that Aminda's arse trembled like a leaf in the storm.

"When you get through, I must suck your prick, too," says the sobbing girl.

Tasso was also greatly excited, for as he looked about him, he saw the handsome Joachim withdraw himself from Pampinea's slit and place his prick, after bathing it in cold water, in Pampinea's mouth. She sucked it with the gusto of a child eating sweets. Robina and Lucia, left to themselves, were tickling each other's clitoris.

Tasso, with his prick in Aminda's cunt, lifted her up, and carried her to where the Mother Abbess was engaged in amorous warfare. Placing the palpitating form of his partner in close proximity to the double fucked Abbess, he ran his finger up her arse and moving it in and out of the darker fringed hole, violently fucked Aminda at the same time.

Meanwhile Pedro's prick, under the tender manipulation of the Mother Abbess' mouth, had assumed its most formidable appearance. When he withdrew his staff, it was red and swollen.

"Put it in my arse-hole," pleads the Mother Abbess, sick with lust. "Fuck my arse-hole! – Oh! For Christ's sake, fuck it!"

As she spoke, Father Ambrose uttered a hoarse shout, and emptied into her a copious supply of rich semen. He then proceeded to suck her mouth, whilst she ran her tongue down his throat.

Aminda now commenced to move her arse with quickened motions, expressive of unalloyed pleasure; for Tasso's fine prick was touching her to the very quick.

"Hurry, Tasso!" she whispered in his mouth. "I am crazy to suck your dear prick."

While she was thus speaking, Father Pedro flatly refused to obey the Mother Abbess' request.

"Two fine cunts are awaiting a prick!" he exclaimed. "I prefer cunt to arse-hole. Therefore, let Tasso's finger answer."

He spoke truly.

Robina and Lucia were reposing naked in each other's arms.

"Oh! I would give the world for a good prick," sighed Robina.

"So would I!" echoed Lucia.

The Spaniard at once went to them. Then placing their cunts on a level with his mouth, he cried,

"By Saint Peter! What glorious cunts! See this one with its jutting lips and scarlet mouth! – Ah! God! What a feast!"

He places his finger in Robina's wet cunt, and epicurean-like he rubbed and felt its satiny softness.

"Oh! What pleasure will I enjoy as I fuck this creamy thing! Sister Lucia, sit up on the couch! Open your thighs wider, and I will suck your cunt as I fuck Robina."

Placing a pillow under Robina's arse, he inserted his prick between the lips of her cunt, at the same time sucking Lucia's slit.

"Dear! Dear! Father!" cried Robina. "Your prick is thick and big! – But it feels perfectly heavenly! – See! You are nearly half-way in! – Oh! Merciful Saviour! It is all the way in! Now your big balls are against my arse!"

"You are indeed enjoying it, Robina, for you show by your countenance that your pleasure is very great. – Oh! Robina! He is sucking my cunt deliciously. Oh! Oh! – I will spend right in his mouth soon."

But Robina was speechless with the pent up bliss. The splendid prick of the Spanish Stallion was giving her the most exquisite joys on this earth. Her vagina sucked it so hard that Pedro could not stroke her quickly: – for when he drew his prick outward, the folds of her lovely cunt came with it, thus giving him indescribable pleasure. As he gazed about he also saw scenes that goaded him to the extremest point of human endurance.

Pampinea and Father Joachim had their hands between each other's thighs and a finger in their respective arse-holes. The Mother Abbess was busily engaged in sucking Father Ambrose's prick, whilst he, in turn, sucked wildly away at Aminda's hot and quivering cunt. On her part, she had Tasso's prick in her mouth, and was moulding it in the most lecherous manner. Tasso had his three fingers in the Mother Abbess' slit, and another finger in her arse-hole. Thus the entire company were now engaged in bestowing upon one another the most libidinous touches.

Lechery was rampant. Prick was king and Cunt was his consort. Here were men of great talents, and celebrated as teachers of the people. Their preachings electrified their hearers. They were looked upon as the servants of God deputed to do His will on this earth. No thoughts of an evil character were ever supposed to have strength enough to wean them for a moment from their priestly ways.

Yet look upon them! – Yea, behold them! – Where is now their boasted strength to resist temptation? Bah! Cunt conquers all men. And the saintly women, to whom a few months since the very thought of contact with man was contamination! – Now they are sucking pricks with the greatest gusto.

Lo! The pride of woman falleth before Prick. When priest and nun throw off the mask of sanctity, they display passion raging beneath with volcanic force. Fucking is but the half way post; sucking is another quarter, and buggering marks the finish.

When the Spanish Stallion had finished Robina, the nun was but partly satisfied. She commenced rolling forward and backward along the floor, gesticulating violently with both legs and arms.

Lucia was spending, and at the same time uttering deep sighs indicative of extreme desire. Her cunt had been well sucked but not yet fucked. A good stiff prick was now an absolute necessity to ease her sufferings.

Pedro saw her anxiously eyeing his prick. He understood her mute appeal. Then, after bathing his tool with fresh cool water, he placed it in her mouth. As he did so, she uttered little shrieks of delight. Finally, her suckings gave him the desired hard-on, and when he removed it from between her lips, it appeared bigger and thicker than ever.

She eyed it with the look of a famished hound, and threw her legs upward, thus exposing the blonde-haired cunnie, plump arse, and broad white thighs.

With a beastly cry the Spanish Stallion falls upon her, and plunges his prick straight into the close-mouthed red-limned mount of Venus, and works his arse without mercy. The greedy cunt takes it all in, and Lucia moves her arse from side to side, and meanwhile utters deep sighs of satisfaction.

"Spare me not, Father!" she cries. "Now fuck all you can! I feel your prick way up in me!"

"Sweet angel!" replies Pedro. "Was ever a man so blessed? Your cunt is so tight and warm that the head of my prick feels as if it were afire. Ah! Christ! Christ! – How I would like to put my balls into you! – Come here, Robina! Let me suck your cunt while I fuck Lucia."

Robina places herself in a position to gratify the lecherous priest, and soon he is sucking away for dear life. His big prick at the same time, is rushing in and out of Lucia's greedy cunt, with speedy thrusts.

The whole apartment now resounded with shouts of vulgar language.

"A prick for my arse-hole!" still pleads the Mother Abbess.

Alas for her! No sodomite is there to gratify her. There are too many enticing cunts in opposition.

Such scenes as we now depict may seem as unreal as they are unnatural; but the keen student of human nature knows well that the most modest of women, when over-excited by a good fucking, will halt at nothing. In their cooler moments, they would be horrified at the very thought, rather than act in the manner in which the present pages now suggest.

CHAPTER IX.

A PRINCESS HAD TO HAVE IT

FOR A short period the company halted. Over-excited nature now demanded a brief respite. Through the forethought of the Mother Abbess, utensils for ablution were plentiful. Priests and nuns could be seen gently bathing pricks and cunts in order to strengthen them for renewed orgies. Wines and light refreshments abounded. Naked forms sat around the banquet board. Shafts of wit with pointed allusions brought forth paroxysms of laughter.

'The arse-hole is still waiting!" shouts Ambrose. "Who will be the first to storm the breach?"

"Yes! Yes!" returns the Mother Abbess. (The wine-glass had been raised perhaps too often to her lips.) "I will take a prick in my mouth, another in my cunt, and still another in my arse-hole!"

"Be not so greedy!" cry the others, indignantly. "Would you deprive us all to gratify yourself?"

"Have no fear, fair Sisters," interjects Joachim. "It would take a regiment to gratify our Mistress. She is a veritable succubus. 'More! More!' is her ever constant cry."

A shout of laughter greets this sally.

"Cunts were formed for fucking, and pricks were made to fuck them!" chimes in Father Pedro. "If it were not so, God would have given us little holes to piss out of. But arse-holes were made for still another purpose, and I for one, have no desire to put my tool in such a dirty place!"

"Bravo! Bravo!" shout the anti-sodomites approvingly.

The Mother Abbess laughed loud and mockingly, in a perfect fit of mirth.

Father Joachim endeavoured to restrain the outburst.

"Madame, I beseech you not to give way to your feelings in such loud tones. We may awake the aged Sisters."

"Quiet your fear," returned the Mother Abbess, restraining her mirth somewhat. "Think you that I have not prepared against such an event? We are now in the unused portion of the Convent.

The other Sisters are locked securely in their cells."

[Father Joachim, Pedro and Ambrose, be it known to you, were not residents of the Convent. They were supposed to dwell in a monastery some distance removed from their present location. Their vocation as Confessors' however, gave them special privileges, and as the reader will observe, they were by no means backward in taking advantage of the opportunities offered them.]

The entire company now became lost to all sense of shame. Once more modesty was thrown to the winds. For wine and full stomachs have a tendency to influence the passions; and the present instance was no exception to the rule.

Would that a painter's skilled hand could depict in glowing colours what the pen is now incapable of fully describing. The beautiful maidens were now mere animals. Plump white thighs were partly lolling on the table and chairs, the atmosphere being so balmy that nakedness was pleasant. Pouting cunts were displaying themselves in such a manner as would have influenced even a hermit, or corrupted a saint, – and the Fathers present were neither. Their hands were playing with the tempting lips and clitoris of each. Deep sighs indicative of exquisite pleasure came from all. Pricks and balls were being handled in the most lascivious manner. Lily-white arses were gently rising up and down in the anticipation of the joys that were to come.

"Ah!" said Father Pedro, whose sturdy tool and large rounded appendages were worked at once by Robina and Lucia. "This is almost as fine as my palace experiences."

This remark attracted the attention of all.

"You excite our curiosity," chimes in the Mother Abbess. "Come, tell us the story. From whence comes your title of Stallion?"

"Yes! Yes!" cry the rest in unison. "Tell us the story."

Father Pedro smiled.

"I will relate to you the cause of the title," he replied. "But soft! Before I commence, sweet Sisters," he added, turning to Lucia and Robina, "restrain your eagerness. Handle me gently, and I will entertain each of your cunts in return. This pleasant dalliance must last until I finish my tale."

Then the entire company, whilst dallying with one another, listened to the following narrative:

"I scarcely need remind you," commenced the narrator, "that for ages the Spaniards have been renowned as adepts in the arts of love as well as of war. Hot blooded and impulsive, addicted to strong jealousies, it is said of us that we are more prone to punish than to reward. A Spaniard will imperil his life and honour for a woman's embrace, yet he will pursue with implacable vengeance the outrager of his domestic hearth. He receives but will make no return. Secrecy is safety – discovery is ruin."

"Bah!" interrupted Father Ambrose. "Have done with such dry details. Come to the point without so much wandering."

Pedro flushed deeply at the reproof, if such it might be termed. But an extra jerk of his prick by Robina restrained his temper.

"Know then, that in Madrid I was in the employ of his Eminence the Cardinal, as Secretary. My employment brought me frequently to the Palace, and it was not long before I was on excellent terms with the King and the entire royal family.

"My conduct was of the most exemplary character; and I was looked upon as a model of propriety. Such was the confidence displayed in me that I became a depository for all the secrets of the Palace. I acted the part of Confessor to the best of my ability, and reproved and rewarded in turn.

"One afternoon I was summoned to the Cardinal's private apartments, and to my great astonishment, was addressed as follows:

"'Father Pedro, you know that we who serve the Holy Father obey him in all things, halting not to inquire the why and wherefore. Therefore, my son, be not amazed at what I now speak of to you. Learn that the Princess Dolores, the fairest maid in all Spain, is in a delicate situation. Her physician informs me that she must perforce have sexual connection without delay, or her life may pay the forfeit. – Do you follow me?'"

"'Perfectly, your Eminence,' I replied.

"'Well,' continued the Cardinal, 'a month hence she will be married to the Prince of Parma. But pending that period, her condition is so serious that nothing but a man can alleviate it. Now the marriage of the Prince and the Princess is of absolute importance, for the reason that the Church will vastly benefit by it. Should the death of the Princess prevent such a consummation, the Holy Father will be overwhelmed with grief. He has set his heart upon this union, as vast interests can thus be maintained. – But, enough of explanations. I now order you to go to the Princess this very evening, and give her that relief which nature so strenuously demands. We know we are safe when we confide in thee. We dare not seek another. What sayest thou, my son?'

" 'To hear is to obey,' I responded humbly, with head bowed and raised hands clasped in prayer.

"With a gesture, the Cardinal dismissed me.

"Now laugh as you will, Brothers and Sisters. Nevertheless, I speak truth when I state that heretofore I had never enjoyed a woman, save in imagination. You well know," he added, with a suggestive smile, "that our text-books which we striplings studied before our entrance into the priesthood, are crowded with descriptive and alluring suggestions. A hundred or more volumes are devoted solely to subjects of a sexual nature, and I can assure you that they can with truth be termed 'An Exposition of the Art of Fucking' in every shape, manner, and form known to civilized and uncivilized nations.

"The maiden I was about to satisfy was the most beautiful woman in Spain. The young gallants of Madrid would have periled their lives and fortunes to obtain her. Yet here was I offered this luscious fruit without an effort."

"Lucky dog!" quoth Ambrose, between his set teeth. "How I envy you!"

A murmur of disapproval quieted the interloper.

It was evident that the company were becoming greatly interested.

"I prepared myself fittingly for the coming event," resumed Father Pedro. "The perfumed bath of the King was at my disposal that evening; for upon my arrival at the Palace, a lovely maid of honour met me and conducted me to that apartment.

" 'I have been commanded by high authority,' quoth she, with a smile upon her lovely face, 'not to lose sight of thee until the destination is reached.'

"And you may be assured she obeyed her commands faithfully. She saw me disport naked in the bath. With gloating looks did she observe my manly beauties, and it was only with great difficulty that she could restrain herself from fondling me.

"When I entered the private chamber of the Princess, I saw the beautiful being reposing on a couch of great magnificence. Two maids of honour were in attendance upon her.

"Previous to my entrance I had not allowed my thoughts to dwell on the subject. I saw only the path of duty. Passion had not yet commenced to play its part.

"The Princess was attired in a silken robe; but

when I fell upon my knees I saw that it covered nakedness only. For when she gave me her hand to kiss, the robe revealed the superb bosom entirely to my gaze. By all the saints!" cried the enraptured Pedro. "Never did I see such a beautiful being! Her white skin would have matched the purest alabaster. Her long black hair fell to her feet. Her coal black eyes pierced me like an arrow's dart. Her cheeks were suffused with the deepest crimson, and her reddened lips were a Cupid's bow, wet with dew.

"I fell upon those lips like a famished dog. I sucked and sucked the velvet mouth, and was sucked in return, for the Princess was overflowing with desire.

"'Pardon my sin, Father,' she whispered softly.

"'The Virgin herself would atone for thee! – Oh! Lovely Princess,' I returned.

"Regardless of the arch-looks of the maids of honour present, I threw off my single garment. The Princess in turn imitates me, and there, naked and palpitating, does she lie before me. With eager hands I seize upon the hemispheres before me, and mumbling cries of excited lust as I press and fondle them, and suck their virgin rubies, and press unnumbered kisses alternately on lips and bosom;

while she, with both hands upon my gloriously stiffened prick, is uttering cries indicative of unbridled lasciviousness.

"Our lips join in one long, long kiss. Our tongues stick together. Then I halt to gaze upon the beauties lower down. – Ah! God! – Sisters!" he cries, halting in his narrative, "Have mercy! Permit me to finish this story with stiffened tool."

"I cannot help myself, Father," returns Lucia.

"Nor yet can I," adds Robina. "Your fingering excites me so greatly that I lose command of myself."

"You break in upon his narrative," cries the Mother Abbess. "Contain yourselves, Sisters. Let us have no more interruption."

"Where was I?" asks Pedro, bewildered.

"You were just about to gaze upon the beauties lower down!" cry Ambrose, Joachim and Tasso in one voice.

A shout of laughter greets this involuntarily concerted answer.

"Ah! Yes!" resumed Pedro. "I gazed at the sight before me like a famished wolf. The white stomach, the magnificent thighs which were opening and shutting in gleeful anticipation, but best of all the mount of Venus, the door of Paradise, the sweet silken-lined cunt. Between its moist and reddened lips nestled a half-blown rose, a symbol of virginity that Princesses of Spain have worn from the beginning of their history. None but a true virgin dare place a bud in such a receptacle.

"I uttered a shriek of delight at this most enchanting sight, removed the bud, and alternately kissed and sucked the unfucked slit. Then I played with the exquisite clitoris until the couch groaned with her motions and tossings.

"My prick was now swollen to an enormous extent. As I glanced at it, I heard a voice say:

"'The King's Stallion cannot compare with it.'

"It was the maid on the left who spoke. It was then that I became aware that the two whom I first saw upon my entrance, were still in attendance.

"'Ah! My mistress will be split apart by such a monster!'

"'Have no fear!' retorts the other. 'She will conquer it shortly, and reduce it to nothingness.'

"The Princess meanwhile was mad with passion. She pulls me vigorously towards her. I mount her, like the stallion that I am. My staff is burning with desire. I push open the tightly closed lips of the royal slit. Not a protest comes from her.

Now I am in. I rage like a bull. I push. I snort. She bids me onward. I fuck and fuck. She foams at the mouth. I fuck and fuck more swiftly than before. My feet are on the floor. I am in a glorious position between her thighs. She then raises her feet, and places them upon my shoulders. Still I fuck and fuck until my balls are all but in the breach. Then I pause for breath.

"A loud shriek, expressive of overflowing joys, comes from her. Then I pounce upon her mouth and suck the sweetness from her lips.

"Thus glued together, I unloosed the long pent-up savings of my loins, and pour them into her inmost depths, so much so as to copiously drench every portion of her womb. Yet I did not withdraw myself. She seeks to throw me off. In vain! I fuck and fuck, she wildly gesticulating with her arms, and pressing me close with her dainty feet.

"Thus we lay, – how long I know not, nor cared. If I could have stayed thus, never would I have removed myself; but as such things must have an end, so it came in my case, too.

" 'Ha!' cries one of the maids. 'Did I not speak truth? See! She has conquered it completely.'

"The Princess was lying in sweet confusion upon the couch. Her attendants did her needed service, and later, I too, was treated like a royal prince. Ere that night of pleasure had ended, I had fucked both the virgin maids of honour, each in turn, straight before the royal face.

"'As these faithful maids have honoured me, so I will honour them!' cries the Princess. 'Father!' she added, 'See! They await your pleasure!'

"By the ten thousand virgins!" swore Pedro. "How I did fuck them! And their sobs of joy linger in my ears even yet! And for a finale, the Princess with her dainty mouth sucked my hard-worked prick into an erect state, and in return I gave her such a bouncing as to completely drive all sickness entirely from her.

"Need I say more? Save that the Prince of Parma espoused the Princess of Spain a month later, and my master complimented me highly for the assistance I had lent in the affair. Some of the details in a mysterious manner became known in Church channels. Hence the title given me."

That Father Pedro's story was highly appreciated needs scarce to be mentioned. All present were infatuated with the tale. The orgies recommenced with renewed vigour, and the apartment witnessed scenes in which unbridled lust figured to an extent unimaginable even to the most depraved of human beings.

Aminda could be seen handling Tasso's fine prick with such vigorous jerks that it seemed as if she would dissever it from his body. He in turn was sucking her burning slit. He imprints long and hot kisses upon it. He implores her to have mercy upon his instrument of pleasure.

"Give me your cunt to fuck!" he begs.

She answers by throwing herself upon his tool, and fucks him with such gusto that he writhes about like a serpent.

Father Pedro has secured a stout birch, and commences to give the Mother Abbess' large fat arse a sound drubbing.

Lucia, Robina and Pampinea are chasing the naked priests Joachim and Ambrose around the apartment. Soon the five forms are intermingled. Cunts and pricks are fondled with eager touches. The prick of Ambrose enters Lucia's cunt. Joachim fucks Pampinea, while Robina enjoys the pleasure of having her cunt sucked in turn by the two priests.

Pedro is once more in superb shape. His large prick inflames the Mother Abbess to passions beyond control. She sucks it until it dwindles to flabbiness, and so the company enjoyed themselves until the faint beams of the rising sun bade them to disperse.

CHAPTER X.

ROSA WINDS IT UP

THE lascivious pleasures which were so greatly enjoyed by all who were present at the amorous orgies just described in our last chapter, were unfortunately never repeated; for, a few days later Fathers Joachim, Pedro and Ambrose received summons from those high in authority, commanding their presence elsewhere.

The Mother Abbess and the Sisters were deeply grieved when the Fathers informed them of this fact.

"Alas!" cried the Mother Abbess, as she affectionately embraced in turn each of these departing priests. "Who shall now give our hungry cunts solace? It was only this very morning that our Tasso left for a month's absence. His aged parent is in a decline, and needs his son's presence to cheer his dying hours."

"Ah!" sighed the beautiful Robina. "What ill fortune is ours!"

"Restrain your grief," said Father Pedro, mournfully, "or you will but add to our own."

The three Fathers then and there fucked the Mother Abbess and the four Sisters until the entire party were deluged with blissful feelings. They fucked and sucked until exhaustion forced them all to halt.

After the departure of the lusty monks, affairs in the Convent resumed their usual state. Two attenuated, wrinkled Friars now acted the part of Confessors. They were lean and shrivelled, and in strong contrast to the strong and sturdy monks whom they had succeeded.

The Mother Abbess was loud in her complaints.

"How dare they inflict such scarecrows upon us?" she protested, indignantly, to the Sisters.

"Their stinking breaths show that their stomachs are starved with improper food," interjected Lucia.

"And one of them," spoke up Aminda, "bade me to sacrifice my appetite and not indulge it so freely."

"The dastards!" exclaimed the Mother Abbess. "They would have our stomachs as foul as their own. I am of the opinion that their shrunken tools would not secure an erection, even if we were to attempt the disgusting task of trying."

"Horrid thought!" said Lucia, laughing. "No doubt," she added, "but they are so virtuous that they fail to pay attention to the calls of nature."

"Then say I," rejoins the Mother Abbess, "may they foul themselves to perdition with their own urine."

Sad indeed were the straits in which the unfortunate band of Sisters now found themselves.

"'Tis more than we can bear," said Aminda to the Mother Abbess some time afterwards. "Pampinea and myself are determined to leave this life. We shall go out into the world, find proper husbands, and be fucked every night."

"Oh! Will not that be truly delightful?" returned the Mother Abbess.

Shortly afterwards they carried out their determination and both were fortunate enough to secure lusty gallants as husbands, who, no doubt to their great satisfaction, plowed them well.

The Mother Abbess, with Lucia and Robina were now forced to seek gratification in each other's company. They often fucked one another in the feminine manner, with tongue and finger, and thus to some extent made up for the loss of the Fathers and Tasso.

About this time, an addition was made to their company in the shape of a beautiful young girl, Rosa by name. She had sought the Convent to escape the machinations of those related to her. A deceased uncle had left her a snug fortune, the possession of which had excited the envy of those closely allied to her. To free herself from their persecutions, she had fled to the Convent.

Lucia and Robina were soon on intimate terms with her.

"She is truly a virgin," said Lucia to her companion. "It was but yesterday that I asked her if she knew what prick meant. – She immediately answered in the negative.

" 'Prick is what men possess,' I explained, 'It is soft at first, but when a woman touches it, the thing grows large and stiff.'

" 'Oh! Yes!' she responded. 'I know now. You mean that which a man pees with. I did not quite understand at first.'

"I asked her if she knew what a cunt was, and she replied in the negative as before. When I told her, she blushed scarlet. I then spoke of the great pleasure to be obtained by joining prick with cunt, and then I further said,

" 'If you will let me, I will play with your cunt to give you some conception of what would happen when a man lies in bed with you.' And Oh!" continued Lucia, hotly, "would you believe it? She permitted me to play with her cunt for a long time. It made me sick with pleasure, and I told her to play with my slit as I did with hers; and soon our arses were bounding away in a manner that would set a man crazy to behold."

"I must play with her too," interrupted Robina, in an eager tone.

"Oh! She is so fresh and sweet!" returned Lucia, "that I would love to see her fucked for the first time!"

"Happy thought!" cried Robina. "You know Tasso returns tomorrow. Would it not be an excellent idea to have him fuck her? A month's absence must have given him renewed strength."

"I will make mention of it to him," replied Lucia.

The next day when Tasso returned, Lucia brought Sister Rosa to him as he was working in the garden with the old gardener. Tasso saw the signal and went at once to her.

The novice was much pleased with the appearance of the gardener; and when Robina and Lucia had told her what he had done to them, she too seemed desirous of testing his ability to please.

"We are all nearly starved," said Robina to

Rosa. "Our cunts are just watering for a man; but we will restrain ourselves in order that you may enjoy the bliss of being fucked. It will also be a source of great pleasure to the Mother Abbess if you will permit her to see you fucked by Tasso."

Now Rosa was as tempting a piece of woman-flesh as the eye of mortal man ever beheld. She was short and plump in figure, with a lovely face, expressive of a mirthful disposition. Her blue eyes were large and lustrous; and there was that in them which would make any healthy man's prick rise very quickly. The lily and the rose fought for supremacy in her cheeks, and the luscious red mouth was one to gloat over, to sigh for, to dream about.

Tasso fell head over heels in love with Rosa at first sight, and when Lucia told him of the feast she had in store for him, he knelt at her feet in worship. He raised her robe and kissed her tempting slit, whilst she in turn played with his fine prick.

"We have determined to deny ourselves," she said, removing herself from him. "You must save yourself for Rosa."

The following evening the Mother Abbess, in company with Lucia, Robina and Rosa, assembled in the apartment which had been the scene of their former orgies. Tasso did not keep them waiting;

for hardly had the four entered than he made his appearance.

The blushing Rosa was as first quite backward, but the hot-blooded Tasso soon cured her bashfulness; for he pressed her tempting bosom and played with her tight little cunt until she was in a high state of sexual excitement.

The Mother Abbess and the two Sisters will now describe the exciting contest.

"See! Tasso is quite naked!" says Robina. "How large his prick looks! – Oh! Rosa! How your backside will jump up and down when his thing is in you!"

"Rosa is bashful! She still has her gown on. – There! That is right, Tasso! Take it off and fuck her naked!"

"Look at her swelling slit! – Is it not lovely?" observes the Mother Abbess. "Tasso likes it! – See him kiss it! – That's right, Rosa. Move your arse about! – There! Lay down upon the couch! Tasso will now work your clitoris until you spend."

"Oh! This is a feast!" interjects Tasso, as he sucks Rosa's mouth, and rubs her cunt in a vigorous manner.

"Play with his balls, Rosa! – Yes! In that manner! For it will make his prick stiffer," advises Robina.

"They are both getting in shape for a good fuck!" she continues. "Look, Mother! Rosa has commenced to spend."

"Play with my cunt, both of you!" entreats the Mother Abbess, who was now in a high state of excitement.

"Tasso, do not tease her so! Her cunt is eager for your prick!" expostulated Lucia. "That is proper," she continues. "See, Robina! His prick is going in, and Rosa is pushing her arse forward! – She wants it so badly."

"How closely her cunt clings to his prick!" said Robina, who was watching the two with eager eyes.

"Oh! God! – This is pleasure, indeed!" shouts Tasso. "Her cunt is like a vice! – Oh! Ah! Ah! My balls will burst with bliss!"

"Now fuck her, Tasso! Fuck her!" almost shrieks the Mother Abbess. "Your big prick has opened her fresh cunt for the first time! – That is why it is so tight."

"His prick is all wet!" says Robina. "She must be spending."

"Ah! My finger is all wet also," cries Lucia. "Mother, you too have come off!"

"Oh! Do but see him!" admiringly exclaims the Mother Abbess. "Ah! That thrust touched her to the very quick!"

And indeed, so it seemed, for the beautiful Rosa became wild with bliss; and when Tasso halted a moment, she twisted herself on top of him and fucked and fucked him until she had drained him entirely.

When he removed his prick the three waiting women took possession of it; and when they were through, poor Tasso was as weak as a cat.

The day following, Rosa, in company with Tasso, fled from the Convent. Tasso feared that he would fade away into a veritable shadow if he continued to dwell amongst such amorous women.

Tasso and Rosa were married without delay, and continued faithful to one another for the remainder of their lives. A large family of children blessed them.

A few weeks after the flight of Tasso, Robina and Lucia followed his example, and were espoused later by two noble gentlemen, who frequently wondered at their wives' marvellous knowledge of the art of fucking. Of course the modest girls always kept them in a complete state of ignorance respecting the school in which they were so ably taught.

The Mother Abbess one day horrified her Confessor with a vulgar remark. The poor woman had been deprived of sexual food so long that she was scarcely conscious of her words.

She saluted him with the following:

"Scarecrow! Your stinking breath would shame a shit-house!"

The horrified priest at once reported this remark to his Superiors, but before the resultant penalty had time to be announced to the Mother Abbess, she had gathered up her belongings, and returned, like a sensible woman, to the world. As she was possessed of large means, and thus being able to gratify her desires, she hired ponderous footmen; and when they were fucked out, she would present them with a handsome stipend, and replace them with others more sturdy. She maintained this state for long years, occasionally varying her diet with a good fat oily friar, until finally her dwelling-place became known to the curious as a "place where fat men got thin," or, in modern parlance, an anti-fat cure. But, as death comes to all, so in due time he came to the Mother Abbess. Her place of burial is celebrated to this day in consequence of the curious monument that ornaments her last resting place. It is an immense stone, partly rounded, and a very close imitation of a stiff prick. Thus can be seen, even the ruling passion strong in death.

MORE EROTIC CLASSICS FROM
CARROLL & GRAF